Lilly Sommers
much of her chil
past is one of her
began writing ab
thing to being t
gardening and
Bendigo, Victor
children.

Also by Lilly Sommers

The Glass House
The Bond
The Dark Dream
When Shadows Fall

FOOTSTEPS
in an
EMPTY ROOM

LILLY SOMMERS

ARROW

An Arrow book
published by
Random House Australia Pty Ltd
20 Alfred Street, Milsons Point, NSW 2061
http://www.randomhouse.com.au

Sydney New York Toronto
London Auckland Johannesburg
and agencies throughout the world

First published 1999

This edition published 2001 by Hinkler Books Pty Ltd.
17-23 Redwood Drive, Dingley, Victoria 3172 Australia

National Library of Australia
Cataloguing-in-Publication Data

Sommers, Lilly.
Footsteps in an emtpy room.

ISBN 1-865-15635-3

I. Title

A823.3

Typeset by Midland Typesetters, Maryborough
Printed and bound in Australia by Griffin Press

10 9 8 7 6 5 4 3 2 1

For my mother

CHAPTER 1

The sun had set like fire. Across the bay, over the You Yangs, the sky was still streaked in orange and red, like something in a dream. Alice Parkin looked towards the paddocks where the sheep threw monstrous shadows. She was pretending to shake the white damask tablecloth but really she was enjoying the evening air with its bite from the bay, and the freedom. Behind her was Colonsay, the house. She felt its presence even without looking. Big, menacing, claustrophobic. She wasn't happy, and although she had only been living in it a month, she knew she could never be happy.

'You'll just have to put up with it,' her father had told her unsympathetically. 'We can't feed you, Alice. You have to make your own way now. You're twelve, girl, twelve!'

Her mother had more compassion—she had had numerous visits from Alice's school teacher informing her of Alice's higher than average intelligence. But, as her husband said, what was the use of being clever? Where would that get girls such as Alice? She would do better with a strong back.

Mira Parkin had eased her own aching back and turned again to her eldest daughter, her eyes pleading. 'Mrs Cunningham is nice, isn't she? And the children are not so bad, are they? You know what children are, Alice, you've brothers and sisters yourself.'

Yes, Alice knew what children were. She glanced at her younger siblings and suddenly wished with all her heart that she was still one of them.

'No, Mother, they're not so bad.' At last she spoke the words Mira Parkin wanted to hear.

Her mother relaxed, her plain linen blouse swelling out over her flat bosom as she took a deep breath. 'Well, there you are, then,' she murmured. 'There you are then, Alice love.'

'There you are, then,' Alice muttered to herself now, and there was a sort of bitter betrayal inside her. She gave the cloth one last shake and, as if she could avoid it no longer, turned towards the house, towards Colonsay.

It was a two-storey sandstone building, solid and square, with a verandah on the front. There was a garden either side of the path up to the front door. Mrs Cunningham had had the old-fashioned borders altered to a new formality, and her husband had promised her exotics from far-away places, but she had left the old honeysuckle which twined around the verandah posts and stretched towards the upper windows. It had been planted by, it was said, the first Cunningham, grown from cuttings brought from China. Alice loved the sweet, heady scent.

The original house had been built in the 1830s by the same Cunningham who planted the honeysuckle, Cosmo Cunningham's grandfather. When he and his sheep settled on the Bellarine Peninsula there wasn't much else, and although Cosmo had now added to the old house extensively, making it bigger and grander, the shell remained. In the cellar there was a brick well, and that was old. Sometimes Mrs Gibbons, the cook, sent Alice to fetch up some water—the well in the cellar gave particularly sweet water. Alice was never happy until she had climbed that final step and had the cellar door closed behind her again.

Dark places had always disturbed her, and now Colonsay had begun to have a similar effect. If she had been a girl of little intelligence and imagination, as her parents seemed to want her to be, she may not have sensed the undercurrents, but she wasn't and she did. It was not even something she could explain. The house was often full of guests, full of noise and life. Mr Cunningham, although he was away for weeks at a time, always brought visitors home with him. He spent an awful lot of money on them. Once Alice had overheard one of the guests say, in a scornful manner, that Colonsay was more like a hotel than a house, and that such lavish entertaining was an 'affectation'. When she asked Mrs Gibbons what an affectation was, she had received a clip around the ear and been told to mind her own. She had looked the word up later in the big dictionary in the library, and mulled over it. Was Cosmo, the Grand Host, no more than a Grand Illusion?

Alice didn't want to think so.

She liked Cosmo Cunningham. He was a big man with a loud voice and greying hair, who smelled of the cigars he smoked. There was kindness in his half shut eyes and he always asked after Alice's family, when he noticed her. He had never forgotten that Alice's father had saved him from an icy death in Port Phillip Bay on a day which had started flat and fine and ended with waves like mountains and slashing rain. Cosmo had been fond of sailing then and Alice's father, a lad himself, had gone with him. Yes, she liked Cosmo Cunningham.

Of Mrs Cunningham she was not so certain.

Everyone knew Cosmo was in love with his young wife, and proud of her, of her beauty. You could tell just by the way he looked at her. And she *was* beautiful, with her dark hair swept up from her slim neck, the family emeralds glinting about her throat. She had so many clothes and shoes Alice's mind boggled. It took her ages to dress. Even her name was beautiful, Ambrosine, although Cosmo shortened it to the more intimate Rosie.

Mrs Gibbons loved her and spoiled her, whipping up special dishes to tempt her appetite, for she was a sickly lady. Delicate, according to Mrs Gibbons. Alice wondered about that. It was strange, she thought, that Ambrosine's illnesses coincided with visits by guests she did not like, usually Cosmo's boring political cronies, but after that clip around the ear she no longer spoke her thoughts aloud.

Cosmo and Ambrosine had two children, a boy and a girl. There was a nanny for the younger child, Ada, and a governess for both children. Bertie, the boy, would be going away to school soon—he was ten. Alice would miss Bertie, he was her friend. Bertie Cunningham, gentle Bertie, she wondered how he would fare at boarding-school. Cosmo Cunningham said it would be the making of him, and his mother, if she thought of it at all, did not seem to care. Poor Bertie, he didn't want to be shuffled off into the care of strangers.

Perhaps, thought Alice, Bertie and I are not so different from each other.

'Alice! Alice Parkin!'

Alice looked up. There was Bertie now, smiling through one of the diamond-paned windows in the attic. He had a hidey-hole up there, where he kept his treasures and his secrets. She waved as she walked towards the house in her sturdy boots. They had cost her father five shillings and were meant to last at least two years. Alice didn't dare tell him they were already pinching and that at night her feet ached. She dreamed of one day having soft, satiny slippers like Mrs Cunningham's. Alice knew they were no more than dreams, but they helped. She was only twelve.

'Alice.' Meggy hissed a warning as Alice slipped into the kitchen through the side door. Steam erupted from a pot over the hearth. The big black wood stove was sending waves of heat into the room. Mrs Gibbons stood at the kitchen table cutting onions, her eyes red and angry. Cosmo had been away to the Federal Parliament in Melbourne but was expected back tonight, bringing guests as usual.

'Where have you been, girl?' she demanded. 'Get about it, then! It'll be time for dinner and nothing done.'

Meggy grimaced and slid, like a ghost, back to her corner and the potatoes to be peeled. Alice followed her.

'Madam is ill tonight,' Mrs Gibbons went on, then sighed and shook her head. 'Sweet, delicate lady. I pray for her every Sunday. You can take up some of my broth, Alice, and careful you don't spill it.'

Alice stood, wiping her hands nervously on her apron.

'Tidy yourself, your hair's wild as a nigger's,' Mrs Gibbons added sharply.

Meggy said nothing; being half 'nigger' herself she had learned to assume a certain deafness in Mrs Gibbons's presence.

Alice smoothed the offending hair, repinning her white cap. She came to stand by the table, watching as the cook arranged a tray, neatly and deftly.

'There. Now, careful on the stairs,' the older woman instructed, mopping her dripping eyes with her apron. The onions were only half done, but Mr Cunningham loved his onions and always praised Mrs Gibbons for her special way of doing them. Alice wondered, mutinously, if he would love them as much if he had to prepare them himself.

Sometimes, her own thoughts surprised her. They were not at all as they were meant to be, as she had been brought up to order them. Sometimes, they did not seem to belong to Alice Parkin at all.

The back stairs rose from the passage outside the kitchen door, beside the scullery, and Alice climbed them carefully, balancing the tray. The stair runners were bare, the banister rail dented and the walls dark, but as they were only supposed to be used by the servants none of this mattered. On reaching the top, Alice was suddenly transported into a world of soft carpet and fancy wallpaper. The glass window at the far end of the upper corridor strained the evening gloom into green and pink and blue. The soft watercolours of a child's fairytale book. Alice peered towards it, adjusting the balance of the tray once more. The window had only been completed last month, and depicted a woman rising out of swirling water, wearing something narrow and restrictive which looked, to Alice, rather like the dark kelp that washed up on the beach after a storm.

This was the east wing of the house, where the best bedrooms were situated, those set aside for the adult family and their guests. The children slept in rooms in the west wing. Ambrosine Cunningham's bedroom was placed at the front of the house, and was large and very feminine. It was the room where madam spent most of her time, second only to her private sitting room on the ground floor. Beautiful, elegant, well-mannered, she was the perfect wife for a man like Cosmo, but beneath the calm surface of her smile was . . . what?

'Emptiness and vacancy,' muttered Alice. 'A selfish, spoiled woman, is Bertie's mother.'

On that note, she knocked and opened the door. And blinked, for the curtains were pulled tightly across the windows and it was even darker in here than on the back stairs. The room was crowded with tiny tables and delicate ornaments, heavy with oriental rugs and cloth-draped chairs and overstuffed cushions, every piece playing its part in this display of Cunningham importance and prosperity. Alice felt as if it were difficult to breathe. If this were her room, she would have flung the windows wide and let the cool evening breeze stir the shadows.

'Who is it?' a light, soft voice demanded. Rosie Cunningham lifted her head from her day-bed and shaded her eyes as if the watery light from the open door were too much to bear. A dog, like a small mop of long, toffee-coloured hair, lifted a head adorned with a blue ribbon and snuffled indignantly.

'Oh, Alice. Have you some of Mrs Gibbons's broth? Bring it in, please.'

Alice did as she was told, setting the tray on a table by the day-bed, trying to avoid upsetting a vase of white roses, a couple of gilt-framed photographs, a tiny cut-glass vial of smelling salts and a larger bottle of perfumed water with a silver stopper. Mrs Cunningham watched her manoeuvres, hand absently stroking the dog, her eyes half closed. They did not look like the eyes of an invalid.

Earlier this afternoon Mrs Cunningham had been sitting for the portrait her husband had commissioned of her. She had seemed perfectly well, but then the artist, Mr Marling, was far more handsome and interesting than any of Cosmo's guests. This cynical thought shocked Alice, and she edged nervously away in case the other woman should read her mind.

'Thank you, Alice.'

Guilt made Alice more solicitous than she would otherwise have been. 'Shall I pour your tea, ma'am?'

Rosie Cunningham's eyelids lifted slightly, her eyes fixed on Alice's. There was surprise in them, and some amusement. 'There's no need for that, thank you, Alice.'

Alice backed away further. As she did so, her boot sent something spinning and rattling under the day-bed. Mrs Cunningham had draped a finely woven silk shawl over herself, the fruit- and flower-patterned cloth spilling over onto the floor. Alice bent down, her hand darting through the slippery silk folds, and closed on a small, hard object. An ivory button, carved into the likeness of a flower. A rose.

Alice recognised it immediately. It belonged to Mr Marling's deep blue waistcoat. She had often admired those buttons when she took his hat and cane at the front door, or led him up the stairs to the room at the end of the corridor, which he was using as his studio. Mr Marling said the light in there was better than in Ambrosine's downstairs sitting room. He said they were less likely to be disturbed by the children or the servants. And, thought Alice, it was only a few steps to madam's boudoir, to her day-bed, where the ivory button had no right to be.

The dog jumped from the day-bed and made a run at her, barking.

'Be quiet, Cleo! What are you doing, Alice?' Mrs Cunningham sounded querulous, but something in the dull gleam of her eyes warned Alice that she'd best be careful. Her fingers closed over the button until the rose was indented into her flesh.

'The heel of my boot caught in the fringe of your shawl, ma'am. I was freeing it.'

Mrs Cunningham met her look. 'Very well,' she murmured softly. 'That will be all now, Alice.'

Alice went out and closed the door. Her legs felt weak. She unfolded her fingers and peered at the button. The rose was fat and full, an opulent thing, rather like the ones madam grew in her garden. Alice slipped it into her pocket, and made her way down the stairs.

'What is it?' asked Meggy. 'You've been quiet as a mouse, Alice.'

Beyond the door they could hear the master's booming laughter, echoed by the colleagues he had brought back with him from Melbourne. For years they had been involved in the drawing up of the Constitution—that important document the old Queen in England had last year, before her death, placed her signature upon. Now they were part of the first Federal Government. For Australia had become a Federation on the 1st of January 1901.

Cosmo Cunningham had told Alice all about it one morning, when he had ridden up to the stables behind the house and almost knocked her over as she carried a bucket of peelings and stale bread to the chooks. Cosmo had explained to her what Federation meant, how the old colonial states had gathered together and were now held tighter than Mrs Gibbons's stays. Federation had made Australia a stronger country, although nonetheless British for that. But everyone knew that the French and the Germans were in the Pacific, looking to extend their empires and, to defend herself effectively, Australia had to have a proper defence force, not the every-state-for-itself situation which had been the way until Federation. There were other considerations, but with his brother-in-law away with the Australian Lighthorse fighting the Boers, defence was Cosmo's current preoccupation.

Only last month in Sydney, Lord Hopetoun, the first Governor-General, had presided over extravagant ceremonies through streets garish with waving streamers and fluttering flags, with British soldiers marching and crowds applauding, while dignitaries vied with each other in clever conversation and diplomacy. Lord Hopetoun appointed Mr Edmund Barton to form the first Federal Government, a temporary measure prior to the first elections in March. One of the men Mr Barton had chosen for his cabinet was Cosmo Cunningham. 'When the election is held,' Cosmo told Alice, 'men will be able to vote for the members they want in their Parliament. The men they want to shape their country. Men with the experience and strength of character to plot a course and steer by it, whatever the temptations to do otherwise.'

'If I were a man, sir, I'd vote for you,' Alice said, carried away into indiscretion.

He laughed, a rumble in his chest, and his eyes gleamed. Why shouldn't Cosmo be Prime Minister? Alice asked herself. It seemed perfectly sensible to her.

'Alice?' Meggy queried again, breaking the spell. 'Alice, what is it?'

'Nothing.' Alice answered at last. 'Just tired. My feet hurt.' She grimaced, stretching out her boots beneath her thick skirt. Meggy winced in sympathy. 'Are you meeting Jonah tonight?' Alice went on, with a glance at her friend.

'Maybe,' Meggy shrugged. Jonah was Meggy's half-brother, and a stockman who had come from the Cunningham's property over the Murray River, where the land was flat and stretched endlessly, and the sky burned bright and hot. Cosmo had visited up there in June last year to see what damage the drought was doing—they were calling it the Federation Drought—and brought Jonah back with him. Meggy and Jonah had the same black mother but different white fathers, and though there was a certain similarity in the shape of their eyes and the curve of their smiles, that was where it ended. Jonah had been sent to a mission school and spoke like a gent, whereas Meggy had stayed in the homestead kitchen.

Alice loved Meggy, but in Jonah's presence her hackles seemed to rise, like Cleo's when she smelt mouse. He had a quietness about him she didn't trust, and sometimes when she was speaking he would smile for no reason other than that her opinions amused him. Surely that was arrogance? And what had a half-caste stockman to be arrogant about?

'Bertie's leaving in a fortnight,' Alice said, out of nowhere.

Meggy giggled.

'I'll miss him,' Alice added, ignoring her. 'He's like a brother.'

'You wait, in a few years he'll be looking down at you like a dog turd, like all the rest.'

'Meggy, your mouth is so filthy.'

'I talk truth.'

But Alice didn't want to believe that Bertie Cunningham would ever look down at her. They were friends. They understood each other. No, Bertie would still be her mate, whatever happened. He had promised to write to her from school. Of course, it wouldn't be the same as talking with him, but it would be a comfort.

Cosmo and his guests had moved into the library and the girls cleared the dining room, carrying the dirty plates and cutlery back to the scullery. Mrs Gibbons left them to it and went to bed, yawning and stretching, pretending to be dead on her feet. But later, in the quiet warmth of the kitchen, the two girls heard the side gate open softly and close with a click.

Meggy giggled. 'Visiting?' she whispered. Her eyes, a curious shade of hazel, opened wide under arched brows. It was a trick she had had off Jonah.

Alice pursed her lips and didn't reply. It was one

thing to think a thing, another to talk about it. Mrs Gibbons might just be going for a night walk—perhaps she couldn't sleep—and if her steps happened to take her down to the swamp where old Harry Simmons had his hut, then so what? It was like the button she had found in Ambrosine Cunningham's bedroom and which belonged on Mr Marling's blue waistcoat. Sometimes thoughts were better not translated into words.

'You're a sweet girl, Alice,' Meggy said abruptly, as if she had read her mind, 'but you need to open your eyes. There's bad things in this house, things you want to keep away from. Bad things, you hear me?'

Later, when she was ready for bed, Alice leaned out of her window and looked up at the moon where it sailed above the paddocks. The moon was big tonight, like a great luminous jelly. Alice had heard that looking at the full moon could send you silly, but she didn't believe it. Instead, she felt as if she were being drawn towards it, as if the moon were pulling at her blood and bones. Above her head, in the governess's room, the floor creaked and someone murmured, and then nothing. Beyond the post and rail fence, Alice saw a broad figure, long skirts trailing through the stubble from the harvest, wandering home. Mrs Gibbons. She was coming by way of the side gate, and to reach it she would have to pass Alice's window. As the cook drew closer, Alice could hear her singing under her breath. Silently, she withdrew her head inside the sill and held her breath as Mrs Gibbons stumbled past, quavering, 'After the ball is over, after the break of day . . .' A strong smell of rum remained when she had gone.

Bad things, Meggy had said. Bad things.

Alice shivered, and closed her window with a bang.

CHAPTER 2

The light hurt her eyes.

Rosamund turned away, hiding her face in her arms with a groan. Outside, the noise of a truck arriving and doors slamming and Silverchair turned up loud reminded her that the day was already well under way. There was no escape. She had to get up.

She lifted her head and looked about her. She was in the east wing, one of the big front bedrooms—Grandma Ada's old room. Why had she chosen it? She had hated Grandma Ada. Besides, Mark had booked her into a good hotel. Why had she cancelled at the last moment and decided to rough it here? Rosamund wasn't usually one to rough it when she had a choice. That was why she had given up her singing career when she married Mark, wasn't it?

The room was a mess, but not as bad as some of the others. A lump of plaster had fallen from the corner of the ceiling and lay, cloudy white, on the bare floorboards. There was an odour of disuse, of neglect, but even as Rosamund wrinkled her nose the scent of honeysuckle swamped it. There must be a plant flowering outside somewhere. It was almost overpowering, almost unpleasant, Rosamund thought as she sat up.

Her head hurt. She'd finished the bottle, even though she'd promised herself she wouldn't. If Mark were here he'd give her that look. Not quite hate, not quite that. Something more careworn, that would leave her in no doubt as to his disapproval and disappointment. That was one of the reasons she was here at the Bellarine Peninsula, ostensibly to oversee the restoration of the house but really to pull herself together.

'We need a break from each other,' Mark had told her. He had been off to a meeting and looked like a commercial for one of the better clothing stores. At least, he had told her he was off to a meeting—Mark was such a liar. He could tell her anything and she would believe it, and it was only when he had gone that she began to doubt. Was there another woman? Probably. Mark was very attractive to women.

Outside, voices rose and fell. Rosamund picked her way to the window and gazed out, expecting to see chaos. And was silenced. She had forgotten she was on the upper storey of the house, she had forgotten the view it afforded. Her gaze travelled across the ruin of the garden, over the windbreak of pines and beyond, where the bay gleamed like molten silver. On the other side, the rounded points of the You Yangs dissected a cloudless blue sky. It was a beautiful day. Rosamund ran a hand through her hair, ignoring the fact that it urgently needed a wash, and breathed deeply. I wonder, she thought, if anyone has breathed this air before. Am I the first?

Laughter reached her. Below, in what had been the old garden and was now a flat expanse of criss-crossing tyre tracks, a couple of workmen were unloading a van. They had stopped and were looking up at her, their faces bright with amusement, their mouths gaping. Frowning, Rosamund stared, and then, as the reason for their laughter struck her, stumbled back into the room.

'Shit.' Helplessly, she looked down at herself. She was stark naked and, between the beauty of the view and last night's bottle, had forgotten it. For a moment she had the urge to bolt out to the car and drive away, but even as she thought it she knew she wouldn't. Couldn't.

'Get yourself together, woman,' she muttered. The packet of cigarettes on the table caught her eye but she resisted. She was trying to cut down. Instead, she grabbed up yesterday's jeans and sweater with shaky hands and, picking her way through the debris of her room, made the journey down the corridor to the bathroom.

The water was hot, thank God, and she luxuriated under the uneven spray, washing her hair thoroughly, soaping her body. She had always been a tall, big-boned girl, but she had let herself go lately. Bits that used to curve in now curved in less, and bits that used to swell out now swelled a lot more. Somehow it no longer mattered to her, or not enough to want to change it. Mark noticed her deterioration, of course he did, but he said nothing.

'Too busy. Always too bloody busy.' Rosamund caught up the towel. The mirror was opaque with steam and she saw herself only as a vague outline. The last time she had stood in this bathroom she had been so young—a girl. She hadn't met Mark then, hadn't fallen in love with him. Hadn't done very much at all.

It never failed to surprise and amaze her, the fact that she was with Mark. He wasn't her type.

He wasn't from her world. He never had been. Rosamund had had so much going for her then, so many doors of opportunity, but she had sat back and watched them close in her face, one by one. While Rosamund had been going down, Mark had been heading up. He had been raised in poverty but his construction company had thrived, everything he touched made money. And when, two years ago, the first mention had been made of him running for Premier, Mark had willingly entered the ring. In one month, he would be the favoured candidate in a by-election which would finally set the wheels of his dream in motion.

Mark had been dabbling in politics since he was old enough to vote, and had been an adviser to the government on this and that. He had a cat's cradle of strings he could pull whenever he felt like it—newspaper barons, television owners, government ministers, transport giants, union bosses, Mark knew them all. Now he wanted, more than anything, to be involved in the decisions that would shape the future Australia.

Although it hadn't always been all hard work. Not in the beginning, anyway. There had been times when it was just Mark and Rosamund, and they had shut the door on the world. But there was a passion in Mark, a belief in himself that Rosamund had always admired. Even when it was taking him away from her. The name of his company, Markovic Constructions, in black bold capitals, was printed on all his stationery, and Rosamund felt it was a statement about the man himself. He always said he was destined for great things, and now he was making them happen.

Rosamund rubbed away some of the steam on

the mirror and peered at herself. The effect was like the sort of takes ageing actresses insisted upon to hide their lines and wrinkles. In the mirror was the girl Rosamund had been, with all her hopes and dreams. She wondered whether she would do what she had done if she had the chance to live her life again.

'Mrs Markovic?'

The voice was curious rather than diffident. Kerry Scott had known her too long, since the days when she was Rose Cunningham. Kerry had looked after Grandma Ada and knew all about the Cunningham family. Theirs was hardly the usual employer-employee relationship, but neither was it close. Kerry never overstepped the bounds, and if she felt sympathy for the child Rosamund had been, she didn't show it. Rosamund couldn't remember Kerry putting her arms about her, and Grandma Ada certainly hadn't. Her childhood had been a barren sort of place.

'Yes?' Rosamund pulled on her clothes and opened the door, letting out a puff of steam. She gave her hair a final rub. It hung thick and dark about her shoulders, making damp runnels on her crimson sweater. Her feet were bare.

Kerry Scott gave her an amused look. 'The builder is here to see you. Mr Markovic arranged for him to come first thing to discuss what has to be done. I've put him in the library downstairs.'

'Good. I'll see him in a moment.'

Kerry smiled and turned to go. She hadn't changed much. The grey hair had always been grey, perhaps she stooped a little more and moved more slowly. She must be close on sixty now, a widow for forty years, Ada Cunningham's companion for thirty. Prison sentences were shorter, and yet Kerry did not seem to feel that her life had been wasted.

Rosamund found her voice. 'Thank you for coming back to stay here, Kerry. I appreciate it.'

Kerry turned, looking surprised. 'It's no trouble. Your husband was paying me to stay anyway, while the work was going on.'

'I believe after my grandmother died you moved into your sister's house?'

Kerry glanced away, her mouth tightening. Rosamund sensed the other woman was more grateful than she let on that Mark had employed her as Colonsay's caretaker during the renovations.

'My sister is used to her own company,' Kerry said at last. 'And I enjoy having someone to look after. If you're sure that's what you want, Mrs Markovic?'

'Rosamund, please. And do you know, I think I might enjoy the experience,' Rosamund replied evenly, but Kerry was following her own line of thought.

'It worried me to see the house so neglected, but Mrs Ada would never sell, never. I'm so pleased you and Mr Markovic are going to live here.'

Rosamund looked about her, giving her hair another half-hearted rub. The corridor was a mess. Wallpaper peeling, stains that didn't bear too much examination, the carpet runner worn so thin she could see the unpolished floorboards beneath it. At the far end, several panes of the stained-glass window were broken and the rain had got in.

'How long is it since I was last here?' The question was aimed more at herself than the other woman, but Kerry answered promptly.

'Eighteen years.'

If there was a hint of reproach, Rosamund ignored it. She let her thoughts go back to that day, eighteen years ago, when she had left Colonsay. She had been how old then? Seventeen, nearly eighteen? Her life, her career had been just beginning, but Ada Cunningham hadn't understood that, hadn't wanted to. They had fought, bitterly, irrevocably. It had been Rosamund's big moment of rebellion, she had never found the courage for another. Afterwards, she had left Colonsay to make her own life. Ada had stayed on there alone, apart from Kerry Scott, growing feebler in mind and body, until she had more or less lived in a couple of rooms in the east wing, the rest of the house closed up. She had been an amazing 102 years old when she died last year, leaving the house to Rosamund.

Rosamund hadn't known whether to be pleased or angry when she received the news of her inheritance. She knew, in her heart, that Ada would have preferred to disinherit her, but blood ties had counted more. Rosamund was the last Cunningham and the house, or what was left of it, belonged to her. There had been no additional money for restoration or upkeep.

'Sell it,' Rosamund had said furiously. 'Bulldoze it. I don't care.'

That had appalled Mark. Mark, who had been born desperately poor, who hoarded his acquisitions like a Spanish conquistador. He'd travelled down to see Colonsay—Rosamund had refused outright to go with him. It was a Friday night and she had been going to a party. Some old friends, lots to catch up on. She had not come home until Sunday. He had been waiting for her, cool, handsome. He frightened her sometimes.

'You should grow up, Rose,' he said, and there was something in his voice, in his face, that was a warning. She had pushed him too far at last. The idea excited her and terrified her at the same time. It was as if she were waiting for something, though she didn't know what it was.

Mark had told her that he wanted Colonsay. He wanted it as he had never wanted anything in his life. It was the family home he had never had, and not just a home. It was a grand house with a grand tradition. The Cunninghams had been instrumental in settling the Bellarine Peninsula and later in making Australia a Federation. He, Mark Markovic, meant to be its new master.

She didn't have the strength to laugh at him, and besides, she understood him. When he put it to her that she should go down and oversee the restoration, she had merely nodded her head. And then he had said, 'I think we need a break from each other,' and made her feel like a balloon, plucked from safe fingers by the wind and heading for certain destruction.

'The builder, Mrs Mark—Rosamund.' Kerry was watching her, eyes puzzled.

Rosamund blinked, bringing her thoughts back to the here and now. 'Yes, of course. Give me five minutes. Perhaps you could make him some coffee or something.'

'Of course.' Kerry turned and went back down the stairs.

Silence filled the corridor, the banging and crashing from the front fading into the sounds of birds and a distant aeroplane. The stillness was heavy and sweet, like overripe fruit; the honeysuckle was back, as potent as before. Rosamund took a deep breath and looked towards the stained-glass window. The nymph in clinging robes stared back at her, hair twisted like rampant vines about her torso. One of her eyes was gone, and there was a crack running down her left breast. Sadness filled Rosamund, the beginnings of depression. The urge to have a drink before she went downstairs was strong, but she stifled it and returned to her room to finish dressing.

'I have to be honest with you, Mrs Markovic.'

Frederick Swann, the builder, made eye contact. Rosamund crossed her legs and waited.

'There are problems with the west wing—I understand it's been shut up for years now—problems with subsidence at the rear, although at this stage I'm ruling out rising damp. The cellar appears in good shape, but the roof has all but collapsed in one section. That's the worst of it, and it could be a lot worse. I know it looks bad, but structurally Colonsay's basically sound. It can be fixed, if you have the money.'

'My husband has plenty of money,' Rosamund replied.

He laughed. 'Well, if he wants to spend it on Colonsay, I won't stop him. I can't pretend the work isn't welcome.' He hesitated. 'Your husband is a builder himself, isn't he?'

'He's more your knock-it-down-build-it-new sort of builder. Renovations aren't his line.'

'Ah.'

'What else needs to be done with the house? You say that it's basically sound, structurally sound, but to me it looks a complete mess.'

'Well, if we put aside what we're going to do with the outbuildings—stables, barns, cottage, and so on—and deal only with the house, we'd be looking at replacement or repair of plaster, ceilings, floorboards, doors, doorframes, a step or two, electrical wiring, plumbing . . . that sort of thing.'

'Excuse me, but it sounds like a hell of a lot, Mr Swann.'

He frowned. He had blue eyes and there was a glint of disapproval in them. He had probably heard about her balcony appearance this morning. Rosamund felt her own lips twitch.

'You'll be staying in town?'

Surprised, Rosamund shook her head. 'No, I'll be staying here at Colonsay.'

'But it could be very uncomfortable, Mrs Markovic. Perhaps you don't realise just how uncomfortable these projects can be.'

'I can always move out if it gets too bad. And call me Rosamund, please. We'll be working together, won't we, Fred?'

'I prefer Frederick.'

She shrugged.

'I understand there are some furnishings stored under the roof. You'll have to move them out before we start work up there.'

'My grandmother called that the attic, though you're right, it's really little more than a crawl space under the roof. God knows what's up there.' When the old lady died, Rosamund had left the sorting of her personal belongings to Kerry Scott. Two pieces—a painting by Streeton and a Charles Rennie Mackintosh table—had been sold. The rest . . . Rosamund had been indifferent.

'Will I get my men to carry it all down for you?' Frederick Swann was saying. 'We could pack it into a couple of the downstairs rooms, out of the way, until you get around to sorting it out.'

'Yes. Thank you.'

She followed him outside. The ground was quite flattened by trucks and other vehicles and, underneath the thin surface layer of mud, felt like concrete. All that remained of the garden was a few half-buried paving stones and a broken piece of crockery. Someone's dog had been out for a run, Rosamund could see its paw prints everywhere.

'I haven't been back here for nearly twenty years,' she said, more to herself than to him. 'I had no idea of the state of the place.' No wonder Mark had been so angry.

'Houses like this need constant upkeep,' Frederick Swann said in a rather prim voice. 'I hear your grandmother closed off the rooms she wasn't using. She would've done better to have sold it to the National Trust, or some other historical body. Too late now, of course.'

'Oh, she would never have sold,' Rosamund informed him. 'The family was everything to her. Her father played a big part in setting up the Australian Constitution, and he was a member of the first Federal Parliament.' She hadn't spent her childhood listening to former Cunningham glories for nothing. 'And then there was the tragedy.'

'I've heard about it.'

'I rarely meet someone who hasn't.'

Ambrosine Cunningham, beautiful and admired, dead from influenza in the days before effective drugs. Her last breath was taken in the arms of her loving husband, who then strode out of Colonsay and into history. He set out in his sailing boat and, succumbing to his grief, gave himself to the sea.

'There was talk once of making a movie, but my grandmother refused to hear of it.'

'I can see her point.'

Rosamund hadn't, not then. Now she could understand how an intensely private woman like Ada would have fought to the death to keep her family's sad past from being turned into sentimental gloss for the public. Still, movies made money.

'Maybe it's not too late.'

Frederick Swann let that pass. 'I'll be back in the morning. We'll start on the roof then.' He hesitated. 'Are you sure you won't move out?'

'I'm sure.'

She gave him a brilliant smile and turned back to the house. It glared at her accusingly. One hundred and seventy years of Cunningham history come to this! She could almost see Cosmo and the rest of them shaking their fists. Several of the upper windows in the west wing were boarded up, part of the tiled roof had sunk and taken a chimney with it. The windows in the attic appeared to be intact, but their diamond panes were too dirty now to reflect the light. The verandah had been ripped down at some earlier date, only the markings on the bricks showing its previous position. The front door seemed exposed without it.

In contrast to the front garden, the western side of the house was overgrown with shrubs and weeds, invaders whose seeds had blown in from other areas. There were a dozen or so stalky-looking plants with reddy-purple tassels—the way they swayed together in the breeze made Rosamund think of women gossiping. Slowly she walked around the west wing, keeping close to the house. Old barns and stables leaned against each other, peering out from their weedy garments. A dilapidated cottage had been used as a storage shed and the remains of a fence leaned against a feral boxthorn hedge. As she approached, a bird flapped up angrily and sat scolding on the rust-spotted guttering above her. Rosamund cupped her hands to the cottage window and peered inside. Old hoes and rakes, a rusted lawn roller and a rotting tennis net. A moth, trapped in a spider web in one corner, fluttered hopelessly.

Whatever Fred Swann said, the job was monumental. She should be unutterably depressed. But she wasn't. Something was stirring in her, something that had been dormant for a very long time. Almost . . . almost she was exhilarated.

Rosamund wandered back to the front door. It stood open, as she had left it, an inky rectangle. She put her foot on the threshold and a wave of dizziness assailed her. She swayed and grasped the door jamb, but misjudging the distance fell against it instead and bruised her shoulder. The pain made her swear. She closed her eyes. Her head felt full of a heavy and suffocating darkness.

'*Rosie.*' A man's voice spoke distinctly in her ear.

'Mrs Markovic?' Kerry Scott was standing in front of her, eyeing her uneasily. Her nose twitched discreetly and Rosamund realised, with a shock, that she was trying to smell alcohol. She thought Rosamund was drunk.

Rosamund straightened, and discovered that the dizziness had gone as abruptly as it had come. 'I'm tired,' she said quietly. 'I think I'll go and lie down for an hour or two.'

She sensed Kerry watching her climb the stairs but no longer cared. If she was hearing voices when she was sober then she was in trouble. Mark was right. She had to pull herself together.

CHAPTER 3

'Here, hold this, will you?'

Meggy held out the bowl and Alice took it, holding the weight of it on her hip as Meggy found a grubby-looking handkerchief in her skirt pocket and blew her nose resoundingly. She said she had a cold but they looked like proper tears to Alice.

The mixture in the bowl smelled good—butter and sugar and eggs. Alice carefully poured in the mound of flour, still managing to spill some. She concentrated on what she was doing, adding first currants and then some of Mrs Gibbons's spices—cinnamon and grated nutmeg. Mrs Gibbons said spices made the difference to an otherwise bland mixture. 'Bit like life,' she had added with a twitch of her lips, so that Alice wondered if she was thinking of Harry Simmons.

'Are they for us?'

The voice, imperious for all its youth, came from the doorway. Alice glanced over her shoulder. 'No, they aren't, Miss Ada. Your governess know you're down here?'

Ada pulled a sulky face. 'I want one.'

Meggy muttered something, mopping her eyes hastily and thrusting her handkerchief back from where it had come. Alice continued to stir the mixture. 'You can't have one. They're not cooked yet.'

Ada strolled into the kitchen. Her boots were tiny button-ups and there was a frill on the hem of her pinafore and a shiny ribbon in her hair. She was a fairy creature, blonde and pretty, with lips as red as cotoneaster berries, but she was not the sweet child she pretended to be when her father and mother were close. Alice had felt the sting of her tongue, and the pinch of her small fingers.

'Bertie'll want one, too,' Ada said now, tapping one toe against the table leg. Her finger traced a pattern in the spilt flour. 'He's crying,' she added, and cast Alice a sly look. 'Up in the attic. You could take him one, if you liked. I won't tell. Not if you give me one, too.'

Meggy snorted and bent to check on the fire. The kitchen was warm compared to outside, where icy gusts of wind were blowing in off the bay, bringing with them rain like shotgun pellets and a cold dampness that crept right into your bones. Mrs Gibbons, who was prone to rheumatism, had taken a dose of her special tonic and gone to bed. She would be up again before dinner, but for now the two girls could manage without supervision.

'Why is Bertie crying?'

Alice knew it was the opening Ada had been waiting for, but she couldn't help asking.

'Because he has to go away to school,' Ada replied scornfully. 'I wouldn't cry, if it were me. I'd be glad! I have to stay here and learn my manners.' Her bottom lip stuck out sulkily.

'Well, go and learn your manners now,' Meggy told her, coming to help Alice place dainty spoonfuls of the mixture on the tray, ready for baking.

'When I grow up I'm going to send you both away,' Ada informed the two girls. 'I hope you both starve.'

Meggy sniffed when Ada had gone. 'Let's hope I'm not here by then.'

'You and Jonah will be back on the property on the Murray,' Alice replied, and set down her spoon.

Meggy's face closed in. 'Not likely,' she muttered, and went to slide the biscuits into the oven. 'These'll only take a minute. You're not really going to take some up to Master Bertie, are you?'

'Why not?' Alice retorted. 'He probably won't get food like this at that school he's going to.'

'His father's paying a fortune for him to go there, they'd hardly starve him, Alice.'

Maybe not, thought Alice, but you can be starved for more than food.

When the biscuits were cooked, Alice defiantly wrapped half a dozen in a fresh napkin and, ignoring Meggy's cynical eye, carried them up the back stairs. There was no-one about at this time of the day and it was easy to slip into the west wing, to the door in the wall that, once opened, disclosed the steep attic stairs. Narrow and dim, they were nevertheless well used. Bertie often came this way.

The air up here was warmer than in the rest of the house, the smells of discarded treasures hung heavily. The light from the diamond-paned windows was muddled, but there was sufficient for Alice to find her way between old boxes and unknown things covered in dust sheets. She was small enough to be able to walk without stooping, but an adult would have to bend if they were not to crack their head on the wooden beams.

'Bertie?' she whispered. The stuffed peacock

which had belonged to Cosmo's mother stared back at her, glass eyes dull and dusty. Bertie was there, hidden in the shadows behind a rolled carpet and a pile of yellowing music. She couldn't see any signs of tears on his face, but when he answered her his voice was scratchy. She laid the napkin down on the floor, and the smell of warm biscuits was released. Bertie smiled.

'Thank you, Alice,' he said, and crammed a whole biscuit in his mouth. Alice sat down beside him without being asked. They were friends, after all. 'What are you doing up here?' she asked curiously.

'Reading old letters,' Bertie said, and pulled over an opened box. The distinctive odour of mice lingered, and some of the paper had been chewed to make a nest. Alice glanced at the envelopes. They were of a thick and luxurious paper, and were addressed to Ambrosine McKay of The Meadows.

'My father wrote them to my mother, before they were married,' Bertie went on. 'He was very much in love with her.'

Alice didn't want to hear about Cosmo and Ambrosine, but she nibbled a biscuit and pretended to listen.

'They were neighbours, and my father and Mr McKay, my grandfather, arranged it between them.'

'Are the letters interesting?'

Bertie pulled a face. 'He calls her his Antipodean Beauty.'

Embarrassed, they smiled at each other.

'We could run away together.'

The words were spoken softly, but Alice heard. She looked at him sharply, wondering whether he was joking her, but he was looking towards the windows.

'Your father would find us and bring us back,' she answered him at last. 'He would still send you to school and I would have to go home to my father, and he'd give me a beating.'

'I know. I'm sorry.'

'I wish . . .' But she bit her lip on her wishes. Wishes were no use to Alice Parkin. A wave of despair swept over her and she wondered whether it was her own or Bertie's, or both.

His hand crept out and found hers, closing over it. His fingers were soft, the nails short and clean. Her own looked red and worn by comparison, already swollen by hard work.

'You'll write to me, Bertie?' she whispered. 'Promise me.'

'I promise,' he whispered back. And after that there was only the rain striking against the diamond-paned windows.

****

Rosamund poked her head through the doorway into the kitchen. Kerry Scott was busy by the stove. It was a modern white stove and looked slightly incongruous beside the remains of the old black range in the fireplace. There was a modern refrigerator, too, and a dish-washer. Mark had had them installed when Kerry had agreed to stay on at Colonsay. Rosamund wondered whether he had realised the restoration work would be quite so extensive and costly, and what he would say when he learned that she had decided to stay at Colonsay while it was going on. Perhaps he wouldn't care, as long as his wife was away from where she could do the most damage to his career.

'Can I help?'

Kerry turned around, her face showing surprise. The door to the back garden was open and the smell of trampled vegetation drifted into the kitchen, to join those of sawn wood and spicy tomato sauce.

'The workmen have all gone home,' Kerry said, by way of an answer. 'I made them cups of tea until I thought they'd leak. They'll be back for more tomorrow, I suppose.'

'Fred Swann should give Mark a discount if you feed and water his men for him.'

Kerry turned back to her sauce. There was a larger pot bubbling beside her. 'I thought we could have pasta tonight,' she murmured, and with a deft hand turned off both hotplates. She proceeded to remove crockery from a cupboard, placing it on the table.

'This room doesn't seem too bad,' Rosamund said, looking around. It was a hotchpotch of styles, nothing really matching, but when you looked at the rest of Colonsay it was almost a pleasure to be in.

'Did Frederick Swann say you could call him Fred?' The question was faintly censorious.

Rosamund shrugged. 'It suits him.' She walked to the door and stood looking out. Here were the remains of a vegetable garden. Stakes, once used for beans and peas and tomatoes, were now covered with weeds of the more rampant kind. Several of the red-tasselled plants lifted their heads through the rank mess. Rosamund felt she should know their name but she had forgotten it. The cottage behind the boxthorn hedge was almost invisible, only the top of the chimney showed. Pines made a windbreak behind the old brick stables, but Rosamund could hear the traffic. Where once had been only paddocks and sheep and silence was now a road, taking evening commuters home.

'The roof needs repairing,' she said. 'They're going to bring everything downstairs from the attic.'

Kerry dropped her spoon with a clatter. 'Good heavens! Do you know how much is up there? No-one's cleared out the attic for years and years.'

'Perhaps it's time someone did. We might find priceless treasures.'

Kerry laughed disbelievingly. 'If you're hoping for another Streeton, you'll be disappointed. There's nothing up there but dust and dirt. After Cosmo died . . . well, everything that was worth anything was sold. Mrs Ada kept what she wanted, no more. She was a frugal old lady.'

'Frugal as in bloody mean,' Rosamund muttered.

Kerry kept silent.

'I suppose you think it was wrong of me, not to visit her?'

The words were out at last, it was almost a relief to say them. Not, Rosamund reminded herself, that she really cared what Kerry Scott thought.

'No doubt you had your reasons, Mrs Markovic.'

Meaning I'm a selfish bitch, Rosamund interpreted. Kerry Scott had looked after Grandma Ada for thirty years and she, Rosamund, her only living relative, had left and never returned, not even for a visit. Maybe Colonsay should have been Kerry's, not hers; she deserved something for such devotion.

A magpie was sitting on part of what must once have been a small glasshouse. It stretched its neck and began to sing, the sweet sounds in harmony with the lengthening shadows. The smell of honeysuckle rose suddenly strong about her.

'*Rosie.*'

Rosamund turned sharply. 'What did you say?'

Kerry was ladling pasta onto two plates. She looked up through the steam rising from the food. 'Say? I didn't say anything, Mrs Markovic.'

Rosamund frowned. 'I heard you. What was it you said?'

Irritation crossed the older woman's face, and something like concern. 'Mrs Markovic, I assure you I said nothing.'

'For God's sake, call me Rosamund!'

Kerry stared at her a moment more and then dropped her eyes. 'Very well, Rosamund. I didn't say anything. Perhaps it was someone outside. Perhaps one of the workmen has come back.'

It was stupid to go on with it. The voice had been distinct, and it had not been Kerry's. Rosamund had known it was not Kerry's even when she accused her of speaking. She had just hoped it was.

'No,' she said at last. 'I'm sorry. I thought someone said "Rosie". It's the second time today it's happened. I . . . I must have been mistaken.' And then, when Kerry's face seemed to pinch in on itself, 'I'm hungry. Shall we eat?'

'I haven't set up the dining room,' she began agitatedly.

'We'll sit here. I don't want to eat in the dining room. It reminds me of Ada.'

Kerry's lips tightened but she said no more.

They were halfway through the meal when the phone rang. Kerry went to answer it in the hallway. After a few moments she returned. 'Mr Markovic wants to speak to you.'

Mark's voice came through the earpiece, smooth and mellow, like old port. 'Rose. I thought you were going to stay in town?'

'I changed my mind.'

'Won't it be inconvenient? Kerry says the place is a terrible mess.'

'It is. What did you ring for? To check on me? For Kerry's report? If you want to know what I've been up to, you'd better ask me.'

There was a pause. 'All right, I will. What have you been up to, Rose?'

She was tempted to tell him about the bottle, about her naked body at the window, but couldn't find the courage. 'I've seen the builder,' she said instead, almost grudgingly. 'There's a lot needs doing. Do you know what you're letting yourself in for?'

'I don't care what it costs.'

She wanted to tell him how stupid he was being, how ridiculous it was to want to own such a place, to think that owning it would turn him into some nineteenth-century sheep baron. 'Is that why you married me?' she heard herself saying. 'Because of who I was? Did you need a wife with my pedigree, Mark, part of the packaging? To go with the expensive suits and the important friends? You must be so disappointed.'

She had never said it before and she felt her emotions bubbling inside her. Mark's silence was more pointed than any words he could have spoken.

When at last he spoke, his voice was calm, urbane, empty. 'You know that's not true.'

'It is, it is,' she hissed. 'I'm nothing, Mark. I'm not a person to you, am I?'

'You're being ridiculous. We'll discuss it when I come down. I have to go now.'

'Go where? I can't cope with this any more, Mark. I can't deal with this any more!'

'Rose. Have you been drinking?'

Fury boiled up and exploded inside her. 'No, I bloody have not!'

She slammed the phone down. Her hand was wet from gripping the handset and she wiped it against her jeans. The silence in the hallway was complete, not even the tick of a clock or the rustle of a curtain. She imagined Mark shrugging and going off to his appointment. She had never felt quite so desolate or alone in her life.

Rosamund had meant to make amends with Kerry by cleaning up in the kitchen, but now she knew she couldn't face the other woman. She opened the door to the library, where she had earlier spoken to Fred Swann, and closed it behind her.

There was still some light coming from the uncovered windows and she looked about her. Books lined the shelves along two walls, though no-one had bothered to read them in a long time. Ada had never been one for reading. The two chairs by the fireplace were leather, old and cracked in places, worn smooth on the seats with use. Rosamund ran her fingers across one of them. The leather felt warm, as if someone had been sitting there and had only just left the room. Wood smoke and cigar smoke mingled faintly in the air. Rosamund sniffed. Perhaps one of the workmen had been having a surreptitious puff. Cosmo used to enjoy his cigars, she remembered Ada telling her so. Ada idolised her father.

'Without my father there would have been no Federation,' she would say. 'Cosmo Cunningham was a powerful and clever man, a giant among pigmies. He told the likes of Prime Minister Barton what to do, not the other way around.'

Such things hadn't mattered to Rosamund. She had neither known nor cared about the past. Her mind was centred firmly in the present and the future, and the songs she was going to sing. Her voice was special, she had been told so a hundred times. Sweet and smoky, it resonated with all the depth of emotion she was incapable of showing in words or actions. It came from deep in her soul. Grown men had been known to cry when Rose Cunningham sang.

Mark hadn't cried but he had been impressed. He'd been on his way to the top when they met. A year or two later and he wouldn't have been seen dead in the pub Rosamund was singing in. It was sheer spur-of-the-moment luck that she'd been there herself. The band's single, 'Grey Skies', had made it into the charts and was soaring. They were about to release an album and promotional tours were lined up. The whole bit. The pub was where they started out, and a combination of exhilaration and nostalgia had brought them back that night.

It was very crowded, but Mark had sat and listened to her for an hour and then walked over to her table. She was sitting with Dave, her manager/lover, and the bass guitarist. Mark told her she sang the way he felt and asked if he could buy her a drink.

Dave told her later that it was boring hovering at the edges of something as intense as the emotion radiating between Mark and Rosamund, only he didn't put it quite that way. 'When you've slept with him get back to me,' he said, as if one night would get Mark out of her system. But even then Rosamund knew it was more than that.

Had Mark's feelings for her intensified when he discovered she was one of the famous Cunninghams? Had he decided, then, that he wanted to marry her? Rosamund hadn't cared. He dazzled her. She had wanted him. There had been a choice to make and she'd made it. Her career vanished overnight and she didn't even mind. She had gained Mark and a lifestyle she enjoyed. It was only gradually that she realised she had given up a great deal more than her singing.

Rosamund blinked. The light was fainter, the room was almost in darkness, but she didn't want to turn on the light. There used to be a sewing box in here, she remembered suddenly. It had been disguised as a small table, but when the hinged lid was lifted there was a cunningly arranged space inside, where Ada had kept her sewing and a jumble of other bits and pieces. She had sewn with a concentration that showed determination rather than pleasure. 'I was taught as a girl to be a good needlewoman,' she told Rosamund. 'I have never forgotten.'

'I thought Cosmo was enlightened where women were concerned,' Rosamund had replied.

Ada gave her a hard look. She had a glare that could freeze fire when she cared to use it. 'I never said that, Rosamund. He was a brilliant man, and he could be a kind man, but he did not believe women were men.'

Ada, for all her age and infirmity, had been a formidable woman and Rosamund had never been very brave. How could she be, when every spark that ever flared had been promptly squashed by her grandmother? Their last confrontation must have come as a shock to the old lady, it had certainly come as a shock to Rosamund. And then she had been out in the world, alone for a time at least, dizzy with the excitement of it. With the freedom of it. Then Mark had come along and she had clung to him, just as she clung to everyone strong in her life. As if, like a plant grown in poor light, she was too weak to stand alone.

The light flicked on, its brightness momentarily blinding her. Kerry Scott stood in the doorway, face creased in a frown. 'Are you all right? I thought you'd gone to bed.'

Rosamund ran a hand through her hair. 'I needed a moment. I'm all right.'

'What did Mr Markovic say?'

Rosamund's hand dropped. 'He implied I was making a nuisance of myself by staying here,' she said drily.

Kerry flushed, her pale skin colouring easily, but her answer was firm enough. 'I'm glad of the company.'

Rosamund hid a smile, searching in her pocket for a cigarette. By the time she had lit it, the silence had grown uncomfortable. Kerry was biting her lip. Rosamund, watching her, felt a sudden tingle in her spine.

'I wondered . . .' Kerry began, 'I was thinking about what you said before about hearing someone speak. I remembered something. Your grandmother often used to say that when you were young you heard voices here at Colonsay. Do you remember that?'

Rosamund shook her head slowly, eyes fixed on Kerry. 'I don't remember that. Heard voices? What sort of voices? Were you here then?'

'It was over by the time I arrived.'

'Did she take me to a doctor, for God's sake?'

'She didn't think they were those sort of voices.'

'What did they say, these voices?'

Kerry looked uneasy. 'Your name, mostly, I think. Rose, or was it Rosie? Maybe both. You were very young at the time. You grew out of it. She assumed it was some childhood fancy. What else could it have been?'

Rosamund drew on her cigarette. Whatever it was then, it's come back now, she thought bleakly. Her mind skittered away, seeking something safer, less worrisome. 'Do you know where my grandmother's sewing box is?'

Kerry started. 'Why yes. I have it in my room.' She smiled nervously. 'She gave it to me, but of course, if you—'

'Oh no, no. It's yours, Kerry. You keep it.' Rosamund felt suddenly exhausted. It had been a long, long day. 'I'll go up now.'

'Of course. I'll lock up.'

The stairs creaked in several places and the banister rail had a crack running down the middle of it. Rosamund watched her feet reach the landing and move, one after the other, as if they belonged to someone else, along the threadbare runner towards her bedroom. As she opened the door the scent of honeysuckle wafted out to meet her.

CHAPTER 4

Frederick Swann arrived the next day with the intention of clearing the attic so that his men could begin work on the sagging roof. He was concerned, he told Rosamund, that the whole lot might cave in.

'A good heavy storm, plenty of rain, and we'd have a massive job on our hands.'

'It looks massive enough as it is.'

He smiled. 'You'll soon see the difference.'

Rosamund let him get on with it. Judging by the smells coming from the kitchen, Kerry was baking, and Rosamund wasn't about to interfere. She decided to spend the morning reacquainting herself with the house.

The original Cunningham home was still there, and formed the central block of Colonsay. To either side were the wings, built by Cosmo for his wife in the late nineteenth century. He had been clever enough not to make Colonsay too big or ostentatious, but nevertheless it was very impressive, and in its day often remarked upon.

Rosamund walked into the west wing and found it as forlorn inside as out. The empty rooms were chilly, with a distinctly damp feel. Some of the plasterwork on the ceilings and walls was host to a grey mould, and water had leaked through the window frames and stained the floral wallpaper. A patch of floor in one room had turned crumbly, and when she unknowingly stepped on it her shoe went through. She was able to pull back her foot without any damage to it.

The downstairs east wing contained the kitchen and library, and two rooms at the back where Fred Swann's men were busy packing the attic treasures. During a lull in the traffic on the stairs, she hurried up.

Dust and noise filtered down from the men in the attic. The house, despite the obvious neglect, was much as Rosamund remembered. If she closed her eyes she could see the heavy furniture, the faded curtains, and Ada Cunningham's unsmiling face. 'This is your heritage,' her grandmother used to tell her.

Rosamund wondered why Ada had decided to make her future in the past, here at Colonsay. A past which had not been kind to her. There had been the deaths of her brother and parents when she was still a child, and then later, when Ada was a young married woman, her husband had died in France, fighting the Great War. Perhaps it had been a combination of the tragedies which had caused Ada's withdrawal from the world.

Voices yelled and timber crashed to the attic floor above Rosamund's head. She jumped. Perhaps upstairs wasn't the place to be just now.

After descending the staircase Rosamund noticed the door to the cellar. It was set in the hall, a low, solid door which Rosamund remembered as always being locked. The cellar ran under the central and older part of the house. Cosmo Cunningham had been famous for his wine collection but Rosamund didn't expect to find that any bottles had been overlooked. She played her fingers against the white painted wood, hesitating for reasons she didn't understand, and then dropped her hand to the doorknob. It turned easily and the door swung outwards. Rosamund stepped onto the small landing and peered down.

There was a light switch, and when she flicked it a bulb above her head came on, as well as several others in the cellar itself. Rosamund ventured down the ladderlike stairs and felt the air grow cooler at every step. Barred windows were set at ground level along the front and back walls, and soil and seepage had come through onto the brick floor. The cellar was actually three rooms, one large and two small. The smaller ones appeared to contain nothing but dust and cobwebs. The large one still retained wooden wine racks against one wall—though they were long empty—a couple of wooden barrels and the well.

The well wasn't a hole in the floor, but a raised circular structure of brick, the top of which was covered by a rotting wooden lid. Ada, Rosamund remembered, had always enjoyed a glass of water from the old well, if she could persuade someone to fetch it up for her. Neither Kerry nor Rosamund had much liked the cellar, Kerry because she suffered from claustrophobia, Rosamund because of the spiders.

Approaching it now, she wondered if there was still water in it. There used to be a pulley mechanism fixed to the brim, with a bucket, but that had gone the way of the wine. Rosamund grasped the lid and pulled until it moved enough to allow her to peer down into the depths. A gleam of something wet slid into view. A piece of crumbling wood dislodged and spun into the well with a soft plonk.

Outside in the front garden an engine revved and doors slammed. Rosamund glanced up towards the barred window but could see nothing. She felt removed from the rest of the house. The silence, the shadows, seemed suddenly oppressive. Rosamund gave the lid a shove, and with a thud it slotted back into place over the well. Dust billowed up and she grimaced, wiping her eyes. At the same moment she heard someone walk across the brick floor behind her.

Rosamund spun around, bruising her hip on the edge of the well. Another chunk of the lid broke off and hit the water with a loud splash. 'Kerry?'

There was no-one there.

She made her way through the smaller rooms, peering about her. They were empty. Of course they were. No-one could have entered the cellar without her seeing them. At the top of the ladder the cellar door was open, but she had the awful sensation that at any moment it might close and trap her.

Rosamund made herself walk normally to the steps and climb them, one at a time, while the adrenalin was surging through her, screaming at her to run, to fling herself onto the ladder and drag herself to safety. When she reached the top, she stepped out into the hall and closed the door behind her with a dull thump.

Relief was short-lived.

'*Rosie!*' This time the voice seemed to come from the back of the house, low and drawn out, almost a sob.

Rosamund lost control and half ran, half stumbled towards the kitchen. She felt as if a huge hand were squeezing her chest, squeezing her lungs, stopping her breathing.

Kerry was standing by the table pouring tea into a dozen strong china mugs, a huge plate of sandwiches on a tray beside her. She looked up, startled, at Rosamund's hasty entrance. 'Is anything wrong?'

Rosamund gave a quick glance towards the open door into the back yard. A man stood in the doorway, leaning against it as if he had all the time in the world. He was wearing shorts and little else and his fair hair curled like a halo around his head. He looked vaguely familiar, but in her present state Rosamund could not place him.

'You look pale,' Kerry went on. Then to the man in the doorway she said, 'Here's your tea, Gary.'

Gary nodded at Rosamund. He had lazy blue eyes and his languid smile stopped her headlong rush as effectively as a levee bank. He waited while Kerry added a jug of milk and a bowl of sugar to the tray, and then he lifted it with surprising delicacy. 'Thanks, Kerry,' he said. 'I'll bring it all back in one piece when we're finished.'

'I know you will, Gary.'

With another nod at Rosamund, he made his confident way outside.

'That was Gary,' Kerry repeated unnecessarily, watching her.

'You said.'

'Don't you remember him? Gary Munro? Enderby's grandson.'

Now the past came swimming back. In the 1920s, Enderby Munro's family had owned the old hotel at the Springs, a couple of kilometres by road from Colonsay. The Springs, or more properly Clifton Springs, had at one time been a popular place for taking mineral waters. Devotees came from Geelong and Melbourne, making the journey across the bay on the steamers which regularly travelled back and forth. The Springs became big business on the peninsula, and Munro's Hotel was more often than not full to the rafters. Rosamund recalled seeing an old newspaper advertisement praising the healing properties of the water, claiming it cured anything from syphilis to tuberculosis.

Munro's Hotel was gone by the time Rosamund was born, flattened under the peninsula housing boom of the 1950s and '60s; the same developers had taken up most of the Cunningham acres. However, tales of it lived on and had given Enderby and Ada a lot to talk about, the former boasting of his grand hotel and the latter her grand family.

Gary Munro had lived in Melbourne with his parents, but every year during the summer holidays for about ten years he came to stay with his grandfather on the Bellarine Peninsula. He had been a moody boy, and Rosamund a quiet, shy girl. As far as she remembered, they had never had much to say to each other.

'Why is he working for Fred Swann?' she asked at last. Her heart had settled to a quieter thump and her breathing was back to normal.

'He needs the money. He's a writer, or trying to be. He used to be with a city newspaper—you must have seen his column. When he decided to write a novel he came here. Now he works for Mr Swann. I expect when he's finished the book he won't need to keep the job.'

Rosamund considered. Gary Munro, famous author? Somehow she didn't think so.

'I told him you were here,' Kerry went on. 'I thought you'd have recognised him.'

'It's been twenty years, Kerry.'

Kerry wiped up a spill on the work bench. 'You always looked forward to his visits.'

O Memory! thou fond deceiver, thought Rosamund. The most charitable emotion she had ever had concerning Gary Munro was indifference. She wondered, suddenly, if Gary had ever heard the voices. Or the footsteps. Footsteps in an empty room.

****

Mrs Gibbons had been out again. Alice heard her pass by the window. She was singing a different song tonight, something about two little girls all in blue. Mrs Gibbons liked a good singsong.

Alice wondered what they found to talk about, her and Harry Simmons. She had heard that Harry used to be a showman, way back in the gold-rush days. He had moved from town to town, setting up his tent, singing his songs, doing his turns.

Alice smiled to herself. Did Mrs Gibbons and old Harry polka together around and around the swamp, kicking up their heels? Did Harry recite to the moon while Mrs Gibbons sat upon the damp ground, her plump white face a reflection, glowing with love?

It hardly bore thinking.

Her smile faded. She was making up silly stories to amuse herself, to divert herself. Because Bertie was gone. He had gone off yesterday and Alice missed him unbearably. She wondered whether he was thinking of her. Meggy would say not, but Alice believed he was. He had pleaded at the last, pleaded with Ambrosine to allow him to stay. In reply, his mother had tried to buck up his spirits, talking about the friends he would make, the fun he would have. When he wouldn't be jollied by that, she had grown impatient and irritably told him that his father had made up his mind and Bertie had best do likewise.

'Mr Cunningham says that the school you go to is as important as the woman you marry,' Mrs Gibbons informed them all at tea. 'I expect young Bertie will be as famous as his father, one day.'

Alice, pretending to chew her bread and butter, had found nothing to reply, while under the table Meggy squeezed her hand.

Outside, a dog was barking. Alice turned over in the creaky bed and stared into the darkness. She could just see the shape of the wash jug and basin, the gleam of the towel, and the squat chest of drawers that she and Meggy shared between them. The top right-hand drawer was the receptacle of Alice's two neatly folded handkerchiefs, a comb, a cairngorm which had once been an earring belonging to her grandmother but was now suspended on a neck chain, a small tarnished bottle of violet water, and Mr Marling's button.

She had thought of throwing the button away, but each time she held it in her hand something had made her keep it.

Her thoughts drifted. Alice had met Mr Marling in the hall this afternoon. She had been coming up from the cellar with a jug of well water, and Mr Marling had been coming briskly down the stairs, as though he were late for something terribly important. Reaching the bottom of the staircase he had turned, seemingly at a loss, and seen Alice.

'Fetch my hat and cane, would you, Alice? I'd call out, but Mrs Gibbons might come and she terrifies me.'

Alice had smiled at that, although she doubted anything could terrify Mr Marling. He had a look in his eye, that one. She hurried to find his hat and cane and handed them to him. He thanked her nicely, he was always nice. And because he was so nice, she was brave enough to ask, 'Is the painting nearly finished, sir?'

He glanced up from adjusting his hat in the oval-shaped mirror on the wall, and raised his eyebrows. Mrs Gibbons said he was vain for a man, but Alice thought he had a lot to be vain about. Not many men were as beautiful as Mr Marling.

'Nearly done, Alice.'

'What will you do then, sir? When it's finished, I mean?'

He had hooked the cane over his arm, and now he hesitated. 'You know, I hadn't thought about it, Alice. I don't know what I'll do then. No doubt something will crop up.'

Once, Alice had heard the governess gossiping in hushed tones to Ada's nanny about Mr Marling. 'They say he's a Bohemian,' the governess had murmured, and the tone of her voice had been at once shocked and excited, so Alice knew a Bohemian was not like a butcher or a baker, or something like that. The next time she was dusting the library, she had looked the word up in the big dictionary.

Mr Marling wasn't from Bohemia, he was as Australian as Alice, although he spoke posh. He must be the other thing, the 'person of free and easy morals'. She could imagine a man like Mr Marling following a different set of rules from everyone else.

Alice blinked in the darkness, her eyes fixed on her drawer. Her thoughts were beginning to shock her less than they used to. Now, when she thought of Ambrosine and Mr Marling together, on the day-bed, she hardly squirmed at all. She had grown quite used to the idea. It was no longer a fantasy or a trick of her imagination. It had become a truth.

It took Fred Swann's men only a day to bring downstairs from the attic what had taken over a hundred years to accumulate. When they had finished, the two rooms on the ground floor at the back of the house were full to bursting with Cunningham artefacts.

Rosamund looked in the first room and some kind of stuffed fowl stared glassily back at her, so that she closed the door again hastily. The past had waited this long, she told herself, it could wait a bit longer.

Kerry looked tired after they had eaten the evening meal. Rosamund sent her up to bed and set about tidying up alone. They had settled on a routine, she and Kerry. Kerry cooked and Rosamund helped. At first Kerry had protested, but Rosamund insisted.

She stared at her pale reflection in the uncovered

window above the sink. Her eyes seemed larger than usual and had shadows underneath. Behind her, the fridge hummed and the dishwasher whooshed softly. Outside in the darkness, the wilderness which had once been the back garden thrashed in the gusty wind, as though some animal ran amok among the thistles and nettles and waist-high grass.

I had a very peculiar childhood, thought Rosamund. A child, alone here at first with Grandma Ada, and then with her and Kerry Scott. No wonder I heard voices. I was probably appallingly lonely. I know I was odd. Other children told me so.

She believed she had changed, rounded her personality out into something more 'acceptable'. But maybe the odd child was still there inside her, like a chicken in an egg, chipping away at the shell until gradually there was a hole large enough for her to peer out.

A particularly savage gust rattled the window pane. The big pine trees that shielded the road shivered and groaned.

Rosamund didn't really remember her own parents. Her father, Ada's son, had died from cancer when she was still a baby and her mother, never mentally or emotionally strong, had had a complete nervous breakdown. She had ended up in a mental institution—it was in the days before such people were treated in the community—and there she stayed until, when Rosamund was ten, she too died. Rosamund remembered the funeral, the dreariness of it, burying a mother she hardly knew, and the silence of the mourners. There had only been a couple, and they had come for Ada's sake rather than Rosamund's mother.

They had thought Ada was very brave to care for Rosamund, at her age. They had thought she was wonderful.

'I'm her only surviving Cunningham relative,' she had replied to their murmured praise. 'It is my duty.'

They assumed she was being modest, but it had been the literal truth. Duty, to Ada, was everything.

Ada had brought her up, Rosamund gave her that, but it had been the upbringing of another era, an era when women married well and said little, and gloried in their men. While Rosamund sat quietly in the library doing her homework, or read aloud so that Ada could correct her pronunciation and her diction, other children were watching television or playing with Barbie and Ken.

Ada had been a strange mixture of the middle class and the eccentric. It was as if she were a left-over from another world. She had no desire to keep up with the present, and could not understand Rosamund being any different. For Ada, the past was enough.

When it came to cooking and cleaning, Ada made do with a series of girls from the town. The house was so big, even then it was never properly clean. Rosamund realised, afterwards, that money had been shorter than Ada let on. Perhaps if she had sold Colonsay then, she might have lived out the rest of her days in a nice little cottage by the sea. But of course she would never have done that.

Several of the girls left after only a couple of days. Rosamund suspected it was Ada's exacting demands which had driven them away. She expected her employees to work hard for the privilege; she didn't seem to comprehend that the modern world was powered by money, not loyalty. In Kerry Scott, however, she found the perfect servant.

Kerry, a timid soul and childless, deferred to 'Mrs Ada' in everything. When she was alone with Rosamund she seemed uncertain how to treat her—there was little empathy. In her way, she was kind, although by no stretch of the imagination could she have been called motherly.

Rosamund attended the local primary school and the high school in Geelong—there was, by then, no money for a private education. She never fitted in, how could she? At first it mattered to her, but after a time she pretended it didn't and kept her own counsel. No-one, according to Ada, was good enough to be her friend anyway, not with the extraordinary Cosmo for a great-grandfather. Rosamund never excelled, but she did enough to get by. Whenever possible, she tried to blend in, to become invisible.

Then, when she was sixteen, Rosamund's life suddenly and irrevocably changed.

A pop concert had been held in a paddock belonging to Colonsay's neighbour. All night long Rosamund listened to the beat of the music and watched the glow of bonfires and stage lights. Her blood stirred to the life and noise; it was like being at the border of a foreign country and she longed to defect.

She had always sung, little songs she made up or those she had heard. Ada owned an old pianola and boxes full of sheet music, and when she played she would ask Rosamund to sing along. They sang 'There's A Long, Long Trail' and 'Roses Of Picardy' from the Great War, Ada's heyday. There were other songs, quite dreadful in Rosamund's eyes, full of death and grieving and mothers being exhorted to send their sons to fight in France. She wondered if Ada thought of her soldier husband when she played these songs. Did she experience again the pain and the grief when he hadn't come back? Did the words tug at her heart, opening wounds invisible to Rosamund? Somewhere, deep in Ada, there must be a pocket of humanity.

It was pointless asking; Ada never answered personal questions. She belonged to the school which believed that displaying one's feelings was bad manners.

Although Rosamund had always been aware of music as a source of pleasure, she had never seen it as more than that. But listening to the sounds coming from the neighbour's paddock, she had realised she could sing like that, too. Was it possible that singing, the one thing she could do well, might be a way of escape for her? A way out of Colonsay?

When morning came, Rosamund climbed through the fence and investigated. The paddock was littered with rubbish and bodies in sleeping-bags. A van was selling cups of coffee and egg and bacon rolls to those on their feet. A few band members were standing around drinking coffee. Rosamund, experiencing an immense rush of uncharacteristic courage, had walked boldly up and told them she could sing, that she wanted to join them.

She cringed now at the memory of herself, a tall and gangly teenager, hair unbrushed, terrified but driven. In the circumstances they had been surprisingly kind. One of them had found a guitar, played a few chords and Rosamund had sung.

Their expressions changed immediately. They

looked at each other, and then looked at her. Dave was always on the lookout in those days. He told her, much later, with a laugh, that he knew from the first moment she was star material. 'You've got a voice,' he said to the teenage Rosamund. 'Have some lessons, learn to control it and not the other way round. And find some songs that will show it off properly. Get back to me when you've done that and I'll see what I can do.'

Rosamund was a bit disappointed—and probably a bit relieved—when they didn't agree to take her with them, but she took the business card Dave gave her and tucked it into her pocket.

For hours after that she wandered along the cliffs in a dream, imagining a life so different from the one she currently inhabited it felt like one of the television serials she was never allowed to watch. Ada had sent her to her room when she got back, but it was worth it.

She plucked up the courage to ask Ada to arrange for singing lessons. Ada never tried to prevent her, indeed she encouraged her. To her, singing was a perfectly acceptable accomplishment in a young lady, as long as it was done for the entertainment of friends and family. She never imagined that Rosamund dreamed of being on a stage, in front of strangers, singing for money. She never imagined that Rosamund might want to leave Colonsay and strike out for herself in the modern world that was little more than a blur to her grandmother.

In a year Rosamund learned a lot. Her teacher had been excited from the first time she heard Rosamund sing. 'I don't pretend a singing career would be an easy step for you, Rose, but you certainly have the talent.'

Lots had talent, it seemed, but you needed more. Ambition and determination, the right temperament and the right contacts. Well, Rosamund had one of the latter at least. She took out the card with Dave's address on it, carefully hidden away in her jewellery box, wrote a letter, and mailed it on her way to her singing lesson the following week. It took a gut-wrenching month for Dave to reply, and when he did Ada opened the letter.

There was hell to pay.

'You will not go to this man. Singing in public houses! I will never allow it, Rosamund.' Ada's voice wavered with anger, up and down the scale. 'Go to your room.'

Despair filled Rosamund.

'As from this moment there will be no more singing lessons. There will be no more singing. I had thought your voice a gift, Rosamund. Now I see it is a curse.'

Despair gave way to anger. She felt it surge through her in a glorious, liberating wave. 'I *will* keep singing, and I *will* keep my appointment with Dave. You can't stop me!'

'Can't I now?' she shrilled. 'Can't I now, girl! You are a Cunningham, and Cunninghams do not display themselves for the pleasure of others.' But she was suddenly so old and so feeble-looking, Rosamund was no longer afraid of her.

'I'm leaving this house now,' she whispered, and her throat felt sore and tight, as though she might cry. 'I'm going now, Grandma Ada.'

The old lady stared back at her with eyes as hard as pebbles. 'If you go now, then I'll never have you back,' she said, and Rosamund didn't doubt that she meant it. Ada never said anything she didn't mean.

'Then this is the last time I'll ever see you.'

There was a gasp from the doorway. Rosamund had not realised that Kerry Scott was standing there.

'You have abused my trust and for that I will never forgive you. You are a Cunningham, the last of us. You are to inherit this house when I die.'

The promise terrified Rosamund. 'No! I don't want Colonsay. I hate it, I hate it.'

Ada's white face went even whiter, her voice a thin reed. 'Your feelings in this matter are of no interest to me.'

Well, she had been true to her word, thought Rosamund, still gazing into her own reflection. Colonsay had come to her. And here she was now, her singing career a joke, her life in tatters, with nothing to do but restore the house to its former glory. Ada would be so pleased.

Perhaps it was Ada's voice which had called for Rosie, and Ada's footsteps in the cellar. Perhaps Ada still could not leave the house she had refused to relinquish in life.

Even as the thought entered her head, Rosamund dismissed it. The voice, so low in timbre, could only be a man's, and the footsteps . . . they had sounded light and quick, like a woman's or a child's.

She shivered, and turned away from the window.

Rosamund had never believed in ghosts. The thought of an invisible world separate from her own was just too much for her to accept. And yet, where had the voice come from? The footsteps?

Upstairs, Rosamund closed her bedroom door. She had cleared away the lump of plaster in the corner, swept the floor and shaken the two worn rugs with their barely discernible oriental designs. With things a little less chaotic, she undressed for bed.

Outside, the wind still moaned through the big pine trees at the back, but here at the front of the house it was quieter. The curtains were tied and Rosamund could see the navigation light on top of the You Yangs flashing on and off. She watched it for a moment, wearily resting her forehead against the cold glass.

She wondered what Mark was doing. Attending a meeting, a dinner? Making friends, finding supporters, smiling the smile that everybody warmed to. Rosamund remembered that smile. She had once thought him the most handsome man she had ever seen. He seemed sophisticated, urbane. She could hardly believe it when she learned of his background, the terrible poverty, the forced emigration, the harsh and brutal day-to-day life of his family, all of which had combined to make Mark a driven and ambitious man. He had his eyes set so firmly on his goals that he had forgotten about Rosamund, and when she had lost her way there had been no-one to help her find it again.

Perhaps he had never realised how much she needed him. By the time she met him in that smoky pub, she had learned to exhibit a kind of sophistication. The years with Dave had done that. Dave had filed the jagged edges from her, filled in the spaces. He had given her the confidence to sing her songs without worrying too much about the audience. Just the singing was enough. It took her out of herself, was almost a spiritual experience. She had told Dave that once, but he had laughed so hard at her she had turned it into a joke, pretending she had meant it to be all along. She and

Dave had been living together when she met Mark, and before Dave there had been a couple of others. She thought herself grown up.

She had been wrong.

Rosamund stared out into the garden without really seeing. The light on the You Yangs winked again. She blinked back. Her bare feet had grown quite cold, the chill from the bare floorboards soaking into her soles. The room itself was icy. As she turned for bed there was a distinct thud upstairs in the attic.

CHAPTER 5

'You're paler than you ought to be, Alice,' Mira said, shifting the baby on her hip. 'Are you well?'

'Yes, Mother.'

Mira sighed. Her daughter had been sullen on the last two visits, but there was nothing wrong with her that she could discover. Twelve was an awkward age.

'We read about Mr Cunningham in the newspaper,' she went on. 'Winning his seat in the elections for the Federal Parliament.'

Mr Parkin gave his wife an impatient look. 'How could he not win, a man like that?'

Alice remembered that her father had saved Cosmo from the sea when they were lads. She wanted to ask him what Cosmo had been like as a boy, but did not quite dare. Her father probably wouldn't answer her anyway, would just tell her to mind her own. Her parents never discussed anything interesting, at least not in front of their children.

'How are the boots standing up, Alice?' he asked her as she took her leave.

The smile felt false and painful on her face. 'Very well, thank you, Father.'

'Look after them, won't you?'

'I will, Father.'

'You're damned lucky, Alice. To be serving a fine family like that. Following in your dad's foot-prints, huh?' He patted her bony shoulder. It was the nearest he ever got to affection.

On the walk back to Colonsay, Alice passed the Old Soldiers' Home. That was the name by which it was known locally, but actually it had a far grander title. The United Services Home for Veterans. It had been built in the 1890s, due, it was said, to Cosmo Cunningham's determination to create an antipodean haven where England's destitute heroes could end their days in the comfort they deserved. He had been presented with a sword for his trouble and it now hung in the library. Alice didn't remember the laying of the foundation stone—she had been only a baby—but it had been a grand occasion, with the Governor aboard the *Lady Loch* steaming over the bay from Melbourne.

The Old Soldiers' Home was built of brick and shaded by wide verandahs. There was a large encircling garden, and the veterans, those not prevented by old age or old wounds, often worked in it. One of the old soldiers was hoeing as Alice passed, meticulously removing weeds from a row of chrysanthemums. He glanced up and she recognised Sergeant Petersham, a soldier of the Crimea. He was one of Ambrosine's good deeds. When he had been ill, two winters past, she had visited him at the home, bringing some of Mrs Gibbons's broth with her. For Christmas she had sent him a new scarlet greatcoat and a new three-cornered hat. When he was well again, Petersham had stumped out to Colonsay to pay his respects, sitting stiff as a wooden skittle in the drawing room while Ambrosine poured tea into dainty cups and chatted about the weather.

He had been smitten by her ever since.

It puzzled Alice how men could be so blind. Tough old soldiers like Petersham who must have seen so much human suffering and brutality, and yet could not see through Ambrosine's shallow beauty to her selfish core. And not just Petersham. There was Cosmo, Mr Marling, even Bertie, who refused to blame his mother for doing nothing to prevent him being sent to that dreadful school.

He was terribly unhappy. Alice could tell by his letters. He wanted to come home. Surely his mother would know that? But she didn't seem to. She was still busy sitting for Mr Marling's portrait, which was taking a very long time indeed. It was Alice who was counting the days until the term holidays. It was Alice who prayed that Bertie would win his mother over, that she wouldn't send him back.

Alice had hoped to get by the Old Soldiers' Home with just a nod and a pleasant smile, but Petersham called out in his gravelly voice. 'Tell Mrs Cunnin'ham I'll pick her the best o' the chrysanths.' And he gestured at the gaudy flowers.

'Tell her yourself,' Alice muttered, but she smiled and nodded again.

'Is she in good health, girl?'

'The best, sir.'

'Ah, now, that's grand, that is, that's grand.'

Alice walked on, kicking at the dusty road until her pinching boots and the hem of her grey skirt were covered in a fine layer of brown. The wind teased her hair out of its knot and into her eyes, and she squinted to stop them watering. The air was chill today, as was proper this far into autumn.

Cosmo was away again, but he would be back next week. Mrs Gibbons had already planned a meal fit for a king. There would be thirty to sit down to dinner, she told the two girls. 'Thirty!' Meggy groaned. Ambrosine had discussed with her cook the more important points of table decoration and food preparation. There had been a moment when it seemed they would never decide between the Potage aux Huîtres and the Consommé à la Victoria. But they did at last, and Mrs Gibbons ordered the oysters. It all had to be just so, just right. This time the Prime Minister was coming, the Rt. Hon. Edmund Barton himself.

Alice remembered that her parents had been terribly impressed.

'Rinse your hair in vinegar,' Mira told her, 'so's it's nice and shiny.'

'Speak only when you're spoken to,' Mr Parkin added. 'Mind your Ps and Qs, girl.'

'Will he be properly welcomed, with a band and speeches and all?' Mira went on, her eyes dreamy.

'It's unofficial,' Alice muttered.

'Ah, unofficial.' Her father nodded, as if he knew all about it. 'No fuss then. Mr Barton must be tired of fuss by now.'

'Mr Cunningham says they're opening the Federal Parliament in May and there'll be lots of fuss then,' Alice chipped in.

Her father gave her a sharp look, but after all didn't tell her to watch her tongue. 'I expect there will be, girl. Mrs Cunningham will wear the emeralds, I reckon. They're famous, them emeralds. Came from India.'

'Unlucky, I heard,' Mira added, still looking dreamy.

Mr Parkin snorted. 'What's unlucky about

being rich and beautiful, like Mrs Cunningham? You talk rubbish, woman.'

Mira sat up straight, her cheeks pink, and for once she held her ground. 'I know what I know,' she retorted. 'I heard from Mrs Sproat they were stolen from a maharaja or some such person, and there was a curse put on them. Cosmo Cunningham bought them cheap because of it.'

'Then he's a better businessman than you or I will ever be,' sniffed Mr Parkin.

Alice, listening intently while she pretended to brush up a little pile of crumbs, saved up this information to impart to Meggy, or Bertie when he came home from school.

She had gone up to the attic yesterday afternoon and sat in Bertie's secret spot, thinking of him. She had found some of his treasures, a pretty rock paperweight and a book on birds. It was warm and quiet up there. When she had finally, reluctantly, come down, Ada had been waiting for her at the bottom of the stairs.

'What are you poking and prying about for?' she had demanded, her chin stuck out aggressively. She really was a most unpleasant child.

'None of your business, young miss,' Alice retorted.

Ada's face went violent pink. 'You're ins'lent,' she hissed. 'I'll tell on you.'

'Go ahead.' Alice brushed past her.

Why hadn't they sent Ada to school and kept Bertie home? It wasn't fair, it just wasn't fair.

* * *

Startled, Rosamund looked up at the dingy ceiling. There was a stain near the plaster rose, as if water had dripped through from the attic at one time. But that didn't explain the thud.

The attic was empty, she knew that. The workmen had cleared everything out, apart from the cobwebs and spiders. There was nothing up there to make a noise like the one Rosamund had just heard. She dismissed it. It was just one of those odd things, an old house settling, or the wind, or her own imagination. Besides, there was only silence now. Colonsay was sleeping.

With a shiver, Rosamund climbed into bed. The sheets felt chill and almost damp. In fact the room was definitely colder than it had been when she first came up to bed. The temperature must be dropping outside. Perhaps there was a change coming in from the south-west. She shivered again, snuggling down, but her eyes kept returning to the ceiling.

The light fitting looked original, a frosted pink lily hung on a single chain. Some of the plaster had come away but the rose was intact, delicate fern fronds and violets. Tomorrow Fred Swann's team intended to begin work on the roof. Kerry was worried. 'They'll be tracking back and forth through the house,' she had said, 'making a terrible mess.' Rosamund had tried not to laugh. As if the house wasn't a mess already! Mark had called again in the late afternoon, but this time had only spoken to Kerry, who had seemed embarrassed that Rosamund's husband hadn't asked to speak with her. But Rosamund pretended she hadn't expected anything else.

'I read all I can in the newspapers about Mr Markovic,' Kerry said proudly. 'I do hope he'll win the by-election.'

'Oh, he will,' Rosamund assured her, full of confidence from the bottle of red wine she had finished over dinner. She had wanted to open another one, but Kerry's sharp eyes had been watching and she didn't want Mark to know she was exceeding her limit. Mark, Mark, everything to please Mark. How many times have I subjugated my own desires to Mark's, repressed my own wishes to please Mark?

The question surprised her. Always before she had taken the blame upon herself. If Mark was displeased then it must be her fault. Had being away from him somehow knocked her viewpoint off centre? And that outburst on the phone the other night, what was happening to her?

Whenever Rosamund imagined Mark as Premier, she found she could picture it very well. It was only when she came to imagine herself by his side that the picture became fuzzy. If Mark's promotional juggernaut had a weak spot, then it was Rosamund. No wonder he hadn't wanted her with him at this crucial time. He could turn her absence around, boast that she so loved her family home she had insisted on overseeing all the work herself. He would draw a picture of her that was much sharper and cleaner than the reality, and she wouldn't be there to spoil it.

Perhaps I can sing him a song when he wins, Rosamund smiled to herself. Sleepy now, her eyes were closing. I can sing him 'Happy Birthday', like Marilyn Monroe did to J.F.K. . . .

The thud jolted her eyes open. She half sat up and switched on the bedside lamp, her heart jumping in her breast. Some flakes of plaster fell from the ceiling and scattered on the floor like overlarge dandruff. The chain which attached the pink lily to the ceiling swung gently, back and forth. It was as if someone very heavy had just leapt onto the attic floor above Rosamund's head.

This wasn't right. She had not imagined it. Someone was in the attic.

Rosamund was still staring at the ceiling, her mind a blank, when there was a tap on her door. The latch clicked and the door swung in a crack. Rosamund shifted her frightened gaze to the dark strip. Kerry's face appeared, her features shadowed strangely by the bedside lamp. She wore her grey hair in one long plait and had an absurd knitted jacket draped over her shoulders.

'Rosamund?' she whispered harshly. 'Did you hear the noise? What is it? Is there someone in the house?'

Kerry was in the room now, glancing over her shoulder nervously. When the thud came again, she scampered across to the bed, her eyes as big as dinner plates. Rosamund noticed, incongruously, that she was wearing woolly blue slippers.

Now they both stared at the ceiling, watching the light swing on its chain. This thud had been louder than the last, more violent. As if whoever was up there was becoming angry, or impatient.

'Someone's in the attic,' Rosamund said at last.

Her voice thawed Kerry's frozen silence. 'We must ring the police.' But it was more a question than a command.

They looked at each other.

'Should we take a look first?' Kerry added unwillingly, biting her lips. 'There might be an animal trapped up there. A possum or . . . or . . .'

Rosamund could understand why she was stumped for possibilities. A possum would hardly make a noise like that, there were few animals in this part of the world which could.

'We'll call the police,' Rosamund agreed. There was no way she was going up those dark stairs to that dark attic. Kerry nodded so quickly that Rosamund knew she felt the same way.

Rosamund picked up her woollen coat from the untidy pile of clothing on the chair and flung it about her shoulders. Cautiously, the two women made their way out into the corridor. The moon was up. Its light shone through the broken stained-glass window at the end of the corridor, making new patterns on the worn carpet runner. Silence now, not even the usual creaks and rattles one might expect in an old house. And it was so cold. Rosamund shivered again, and felt Kerry's breath warm on her cheek as they huddled together.

From the landing they looked down into the entrance hall. It was dark there, only the lighter squares of coloured glass beside the main door giving some relief. Somewhere a cricket chirruped. Kerry flipped the light switch.

The pale glow of the hall light seemed very comforting. They paused a moment, surveying the scene. Everything was as Rosamund remembered, the front door closed with the chain across, the telephone on the hall table, a couple of lengths of wood propped against the wall. Nothing had moved. The bare, scuffed floorboards were covered in dried bootprints where Fred's men had been coming and going all day. Amongst the tread of heavy feet were smaller marks, weaving an uneven pattern. Did one of the men own a dog?

The thud came again. It was above and behind them, definitely from the attic. Only now it seemed softer, more insidious, like a warning. Kerry slipped her arm through Rosamund's and they went quickly down the stairs. Despite the circumstances, some part of Rosamund's brain registered amusement. Kerry had hardly ever touched her when they lived here before and now here they were holding hands.

Rosamund went straight to the phone and picked it up. She heard the dial tone with relief and glanced at the list of numbers on the wall in front of her. Police. It rang twice at the other end before it was answered.

Kerry stood as close as she could, listening. Every few seconds she glanced up the staircase. The silence up there was tangible. Watchful. When Rosamund hung up, Kerry whispered, 'Should we wait outside?'

Rosamund shivered in the cold. 'We'll wait near the front door.'

The thud came again. Loud. The sound vibrated down the walls and inside them. The crockery in the kitchen clinked and chimed as the whole house trembled. Once, twice, three times. Something upstairs fell with a crash. Rosamund heard glass break. The squeezing feeling was back in her chest, stopping her breathing. She had never been so frightened in her life.

Kerry was fumbling at the chain on the front door and then the deadlock. At last it swung in. The air smelt of wet soil and the sea. The wind had dropped and a ghostly mist had formed in the hollows outside. The darkness was impenetrable and as frightening as the thing upstairs.

They compromised and stood in the doorway.

The police arrived seven minutes after Rosamund's phone call—they counted every one of them on Kerry's wristwatch. When finally they saw the lights of the car on the driveway, arcing brightly across the front of the house, their relief was palpable.

'Where is he?' the young constable demanded when he reached them. He was pulling a parka over his shirt and shivering.

'In the attic.'

'Did you see anyone?'

Kerry and Rosamund exchanged a glance. 'We didn't look.'

He didn't comment, only waited until his partner, a woman with short black hair, joined him. 'Where is it?' she asked, glancing up the staircase.

'At the top of the stairs,' Kerry said, clutching her knitted jacket together. 'There's a door to your right which leads to the west wing. The first door after that opens onto the stairs to the attic. There's no light up there. You'll need a torch.'

When one had been fetched from the car, the two police officers creakily ascended the stairs. Kerry and Rosamund could hear their footsteps moving about overhead. Reluctantly, Rosamund edged halfway up the stairs herself, listening for voices, for sounds of an arrest being made, for some sign that the police had made everything all right again. Kerry stayed by the newel post, her eyes wide and unblinking.

In no time at all, it seemed, the footsteps were coming back. The policewoman laughed at something her partner had said. A door slammed. Rosamund's heart sank. They stood shoulder to shoulder at the top of the stairs, grey with dust and cobwebs festooning their hair, and looked down at the two women. 'Nothing.'

'Nothing?' Rosamund stared, her face drawn and white. 'I don't understand it. We both heard the sounds. There was something up there.'

'Something?' Did she imagine it, or did they look at her differently?

Kerry chipped in. 'She means an animal or a person. We didn't hear it speak or . . . or . . . We couldn't possibly have imagined it!'

Rosamund managed to nod. She suddenly felt very tired, her limbs heavy; even her neck was tight with exhaustion, barely able to hold up her head. She badly wanted to sit down on the stairs.

'What sort of sound did you hear?' the woman was asking.

Kerry tried to explain. 'A bang. Like someone jumping in boots or, or hitting the floor with a, a mallet. A dull, banging sound. It shook the whole house.'

They said nothing, but Rosamund sensed a new air of scepticism about them. Even as she felt frustrated by it, she couldn't blame them. If she hadn't heard the noises herself, she too would have doubted Kerry.

'Like someone jumping up and down,' Rosamund reiterated. 'The ceiling was shaking.' She remembered, then, the crash, and with a murmured exclamation climbed back up the stairs towards her room.

It was as she had left it, the bed turned back, the bedside lamp on. But now the ceiling light with its chain still attached lay on the floor in a white cloud of broken plaster. The lily was smashed, dangerous shards of pink glass glittered amongst the white powder. In the ceiling, where the decorative rose had been, was now an untidy hole through which showed the old wooden laths.

It was a mess, but a solid mess, a real mess. Not a figment of her imagination. Evidence.

The male constable came and stood beside her, Kerry peering over his shoulder, while the policewoman prowled around the room. They said nothing for a long moment, taking in the devastation.

'Let's go downstairs again,' he said at last. 'Now, you two ladies stay in the kitchen while we have a look around.'

They proceeded to check doors and windows and investigate the jungle of back garden. For a long time the beam of the torch flickered back and forth, while Kerry made tea and opened biscuit tins. Once, they heard the woman give an excited shout and they both tensed, waiting. But nothing more happened, and when the two police finally returned it was with nothing more tangible than nettle stings.

'Sorry,' the woman murmured. 'Nothing to be seen. No jemmied locks, no broken panes of glass. The house is as secure as it can possibly be.'

'Old houses make noises,' the male constable added kindly. 'I'd get your electrics checked. Maybe something blew, caused the light to fall. Maybe that was the noise you heard beforehand. We haven't heard it since, have we?'

'No,' Rosamund admitted carefully, 'we haven't.' It made a kind of sense, a comforting explanation.

After they'd drunk the tea and eaten the biscuits, the police returned to their car. The policewoman opened her door and then seemed to remind herself of something. 'Your dog's out there at the back. When I caught sight of it, I thought for a moment I had something. Looked a bit bedraggled.'

Rosamund shook her head at the accusing note

in the other's voice. 'I don't have a dog. Kerry?'

But Kerry was also shaking her head. 'Must be a stray.'

'Well, I'd get it put into the shelter. Kinder than letting the poor thing starve to death.'

Something made Rosamund ask, 'What sort of dog is it?'

'A terrier. Long hair. Must have been someone's pet, it had a topknot tied with a ribbon.'

The door slammed. The sound of their car engine took a long time to fade away.

Rosamund relocked the front door, testing it to be sure. 'The light-fitting *was* old,' Kerry said, turning off lights. 'Everything is old. And plaster is always falling. We hadn't lived upstairs for some time, Mrs Ada couldn't manage the stairs. Everything has become so dilapidated.'

Slowly, they climbed the stairs. 'The house feels different,' Kerry murmured, more to herself than Rosamund. 'I'm sure it didn't feel like this when I was here with Mrs Ada.'

Rosamund, though tired, found the energy to ask, 'What do you mean, different?'

The question appeared difficult for Kerry to answer, perhaps she couldn't answer it. 'Just different,' she said lamely at last.

Rosamund's room was silent. The faint scent of honeysuckle tantalised, and was gone. She was so tired. She carefully avoided the mess on the floor from the light, climbed into bed and lay down. There were no sounds from above, there was nothing. She closed her eyes and was instantly asleep.

CHAPTER 6

Alice sat down on the low stool and held her breath. Her feet were aching so badly she wondered if she would ever be able to walk again. The dinner guests had either taken themselves off to bed or retired to the library with port and cigars. Mr Barton, the Prime Minister, was in there with Cosmo, and an occasional rumble of laughter could be heard as far away as the kitchen.

Mrs Gibbons considered the dinner a triumph. The extra staff from the town had been goggle-eyed as she carried in dish after dish, to the admiration of servants and guests.

'Of course, we're used to serving famous people in this house,' Meggy boasted, nose in the air.

'That's enough of that.' Mrs Gibbons spoke sharply. She was putting the finishing touches to a pink castellated jelly in a moat of sugared green grapes. Alice felt her mouth watering.

Now she rested her back against a big jar of lye and closed her eyes. She was very tired. Meggy had gone to bed. Mrs Gibbons hadn't had the energy to go visiting Harry Simmons and had waddled off to her cottage. Only Alice remained.

She should go to bed, too, but the effort involved was more than she could summon just yet. The fire in the big black stove was damped down but still gave off a pleasant smoky warmth. A sleepy, muffled call came from upstairs. It reminded Alice of last spring, when Bertie had kept them all awake with his screams.

'Any wonder he has nightmares,' Meggy had said, rolling her eyes. 'His father takin' him out on the bay on a day like that.'

Cosmo had been sailing and had taken Ada and Bertie with him. Ada had loved it, face turned to the wind, hair streaming out behind her. Bertie had sat rigid with white-faced terror and was eventually taken off onto the pier at Clifton Springs. Cosmo treated him with disgust.

'I was afraid of nothing at his age!'

Cosmo and Ambrosine had been taking afternoon tea in the sitting room not long after the sailing episode. Alice had just lit the fire and it was crackling nicely. The table was laid out with sandwiches, scones with blackberry jam and Battenberg cake. The rich, bitter fragrance of coffee filled the room. Alice pushed a burning sliver of wood further into the heart of the fire with the poker; the sudden burst of heat made her eyes sting.

'The bay *was* rather rough.' Ambrosine's voice, as mild as usual, held no inflection of censure or anger.

Cosmo gulped at his hot coffee and took a sandwich. 'The boy needs to show a bit of spirit,' he replied with his mouth full. 'No use babying him.'

Ambrosine sipped from her cup, her beautiful face impassive. Alice felt her hands trembling. She doesn't care, she thought bitterly. She just doesn't care.

'Next time there's a good fresh south-westerly, I'll take him out again,' Cosmo went on. 'That should sort him out.' And he laughed. 'Did I ever tell you how Alice's father saved my life, Rosie?'

Ambrosine smiled faintly.

'Now there was a brave lad. He'd been touching up the paint work on the boat for me, so I took him for a sail. Hauled me back over the gunwale when I thought I was done for. We were reaching and the sail swung round, sudden gust, and the boom cracked me on the back of the head. I saw stars, I can tell you! Could have drowned that day. Who would you have married then, eh Rosie?'

Ambrosine took another sip of coffee and smiled again.

Now, alone in the quiet kitchen, Alice murmured, 'Mr Marling, that's who she'd marry if Cosmo were dead.' She still had the ivory button hidden in her drawer. To look at it gave her a feeling of dread mixed with excitement. A clenching in the pit of her stomach.

Alice sighed and sat up straighter. The ache in her feet had eased slightly, enough to take her to bed. As she stood up she knocked against the slop bucket. She cursed it under her breath. Would it wait until the morning? But of course it wouldn't. Mrs Gibbons would accuse her of being lazy, of attracting vermin into her kitchen.

Alice heaved it up with both hands and went to the door. Outside the night was clear and cold. The garden was in its final autumn flush, with the sweet perfume of tea roses and honeysuckle filling the air. Tall stalks of love-lies-bleeding mingled untidily with spent Easter daisies. Ambrosine disliked the ungainly red plant with its tassels, and had the gardeners pull them up, but somehow love-lies-bleeding always managed to seed itself somewhere else.

Alice carried the bucket to a safe corner and left it there. At least it was away from Mrs Gibbons's kitchen and there'd be time enough in the morning to empty it out. The stinging smell of tobacco made her stop and turn. Someone was standing by the lilac bushes. Alice recognised the rangy body and easy stance of Jonah. He drew on his pipe and Alice saw the red glow. His stillness, his watching silence, made her skin prickle. 'What are you doing here?' she demanded, her voice sounding all the more brave because she was afraid. 'Meggy's gone to bed, she won't be out tonight.'

Jonah didn't answer.

'You go back to your own bed,' she told him sharply. Jonah slept in the room off the stables so he could keep an eye on the horses. As a child, he had been taught in a mission school run by white people. Meggy said he found it difficult to fit in with whites or blacks, because he was a bit of either and neither wanted to own him—Alice wondered whether Meggy understood so well because she was the same. He was twenty-eight now, older than Meggy by fifteen years. When Cosmo had visited his Murray property last year, he'd found Jonah working there and brought him back to Colonsay to care for the horses. Cosmo called him a natural.

But Alice couldn't like him. He was so quiet, and he watched everyone and everything. Not like Meggy, not a bit like Meggy. No, she couldn't like him, and neither did she trust him.

Still Jonah smoked his pipe and neither moved nor spoke.

'I know what you're thinking,' Alice burst out. 'You're thinking there are things to steal in this house. That's what you're thinking, isn't it?'

He laughed, as if she'd made a funny joke, and his laughter went on and on.

Her heart beating hard, Alice slipped back inside. What had made her say such a thing? It was fright, that's what it was. Jonah frightened her and her mouth had run away with her. The way he had stood out there in the darkness, in the sweet salt air, with his silence. Somehow it wasn't . . . right.

****

The weather had remained fine and the work on the roof was now well under way. Mark wanted the restoration to be as near as possible to the original, and Fred was obliging. Rosamund could hear the voices of the men as they picked their—it seemed to her—precarious way about so far above the ground. The rattling, screeching noise as old tiles and timber were prised away from Colonsay was truly excruciating. The hammering, as a new timber framework went up, was nearly as bad.

The morning following the noise in the attic, Rosamund had insisted the ceiling in her room be thoroughly checked. The report was as she had expected: the weight of the light-fitting had been too much for its fixture. The house was old and neglected. Such an event was inevitable. Fred had already sent up an electrician to repair the wiring and put in a temporary ceiling light, and it now remained for one of his workmen to cover over the hole in the plaster.

Rosamund was brushing her hair after her shower when there was a knock on her bedroom door.

'Hello, Mrs Markovic,' said Gary Munro. 'I've come to fix the ceiling.'

His eyes were just as she remembered. Narrowed, blue, their expression guarded. His hair had always been curly but now it seemed more so. He was taller than her, and looked a lot fitter.

'I expected to see a plasterer,' she told him stupidly.

'That's me. Man of all trades.'

'I thought you wrote books.'

'That too.'

'But not at the same time.'

He laughed, and suddenly all resemblance to the sullen boy she had known vanished. 'Are you going to let me in, Rosamund?'

She opened the door. He brought in a ladder and stood it under the hole in the ceiling. They both stared up at where the delicate plaster rose had been. 'Not much point doing too thorough a job,' he said. 'The laths need replacing. Probably the whole ceiling needs replacing. I'll patch it up a bit—just so that the spiders don't fall through.'

She watched him work, knowing she should go away and leave him to it. He didn't seem to mind, being lost in his own thoughts, and for a long time there was silence. Rosamund pictured Gary as he used to be—weedy, hair untidy, mouth turned permanently down. She couldn't believe this man had grown out of that boy. What had happened to him in the years in between? She wanted to know, but at the same time felt awkward questioning him.

Finally it got too much for her, and she asked,

'When did you learn to do this?' It was a relief to speak.

He didn't stop what he was doing. 'Before I went to uni. Did a bit of part-time work for a builder. When it comes to earning money, it's been more useful than English lit and philosophy, believe me.'

She smiled. 'Kerry said you quit the newspaper to write a novel.'

'I did. It's been a long time, Rosamund.'

'Yes, it has.'

He looked down at her and smiled. They had never been friends, and yet he was someone from her past, someone almost familiar. She felt as if he knew her, that she didn't have to explain to him who she was. It was not a sensation she was used to.

'I heard about the other night,' he was saying, peering up at his makeshift patch.

'You mean the noises we heard? The police thought they might have been caused by an electrical fault.'

He shrugged, balancing on the ladder with the ease of long practice. 'Hard to say. Maybe. Have you heard anything since?'

'No,' she admitted.

'Well then, maybe that was it.'

She had hoped he'd be able to tell her one way or the other. All had been quiet at Colonsay these past few days, and Kerry had clearly put the incident from her mind, but Rosamund wasn't able to. Not that she wasn't glad the noise hadn't started up again, she was. Very glad. And she had told the police constable so when he rang to enquire the morning after his visit. But—and she hadn't told him this—there was something in the air, a sense of waiting, of holding your breath. The house, as Kerry had said, felt different.

'All done.' Gary's voice interrupted her thoughts.

Rosamund looked up. He had finished. For a moment she mourned the delicate pink lily and the plaster rose, and then put it from her mind. If Gary was right, the ceiling would have to come down anyway.

'Thank you.'

He climbed down and began to remove the ladder. When he reached the door, he turned and gave her a quizzical look. 'Why did you come back, Rosamund?'

She had been searching in her pocket for a cigarette and now she looked up at him, startled. 'What do you mean?'

'I used to hate coming here to Colonsay with my grandfather. You and that crazy old woman. It was like a house in a horror movie, I kept expecting something awful to happen.'

Rosamund didn't know whether to laugh or get angry. 'I didn't realise it affected you in that way. I thought you were just naturally unpleasant.'

'I don't like this house,' he went on, as if he hadn't heard her. 'I never did. I can't believe you've come back by choice. What's happened? Marriage on the rocks?'

Anger pulsed through her. 'Get out,' she whispered furiously.

He half smiled and suddenly she realised he hadn't changed at all. 'My pleasure,' he said, and closed the door.

****

The paddle-steamer *Ozone* rested at the pier, swayed by the rolling swell. Cosmo and Ambrosine were speaking with Mr Barton. The two men, in their dark clothing, were a foil for Ambrosine's lilac skirt, high-necked white blouse and straw hat. The narrow belt about her waist accentuated its tininess. The other guests hung back a little, holding on to their hats, their coat-tails and skirts flapping like angels' wings in the brisk breeze.

It would be a choppy journey back to Melbourne.

Alice wondered if Mr Barton was a good sailor. He was a rather portly but handsome man, with grey wavy hair and charming manners. He had, he said, enjoyed these two days at Colonsay: the food and wine, the conversation, the company. Alice couldn't imagine the Prime Minister doing anything as vulgar as being seasick.

Alice looked to the steamer, the cold wind making her eyes water. A continuous stream of black smoke came from the *Ozone*'s single funnel, the smell of burning mingling with the salt. Passengers in holiday clothes lined the rails, eager to see the important travellers.

The Colonsay people had been permitted to come down to the Clifton Springs pier to watch the Prime Minister leave. There were other folk, too. In May, when the Federal Parliament opened in Melbourne and sat for the first time, they would read about it in the newspapers and say, 'I've seen Mr Edmund Barton in the flesh.'

Beneath Alice's feet, through the uneven gaps in the pier, she could see shoals of darting fish and dark gleaming mussels clinging to the piles below the high-tide mark. Back on the sandy beach, seagulls strutted, seeking tasty morsels. Two of them duelled over a crab, screaming and thrusting with their sharp orange beaks. If Bertie were here, Alice thought, he wouldn't be interested in Mr Barton. He would prefer the birds and the fish. He would look them up in his book and make pencilled notes in his neat handwriting. Bertie was fascinated by animals and birds, by shells and rocks and plants. People frightened him. He said that people were unpredictable and untrustworthy.

Alice agreed with him.

The Prime Minister's party was climbing aboard the paddle-steamer. Further offshore, waves were chopped white by the wind. Alice tasted the salt on her lips. The big paddle-wheels began to turn.

Behind her, Jonah lounged against the railing, brown boots crossed, arms folded. He wore a red scarf about his throat and an old scuffed jacket that had belonged to Cosmo. He looked at Alice, eyes dark and amused, but she pursed her lips and glanced away, though not before she had seen Meggy tuck her hand firmly into the crook of Jonah's arm.

Alice supposed, grudgingly, that there was a handsomeness about him. Not the breathtaking looks of Mr Marling, but nevertheless an elusive attraction. She wondered, idly, why he had no wife. There had been a girl from the town a month or two ago who had taken to loitering in Jonah's vicinity. Meggy had been scornful, but Meggy did not think any woman good enough for her brother. 'Besides, he won't stay down here forever,' she had said. 'He'll go home, where he belongs.'

'Back to the bush,' Alice retorted. The girl from the town had given up her dreams and the loitering stopped. Just as well, Alice thought. How would a girl used to the relative civilisation of the Bellarine Peninsula cope with life in the bush? Not the romantic sort of bush portrayed in the poems of Mr Paterson, but the real bush, so harsh, so cruel.

Alice didn't fancy the bush herself. She wanted to live in the city, where things happened. Not as a servant, never as a servant. No, she wanted to live her own life. More dreams, more wishes. The wind twitched at her hair again and she pushed at it impatiently.

The steamer was belching more smoke as it moved away, paddles splashing; it blew a mournful farewell on its whistle. Cosmo and Ambrosine were making their way back up the pier, Ada trailing behind with her governess. Cosmo turned with a laugh to one of his guests, while Ambrosine kept one hand firmly on her straw hat. Her hair was swept up under it, full at the front, so that the unbroken line of her back and neck curved gracefully. The wind moulded the full sleeve of her white blouse to her arm, and there was an inch or two of bare flesh between the lace at the cuff and the button of her white glove. She did not have to try to be beautiful, thought Alice angrily. She just was.

Cosmo winked at Alice as he passed; she smiled back. Ambrosine also looked at Alice, but she didn't smile. Her face was smooth, expressionless. Their eyes met and then Ambrosine's gaze moved to a point beyond Alice. A faint wave of colour stained her cheeks and she bent her head slightly, so that the brim of her straw hat concealed her flushed face.

****

With the men working inside the house, and Kerry busy in the kitchen making endless mugs of tea and coffee, Rosamund wondered whether she should make the garden her province.

The front garden was beyond her limited abilities—Mark would have to find a good landscape gardener—but the back could do with some weeding before anything was decided. Rosamund remembered reading an article in a gardening magazine which instructed would-be restorers not to act in haste when it came to old gardens. 'Remove weeds and prune overgrown shrubs, and then stand back and take a good long look,' it had advised. And that was what she intended to do.

She began with the far left back corner, where the big pine trees loomed up before the wire fence, and what was left of the brick stables slowly returned to earth. She spent the whole day, clothed in old jeans and a long-sleeved shirt and thick gloves, hacking out head-high thistles. There were gardening tools in the cottage behind the boxthorn hedge—itself in desperate need of taming. Someone had hammered shelves along the walls and on them a variety of rusting, dust-covered objects lay jumbled. The larger things, such as shovels, hoes, rakes and the lawn roller, were on the earth floor. A rusted sword, which looked as though it had been used to scythe grass, had been tossed into a corner with wooden stakes. An old stained coat, stiff with dirt, hung at the back of the door. Rosamund touched it gingerly with her fingertips and thought it might once have been someone's best—in the folds, where time hadn't faded it, the cloth resembled blue tweed.

She couldn't remember entering this cottage more than once or twice in her life. Why should she? Ada had hired a man with a slasher to come in and control the wilder parts of the property, and what remained of the garden was tidied irregularly, when she was able to afford the labour. And as time went on that had been less and less often. There hadn't been a full-time gardener since Cosmo's day—probably the owner of the stained coat.

Rosamund had done a little gardening when she first left Colonsay: a window box and a patch of vegies that Dave had prized. The band had been into fresh food—strange that, when she considered the drugs they were also into. When she was married to Mark she had done nothing beyond the perimeters of the house. He wanted perfection, so he hired the perfect garden designer. But then Mark wanted perfection in everything, Rosamund thought grimly as she hacked viciously at another thistle.

There had been no sign of the dog which the policewoman had spotted in the garden. Rosamund and Kerry had called it the next morning, to no avail. Either it had found its way home or sought shelter elsewhere. Rosamund had put it out of her mind. She felt tired but invigorated, as if she was achieving something. A sense of well-being filled her. Perhaps Colonsay is good for me, she thought.

She'd meant it as a joke, but the absolute truth of it shocked her. The realisation would take some getting used to. She let it seep in. Colonsay *was* good for her, and it was hers. Not Mark's, although he thought of it as his, and it was his money being poured into the restoration of it. By law it was Rosamund's house. She smiled. Perhaps she had something to thank Ada for after all.

She stood up and mopped her brow. The air was still and clear, the sky turning an azure colour before the pinks and mauves of dusk crept in. The men were still on the roof and she had noticed one or two of them working around the west wing. One of the men was a woman. She had grinned at Rosamund in passing, as if they were conspirators. Rosamund had noticed that Fred's crew were all shapes and sizes and ages. No doubt they all had their faults, even Fred Swann. They were a microcosm of humankind. Not one of them perfect—no-one could be, and no-one should expect to be. Perhaps that was part of the problem between her and Mark. He wanted something it was not within her to give, something she did not want to give.

The evening drew in. Rosamund gave up her task and collected her gardening tools. The cottage was secret and shadowy, with a strong smell of rusting metal. It must once have housed someone, one of the servants perhaps, or the head gardener. As she pulled the door to, boxthorns caught at her shirt and tore it. Blood beaded on her arm and she licked her finger and rubbed at the drops.

Something rustled in a clump of the red-tasselled plants and Rosamund turned to look, but all was still. She reached out and snapped off one of the plants halfway down the thick stalk. Suddenly the name came to her. Love-lies-bleeding. Appropriate, she thought with a smile. Another memory tugged at her tired brain, herself as a small child running through the neglected garden beds at dusk, ducking behind a big mound of philadelphus and coming upon a man standing there. She had been afraid, more than that, terrified. Because although the man had been there, he had also not been there. She had run to tell Ada, but Ada had told her it was just someone taking a short cut through the garden. Young as she was, Rosamund had thought it a poor explanation, but she hadn't questioned her grandmother. One didn't. Now Rosamund told herself that perhaps she was mistaken, and Ada was right. Besides, she was feeling too pleased with herself to ruin it with odd thoughts.

The men on the roof had gone home; Rosamund heard the last truck pull out and roar away. Something delicious was cooking in the kitchen and Rosamund was looking forward to opening a bottle of red wine. She had promised herself that treat after all her hard work.

Two sets of casement windows looked out onto the back garden, their glass dull and smeared, but surprisingly intact. Rosamund glanced up at the first of them as she passed. This was one of the rooms where the treasures from the attic had been stored but she could see nothing. The windows were covered with a combination of old blinds and sheets.

A stirring of guilt muddied her new confidence. Everything would have to be sorted, and it wasn't a job she could fob off on someone else. This was Cunningham business, Rosamund's business. 'Later,' she muttered. The smell of Kerry's cooking was making her mouth water. Almost as an afterthought she peered in through the second windows.

Someone was looking back at her.

For an instant Rosamund believed her memories of the stranger in the twilit garden had summoned him back, then almost immediately afterwards that it was her own reflection she was seeing. But neither was the truth. There was a strange girl standing inside the room looking out at her. A girl with straight brown hair and brown eyes and pale skin, wearing a dress with a high collar and buttons all the way up to her throat.

The unexpectedness of it froze her to the spot, then adrenalin rushed through her. She turned and bolted towards the back door, into the kitchen. Kerry looked up, startled. White sauce dripped from her wooden spoon onto the floor as she turned to watch Rosamund run through the room and into the hall.

It was the room at the back, on the left, and Rosamund found it within seconds. Her clammy hand closed on the brass doorknob and turned it before her fear could catch up with her actions. The door was unlocked. With a noisy breath, she heaved it open and stood peering into the shadowy room.

Dust, stirred by her entry, spun in the shafts of light from the windows. It made everything seem coloured in sepia, like an old photograph. A cold photograph—the air was icy. There were pieces of furniture, boxes, heaps of old magazines and newspapers, a dressmaker's dummy with a moth-eaten fox fur draped around it. But nothing living, no girl with long brown hair and a high-collared dress. Why was she not surprised?

'Rosamund?' Kerry's voice made her jump. She was standing behind her, still in her apron, her eyes enormous in her pale face. 'What is it?'

Rosamund didn't answer. Instead she took one step into the room—it was all she could manage. The floor was completely covered with Cunningham artefacts, and in places they had been stacked in tiers halfway to the high ceiling. It would have been impossible for anyone to have stood looking out of the window. A sudden wave of nausea swept over her and she put a hand to her mouth to hold it back. Her only thought now was to find a suitable lie, to buy herself time.

'What is it?' Kerry asked again, her breath hot at Rosamund's shoulder.

'I was looking through the window and I thought I saw something.'

Kerry's breath caught and held, she strained to see past Rosamund into the room. 'What did you see?' she whispered.

'A rat.'

The two words sounded flat and she was grimly amused by Kerry's swift retreat. 'Oh! Close the door so it doesn't get out,' she gasped. 'Tomorrow I'll get some poison.'

'Good idea.' Rosamund moved to close the door and stopped. Something had caught her eye. She reached out, stretching her arm to the limit, and closed her hand over a small object resting on one of the stacks of newspapers. It felt warm, as if it were alive. She and Kerry silently peered down into her palm.

'Perhaps it fell out of one of the boxes,' Kerry volunteered. 'Rather fancy, isn't it, for a button?'

Rosamund said nothing, smoothing her grubby thumb over the worn surface. Yellow, the yellow of the old newspapers. There was some sort of carving on it, but age and wear had almost worn it smooth.

'We could clean it up,' Kerry went on.

Rosamund nodded and slipped the button into her pocket. 'Maybe later. I'm starving.' She closed the door firmly and followed the older woman back down the hall.

Upstairs, Rosamund washed and changed into

loose trousers and a silk blouse. She stood at the bedroom window brushing her hair. The sickness had passed, she simply felt tired. The girl, whoever she had been, was gone, but her face remained and Rosamund knew she would see it in her dreams. Smooth and pale and secretive, with its curtain of long hair and childishly rounded chin. It hadn't been like looking at an old photograph, rather it had been like facing a real person, a person who was looking back at her, seeing her, assessing her.

Was that what ghosts did?

The question shocked her. Why was she assuming she had seen a ghost? Was she discounting all other possibilities? Was she ready to do that? It had been almost dusk, the window was dirty, there were shadows, the clothing dummy may have tricked her somehow with its human shape, she was in a susceptible state of mind ...

No, I'm not ready to admit to ghosts, she decided. Still she found herself asking Kerry, as they sat down to their meal, if there were any family photographs Ada had kept.

'Quite a few went to the State Library, but I do remember an old black book Mrs Ada would occasionally bring out.'

Now that it had been mentioned, Rosamund also recalled the big black book full of stiff, studied poses. 'Where is it now?'

'About somewhere. I'll look.' Kerry hesitated, and Rosamund knew it was on the tip of her tongue to ask why she was suddenly so interested in a family she had ignored most of her life and abandoned when she was seventeen.

'Just curious,' she answered anyway, and shrugged. 'I can't remember really looking at them.' That was true enough, she had glanced at those faces, the old-fashioned clothing, the fake backgrounds in the photographer's studio, but never really taken them in. Perhaps . . . perhaps if she saw a face like the face which had looked at her through the window this evening, if she were to put a name to it, it would be a start. But the start of what?

'I don't want this,' she muttered to herself.

Kerry glanced up with a frown. 'I thought you said you were hungry, Rosamund. Leave it, if it's too much.'

'Oh, no . . . I didn't mean that.'

She swallowed some of the wine. It was sweet, too sweet, but that didn't matter. Experience told her a couple more glasses and her thoughts would become pleasantly blurred.

'Are you all right, Rosamund? You seem vague this evening?'

'Vague?' Well, that was a new one. 'I'm tired, that's all. The gardening.' She made an effort. 'Once the weeds are gone, I'll be able to decide what shrubs to save and what to let go. I remember Ada saying there was an arbour somewhere out there, in her father's day.'

Kerry opened her mouth as if to say something, and then changed her mind. 'It must have been beautiful once,' she murmured instead. 'I believe Mrs Ada's father was very proud of the garden. There were walks and fountains, even a summer house. And flowers. The house was always full of fresh flowers. Especially roses, white roses. Mrs Ada's mother was very fond of white roses. I understand when she died her casket was completely covered with them.'

'Good God.' Rosamund found a cigarette and

lit it, ignoring Kerry's pained expression. Ada, if she recalled rightly, had kept newspaper cuttings of the funeral. Did they still exist? Rosamund had found it terribly morbid at the time, but Ada belonged to a generation for whom the trappings of death held an importance all their own. Black-bordered mourning cards, locks of hair snipped from the dead one's head, jet jewellery, black lace veils, widows' weeds ... Now everything was sanitised for public consumption. Death, unless it was the messy sort gloated over on the nightly news, was something to be avoided by anyone other than the bereaved. Death made people awkward and uncomfortable. It reminded them of their own mortality. Perhaps it had been healthier in Ada's day, when death was a kind of celebration.

The cigarette was making her feel sick. Rosamund stubbed it savagely until the smoke stopped curling and pushed the ashtray away in disgust. She stood up, her muscles protesting sharply.

'I think I'll go up to bed. I'm dead on my feet.' The irony made her smile. 'Can you manage the dishes?'

'Yes, of course. I have the dishwasher Mr Markovic installed. So thoughtful of him.'

'Yes, sooo thoughtful.'

She picked up the second wine bottle as she turned to go, ignoring the censorious look on Kerry's face. The stairs creaked but Rosamund was only aware of her creaking legs. Her room was still warm from the afternoon sun, though it was quite dark outside. She leaned against the sill and drank from the bottle. The face came into her mind, she pushed it away. Ghost, imagination, hallucination or trick of the light, she wasn't going to let it get to her. The wine was doing its job. She could sleep now, the dreamless sleep that alcohol would give her.

Rosamund fumbled at her clothes, pulling them off. She had climbed under the bedclothes before she realised she was still wearing her bra and panties, and after a brief struggle tossed them out onto the floor. The sheets were cool on her bare skin, and with eyes closed she ran her hands over her body, imagining it was Mark.

Where was he tonight? Was he thinking of her? He probably didn't even miss her, except in the worry it cost him every time she drank too much and said the wrong thing. He would be better without her. Why, Rosamund asked herself hazily, did that thought hurt so very much?

She was sinking into darkness, spiralling down towards unconsciousness, when suddenly she was brought up short, halfway between awake and asleep, and yet fully aware, and powerless to escape in either direction. She was no longer in her bed in Colonsay. The place she was in was pitch-dark and small. She felt it enclosing her, although she could not move so much as a finger to touch her surroundings. She was frozen, numb, and yet frighteningly aware. All about her was a heavy perfume, honeysuckle, and with it the smell of sawn wood and varnish and roses. White roses.

She was in a coffin. She was dead. She was Ambrosine Cunningham.

They don't understand, Bertie had written. *Not like you do. Why don't they understand? I can't be like the others. People aren't like sorting shells, Alice, but if they were, I wonder which pile I should be put in? The smaller shells, probably, the colourless ones which no-one notices very much. A wink, perhaps. My father would be a big strong shell with fine markings, a helmet shell washed up from deep water after a storm, and my mother would be a Rose Crassatella, smooth and beautiful, the colour of dawn over the beach. And you, Alice, I don't think you'd be a shell at all. You would be a little crab, hiding among the rocks, scuttling to and fro, with one eye on us shells and the other watching the sky for hungry birds.*

My father writes that he and my mother will visit me when they come to Melbourne for the opening of Parliament on the 1st of May. And then, afterwards, I will come home to Colonsay with them, until next term. Can I wait so long? Five weeks. Thirty-five days and nights. I asked my mother to send me my book on birds, but she says she can't find it in my room. I think I might have left it in my secret place. Can you fetch it for me, Alice, and give it to her? I don't want her to go up there. It's my place, our place.

****

In the garden the next morning Rosamund cleared an area of about three square metres. Her head was pounding from the night before and there was a sour taste in her mouth, but she worked on regardless under the blue sky and warm sun. She had decided the dream-hallucination was best forgotten. She had been drunk, that was all. The terror she had felt when she realised where she was, and then the long moments until the black emptiness of sleep finally helped her escape—they were best blanked out.

A truck rumbled along the road beyond the pines and Rosamund turned towards the sound. There was an agitation inside her, like the shuddering of some domestic appliance. She held it in, keeping an outward calm. Earlier, when she got up, she had collected yesterday's soiled clothing to give to Kerry. She had remembered the button and searched her pockets for it several times, but without success. It was gone.

'Lost,' she muttered. She had dropped it. It would turn up. The agitation inside her increased and it was only by a tremendous effort of will that she stilled it.

She considered the giant philadelphus against the side boundary fence, its softly drooping branches, now that they were no longer supported by weeds, brushing the ground like a woman's long hair. In spring the white perfumed flowers must be glorious. A seat would be nice here, somewhere peaceful to sit and rest.

'Didn't he tell you?'

She looked up, angry that he had come up to her without her being aware of it. Gary Munro was wearing stained jeans and a faded blue shirt, and had no right to look so good. He was smiling at her, but there was something in his eyes that had more to do with mischief than amusement.

'Didn't he tell you?' he repeated. 'Your

husband? He's going to level all this and put in a pool. It's in the plans.'

Disappointment knocked her like a boxer's glove. All her ideas finished before they had even begun. Mark had already made up his mind, and everyone knew but her. Rosamund felt like a fool.

'No,' she said at last, aware of the bitterness in her voice. 'He didn't tell me.' She half-heartedly pulled at a piece of shrub. 'It seems a shame,' she added, 'to live this long and then die for the sake of a swimming pool Mark will never use. He's afraid of the sea, and swimming pools come a close second.'

'Why is that?' Gary sounded only mildly curious. 'Did he have a bad experience at Bondi?'

'No. Nothing like that. Nothing he can remember. That's the strange thing. There's no reason for it.' She felt calmer now, more in control of her shaky emotions. 'He's had all sorts of therapy, but nothing works. He breaks out in a sweat just at the thought of going to the beach.'

Gary laughed. 'The admired Mark Markovic scared of the surf. What a headline that would make!'

Rosamund looked at him sharply, aware she might have said too much. As usual.

But Gary was glancing back over his shoulder towards Colonsay, and following his gaze Rosamund saw Fred on the roof, silhouetted against the sky, watching them.

'Fred Swann doesn't employ the usual sort, does he?' she said drily, changing the subject.

Gary shrugged. 'He likes to help people, usually to the detriment of his own business. It's part of his religious philosophy.'

'I thought it was part of most religious philosophies.'

Gary laughed.

'So he's a pied piper for the helpless and needy.'

He looked at her curiously and she felt her face colour. There had been real vinegar in her voice. 'Sorry,' she muttered. 'Don't listen to me. I've become very cynical. It's Mark's influence. He thinks everyone must be out for something. Perhaps Fred isn't like that, perhaps he's a truly good man.'

'Or a self-deluded fool.'

Rosamund looked at him. His familiarity made the temptation to confide in him almost unbearable, but she resisted. She didn't really know him. He could just as easily turn around and sell the story to the newspapers—he was an ex-journalist after all, and she had already supplied him with some pretty juicy material. And then what? God, and then what!

'Maybe. I'll try to keep an open mind.'

Gary smiled. 'So will I. You need to talk with my grandfather.'

Rosamund stared at him, everything else forgotten. 'You mean Enderby's still alive?'

'Well and truly. He's a bit more bent and wrinkled, but his mind's as sharp as it always was. He wants to see you.'

Rosamund wondered if she wanted to see him. No, was her first reaction. It would be rather like resurrecting Grandma Ada from the grave. 'If I have time while I'm down,' she answered with suitable vagueness.

Gary raised his eyebrows but didn't pursue the matter. 'I'd better get back or Frederick will dock my pay.'

'His charity doesn't extend that far, then?'

He began to walk away, then stopped and said over his shoulder, 'Do you ever sing now?'

Rosamund frowned. 'Sing?'

'I heard you once in a pub in Melbourne. I went there by chance, saw your name on a poster on the door. You didn't see me. You were a million miles away.'

Rosamund laughed self-consciously. 'I tended to do that. No, I don't sing now. I grew up.'

Gary shook his head slowly, as if he couldn't believe it. 'I thought I'd never heard anything like your voice. You were singing an old blues number, when everyone else was into heavy metal. It was . . . unworldly.'

'Well,' Rosamund shrugged, flattered despite herself, 'I was always different. I left the band just after their big hit, before the album was out. Dave's never forgiven me for it. He still crosses the street when he sees me.'

There was a silence. She wondered why she had given him that piece of information. It must be confess-your-sins day.

Gary turned and faced her properly. 'There's a talent quest every Saturday night at the pub here. Nothing too serious. Winner gets a free bottle of drink—'

She was shaking her head even before he had finished. 'I told you, I don't sing any more.'

Gary smiled without humour. 'Pity. If you change your mind . . .'

Rosamund let her eyes drift past him as he walked away towards Colonsay. The house was dark against the bright sky, the windows opaque and sightless, the roof a criss-cross of bright new timbers where the tiles had been removed. It looked like a patient on an operating table whose chest wall had been peeled back to expose the ribs.

The thought of getting up in front of an audience, of exposing all her vulnerabilities and inadequacies to strangers, was almost more than she could bear. 'No, Gary,' she whispered after him, 'I don't sing any more. I don't do much of anything, any more.'

CHAPTER 7

The day had been so busy, Alice had not had time to make her way to the attic to find Bertie's book. In the morning, Mr Marling had arrived to put the finishing touches to his portrait of Ambrosine, and then Ambrosine had called the entire household in so that he could give them his news. The Prime Minister had asked that a painting be made of the official opening of the Federal Parliament, and that Mr Marling be the painter. Months of work, possibly years, would be required. He would need to paint portraits of all the major participants, gradually assembling them into one enormous canvas. It would, said Mr Marling, ensure his name was remembered for generations to come.

Mrs Gibbons gave a little shriek when he announced this, and Meggy clutched Alice's arm, shaking with suppressed laughter. Ada had danced over to Mr Marling and looked up at him, her blonde pigtail hanging down the centre of her back and making her look for all the world like a miniature Chinaman.

'Will I be in it?' she asked.

Mr Marling had laughed and Ambrosine had smiled. Like proud parents, Alice thought, before she could stop herself. 'Perhaps you shall,' Mr

Marling said. 'Or would you prefer a portrait of your own, Miss Ada?'

Ada clapped her hands. 'Yes, yes, an 'normous one!'

'Young Miss Ada bids fair to become as lovely a woman as her mother,' Mrs Gibbons sighed when they returned to the kitchen. 'Such an engaging child.'

Meggy rolled her eyes, but this time the cook saw her. 'We need onions for the master,' she told Meggy with a cold smile. 'And plenty of them.'

In the afternoon, Cosmo returned as expected, but he had brought unannounced guests with him. Now there were rooms to clean, beds to make up and food to be prepared. Alice had not stopped again until it was very late, the clearing up had been done, and everyone else was asleep. Only then did she climb the back stairs with aching feet and find her way to the door in the west wing, and the narrow stairs which led up to the attic.

There was no sound. Her candle wavered in the shadows, and the moonlight was like cold breath against the diamond-paned windows. She crept past the ghostly shapes of old furniture and the stuffed peacock, its eyes softly glowing, and crawled into Bertie's special place. Alice huddled there, listening to the rustling of mice among old newspapers and the hoot of an owl outside in the trees. The book was here, as she had known it would be. Alice placed her hand gently on the cover and closed her eyes. Bertie's face came to her, plump and bespectacled, but all the more beloved for that. Memories turned to dreams. Gradually, her head sank lower onto her chest and she dozed.

It was the distant sound of the clock in the hall striking the hour that brought Alice to her senses. As the last of the noise died away, the silence seemed all the more suffocating. Her candle had burned down to a stub and she realised how very late it must be. The attic stairs creaked under her feet, and as she paused in the west wing she heard Ada's high, demanding voice interspersed by her long-suffering nurse's murmur.

In the east wing the corridor was dark, the stained-glass window the only illumination. Usually there was a lighted lamp on the table on the landing, but tonight it was cold. Alice had her hand on the stair rail, ready to descend, when she sensed a movement behind her.

Someone in a loose robe was moving stealthily, keeping to the darker shadows.

Instinctively, Alice stepped back against the wall and held her breath. The figure had paused as if it, too, sensed another's presence, but now it came on, silk whispering very softly. For a shocked instant Alice thought the nymph in the window had climbed out of her glassy home and was on the loose. A pale hand reached out and closed on the porcelain doorknob of Ambrosine's bedroom door. There was a gentle click as it turned.

There must have been a lighted candle in the room, because when the door opened the light spilled out and illuminated both the robed figure and Alice.

It was Ambrosine. She turned, her hair loose about her shoulders, her feet bare, and her pale silk bedrobe reflecting the watery candlelight. As she stared back at Alice, her eyes dark and unreadable, Alice remembered that Mr Marling was also staying the night at Colonsay. And then Ambrosine turned and stepped into her room. The door closed softly behind her, leaving only the lingering sweetness of her perfume.

****

After what Gary had told her, there didn't seem to be much point in continuing with the garden. Rosamund returned to the house, longing for a hot bath to soak away her frustrations. Due to a lull in the hammering upstairs, the hall seemed unnaturally quiet. She paused, her foot resting on the bottom step, her hand on the banister. Something small and roughly circular came rattling down the stairs towards her and struck her on the shoe. She looked down.

The old button.

Rosamund stared at it, doubting her own senses. It must be another, similar one, she thought, but knew it wasn't. Someone must have thrown it, she thought, but upstairs there was only empty silence. Slowly, reluctantly, as if it might bite her, she leaned down and picked it up. The button was warm, as though someone else had been holding it and had only just relinquished it. She stared down at the worn yellowed face of it. The light was better here than it had been last night in the back room. She could see that there was carving on it, a round shape, with another circle at its centre.

Abruptly, she slipped the button into her pocket, keeping her fingers clasped tightly about it. Her chest was hurting, as if someone were squeezing it, and the agitation inside her was almost unbearable.

****

Ambrosine was in her downstairs sitting room. 'Madam asked you to bring the tray today,' Mrs Gibbons told Alice, eyes sharp and curious. It was unusual for Ambrosine to ask for anyone particularly.

'There's some jam sponge, if she cares for it,' the cook went on, fussing with the linen napkin and shifting the plate of sandwiches an inch this way, then an inch the other. She surveyed the silver tray one last time before flapping her hands. 'Well, go on then!'

Alice set off for the door. Meggy grinned at her as she passed, and then darted an anxious glance in Mrs Gibbons's direction, in case the cook saw the exchange and took exception. But Mrs Gibbons was busy making Venus pudding, humming under her breath as she broke the eggs and set aside the required twelve yolks and six whites.

Alice made her way down the hall. She could feel Bertie's bird book snug in her pocket, bumping gently against her thigh. She had been carrying it around for just such an opportunity as this. Anyone would think Ambrosine knew of it. But, as Alice was aware, it was something else entirely which had led Ambrosine to ask for Alice to bring the tea tray to her sitting room.

Her heart began to beat with a sort of unpleasant excitement. I know, she thought to herself. You can't fool me, madam, *I know*. And now you're afraid of me, that's it, isn't it? You're afraid of what I'll say.

The last time she had been in the library she had found a word in the big dictionary. 'Omnipotent.' That was how she felt right now.

Ambrosine didn't look up from her letter when Alice tapped and entered. She was wearing a green day dress with a high-boned collar, and a matching green bolero trimmed with dark braid. The colour accentuated her pallor. Cleo, a bundle of toffee-coloured hair and bright eyes, watched from Ambrosine's lap.

The sitting room was very warm. There was a fire in the small fireplace, although Alice thought it was hardly needed. Sunlight filled the room, filtered through the lace curtains onto the polished floor and brilliant rugs. White roses wilted in a tall white vase.

Alice set the tray down on a table and glanced at Ambrosine, seated on the button-back couch and still absorbed in her letter. It had come from her brother, who was fighting the Boers in South Africa—Alice had seen the postmark when she collected the post. Mrs Gibbons had read a piece out of the newspaper about the Victorian soldiers, and Ambrosine's brother's part in the fighting at Elands River last year. The Boers, it seemed, had no honour. They did not fight like proper British gentlemen; they hid and ambushed their foes like wild animals. It was no wonder General Kitchener had decided to burn and starve them, like animals, into surrender.

'Thank you, Alice.' Ambrosine was folding her letter precisely along its original creases, as if it were terribly important to do so. Alice took the opportunity to slip Bertie's book from her pocket.

'Madam, I wondered if—'

Ambrosine looked up sharply and Alice noticed the shadows beneath her eyes. 'What is it, Alice?'

It was a game, Alice realised. Ambrosine was waiting for something, although for what Alice wasn't sure. She held out the book, feeling suddenly much less omnipotent than she had thought. 'Master Bertie left this, madam. I wondered if he might need it at school.'

A little frown marred her brow and was gone. Ambrosine stretched out a hand and took the book. She glanced through it a moment, turning the pages with the same elaborate care she had shown the letter.

'Bertie is very fond of nature,' she said at last, and there was a strange smile on her mouth.

'Madam?'

'Bertie would say that all birds and animals live by the laws of nature. Survival of the strongest and fittest, as pronounced by Mr Darwin. Can the same be said for human beings, Alice? Must everything be sacrificed in a bid to survive? Where then is music and art and literature? Some would say they are just as necessary as food and shelter. And what about love, Alice? Can one survive without that?'

Alice wondered if Ambrosine were quite well. The smile she had thought odd had been replaced by a look that was wild, almost hunted.

'My husband often tells me that your father saved his life.'

'Yes, madam, he did.'

'For that reason he would never dismiss you, Alice.'

Alice lifted her chin. 'I know that, madam.'

Ambrosine laughed, and put her hand to her mouth to stop. 'You know that? What else do you know, Alice?'

Now was her chance to explain how Bertie felt, how unhappy and how miserable he was. But before she could open her mouth, Ambrosine had placed something on the table before her. Alice stared down at it, puzzlement turning to amazement. It was a five-pound note, folded as particularly as Ambrosine's brother's letter. Five pounds was more money than Alice had ever seen in her life.

'Is that what you want?' Ambrosine whispered behind her hand, her eyes burning and bright.

'I want some new boots,' Alice said slowly, as if testing out the words. Her mouth felt stiff and strange.

Ambrosine fingered her boned collar. 'Then take the money and buy some.'

Alice hesitated.

'Take it!'

Cleo barked shrilly. Alice snatched it up, crushing the paper in her hand, and bolted for the door. Once there, however, her training reasserted itself, and she bobbed a curtsey. Ambrosine gave a gasp of laughter as the door closed.

Something like anger rose bitter in Alice's throat, but she swallowed it back down. She had not asked for what she really wanted. She hadn't asked for Bertie to be allowed to come home. Her feet had betrayed her. At least Bertie will have his book, she told herself guiltily, and soon, soon he would be home. Then she would tell him what had happened.

No. Alice stopped the thought. She couldn't do

that, no matter how much she wanted to. Ambrosine was Bertie's mother and he would never believe ill of her. Alice must keep her own secrets, and now it seemed that she must keep Ambrosine's as well.

****

'It looks like a flower.'

Kerry frowned down at the button, her face flushed from the stove. She had been cooking corned meat for the men's sandwiches. She seemed to feed them regularly on the hour, like overgrown babies. Rosamund had no patience with such things but she understood that Kerry was the kind of person who needed to feel useful, and feeding people was her way of doing it.

'It looks like ivory, although it's very discoloured,' Rosamund added. She hadn't mentioned the manner in which she had found the button this time—or it had found her—and Kerry just assumed it had never been missing.

'We could try cleaning it with cotton wool and methylated spirits. Very gently of course.' Kerry glanced at her sideways. 'Would you like me to do it?'

'Yes, all right. I'll go and have a bath. I'm filthy.'

Kerry's face formed a look of almost comical dismay. 'You can't. They've turned off the water.'

The cloud of depression resting on Rosamund's shoulder grew a few extra kilos. She left the button with Kerry and walked out into the hall. She stood still, fighting tears. Further down the hall, at the back of the house, the two rooms full of the attic's contents waited. They held secrets, she knew it, secrets that only she could unlock.

'Well, I'm already dirty,' she muttered to herself. 'What will a bit more dust matter?'

It was time to begin turning the key.

****

The finished portrait had been hung ceremoniously, before the entire household, in the drawing room. There were gasps when they saw it. Alice wondered, as she listened to Mrs Gibbons's coos of admiration and Cosmo's laughing good humour, how they could all be so blind. Such a picture could only have been painted by someone who knew the subject well, intimately well. Why could no-one else see what was right in front of their eyes?

It was a large portrait, and easily covered the wall above the mantelpiece. The background was quite dark—Alice wondered why Mr Marling had been so insistent upon light when he meant to paint something so dark. The central figure, Ambrosine Cunningham, was seated on a double-sided settee, leaning forward across the arm, leaning towards the artist, towards Mr Marling. She wore one of her high-buttoned blouses, the cloth light and silky, its tucks and scallops failing completely to disguise the swell of her full breasts. Her hair was in soft disarray, with wisps of curls at her forehead; her cheeks were delicately flushed and her lips faintly parted as if she might be about to speak. She seemed to be looking out of the portrait into the room, but the expression in her eyes was difficult to read. Alice thought, at first, that it was fear. But how could that be right? What was Ambrosine afraid of?

****

Rosamund had no choice but to begin at the beginning. That is, the doorway. Until she cleared the immediate area, she couldn't get any further into the room without standing on objects which might not take her weight.

The first thing she pulled out was a doll's cradle made of timber and painted mustard yellow. The bedding in it was holey and pungent with mice. With a grimace of distaste, she dragged it well down the hall.

Returning to the room, Rosamund glanced towards the casement windows. It was still full afternoon and outside the sun was shining. No ghosts, no girls with straight brown hair, nothing to fear. But still she was edgy, and when one of Fred Swann's crew clattered past the window with a ladder she nearly jumped out of her skin.

A cylindrical papier-mâché umbrella stand was an interesting find, even if someone had pierced it with the point of their umbrella. A small box, when she forced it open, was full of old cigarette cards depicting British Army uniforms, mainly from the Boer War and World War I. Rosamund went to set these aside as possible saleable items, and then changed her mind and drew them back.

There had been few children in this house in the early part of this century. Perhaps the cards had belonged to her grandfather, Ada's soldier husband. She touched them again, bending close to examine the tinted, stern faces of the soldiers. They must have belonged to him. She couldn't imagine Ada beginning such a collection, and besides she had never smoked.

Rosamund decided that a basket of coloured tapestry wools probably did belong to Ada, most of them a meal for long-dead moths. The half-finished tapestry which went with them was so faded and stained it was barely recognisable, but Rosamund made out the obligatory cottage with flowers about the door.

An ancient Remington typewriter, grimy with dust, sat on a cane rocking-chair. Rosamund set the typewriter aside and dragged the rocking-chair further down the hall towards the stairs. It would do for one of the rooms, when they were habitable. The stuffed peacock was next. It was in such a state she could hardly bear to touch it, the feathers shivering with microscopic life. That would definitely have to go. Then there was a commode, a lampshade she vaguely remembered, a cigar box full of shells, a chest of smelly old blankets—the chest was reasonable—a dozen or so cracked cups and saucers, and a potty.

She worked on.

Most of the things were either broken or ruined by mice, moths or damp—the sagging roof had leaked. There were a couple of paintings, but Rosamund's initial excitement quickly evaporated. One was a bad copy of a Rembrandt and the other an amateur effort with sailing boats and poor perspective. She soon came to the conclusion that if the Cunninghams had owned anything of real worth, it had been sold either by Ada or her trustees, when she was a minor. All that was left was junk. She could already foresee numerous visits to the local tip. Well, she had known it all along, hadn't she? But that didn't mean the task wasn't a necessary one.

'I thought you could do with this.'

Rosamund looked up, pushing her hair out of her eyes, and gave a violent sneeze. Kerry bit her lip to prevent a smile, but her brown eyes were warm with laughter. Rosamund blew her nose. 'I'm a mess,' she announced self-consciously. 'Is the water back on yet?'

'Just. Leave it a bit so that your bath is nice and hot.'

Rosamund took the mug Kerry was holding and sipped gratefully. 'Thanks.' She gestured into the room and pulled a face. 'Nothing here, just junk.'

Kerry sighed. 'I suspected it. Mrs Ada sold anything she could make money out of. She brought in an antique collector one day and he stayed the weekend. I don't know how much she got but it was enough to keep us for a year.'

'Do you mean keep you in luxury or penury?' Rosamund put the mug down and found a cigarette, lighting it and drawing deeply. 'I was wondering whether these belonged to my grandfather,' she said, exhaling smoke and pointing towards the box which contained the card collection.

Kerry bent and inspected the cards, turning them over carefully. 'I'm surprised these are still here. They're probably worth something.'

'I thought Ada might have kept them for sentimental reasons.'

Kerry looked so doubtful, Rosamund smiled.

The dust lay thick on the floor about their feet, and more of it floated in the air. Rosamund could feel another sneeze gathering strength.

'That button . . .'

Rosamund looked up and saw that Kerry was holding out her hand, palm up. The button had been cleaned, and although it was still discoloured the design was now much easier to make out. It was obviously a flower. A rose, the curled petals making an irregular sort of circle. What sort of garment had buttons like these?

'Rather ostentatious,' Kerry echoed her thoughts.

Outside, the man with the ladder clattered back the other way. Fred Swann's crew were preparing to go home. Hastily, Rosamund dusted herself off. It was getting late, the light was fading to sepia. The air had suddenly become quite chill.

'I think I'll have that bath now.'

The kitchen was much warmer and full of cooking smells. Rinsing out her mug Rosamund caught sight of her reflection in the window above the sink.

'The wild woman of Colonsay,' she murmured. 'If Mark could see me now.'

'Perhaps you should ring Mr Markovic,' Kerry said from behind her.

Rosamund turned and gave her a long look. Kerry dropped her eyes and became conspicuously busy with one of the pots on the stove.

'No,' Rosamund replied softly at last. 'I don't think so.'

Upstairs in the bath, she washed her hair then emptied half a bottle of perfumed oil into the water and soaked for ages. Musk-scented steam filled the room each time she added more hot water. Rosamund closed her eyes and rested her head back against the cool rim of the tub, letting her body go loose. Mark's face insinuated itself into her thoughts but resolutely she pushed it out again. Instead she turned them to the Cunningham family tree.

Ada, despite her tragic past, had probably expected the usual share of happiness. She had grown up and fallen in love—this was pure speculation on Rosamund's part—and married her soldier fiancé. But he had been killed in France and Ada had had to raise her son Simon alone. They remained at Colonsay, and Ada called herself Mrs Cunningham. Her married name—Rosamund vaguely recalled it as Evans—was forgotten. The name Cunningham had always been so much more important to Ada, and those who knew of Cosmo had never thought of her as anything else.

There had been more money at Colonsay in those days, enough to send her only son to a good school, but Simon had never aspired to much. Perhaps Ada's ambitions were beyond him. Who, Rosamund asked herself, could live up to Cosmo in his daughter's eyes? Then World War II had come along, a chance for Simon to cover himself in glory. He had done a fairly reasonable job of it, too, but after the war had seemed to drift. As if he had no centre, no anchor.

Simon had married late. Almost too late—he was fifty when Rosamund was born. Maybe being brought up by Ada Cunningham had lessened his urge to play happy families. The woman he married, Janet, was young and pretty, but unstable. No money, either. Ada despised her, and didn't quibble at letting Rosamund know it.

'Weakness is something I will not tolerate,' she

had said. 'My brother Bertie was weak, too. Better to be vicious.'

And so Simon had died, and then Janet had died, and Rosamund and Ada were left. And now there was only Rosamund. The last Cunningham. What a legacy!

'Not a happy family then,' Rosamund murmured to herself, covering her face with a face washer. Happy families? Well, there was a joke. The Cunninghams must be one of the most unhappy families she knew.

A soft thump sounded above her head, in the ceiling, in the attic.

Rosamund sat up, water cascading over the sides of the bath, the face washer slipping from her face. Above her, through the steam, the greyish ceiling looked innocent but she was not deceived. Rosamund held her breath.

She didn't have long to wait. The thump came again, still relatively soft, but firm, insistent. Downstairs the telephone began to ring.

Breathing quickly, Rosamund stood up, grabbing her robe to wrap around her, her wet hair clinging to her arms and shoulders. She slipped on the spilled water as she climbed out of the bath, catching at the edge of the pink wash basin to steady herself. Her eyes looked back at her from the fogged mirror, distorted, terrified.

Thump! Above her head the noise reverberated. Once, twice, three times. Rosamund fumbled at the handle with slippery hands and flung the door open. Dusk was a spectacular array of purples and mauves and violets, the colours shining through the broken stained-glass window at the end of the corridor. The beauty of it touched Rosamund even in her fright, causing her to pause, confused, water dripping from her body onto the faded carpet runner.

Another thud, so loud it was like the blow of a huge hammer. The glass in the window appeared to shimmer, fragment. Rosamund bolted for the stairs.

'Rosamund!' Kerry was down in the hall, her voice full of panic. 'Rosamund, are you all right?'

'Yes,' she said, her voice a frightened squeak. The thuds came again, continuous now, even louder than before, until the whole house shook about her. She felt a scream well up inside her and was powerless to stop it. The voice came immediately afterwards.

'*Rosie*!' It was an anguished moan, enveloping her.

Rosamund slipped halfway down the staircase and slid on her shins the rest of the way, scrabbling at the banister with wet hands to stop herself from falling head first. Kerry was there, pulling her to her feet, half supporting her, making for the kitchen. Once inside, she slammed the door and turned the key. They stood shoulder to shoulder staring at the blank wood, listening to the thunderous noise from the attic, almost too afraid to breathe.

'Gary Munro was on the phone when it started,' Kerry was saying. 'He's on his way over.'

The banging had increased to an unbearable pitch, a frenzy. The noise of it was hollow; it echoed as though they stood at the mouth of a huge abyss. Rosamund put her hands over her ears and squeezed her eyes shut. It seemed as if the whole house were collapsing, as if every stick of it must be smashed. And then, as abruptly as it had begun, the noise stopped.

The silence was just as shocking.

'It's gone. It's gone!' Kerry cried hysterically, her voice going up and down the scale.

'Is it?' whispered Rosamund, too afraid to move in case she somehow brought it back again.

A volley of knocks on the front door caused them both to jump violently.

****

'That was kind of Mrs Cunningham,' she had cried on seeing them. 'Wasn't it kind of Mrs Cunningham?' Mira sat back, her hands folded in her lap, and surveyed Alice's boots. They were tan button boots, and had cost 13/9. And they fitted perfectly.

Mr Parkin had glanced at them sideways, as if they might strike out at him and bite.

'I said, that was—'

'I heard you, woman. Yes, they're fine enough,' he admitted grudgingly. Alice realised her father would never openly criticise Ambrosine. 'What did you do with the others? Perfectly good pair of boots, those. Cost me five shillin', they did.'

'I know, Father. I have them safe. They're my second best pair now.'

He was a little mollified by that. She couldn't tell him the truth, that she had given them to Meggy.

Neither of her parents thought it strange that Ambrosine should bother to buy her servant a new pair of boots. They considered it natural, consistent with their belief in her goodness and sweetness. If only they knew, thought Alice bitterly.

****

Gary was wearing jeans and a parka, his hair a mass of wild curls. He gave Rosamund, in her wet robe, a startled glance but made no comment. 'Where's the noise coming from?'

'In the attic.'

He brushed past them to the stairs. Light from the open bathroom door gave out a soft glow. Very little time had passed since she made her wild escape, though it seemed like hours. Her head was aching and she felt the wave of exhaustion which was becoming almost familiar.

She and Kerry stood and waited, listening to the silence, every moment expecting the chaos to begin again. After a short time Gary reappeared from the west wing and came quickly down the stairs, grinning at their expectant faces. 'Nothing,' he said. And then to Rosamund, 'Get some clothes on, for God's sake.'

Rosamund hesitated, her hand on the rail, but Kerry was beside her. 'I'll come with you,' she murmured, although she looked as if she would rather not.

Upstairs, Rosamund threw on her red sweater and jeans, and was still drying her hair as they re-entered the kitchen minutes later. Gary was making instant coffee, setting out mugs, sugar and milk on the table. He looked from Kerry to Rosamund.

'Should we call the police?' Kerry whispered, leaning confidentially across the table to him.

Gary sighed. 'There was nothing up there.'

'There must be!'

'Old houses make noises,' he said tentatively.

'Not like this they bloody don't,' Rosamund managed, her voice still shaky. She put her head in her hands. 'It was horrendous. What does it mean? What does it want?'

'Ah.' Gary sounded as if she had said exactly what he wanted to hear. She looked through her fingers and then carefully lowered them to rest on the table. He was watching her like a cat watches a mouse, waiting, patient.

'You know,' she breathed. 'Don't you?'

'I told you that I always hated this house, but you didn't ask why.'

'Have you heard the noises before?'

He smiled without humour. 'I've heard things, and seen things, and felt things.'

'Things?' Rosamund felt the flesh on her arms creeping and rubbed them vigorously with her hands.

'I saw a man once, in the library.'

'A real man?'

He snorted and sipped his coffee. Kerry, who had been looking from one to the other of them, her head turning from side to side as if she were watching a tennis match, cleared her throat.

'Are you saying the house is haunted, Gary? Because if you are, then I can't believe it. I *won't* believe it. I'm sorry, but I've lived here for thirty years and there has never been anything in the least ghostlike at Colonsay. I'm not saying this house hasn't had its share of tragedy, all houses have tragedy in varying degrees, but there has never been anything at all supernatural at Colonsay. Mrs Ada would not have allowed it.'

Rosamund laughed but Kerry ignored her, her face pink with the effort it had taken her to make such a speech. Gary reached across and covered her hand with his own.

'I don't know what I'm saying,' he said. 'I'm trying to make sense of something that makes no sense. I don't know what a ghost is, I don't know what you have here at Colonsay, but you have something. Rosamund knows that, don't you? Or are you going to pretend it was all in your mind?'

She wanted to, oh God she wanted to, but when she met Gary's eyes she knew her hiding days were over.

'What are we going to do then?' she asked wearily.

'I don't know. Nothing now.' He eyed her cautiously. 'I'll stay tonight.' When neither Rosamund nor Kerry objected, he went on, 'I've some gear in the car.'

'Oh, you came prepared then?' Rosamund couldn't resist.

'I've been down on my boat. It just so happened I was bringing some stuff home and left it in the car. Okay?'

She nodded and looked away. The weariness pulled at her muscles. She hardly heard Gary get up and go out into the night. A warm hand covered her own, and when she looked up Kerry was watching her with a mixture of unease and determination.

'Rosamund, I don't know if you've heard . . . if you realise, but Gary had a sort of breakdown in Melbourne. That's why he left the newspaper and came home. I don't think you should give credence to everything he says, and I don't think you should encourage him in his belief that Colonsay is haunted.'

CHAPTER 8

'I think we all understand the need to keep Australia pure. White. I sympathise with the arguments of our northern relatives, who need to bring in labour to work their cane fields, but the purity of the race is all important. We must think of the greater good. If we open the immigration gates now, we'll be overrun. That was one of the reasons I worked for a Federation, Marling. I want a strong country, a white country. We must keep our European traditions and our Anglo-Saxon blood undiluted, we must preserve what we have or we are surely lost.'

Cosmo drew on his cigar, eyes half closed through the grey smoke, watching for Mr Marling's response.

Alice pulled the curtains on the still, shadowy garden. It was difficult to believe that last night the rain had come in squalls, thrashing against the windows, leaving in its wake a legacy of broken stems, torn leaves and sodden petals. The gardeners had long ago tidied the mess away. Behind Alice, the fire she had made crackled pleasingly in the hearth, filling the library with warmth.

Mr Marling settled back into his chair, his fair hair bright against the dark leather. Above him, on the wall, the sword the old soldiers had gratefully presented to Cosmo glowed with polishing. Cosmo poured another brandy from the glass decanter and handed it across. Mr Marling took an appreciative sip and smoothed the already smooth line of his trousers. The firelight lit up the faces of the two men, gleaming here on a button, there on the polished toe of a boot. Cosmo, bluff and handsome, his luxuriant grey hair swept back from his broad forehead, had the loud, uninhibited laugh of a man used to having things his own way. Mr Marling was more watchful, his smile like a testing of the water.

'Then you do not feel, sir, that those races other than the Anglo-Saxon have anything to offer us? As you say, the north requires labourers, and everyone knows Coolies and Kanakas work better in the hot tropical sun. White men are too refined for it. And I quite understand that our intellectual and creative abilities are far superior. It is comical, is it not, that these people cannot grasp their own inferiority? The Chinese, to take but one example. Who are they? Do they think that building a wall fifteen hundred miles long makes them special? Or making silk from worms, or inventing gun powder, or manufacturing porcelain so fine the light shines through it? I have heard that they have managed to exist for thousands of years in a state very close to civilised, but surely that is just sheer good luck?'

Cosmo grunted and sipped his brandy. They eyed each other warily. It occurred to Alice that Mr Marling was being ironical and Cosmo knew it.

'And what of our own black race?' Mr Marling went on. 'The Aborigines? What will become of them? We can hardly send them back to where they came from, for they come from Australia. What do you propose to do, sir?'

His tone of worried concern fooled no-one. Cosmo frowned. 'You must lack a proper understanding of the matter, Mr Marling, or you would not be so flippant. Look at my own servant, Jonah. He is half white—the better half—and has been educated as a white man. Whenever I see any trace of black man in him, I make sure to beat it out. He knows better than to play the savage with me. And he is grateful for it, sir. Where would he be now, if it were not for me? Think on that, Mr Marling, just think on that.'

Mr Marling appeared to be thinking on it as Alice's new boots tapped satisfactorily across the library. She closed the door behind her. Jonah, she thought to herself, would be better for a beating. Secretive Jonah. How could Meggy and the others love him so? No, if anyone deserved a beating, it was Jonah.

****

Gary Munro carried his gear up to one of the bedrooms in the east wing. The room was untidy and dusty but he didn't seem to care. Rosamund and Kerry watched him look about and give a nod of satisfaction, as if the chipped plaster and holes in the wallpaper didn't exist. Grubby windows reflected the three of them standing grouped inside the doorway.

The three musketeers, Rosamund thought with a wry humour.

'Any damage this time?' Gary asked. He was looking at her—his eyes really were extraordinarily blue. She found herself remembering what Kerry had said, and it took a moment to realise he meant any damage from the violence in the attic.

'We haven't looked.'

'Well, perhaps we should.'

But this time the light in Rosamund's room had withstood the onslaught. The bathroom door was still open, the bath water now cold. Rosamund pulled up her sleeve and slipped in her arm to pull out the plug. As Kerry and Gary checked the other rooms, she stood in the empty corridor. There was something ... something she should remember. Her eyes fixed on the stained-glass window at the far end. Rosamund blinked.

'The window!' she called. 'I saw it shatter. At least, I thought I did.'

Gary followed her over to the window and they both inspected it. The glass was still in place, although the lead looked brittle in parts. 'Was it like this before? I mean, with this piece missing and the crack down here?' he asked.

Kerry nodded. 'Frederick Swann has made arrangements for it to be restored. Someone's coming next week to take it away to their workshop. I believe it's rather valuable. An early attempt at Art Nouveau.' She sounded surprised, as if it wasn't her idea of art.

Rosamund hardly heard her. She had seen the glass dissolve. Or had she? It seemed that she could not believe her own eyes these days. Perhaps everything she had so far experienced was an illusion. Perhaps she was having a breakdown, like Gary. She hugged her arms about herself. How much should she be telling him? How much could she afford to tell him?

Gary was watching her, and as if he had read her mind, said, 'I think we should talk about it. Now. Tonight.'

Rosamund shook her head, avoiding his eyes. 'What's to talk about? I'm tired.' And she realised suddenly that she was, soul-drainingly tired. Her legs wobbled, barely able to hold her up, and her head ached. She needed sleep, she needed time to think.

Gary was eyeing her curiously. 'Tomorrow's Sunday,' he said. 'Frederick's day of rest. Colonsay will be quiet. We'll talk then.'

It sounded like a threat. 'Whatever,' she muttered, and brushed past him towards her bedroom. 'I need to sleep now.'

She heard the murmur of their voices outside in the corridor long after she had closed her door and flung herself, still fully clothed, into her bed. And then, just before sleep, a faint scratching noise near her door. 'Mice,' she muttered, and didn't open her eyes. This time there were no nasty hallucinations about coffins. She slipped straight down into nothingness.

'From the beginning, then.'

Gary was watching her expectantly. Behind him, Kerry looked up from stirring scrambled eggs and caught Rosamund's eye. Be careful, she seemed to say. Remember what I told you. Gary Munro is not the safe shoulder to lean on that he appears.

'I think you should go first,' Rosamund said, cupping her hands around the cooling coffee mug.

Her cigarettes lay on the table beside her but she had no urge to light one. There was a faint queasiness in her stomach, and her muscles were aching as though she had had a seriously heavy workout. Perhaps she was coming down with something.

'Me?' Gary demanded. 'Oh, no you don't. I need to hear you first. I don't want what I say to colour your story.'

Rosamund frowned. 'I could say the same for you. How do I know you won't alter your story to fit in with mine?'

Gary snorted with disbelieving laughter. 'Why would I do that?'

'You're a writer, writers tell lies. You might be planning a book about a haunted house. You might want to write a "true" account of Colonsay à la *Amityville Horror*. You might have trouble differentiating between fantasy and reality. How would I know?'

Gary stared at her hard. 'You mean I might be mad?'

Kerry looked up sharply, her irises completely surrounded by white. Before she could stop herself, Rosamund met her gaze. Gary glanced from one to the other of them suspiciously. And then, as realisation struck, his face went slack. He covered it with his hands and shook his head.

'I get it,' he cried. 'I get it.' His hands dropped away, his expression a mixture of anger and embarrassment. 'You think I'm gaga. You think I've convinced myself, in my warped, sick mind, that Colonsay is haunted, and if you tell me what you've seen you'll only encourage me in this pathetic fantasy? Is that it?'

Kerry's fair skin coloured tomato red and she turned back to her eggs, stirring them furiously.

Rosamund forced herself to meet his eyes without flinching. There were deep creases around them, and more about his mouth. They were smile lines. There was another line, particularly deep, between his brows which had little to do with laughter. But his skin was tanned and clear—he looked healthy. He looked like the sort of man who was up at six to jog along the beach and then sat down to a hearty breakfast. She could not convince herself, despite what Kerry had said, that there was anything mentally wrong with Gary Munro.

'Let's clear the air,' he said. 'Secrets out in the open.'

Rosamund nodded and watched curiously as he drew a deep breath.

'I was under a lot of stress,' he began. 'The job at the newspaper, and a lot of other shit going on in my life at the time. A friend committed suicide, a girlfriend walked out on me.' He shrugged, as if this happened all the time. 'One morning I woke up and got ready for work as usual, but when I walked out of the door I just . . . I don't know, lost myself. I don't remember anything beyond walking out of the door. It was as if something in me switched off. I lost a whole day, and although I've tried to piece it together from things other people have told me, I still can't remember it. Evidently I drove to a friend's house and had a coffee and spoke about greenhouse emissions, and how I expected the sea to begin rising very soon. And then I went to Parliament House and tried to see the Premier to discuss it with him. I had a boat, you see, and I thought it might come in handy. Not surprisingly, they threw me out. I'm lucky they didn't call the police—or unlucky.' He shrugged again.

'After that, who knows? A couple of friends found me sitting on the beach at St Kilda, staring across the bay. Waiting for the sea to come in and sweep me away, I suppose. They took me to hospital, where the doctors pumped me full of drugs, and there I was kept incommunicado for a week. Then I came home. I was in therapy for a while, but I stopped when I came back here. I find I don't need it now. I have a job, I've started writing, I go sailing a lot. All the things I should have done much earlier. I think that's what my mind was trying to tell me. It was saying "Enough!" but I just wasn't listening. So it made me listen.'

He was watching her, Rosamund realised. He was smiling, his body language was relaxed, calm and collected, but behind all that he was watching her to gauge what she was thinking. She couldn't blame him for that. Most people were uncomfortable with mental illness, he must be used to being rejected. He had learned to be careful with his secrets and she and Kerry had more or less forced this confession.

He spoke again when Rosamund didn't comment.

'What's happening here, now, at Colonsay, and what happened here years ago, has nothing to do with what happened to me in Melbourne. Believe me.'

The blue eyes were begging for some sign from her, and Rosamund responded. She smiled.

His own mouth curved up at the edges. 'I know,' he went on, 'we were never friends before, when we were children. But I want us to be friends now.'

He held out his hand across the table. Rosamund found herself reaching towards him, mesmerised by his eyes and the promise of having someone, anyone, on her side. His fingers closed on hers, strong and warm, the skin callused and dry. She felt a frisson at his touch, but it was pleasant rather than nasty.

Kerry was standing over them with two plates of egg, her expression non-committal, but she avoided meeting Rosamund's gaze. 'You should eat now,' she said firmly.

After eggs and toast and coffee, Gary and Rosamund went out into the back garden. The sun was warm and the day calm. Bees buzzed in the abundant flowering weeds, birds launched an assault on the red berries dripping from the straggly branches of a cotoneaster. Colonsay was wonderfully quiet after the racket made by the builders, the only mechanical sounds the hum of a passing car and the whine of an aeroplane. Rosamund lit a cigarette and drew in, feeling the nicotine firing her brain even while it soothed her nerves. God, how was she ever going to give up?

Saucepans rattled. Kerry was already starting lunch. Rosamund had tried to persuade her to join them, but it was obvious she didn't want to. Talk of the happenings at Colonsay made her nervous. She didn't believe it was anything supernatural; she didn't *want* to believe it. Rosamund desperately hoped she and Gary would come to the same conclusion.

'Voices,' she began at last. 'And the attic, the banging in the attic. That happens at night or in the evening. Maybe the darkness brings it on. Cold, a terrible bone-chilling cold, the sort you read about in horror stories. That comes with the noises in the attic. Once I heard footsteps in the cellar. And I've seen a girl at the window in one of the back rooms.'

'Do they have anything in common?' Gary asked, watching her face. 'I mean, was there a particular moment when it all began?'

Rosamund shook her head. 'I don't know. I would have said it all began the day Fred cleared the attic, except that I heard the voice before that.'

'Voice? You said voic*es* before.'

'Did I? What does it matter?' But it did matter, she knew that. She just didn't want to think about it; she was like Kerry in that. She held a childish fear that discussing these things might make them worse.

'What does the voice say?'

Rosamund drew on her cigarette before she answered. 'Rosie,' she said finally. 'Only not at all like that. It's a cry, a . . . a plea. Do you know what I mean? Whoever says it—said it—is in some sort of pain, I think. Maybe not physically, but certainly mentally.'

She glanced at him sideways to see whether he was laughing at her. He wasn't. He was staring at his shoes, deep in thought. Next he asked her about the girl and she answered as best she could, describing the long brown hair and the old-fashioned clothing, the sense Rosamund had of being inspected by something with intelligence rather than viewing an inanimate picture from another time.

Gary lifted his face to the sun. It caught in his hair, picking out silver strands among the gold. Rosamund watched him, waiting. His jeans had a hole at the knee but they were clean. His shirt was unironed but the colour suited him and it was also freshly washed. He was so different from Mark, who was always so perfect. Rosamund realised that Gary was looking at her. He smiled, and involuntarily she smiled back.

'All right,' he said. 'Let's start with Enderby. My grandfather is fascinated by Colonsay. I don't know why. It's more than the history of the place. He has cuttings about your family, books of them, going right back. Enderby was something in the government in his younger days. Nothing as flamboyant as Cosmo Cunningham, of course, but maybe that was the beginning of it for Enderby. Fame by association, first with Cosmo, then Ada, now you.'

'Me?'

Gary raised a pale eyebrow. 'Why not you? Apart from being the wife of Mark Markovic, hot contender to be our next Premier, you are a Cunningham.'

'Enderby loved visiting Colonsay,' he went on. 'He brought me along because he considered it a treat. He never understood my reluctance—didn't want to. He certainly never *saw* anything. I told him a couple of times what I had seen, but he didn't like unpalatable things thrust in front of him like that. He probably thought I was just over-imaginative, or a liar. He did everything he could to avoid the subject or turn it back on me. So I just stopped telling him. I came to the conclusion that it was my cross to bear, just another thing to make me different from the others.'

A jolt of recognition went through Rosamund, but she stayed quiet.

'I remember, once, I was in the library and a man appeared. One moment I was alone, the next he was there. He was sitting in one of the leather chairs, but I could see the chair through him. He was wearing a suit, but it wasn't modern. You know, high collar, waistcoat . . . Could have been Victorian, I suppose. I don't know much about period clothing, and men's clothing never changed that much anyway, did it? I know he had pale hair but I couldn't tell you the colour of it, because he was grey. Grey all over. He didn't seem aware of me, not like your brown girl. He was more like a still photo. I always explain it to myself as an overlap in time, or God putting the wrong reel of film on his projector and creating a celestial cock-up.'

'Did you ever . . . did you find out who he was?'

Gary laughed. 'God no. I was just glad that he went. I got out of there as fast as I could. But after that I hated coming to Colonsay even more.'

'I thought you hated me.'

The lines about his eyes creased up as he smiled. 'You didn't seem too fond of me, either.'

'I wasn't. But if I'd known . . . if you'd told me . . .'

Gary shook his head. 'And have you piss yourself laughing at my expense? No, thank you.' He paused, his gaze slipping beyond Rosamund into the past. 'I heard a woman once. She was weeping, and it was the saddest, most gut-wrenching thing I'd ever heard. And another time, when I was looking for you in the garden—you used to hide, do you remember?—someone was following me. I couldn't see them but I could hear their footsteps crunching in the leaves. Bloody creepy. I took off like a shot from a gun, expecting any moment to feel a hand on my shoulder. A bony, skeletal hand, mind you.'

Rosamund placed her cigarette butt carefully on the ground and pressed it into the dirt with her shoe. The benefit from the nicotine was already fading. She looked back to the house. It had the brooding look of any number of the haunted houses in folklore and literature. Gary didn't seem to notice, he had returned to the days of his unhappy youth.

'Those sorts of frights were few and far between, thank God. Most of the time it was just the feel of the place that got to me.'

'What do you mean?'

For the first time Gary looked stuck for the right words. 'A *feeling*. I don't know if you . . . Oh shit, let me try and explain.' He bit his lip, thinking. 'When I was in the psychiatric hospital . . . I don't know if you've ever seen one of those places? You have all sorts in there, from minor breakdowns like me, to the very complex cases. Anyway, I used to amuse myself by thinking of it as a sort of toy hospital, you know, where the broken ones went to be fixed. Some of the patients were a lot more broken and a lot harder to fix than the ones who just needed a new bit of elastic.' His smile faded. 'There was a woman in there. I don't know what had happened to her, but there was a sense, a *feeling* about her. Honestly, the pain and suffering sloughed off her in waves. You could sit down next to her feeling fine and within a minute you'd be as bloody depressed as it was possible to be. That's how Colonsay used to make me feel, Rose. There was an air about it—I don't know, a cloud! And once you walked into it you felt depressed. Unbelievably depressed.'

'I never felt like that,' Rosamund replied, fascinated and curious at the same time. 'Does it still make you feel that way?'

Reluctantly, Gary shook his head. 'No. At least, I didn't feel it at all when we started work on the place, but I'm beginning to sense it now. Like a tremor in the soles of my feet, but not strong enough yet to affect me.'

They were silent for a time. A magpie sat on the boxthorn hedge and watched them, head cocked, hoping for a treat. It waited a moment and then hopped down to the ground, coming closer, trusting them not to harm it. I'm trusting Gary in the same way, Rosamund thought, and I think—I know I'm right. He's a loner, like me, and he's struggling to find a safe path through life's minefield, like me, and he's hurting inside. Like me.

The sound of her own voice surprised her. 'When I was very young I heard voices. I don't remember it but Kerry does—she says Grandma Ada used to discuss it. I grew out of it, evidently, or it stopped as I got older.' She shuddered. 'Now it's come back.'

'No.' Gary was looking at her strangely. '*You've* come back, Rose. You've brought Colonsay back to life. The house has changed since you've been here. I've felt it, Kerry's felt it. Whatever was here has been here all along, but it wasn't able to make its presence felt until now. Somehow your arrival has been the catalyst.'

Rosamund stared back at him, knowing it was true, feeling the warmth drain slowly out of her, as if the sun had gone under a cloud.

'But why?' she whispered.

Gary shook his head. 'I don't know why. I have a friend who's into all this . . .' He hesitated and then said, 'Stuff,' as if he couldn't find a better word. 'She tells me that we're arrogant to think our world—for want of a better word—is the only one. There are others. And some of us can tune into them, some of us have a thinner veil between us and them. Perhaps,' he added ironically, 'you and me are two of the lucky ones.'

*

Gary went out for a couple of hours in the afternoon, and returned carrying bags from a local hardware store. They held string and fine cord, tacks, hooks, and several large containers of baby powder.

'I wrote an article once on ghost-hunters, so I know a few of the strategies they use. I'll set everything up before we go to bed. If there's a practical joker at work here we'll flush him out.'

'You're staying again tonight, then?'

He looked at Rosamund, surprised. 'Of course. I want to know what's going on as much as you do. You do want to know what's going on, don't you?'

'Yes,' she said too quickly, and this time avoided glancing Kerry's way. While Gary had been out, Kerry had warned her again about trusting him too far.

'I thought you liked him,' Rosamund had retorted.

'I do like him, but he was never an easy young man to understand.'

'I understand him.'

Kerry looked sceptical.

'Why won't you acccpt somcthing is wrong with this house?' Rosamund burst out angrily. 'At least Gary is willing to accept that, and to try and work out what it is.'

Kerry flushed, but her mouth was stubborn. 'Mrs Ada and I lived here for—'

'Ada! You're not going to bring her into it again, are you? She was as crazy as a hatter. She never managed to drag herself past 1918.'

'She suffered such terrible loss,' Kerry muttered angrily. 'Her parents dying when she was a child, and then her husband killed in France—'

'Don't you think my childhood was just as traumatic as hers? I lost my parents, too.'

Kerry's mouth became even more stubborn. The silence drew on. Rosamund could hear her breathing.

'You think I deserve my misery, don't you?' she whispered, the anger draining out of her. 'You think I was wrong, leaving here? Running away?'

'You had more than other girls.' Rosamund was taken aback at the tone of resentment. 'You threw it away for a whim. Singing,' and she raised her eyes to heaven. 'Ada Cunningham loved you and cared for you, and you deserted her. Her last words were of you, did you know that?' Rosamund shook her head dumbly. 'Well, they were. I held her hand at the end, and I made the burial arrangements and sorted through her bits and pieces. You didn't even come to the funeral. You didn't even come back afterwards, to take what was rightfully yours. She lived here all those years on a pittance so that she could save the house for you. For *you*!'

Rosamund had never heard Kerry raise her voice, she would never have believed her capable of it. 'Not for me,' she answered dully at last. 'She did it for herself. The past was her world, and Colonsay was her past. She wouldn't have known how to live anywhere else. Could you have seen her fitting into your typical nursing home? Watching *Days of Our Lives*, and playing cards, and knitting bootees for the yearly fête? She did it for *herself*, Kerry, just as she did everything for herself. She took me in and cared for me because it would have been a slur on the family name if she hadn't. Not because she loved me. She never loved me.'

Kerry shook her head, brown eyes glittering like wet pebbles. 'You're as pig-headed as she was. You're so like her, Rosamund! Can't you see it?' She turned and walked away.

Frozen, Rosamund stared after her. Like Grandma Ada? What a fate worse than death! As the quiet pressed down on her she realised she hadn't asked what Ada's last words were. Perhaps it was safer not to know.

By the time Gary returned with his ghost-catching gear, she and Kerry had managed to forge a sort of truce. Kerry bustled about in the kitchen, speaking as little as possible and avoiding Rosamund's eyes, while Rosamund sat in the doorway, smoking and drinking coffee and doing the same.

But there was another unpleasant incident during the evening meal. 'If Mr Markovic rings,' Kerry asked innocently, 'should I tell him Gary is staying?'

Rosamund speared a green bean with her fork. 'Why not?'

Gary looked up from his plate. 'Is my staying going to be a problem?'

'Not for me,' Rosamund announced.

He inspected their closed faces and a shadow of uncertainty dulled his eyes. 'Maybe I'm assuming too much here? Maybe you don't want any help on this? I can leave now, and if you have any further trouble you can just ring the police.'

'I want you to stay.' Rosamund's voice was too loud, with more than a hint of fear. She toned it down. 'I want you to stay,' she repeated, softer, and managed a smile. 'I don't mind admitting I'm frightened, even if Kerry won't. And if you can help us sort this . . . this thing out, then I will be most grateful. Please stay.'

He stared at her a moment more, as if judging her sincerity, and then nodded his head. 'All right then, I will.'

Kerry said nothing, eating her way silently through her meal.

They took their coffee into the library. It had become the room Rosamund preferred. There was something cosy about the bookshelves, untended as they were, and the leather armchairs, and the long windows looking out over what must once have been a beautiful garden. With the faded velvet curtains closed she could pretend the garden was still there. White roses, Rosamund thought. That was what she could picture out there. Hadn't white roses been Ambrosine's favourite? A circle of white-rose standards, with a statue as a centrepiece. She pictured the women in their long skirts and large hats, strolling among the perennial borders and the shrubbery. Colonsay had been full of visitors in Cosmo's day, rich and influential people, politicians and artists. Rosamund understood more fully than she would admit why Ada had wanted to preserve those memories.

Gary wandered along the bookshelves, making the sorts of noises avid readers do when they come across old favourites, or long sought-after titles. He had been a bookworm when he was a boy—Rosamund had often come upon him in here browsing. She wondered with wry amusement whether this was the first time he had returned since his encounter with the ghost. She lit a cigarette, sipped her wine, and watched the fire crackle in the sooty hearth. Autumn had really arrived. At home, in Melbourne, Mark would have the central heating set at 25°C. He hated the cold, he said it reminded him of his childhood when he was never warm. Rosamund, brought up to Colonsay and fierce weather, used to laugh at him; at least, she did when they were first together. Lately, neither of them had had much to laugh about.

'These belonged to Mrs Ada.'

Rosamund looked up, startled out of her reverie, to see Kerry grasping a cardboard box. It was of medium size but when Rosamund took it from her it was heavy. Inside it was full of papers, their musty smell indicative of their age. A black photo album rested on the very top, its edges and corners scuffed and worn. Rosamund set the box down on the floor beside her chair and lifted the album onto her lap.

The front cover had faded in places to a rusty colour. It crackled when she opened it, as if it might separate completely from the rest of the book. Rosamund bent to read the single line of copperplate writing. 'Cunningham of Colonsay'. The two went together without question, as if one was nothing without the other. The skin at the back of Rosamund's neck prickled.

The photographs were not labelled. Ada had known who they were, and so had Rosamund, once. She turned the pages slowly, carefully, examining the set poses of groups in long dresses, smart suits, picture hats and straw boaters. Informal outings at the Springs, or more formal times at Colonsay. One grouping included numerous politicians from the early 1900s—Rosamund recognised the faces but had trouble with the names. A photo of a child with long blonde sausage curls and a sweet smile—Ada. A little boy, booted and buttoned to within an inch of his life—Ada's brother, Bertie. Then a family photo of Cosmo and Ambrosine and the two children. Incongruously,

Cosmo reminded her a little of Stalin, with the thick grey hair and intimidating moustache, but his face was more amiable, his eyes more humorous. Ambrosine was perfectly dressed in the fashionable Gibson Girl skirt and blouse, her dark abundant hair twisted up on top of her head, her gloved hands clasped about the bone handle of a parasol. There was an air of unreality about her which puzzled Rosamund. As if, behind the perfect face and figure and reputation, there was an emptiness ... a nothingness. One knew, just looking at Cosmo, exactly what he was and what he thought, but the same could not be said for his wife. Ambrosine was an enigma.

Rosamund turned the page, blind and deaf to Gary and Kerry as they refilled their coffee cups and made conversation. Gary added a log to the fire and poked at it inexpertly, until Kerry clicked her tongue and took over.

There was a small photo of a man in uniform, his face smooth and young and untouched. Ada's husband, Rosamund's grandfather. How many times must Ada have stared at this face and wished? What would her life have been if the war had not taken her husband? The next face Rosamund recognised was that of her father, Simon, also in uniform, clean-cut and solid, before he left for the Middle East. Then Ada again, alone, in a '50s skirt and jacket, her smile determined for the camera. There were a couple of photos of Rosamund's mother, Janet, tall and gangly with a tentative smile. There had not been much happiness for Rosamund's parents, either, and the lack of photos declared it. And finally, Rosamund herself. First as a baby, then as a toddler, and then a tall, lumpy, sullen teenager standing in the already overgrown garden, glaring at the camera lens with dark, resentful eyes.

Something stirred in Rosamund. Was it possible, all your life, to see a thing from a certain angle and then, for some reason, suddenly to have that angle change, your perspective change, so that everything shifted into a new focus? Had her loneliness and her oddity as a child made her believe things about Ada that weren't true? Was Kerry right and Rosamund wrong?

'Anything interesting?'

Gary was standing close beside her chair. Rosamund looked up, willing her confusion not to show on her face. 'Depends on your point of view,' she replied with a brief smile. She turned the pages again, from back to front this time, while Gary peered over her shoulder.

'There's Enderby,' he said.

Rosamund looked more closely and saw that he was right. His grandfather stood by Ada's chair, with Simon. The house was behind them. They were all smiling.

'Happy days,' she murmured.

Back at the first photograph she closed the book. The brown girl hadn't been in there; she hadn't expected her to be. Her face was not a Cunningham's. In her heart Rosamund knew, whatever she had believed to the contrary, that she would have remembered it if it was. No, the brown girl was a stranger. A mystery waiting to be solved.

'Did you see your ghost?' Gary asked her softly.

Rosamund shook her head. 'What about you?' She smiled despite herself. The conversation was becoming ridiculous.

'It wasn't Cosmo, or any of the Cunninghams.

I'm sure of that much. Perhaps it was a visitor who had a miserable time here and comes back to haunt the scene of his humiliation. From what Enderby says, Cosmo could humiliate with the best of them.'

'He *was* a politician,' Rosamund murmured, and wondered if she was trying to make excuses for Cosmo or Mark.

Gary gave her a strange look. 'I forgot, you're married to one—an almost one. History repeating itself?'

Rosamund shrugged and put the album back in the box. There was plenty more material in there to be gone through, but it was late and she was tired. She realised, with sharp relief, that so far whatever made the noise in the attic had remained silent. She had even forgotten about it, for a time. Perhaps Gary's presence was inhibiting their unwelcome visitor and they would be given a respite tonight.

Before bed, Gary went around the house to set his ghost traps. He hammered in tacks, and tied lengths of strong cord and string across windows and doors and at various points along the hall. He fastened another string at the top of the stairs, and constructed a simple but ingenious home-made alarm with a chair and saucepans just inside the staircase to the attic. Anyone opening that door would pull on the cord holding the chair and bring the whole lot down with a clatter. In the attic itself he stretched more lengths of string back and forth within the wide, low space, so that it would be impossible for anyone to move freely without tripping. When he had done all that, he proceeded to sprinkle powder on the floor surfaces—all the main thoroughfares—so that anyone walking through the house would leave footprints, evidence of their passing.

When he reached the east wing's corridor, Kerry and Rosamund were standing inside their doorways, watching him as he completed the powdering of the floor. He had pulled aside the old carpet runner, rolling it up haphazardly so that the floor was bare. Kerry's eyes were dark shadows in her face, her arms folded tightly across her knitted bed jacket. No doubt she was thinking about cleaning it all up in the morning, thought Rosamund.

'I won't tie any string across our doorways,' Gary said as he worked. 'In case we have to make a quick exit.'

'Doesn't that rather defeat the purpose?' Rosamund asked. 'Kerry could be making the noise in the attic. Or me.'

Gary glanced at her, eyebrows raised. 'I defy either of you to leave your rooms tonight without me knowing about it.'

He had powdered his way to his own room now, across the hall from Rosamund and Kerry. They stood awkwardly, staring at each other, as if reluctant to part.

'Goodnight,' Kerry said at last, and closed her door.

Rosamund moved to close her own and hesitated. 'You don't think this is completely crazy?' she ventured.

He shook his head. 'Not completely. Let's give it a go. See what comes up. What's happening may have a completely rational explanation.'

'I hope so.' She saw him smile before her door closed.

Rosamund climbed into bed and lay on her back, staring up at the ceiling. Outside, wind stirred in the pine trees and an owl hooted. Colonsay was still, even the usual creaks and groans of an old house were silenced. Rosamund closed her eyes and allowed her thoughts to drift, floating out of the window, away from Colonsay, to the cliffs. Out across the bay, where the bright lights of tankers and other craft shone over the dark wash of water. Seamen steered their ships and boats safely through the shoals and sandbanks, towards the Rip, that shallow tidal stretch which was the gateway from Port Phillip Bay to the sea. These were dangerous waters, filled with wrecks and tales of misfortune.

'*O hear us when we cry to Thee/For those in peril on the sea*.'

The words rang in her head, clear and true. Where had that come from? Her eyes flickered but she kept them firmly closed. Near her bedroom door the faint scratching began—mice? It must be mice, what else could it be? If she didn't look, then she could pretend it was mice . . . Even when the terrible, now familiar chill began to creep into the room with her, she refused to open her eyes, hoping if she paid it no heed it would simply go away.

The first thud from the attic caused her to stiffen, lying like a board beneath the quilt. The second had her up and running for the door.

****

Mrs Gibbons was singing 'Those Endearing Young Charms' in a wavering soprano.

Meggy rolled her eyes as she grated nutmeg carefully into a bowl. Alice cleaned knives, forks and spoons, laying on hartshorn paste thickly and rubbing carefully with a soft cloth. The silverplate at Colonsay seemed to tarnish almost as soon as it was cleaned—Mrs Gibbons said it was the salt air.

Ambrosine had been out riding this morning. She had been caught in a heavy shower and had come home dripping. Mrs Gibbons had fussed, sending up hot water for a bath, and then warm broth, and now, still singing, she was busy making some tea to tempt Ambrosine's appetite. She added a hefty dollop of influenza tonic to the cup.

'Madam may take a chill, and my tonic is the best thing to prevent it,' she announced to the kitchen at large.

'That tonic'd prevent breathing if you drank too much,' Meggy muttered grimly. 'God knows what's in it!'

Alice had a fair idea. She had seen the cook make it up and the ingredients had included liberal quantities of stout, wine and malt.

'What about poor Jonah,' Meggy continued under her breath as Mrs Gibbons sang on. 'He was out with madam and got drenched, too. No-one cares enough to make *him* tea and soak *his* feet in a bowl of hot water.'

'Why didn't they take shelter?' Alice retorted.

Meggy grated her nutmeg vigorously. 'Wouldn't be right, would it?' she muttered. 'There might be talk.'

Alice almost laughed. 'Jonah's a *servant*, Meggy.'

Meggy lifted her eyes and Alice could see she was bursting to tell her something.

'Enough chatter!' snapped the cook, and once again silence reigned.

****

Gary caught her at the head of the stairs. 'Whoa! You'll break your neck.' He yanked free the string trip-wire.

Above them the thuds continued, louder now, a fury of sound shaking the entire house. Gary had a torch. He shone it through into the west wing, where the stairs to the attic were situated. The beam trembled, but they could both see that the powder on the floor was perfectly intact. Gary took a step forward, as if considering going up them.

'Don't!' Rosamund shouted above the noise. 'Gary, don't!'

Colonsay shuddered under the fury of the blows. Kerry had arrived and was now huddled against the wall, hands over her ears, eyes squeezed tightly shut. Rosamund slid an arm about her, feeling comfort in comforting. They began the descent. The noise changed; once again it began to echo, and it was as if they were standing at the mouth of an immense cavern. In the kitchen, they flicked on the light and locked the door. It gave an illusion of safety. Gary's arms around them both felt safe, too.

The crashing and banging went on for perhaps another two minutes and then stopped as suddenly as it always did. The resulting silence was like a sound in itself.

Gary took a deep breath. 'We'd better check out the rest of the house.' There were shadows under his eyes and he was dressed in the same clothes as earlier. Obviously he had been sitting up, waiting. Kerry, her skin pale and sickly looking, followed him towards the door. Rosamund had no choice but to go too, but she did so unwillingly.

She and Kerry stood in the entrance hall together while Gary checked that his traps were all in place on the ground floor. 'Looks like something small's been here,' he called back to them, sweeping the torch over the floor where Rosamund had been sorting the Cunningham treasures. 'Do you have a cat?'

'No, no cat.'

'Something small, anyway.' He dropped his voice.

'What?'

'I said, whatever it was couldn't have made noises like the ones we've just heard.'

They followed him upstairs. The powder was untouched apart from where the three of them had left their rooms. There were no footsteps leading into the west wing, and the saucepan alarm on the attic stairs had not been tripped. When Gary opened the door, several pans fell with a shocking clatter, making them all jump nervously. He swung the beam of the powerful torch up the stairway, cutting the darkness. 'Come on,' he said. Slowly, nervously, they followed him into the attic.

Gary shone his torch across the low, sprawling area. The roof seemed to press down on them, even the blue tarpaulin Fred had fastened over the new framework in case of rain. Torchlight swept across dusty floors and a litter of wood, tiles and builder's paraphernalia. The powder lay white, faintly gleaming, undisturbed. The maze of string was in place, a giant spider's web.

Rosamund could hear the sound of Kerry breathing behind her, and Gary muttering, his head narrowly missing a low beam as he moved further into the attic. His feet scuffed up powder and he sneezed, the sound magnified in the silence.

'No-one could've been in here,' he said, his voice echoing. 'It'd be impossible without leaving some evidence. And I can't find any microphones or sound equipment, no Steven Spielberg technology. Just an ordinary, empty room.'

There was something almost triumphant in his voice, and Rosamund swallowed her irritation.

'*You* could have done it,' Kerry said with forced conviction.

He made his way back to them and looked at Kerry from behind the torch, the shadows on his face making it as unfamiliar as a stranger's. 'Why? Because I'm a nutter?'

She avoided his gaze.

'Even if that were the case, why would I be doing this?'

Kerry did not answer. The three of them stood there, the torchlight reflected back at them from the grimy, diamond-paned windows. The tension between them was as tight as one of Gary's strings. The attic felt claustrophobic—Rosamund couldn't remember ever being up there before. Ada had never encouraged it, but even so she must have been an unnatural child, because it had never struck her as a possible hiding place or cubby. She had never liked the feeling the attic stairs gave her, and she had had no desire to climb them.

'It's empty,' she announced, sounding angry

because she was frightened. 'I'm going back to bed.'

She brushed by Kerry and padded on bare feet down the dark stairs, avoiding the teetering saucepans. The west wing was silent, the rooms which had once been the Cunningham children's nursery were musty with disuse. Rosamund felt the emptiness, and yet . . . there was a sense of being watched, of being spied upon. Why was this happening? Was someone trying to drive them away from Colonsay? And if so, for what purpose? Or was it an attention-getting exercise? A bored poltergeist?

She half smiled at the notion. It was an effort. She was so tired she could hardly lift one foot after the other. It was always the same after the banging had stopped and she wondered for the first time if there could be some connection. Strange it had not occurred to her before. Was whatever was creating this havoc syphoning strength from Rosamund, using her as a sort of power socket and plugging into her whenever it felt like it?

She shivered, hugging her arms about herself, and heard a soft footstep behind her. Kerry. Perhaps they could make themselves a warm drink before going back to bed, or pour a stiff brandy. She turned around to suggest as much.

And froze.

The brown girl was standing behind her. Rosamund found herself thinking, absurdly, that she didn't need a torch. She was glowing with a light all her own.

CHAPTER 9

'Mademoiselle Sombreuil, that is. Last of them before winter. She's a grand French beauty, ma'am.'

Petersham nodded proudly at the white roses Ambrosine was arranging in a vase brought by Alice. Their scent was lemony and sweet, and they were saucerlike in shape rather than with the elegant slender points of the other tea roses.

Ambrosine cupped them in her hands, bending to press her nose into the foam of petals. 'Wonderful,' she murmured, and lifted her smiling face to the old man.

He cleared his throat as though embarrassed, but Alice saw the faint colour in his cheeks. All men were such fools when it came to Ambrosine.

'My mother grew roses when I was a child,' she was saying. 'Comtesse de Murinais, Semi-plena, Madam Hardy . . . always the white ones. They only flowered in the spring but they were sweet, so sweet. Water was precious and she saved every drop from our cooking and washing, hoarding it like a miser. Sometimes there was only a single bucketful, or less, at the end of the day, but she would carry it out into the garden and ladle it onto her roses. The plants struggled in those hot, dry summers, but they survived. Rose flowers are so delicate, we believe a puff of wind will destroy the plant, but in fact they are very hardy. Exquisite and strong. Their strength, Sergeant, is in adapting to the conditions in which they find themselves, not fighting against them.'

Petersham, his big gnarled hands clasped between his knees, sat frozen in the brocade-covered chair as if afraid he might damage it, while Ambrosine continued. There was a pensive quality about her today.

'You see, I am not unused to difficult times. We lived north of the Murray, on the plains. My father yearned for land of his own. When his business failed, he bought a property with what he had left. My mother and my brother and I joined him, leaving civilisation behind us. I was thirteen. It was a life so very removed from what I was used to, my friends thought I would be unhappy, and yet instead I felt as if I had been given my freedom.'

Alice moved softly about the room, setting more wood on the fire, placing the roses on a table by the window, rearranging the delicate plates of sandwiches and cakes which Mrs Gibbons seemed to be able to produce in no time at all. Ambrosine did not notice her, or, if she did, chose not to show it.

'Is it right that Mr Cunningham's from up that way, too?' Petersham queried.

Ambrosine shook her head with a glance that was almost flirtatious. 'No. My husband is from Colonsay. He has land on the Murray, yes, but he has never lived there. He finds that country harsh and unyielding. Here, by the sea, is much more to his taste.'

''Tis a beautiful place, is Colonsay.'

'Indeed it is. Yes, you are right. But sometimes

I long for my plains stretching to the horizon. I long to see the sun sinking lower and lower in the great arc of the sky, with the shadows lengthening . . . where giants walk.'

She sipped her tea, smiling, but Alice thought that her hand trembled slightly.

Giants! she scoffed to herself. But it surprised her that Ambrosine had come from such harsh and uncompromising surroundings. Alice had always believed Cosmo's wife was the product of easy Melbourne living, a spoiled child first, and then a cosseted woman. The image she had now sat uneasily upon the previous one.

Petersham took a sandwich and snapped it up like the grizzled old hound he was. Ambrosine watched him and her smile did not waver, the polite mask back in place.

****

Frederick Swann and his team were at Colonsay bright and early. Their cheerful noise woke Rosamund from a sound sleep, which she had finally managed to achieve about three o'clock that morning.

She lay listening to the voices calling back and forth, the laughter. Strange how some people seemed naturally cheerful while others saw only gloom. Why was that? Were people born with their characters set, or were the lessons learned in childhood essential components of the adult?

Rosamund thought of her own childhood, the loneliness, the feeling of being unloved. Could that alone explain the weak and dependent woman she had become? She was certain Ada had not wished her to be like this. Snippets of conversation returned to her. 'Make your decisions wisely, Rosamund. They will be with you until you die.' Ada, dispensing advice between the soup and the main course. 'Marry with caution, Rosamund. If you marry for love, you marry with your eyes shut. I married for love, as did my father.' Ada, sitting straight-backed in her chair, profile sharp and birdlike. 'I have always stated my beliefs openly, Rosamund. I abhor secrets, perhaps because I'm not good at keeping them.'

I didn't understand, Rosamund thought now. I didn't listen. She was trying to help me in her own way, offering me what advice she had available from her own bitter experience. How could she have been a warm and loving woman when her own life had been so tragic? But I was a child, and children don't understand.

It was unproductive, now, to berate herself or Ada. Just as Rosamund had failed to see her grandmother's point of view, Ada had made no allowances for her youth and inexperience. She had been impatient with children. Rosamund had sensed that impatience and, being an insecure girl, had acted accordingly.

A cement mixer started up in the front garden, rattling away as someone shovelled in sand and cement. Rosamund sighed and sat up, pushing her hair out of her eyes. She was thinking about Grandma Ada because it stopped her thinking about the brown girl, but she would have to think about her eventually.

Last night, Gary and Kerry had put her to bed. They had found her semi-conscious, slumped against the wall. She had muttered about ghosts but Kerry hadn't wanted to know. Gary had carried her—good God, had he really?—to her room. As she lay trembling and dry-lipped on the bed, she had heard Kerry murmuring to him near the door. Probably telling him about her drinking, and what a nuisance she was being to Mark, and how she was only here at Colonsay to be out of his way. Well, it was the truth, why shouldn't he know? And Gary wasn't exactly spotless, was he? They were well matched.

The thought comforted her and she moved to the window, cautiously though, remembering her first morning here when she had unwittingly given the workmen a peep-show. So much seemed to have happened since.

The brown girl. Rosamund put her hands over her face. It was the eyes that had frightened her. More than the grainy quality of the apparition, more than the inner glowing light, even more than the fact that she was a phantasm—the essence of something that had lived once and now was dead. The eyes were *alive*, seeing not some scene from a dead past, but Rosamund.

'She wants me,' Rosamund whispered to herself. 'For some reason she wants me, and I don't understand why.'

'Then you must find out!' Grandma Ada's voice echoed in her head, harsh and shrill. Whoever the brown girl was, and whatever had happened to her, she was here for a reason. Find the reason, solve the puzzle, and the ghost would disappear in a puff of ectoplasm. That was the theory, anyway.

Rosamund took a deep breath. Yes, she thought, I must find out. Last night, after it happened, she had decided she must leave Colonsay as soon as possible, but this morning she was asking herself where else she could go. And apart from that, the old house had become her home and she did not want to be driven out. 'I'm the last Cunningham of Colonsay,' she murmured. 'No-one has more right to be here than me.'

She heard the clatter from the kitchen as she descended the stairs. Kerry was indulging herself in her own brand of therapy. There was a warm meaty smell drifting through Colonsay, mingling with the usual breakfast ones.

'Coffee?' Kerry called as Rosamund hovered in the doorway. 'I've just made some for the boys.'

Rosamund presumed the boys must be Fred Swann's workmen, none of whom would see twenty again and few of whom would see thirty.

'Thank you. No, don't stop, I'll get it. I want to do some more sorting in the back room.'

'Are you sure you're well enough?' Briefly, the brown eyes met hers before sliding away again. Kerry bent over a thick roll of pastry, pushing and pummelling it with her hands.

'Yes, I'm fine.'

Rosamund took the cup and left before Kerry could ask any more questions. She went down the hall and stood in the doorway, sipping her coffee and viewing the remaining treasures. It was amazing what a difference even the small amount she'd done had made. She was surprisingly eager to continue. The secret to the brown girl was here in this house, she knew it.

During the hours before lunch, Rosamund discovered several old toasters, a stack of calendars from the 1950s, a broken cricket bat and torn gloves, newspapers from the 1960s and '70s full of girls with too much eye make-up and not enough skirt, a table with three legs, a chair with two, and a stack of shellac long-playing records in torn, flimsy sleeves.

Fascinated, Rosamund turned each one over, reading the labels. Scottish ballads, mostly, with a couple of marching tunes. A Cunningham nostalgic for the old country? Rosamund hummed 'Loch Lomond'. 'Rosamund Cunningham sings Cunningham classics,' she murmured to herself, and smiled.

The smile faded. Was this what the Cunninghams had been reduced to? Dusty objects in a dusty room? Was all life reduced to this, eventually? What would remain of her, when she was dead?

'Rosamund?'

Dazed, she looked up at Kerry standing uneasily in the doorway, eyes shifting about the room as if she expected to see something nasty. Her apron was spotless.

'What is it?' Rosamund heaved herself up, feeling dizzy. She went to push a hand through her hair, but stopped when she realised her hands were filthy.

'Do you remember that ivory button? The one I cleaned?'

Rosamund nodded.

'Gary wanted to see it, but when I went to get it, it wasn't there. Do you have it?'

Rosamund's eyes narrowed. 'You know I don't.'

'I just thought . . . I wondered . . .' She bit her lip and turned away. 'It doesn't matter. I must have misplaced it.'

Alone now, Rosamund stood looking around her as if the button might spring out at her. This disappearing-reappearing act had happened too many times to be a coincidence.

'What are you trying to tell me?' she whispered. But of course no-one answered.

After lunch, Rosamund continued sorting. There was an old phonograph, broken unfortunately, or she would have played the records, and a newer stack of vinyl albums, this time mostly blues and soul, belonging to her father.

I'm discovering my roots, Rosamund told herself with grim humour. I was never interested before, I was more or less forced to come here, and now I'm even enjoying it. Except for the ghosts. The past is me, it's what made me. It's me and I'm it. Cosmo Cunningham, and now three generations later, Rosamund Cunningham. Are we alike at all?

She doubted it. Cosmo had been an ambitious man, full of his own importance, secure in his place in the world. What was Rosamund? A shadow, the blurred shape behind the brilliant husband. Not a person at all, really. Though for a time, she had been.

When I sang I was real, she thought. And then Mark came and for a time that was real, too, before his ambition took him elsewhere and I was left behind. I'm as much a ghost as the brown girl, only more trouble. A troublesome spirit.

Rosamund carefully replaced the record she had been holding on the rickety pile. She had divided the hall into several areas now, categorising each item as she sorted. The area designated the tip needed a lot of space, and then there were the items for possible sale—that pile was small. Finally, there were the things to be kept, which had grown far bigger than she had imagined. 'One man's junk is another man's treasure,' she muttered to herself. 'Or something like that.'

She had reached the back wall of the room before she saw the couch. It was of a dark and sumptuous wood, with scrolled arms and a red velvet cushion seat, stained and squashed by the pressure of numerous Cunningham buttocks. Fred Swann's team had all but covered it with boxes and bags, but they were soon cleared. When she had liberated the couch, Rosamund dragged it towards the door and sat on it. A puff of dust rose around her and she sneezed. She tucked her legs up under her and searched in her pocket for a cigarette.

Outside the grimy window, the day was cool and windy. A magpie sat on the boxthorn hedge, perhaps the same bird she had seen before. The hedge was full of red fruit, and the birds were enjoying its bounty. The noise of Fred Swann and his men was muted here. They had begun work on the west wing and had been up and down the stairs all day. Kerry had given up trying to keep the floor clean, and complaining about men and dogs with dirty feet had retreated to the sanctuary of her kitchen. The smell of baking permeated Colonsay. The way things were going, Rosamund thought, they would soon have food rolling out of the doors and windows.

The light glanced across the wooden floor in front of her. She could see her own footprints where she'd walked back and forth, and the drag marks of the various treasures. There were other prints, too. Odd ones. What had Gary said last night—a cat? Rosamund squinted through the smoke, trying to make sense of the small paw marks running in circles through the dust.

Further down the hall the telephone gave a shrill ring. Rosamund didn't move, smoking quietly. Let

Kerry get it, give her a change from whipping up scones and icing cakes. The room was so quiet, so peaceful. She'd think about the prints on the floor later. Later . . . She felt her eyelids begin to flutter. So easy to drop off for a moment. So pleasant. So restful.

'Rosamund?'

Kerry's voice was sharp, and Rosamund lifted her head with barely concealed irritation.

'Mr Markovic is on the phone. He wants to speak to you.'

With an effort Rosamund stumbled to her feet. 'To me?' she repeated, and then frowned impatiently at her own idiocy. Why shouldn't Mark want to speak to her? He was her husband, after all.

When she reached the hall table where the phone was situated she waited until Kerry had closed the kitchen door, and took her time stubbing out the last of the cigarette before she lifted the receiver.

'Mark?'

'Who's this Gary Munro?'

So Kerry had told. Rosamund wondered, briefly, irritably, exactly what agenda the other woman was running. She took a breath. 'He's someone I used to know.'

'Why is he staying at Colonsay?'

He sounded impatient rather than curious, as if he had been interrupted at a meeting. Rosamund found her own heart rate rising, his mood affecting her.

'Didn't Kerry tell you why?'

'Only that you've had animals or some such thing getting into the attic, making lots of noise.'

Rosamund didn't answer; she heard his impatient exhale of breath.

'Rosamund? What's going on? I sent you down there to oversee the restoration of the house, not to pick up strays and give them a home.'

'Colonsay is my house. I'll pick up who I like, Mark.' Had she said that? Her heart was thumping, but she forced her fingers to relax on the telephone receiver.

'Rosamund.' That letting go of breath again, as though he were a balloon and she a sharp object. Some of the tension went out of her.

'Really, he's a friend. A perfectly respectable friend. He's a writer and his grandfather has lived on the peninsula forever.'

She had made him respectable, tidied up all the questionable truths about Gary. She had told Mark what he would want to hear.

'Oh.' He was grateful, she could hear it in his voice. She had saved him having to sort out another messy problem, another of her embarrassments.

'Was there something else you wanted to speak to me about?'

'Did you see the piece in the *Age*?'

She hadn't. He told her. The journalist had been very generous, the photo was flattering. There had been a new poll, too, on the possible outcome of the by-election and that was looking good. Mark was way ahead. Rosamund stared in front of her at the cork board full of names and numbers, pretending to be interested. I shouldn't need to pretend, she told herself. But with every poll, with every 'piece', Mark moves further away from me. He doesn't need me any more, except as a cut-out figure by his side. The perfect wife. And I was never that.

'I have to go,' she said suddenly, and now she was breathless.

Mark stopped mid-sentence. The silence between them was alive.

'I can't get down there this week,' he said at last. 'Maybe next weekend.'

'I thought we needed a break from each other?'

'I want to see you. What you said last time—I want to talk.'

The numbers on the cork board swam before her. Rosamund closed her eyes. 'Can't you talk now?'

'I've a meeting.'

'Of course.'

'Rosamund—' But whatever it was he wanted to say, he did not finish. She could hear the voice of his secretary in the background and Mark's murmured reply. She put down the phone; it gave her the illusion of being in control.

Darkness settled around her. Night. Rosamund moved restlessly, caught in a dream of toasters and old records and scones and cream. Gary was there, winding string around and around her until it was impossible to move. He had sown the missing button onto his shirt, and when Rosamund looked closer she saw not the rose but a pale face with watchful eyes. As she screamed Gary was laughing, and banging saucepans together, louder and louder and louder . . .

Rosamund woke, gasping for breath. The echoes of clattering metal drifted up the stairs. There came another terrible crash, this time interspersed with shouting voices. She jumped out of bed, fumbling for her coat, her cold toes curling on the threadbare rug.

Footsteps pattered by Rosamund's door, and

when she ran to open it Kerry was at the head of the stairs, peering down into the hall. She raced to join her and saw that the light was on, the front door wide open. A man lay sprawled, arms and legs tangled in Gary's arrangement of string, an avalanche of saucepans around him. Another man was bent over him, attempting to free him.

'Oh, my!'

Both men looked up at the sound of Kerry's cry. Shocked, Rosamund recognised the white face of Mark's driver. That meant the man on the floor must be—oh God! She closed her eyes briefly on the nightmare.

Kerry, recognising Mark herself, was already down the stairs, blurting out apologies. Mark, with Kerry's help, finally managed to unravel himself. He pushed aside the fallen chair and stood up, brushing down his clothing with brisk, angry movements. Rosamund sensed someone behind her and glanced over her shoulder. Gary hovered in the shadows, and she saw the laughter in his blue eyes before she turned again to the scene below her.

'Mark?'

He lifted his head, and too late she wondered how she must appear in her fawn coat with her hair wild about her and her bare, size-nine feet. Maybe a down-market version of Carmen? Mark, of course, despite his run-in with the kitchen utensils, was immaculate in a dark suit and white shirt. His dark hair was only faintly untidy, cut fashionably shorter than the last time she had seen him. But his face seemed white and drawn, the shadows under his eyes a lighter grey than his eyes.

'Rose.'

His gaze shifted sideways and she knew Gary

had come to stand beside her. For his mouth to harden like that, the two of them together must look pretty damning. Rosamund decided not to explain, not to make herself even more foolish with guilty excuses. She was innocent of *that*, whatever Mark might think.

'You said you weren't coming until next weekend,' she said instead, descending the stairs. The air from the open door was freezing and she pulled the coat closer about herself. She could see Mark's BMW out there at the front, lights still on. There was an overnight bag by the bottom of the staircase.

'I changed my mind,' he snapped. 'What's this meant to be? A burglar alarm?' He was looking at Gary, and Gary answered him.

'We've had some problems. I set up a few traps to try and catch the culprits. Sorry. If you'd let us know you were coming, I could have deactivated this one.'

'I'll make some coffee,' Kerry murmured, and headed for the kitchen.

'They seem very effective.' Mark's mouth twitched into a smile.

'It's the first time they've been tested.'

The two men watched each other, outwardly polite, but with a tension Rosamund could taste. She came down the last few steps and reached to pick up Mark's overnight bag. He stopped her, bending first, his fingers closing over hers. The touch of his skin was faintly shocking, and nervously she glanced sideways, suddenly aware of the warmth of him, the smell of him. Something inside her sparked into violent life. She straightened clumsily and took a step back, out of his way. At the same time, Mark turned to his driver.

‘Thank you, Lance,’ he said calmly. ‘I’ll see you tomorrow at ten.’

‘Yes, sir.’ The man nodded and went outside, closing the door behind him. Rosamund heard the soft but powerful roar of the car as he drove away.

‘We have plenty of rooms.’ Kerry had come to the door, holding a tray heavy with mugs and a plate of biscuits. She looked worried. ‘Really, I don’t mind making up another bed.’

‘He has a sister in Queenscliff,’ Mark explained, smiling, putting her at her ease. ‘She’s expecting him; he rang ahead when I ordered the car for tonight. But thank you, Kerry, for your kindness.’

Rosamund could see Kerry responding to his verbal stroking, her shoulders relaxing, her mouth curling into a half-smile. God, he was a master at it!

‘Here, let me.’ Not to be outdone, Gary relieved Kerry of the tray. ‘The library?’ he asked, with raised eyebrows. She nodded, and hurried to open the door for him.

Mark and Rosamund were left standing alone in the hall. She felt him watching her but didn’t want to respond. Why had he come here tonight, without warning? What had prompted such a spur-of-the-moment gesture? Mark never did anything on the spur of the moment. Rosamund was suddenly afraid, but with the fear came a wave of something else. A courage that originated not from within but from outside. Colonsay. The house enclosed her like another skin, protective, strong. Rosamund lifted her chin and faced him.

‘What have you come here for?’ she demanded, and registered the surprise in his grey eyes.

‘I decided our talk couldn’t wait.’

‘That’s a first.’

'We need to discuss our relationship.'

'Do we? Have you decided to divorce me? Or is it strategically better for you to have a wife by your side, loving or otherwise?'

He actually laughed. Shaking, Rosamund turned away and hurried after the other two, afraid if she stayed she might physically assault him, or burst into tears on his Gucci-plated chest.

Kerry already had the fire crackling and the curtains drawn. She had left the main light off but turned on two of the smaller lamps, so that the atmosphere was mellow and warm. Inviting. Rosamund went to stand beside Gary. He was wearing an old pair of jeans and a green jumper. She found his presence comforting and reassuring.

'You all right?' He was looking at her as if he understood her better than she did herself.

'Yes,' she murmured, and took a deep breath.

'Did you know Superman was coming?'

'Mr Markovic.' Kerry's louder tones drowned out Rosamund's reply. 'Come and warm yourself. Sit here. You haven't met Gary properly, have you?'

Mark sat down and thanked Kerry for the coffee. 'No, I haven't.'

'Mr Markovic,' Gary nodded. There was a definite animosity between them.

'This is Gary Munro,' Kerry went on. 'He was a journalist in Melbourne. Now he's a writer, although he's presently working for Frederick Swann. He used to come to Colonsay as a child, didn't you, Gary? His family owned the old Munro Hotel at Clifton Springs.' She stopped, as if aware she had been gabbling, and held out the biscuits. Mark took one with a smile.

'You've come here to write?' he asked. 'Have you had any books published?'

Gary grinned. 'This is my first.'

'Fiction? Non-fiction?'

'Fiction, I'm afraid.'

'Why do you say that?'

Gary crouched by the fire, warming his hands, and the flames touched his hair with gold. 'Well, non-fiction is selling so well lately. Especially biographies. So many politicians willing to tell their stories for the right advance.'

Mark watched him expressionlessly. Then he tilted his head to the side and suddenly smiled his most devastating smile. 'Are you taking the piss out of me, Gary?'

Gary laughed. 'Not entirely.'

'What did the police say about the problems you've been having at Colonsay?' This to Kerry.

She fussed with the fire. 'They were very kind, Mr Markovic. They searched the house. But there was nothing—that is, nothing they could find. An animal, I thought, or a bird. And old houses can be so noisy at night, settling, you know.'

He waited politely for her to finish before he turned again to Gary. 'Is that why you're staying here? Because the house is so noisy at night?'

Gary shrugged. 'I'm investigating the matter. Rosamund asked me to stay. It's her house.'

The grey eyes lifted to Rosamund, who stood in the shadows by the corner of the mantelpiece. For a moment she was transported back in time to the pub where she and Mark first met. She'd been wearing a tight red dress—she had smaller curves in those days—and Mark had looked at her as if he'd found paradise. Rosamund could remember the gritty, smoky feel of the place, the sour-sweet smell of beer and sweat, and the warmth of Mark's hand as he gripped hers.

The silence stretched out unbearably. 'Yes, it is her house,' Mark said at last, soft as cashmere. 'And she's my wife.'

Kerry cleared her throat and moved to collect the empty mugs. 'I think I'll go back to bed now, if no-one wants anything else?' She gave Gary a meaningful glance.

He straightened abruptly, and with astounding litheness. 'Yes, me too. God, is that the time? Goodnight.' And his smile slid, brief and meaningless, over them all as he followed Kerry out of the door. A chunk of wood shifted in the fire, sending up sparks and causing one to catch in the hearthrug. Rosamund moved to stamp on the smouldering cloth and then stopped, realising her feet were bare. But Mark was there.

'Careful,' he murmured. He ground his shoe against the burning spot until it was black and dead, and then pulled the guard around the fire to prevent further mishaps. His arm brushed Rosamund's. She closed her eyes. She knew she should leave him, go to bed, but her brief strength seemed to have deserted her.

'What's happening to us?' His voice was so close to her cheek that she felt his warm breath, smelt the coffee on it.

'I don't know,' she whispered.

Mark's kiss touched her skin, and long before he reached her mouth her lips had parted, waiting, wanting him. His arm came around her waist, under the coat, and he pulled her tight against him. He had always liked to do that, to show how well their bodies fitted together. Like chewing-gum on a shoe, he used to joked. Mark wasn't a tall man, no taller than Rosamund herself, but he was broad-shouldered and well muscled. He had kept himself in shape these past years, while Rosamund had let herself slip, like an earth slide, an inch or two every year, until suddenly everything just careered away downhill.

'You've lost weight,' he said.

Startled, Rosamund laughed. 'Not from lack of food, believe me. Kerry's cooking is superb, and there's plenty of it.'

'What then? Hard work?'

'Perhaps I miss you.'

Mark went still. The grey eyes narrowed, assessing her words for their value and their honesty. His arm tightened. 'Where's the bedroom?'

They stumbled upstairs. He tossed his clothes over the chair and pulled her down onto the bed. The springs creaked alarmingly. He reached up under her negligée and cupped her breasts and then his mouth was on hers.

He was familiar and yet different. A stranger in Mark's clothing. The thought made her smile under his lips, and she felt him smile back. His hand slid down between her legs. 'Knock, knock?' he whispered, another old joke. Her laugh was almost a sob, and he rolled her over in his arms, kissing her. The darkness held them enfolded, until Rosamund lost her sense of time and place, until it seemed as if she wasn't Rosamund any more, and Mark wasn't Mark.

****

Alice stood in the darkness, the shapes of Cunningham cast-offs all about her. The attic was still full of the day's warmth, but airless. There were no fresh breezes up here, no ozone for ailing lungs. The diamond-pane windows were rarely opened; no-one ventured into this place. Except Bertie and Alice. She pressed her face to the windows now, peering down over the moonlit garden. All was still. If Jonah had been out there, he had long since retired to his separate quarters. Even Mrs Gibbons would be tucked up in her bed in her cottage behind the boxthorn hedge, dreaming of music halls. All of Colonsay was sleeping, apart from Alice. Not long now, she thought, until Bertie is home. Downstairs the grandfather clock chimed, the sound muted and far away, before the stillness regained its ascendancy.

****

The sound died away, a measured bong that resembled a clock striking. A heavy, mournful sound. Rosamund tried to open her eyes but couldn't. The scent swept over her, sudden and overpowering. Honeysuckle and roses. White roses. The air was full of them. Her fingers wriggled, just a tiny bit, it was all she could manage, and felt the soft padded lining. She gasped then, because she knew where she was. They were burying her. She was Ambrosine and she was dead, and they were burying her.

'Rose? Rose!' The hands shook hard, fingers digging into her shoulders, bruising her flesh. Rosamund's eyes snapped wide, but for a moment all she saw was blackness.

'Mark?'

Confusion. How could Mark be here? And then, remembering, relief, and his cheek against hers, his arms around her, the warmth of his body pressing to hers.

'Mark.'

'Are you all right?' He sounded strange, as if he had fallen into her dream and been infected by it.

'Yes. What time is it?' She asked it only to stop his questions, and lay watching as he reached over to switch on the lamp and peer at the clock. The line of his bare back tempted her, but she kept her hands clenched by her sides. How could you still be in love with someone and yet not trust them? Surely it was a contradiction in terms?

'Nearly two,' he said, and turned to look at her over his shoulder. The lamp silhouetted him, his face a blank. 'Nightmare?'

Rosamund ignored the question. Her hands clenched harder. 'Why did you come?' she asked suddenly.

'I told you, to see you.' His answer came smooth and easy, as if it were the truth.

'Do you want me to come home?'

His hesitation was small but she had been waiting for it, so wasn't fooled. 'If you want to. What about Colonsay? I thought you were enjoying yourself here, picking up the past?'

Enjoying herself? The comment seemed wildly inappropriate given what had happened here so far.

'I'll give the police a call, make sure they're keeping an eye on the house, on you. What is this Gary character doing barricading all the doors and windows? What's been going on, Rose? I want the truth.'

She sat up so that she could see his face. He was frowning, concerned. She almost believed him. 'We told you. There have been noises, unexplained noises. Kerry tries to believe it's a bird but I don't, and neither does Gary.'

'Do you think someone is getting inside?'

'That's one theory. Gary has just about disproved it, apart from you tonight.' She forced a smile but he didn't echo it. 'We believe there is something . . . unusual going on. Something supernatural, if you like.' There, she had said it. She waited, holding her breath, watching him for the expected reaction.

'You mean ghosts?'

Rosamund nodded.

He smiled. 'The guy's having you on.'

'I hear things. I see things, too. It's not Gary. I'm the one who's started it happening. I'm the switch, Mark. Me. And I'm not leaving, even if you want me to, and I know you don't. There's something at Colonsay I don't understand, and I want to. I'm going to, with or without your consent.'

His smile had long ago faded. His face was guarded, his eyes watchful. 'I wouldn't make you do anything you didn't want to,' he said mildly. 'What makes you think I would?'

Blindly, Rosamund shook her head, moving to get out of the bed. He reached up and caught her hand, holding it tightly.

'It's still there, isn't it?' he murmured. 'Whatever it is that happens when we're together. It's still there.'

'No,' she whispered, her face turned away.

'When I saw you tonight, on the landing . . .'

She let him draw her down, into his arms. Her

heart was hammering. There was confusion on his face, something she rarely saw in Mark. She already knew, instinctively, that he had come here tonight with the intention of telling her it was over. That he had decided the handicap of having her as his wife was greater than the benefits of having 'a wife'. What had really changed his mind? Colonsay? Was the idea of losing Colonsay enough to sway him back?

'You should have done it over the phone,' she said, tears shining in her eyes.

'Rose . . . Rosie,' he groaned. And bending his head, Mark began to kiss her.

CHAPTER 10

The ground was wet with dew and mist lay in the hollows. Rosamund dug her hands into the pockets of her jacket and concentrated on watching the toes of her boots slowly darken with moisture. Beside her, Mark's breath was a white cloud.

They were walking briskly down the driveway from Colonsay. Rosamund gulped in cold air, her lungs aching. Mark was hardly puffing. Ahead of them was the Geelong road, and to their left, like a sentinel across the bare paddock, the tall monument that marked Cosmo's grave. It was part of the family graveyard, and even from here Rosamund could see it was neatly kept, the grass mown, the picket fence painted white. The local Historical Society made certain Cosmo's final resting place was presentable. The little Cunningham graveyard faced onto the road, handy to passing motorists. Ada had never minded people stopping to pay their respects, and had been more than happy to accept the Historical Society's contribution.

'I'm sorry I couldn't stay longer.' Mark broke the silence.

He had politely refused Kerry's offer of breakfast, making do with coffee, and then suggested they walk. Now, gratefully, Rosamund stopped, using conversation as an excuse. It took a couple of breaths before she could reply evenly. 'You're busy.'

'I cancelled two appointments to come here, and I've neglected other business—I'm sorry, it sounds as if I'm putting you last.'

'I understand.' And the thing was, she did. She always had.

The monument really was too large, Rosamund decided, even for Cosmo Cunningham. It dominated all the other headstones. She recognised most of them. Ambrosine's was a pink coloured marble with an angel carved into the face. There were the older graves, the original Cunninghams and their families. Ada wasn't buried here, she had been cremated, her ashes strewn about the grounds.

Rosamund blinked. There was an elderly man bending over one of the graves. He wore a big crimson coat with gold trimming, its brilliant colour startling on this dull morning. She watched as he moved about placing flowers, tidying. He must be one of the members of the Historical Society. Rosamund, who had planned to walk over that way, now decided against it. She didn't feel like discussing Cosmo's merits, and she sensed Mark also preferred his privacy.

They had only twenty minutes to themselves before his driver came to take him back to Melbourne. It might be all they ever had. Once away from her and Colonsay, Mark might decide he had been foolish and short-sighted to reconcile with her. Rosamund accepted it numbly. Divorce seemed inevitable, even after last night's passion. Perhaps because of it. Mark's lovemaking had been the equivalent of saying goodbye.

Mark blew into his gloved hands, watching her over his fingers. 'I was thinking about what you said last night.'

'What was that?'

'About Colonsay, about the noises.'

Rosamund tensed. 'And?'

'It wouldn't be a brilliant idea for stories of that sort to leak out to the press, not just now. A haunted house? You can imagine what they'd make of it, of you. This Gary Munro, he *is* a journalist.'

'*Was* a journalist,' she corrected, searching her pockets for her cigarettes.

'I don't think it's something you can shrug off that easily.'

'Like the flu, do you mean?' She tried to joke, but he didn't smile. Rosamund sighed, jamming her hands into her jacket pockets—she must have left the cigarettes in the house. Last night had been last night, and now they were back to business as usual. She couldn't really blame him for not trusting Gary; she had felt the same.

'You mean you don't think he'd be able to resist a good story? A chance to make you look a fool because of me? "Mark Markovic's Mad Missus". I see your point.'

He caught her arm as she turned away, swinging her around and gripping her shoulders. They stood face to face. The cold had drawn all of the colour out of Mark's skin and turned the tip of his nose faintly pink.

'I want this seat in Parliament,' he told her with quiet anger. 'I've worked hard for it, I deserve it. And I won't let anything stand in my way. Do you understand me, Rose?'

His fingers made her shoulders ache, his eyes

were bright, fanatical. Rosamund bowed her head so she didn't have to look at him, didn't have to see the stranger in Mark's face. 'I understand.'

'Good.' He touched her cheek with a gloved finger, a meaningless caress, and then dropped both his hands from her, releasing her. Rosamund turned her back, staring blindly towards the graveyard. Some part of her brain noted that the old man in the crimson coat had gone. There was a large bouquet of flowers on Ambrosine's grave. White roses.

'You should have phoned me instead,' Rosamund whispered.

If he heard her, he pretended he didn't. 'Lance will be here soon. Let's walk back. Rose?'

He was holding out his hand, smiling his smile. Rosamund silently called herself every sort of fool, but she still gave him her own hand, and felt the hard grip of his fingers.

****

The sun shone brightly but the breeze was cool. The blue-grey of the bay was flecked with white, and closer to shore the beds of straplike kelp made shadows beneath the water. A steamer ploughed through the channel heading for Portarlington, the smoke from its chimney a ribbon of grey, the passengers no more than bright dots of colour lining the rails.

The Cunninghams had come on a picnic with their guests and servants to Fairy Dell. It was a yearly event, a 'self-indulgence' Mr Marling called it in Alice's hearing, but she was puzzled as to his meaning. She believed Cosmo kind and generous for carrying on the yearly picnic—it had been his father who began it.

Fairy Dell was a local spot of particular beauty. The Dell, as it was known affectionately, was a concavity in the cliffs at the Springs, a grassy amphitheatre complete with shady trees and a view over the white sand and the waters of the bay. A path led along the foreshore to the old kiosk and sulphur baths and, beyond them, the long pier stretching out into deeper water.

Cosmo held a teacup, his big hands making it seem very fragile. He was laughing at something one of his guests, Mr Hastings, had said, while Ambrosine politely offered around a plate of dainty sandwiches Mrs Gibbons had made. The cook sat on a small rise some yards away, her skirts spread about her, an old flower-trimmed hat shading her round face. Meggy and Jonah had wandered down to the sand, which at low tide was as clean and white as a tropical island. Alice could see the darker indent of their footprints along the shore, just above the lap of the waves. Ada had followed, and was attempting to make a miserable-looking Cleo fetch sticks.

The passing steamer blew its whistle, a deep and sombre sound. Nearby, Mrs Hastings's chattering voice rose and fell, reliant upon the whim of the breeze, while Ambrosine's answers came less frequently, her pale face bored and withdrawn. It occurred to Alice, as it had before, that Ambrosine was a poor hostess. She was beautiful, of course, but didn't an important man like Cosmo require more than an ornament? It was a wonder he put up with her, and yet he did not seem to mind her moods or the headaches which coincided with his guests. Perhaps he did not want to see. Alice wished, just once, he would open his eyes. She longed, just once, for Ambrosine to receive her just desserts.

Mr Marling had strolled down from the upper reaches of the Dell and now joined in the ladies' conversation. Ambrosine gave him a smile brilliant with relief, while Mrs Hastings twittered. Alice watched him strike a pose, one hand lifted to tilt the brim of his homburg and shade out the glare. He was sporting a dashing new checked, double-breasted waistcoat, his shoes were of an elegant light tan over silk socks, and he carried a new ivory-headed walking cane.

Alice's legs were cramped from sitting so long. She rose, shaking out her plain dark skirt, intending to follow Meggy down to the beach. However, as she reached the shellgrit path, Mr Marling caught her up.

'Do you intend to take the waters, Alice?' Laughter sparkled in his eyes.

'No. I . . . I find them nasty, sir.'

She expected him to tut-tut and tell her how good they were for her, as everyone else did, but he only smiled. They walked slowly along the path, Alice wondering with some trepidation why the famous painter had decided to favour her with his company.

'I believe your father saved Mr Cunningham's life when they were lads?'

'There was a sudden change in the weather, sir. A squall. My father saved Mr Cunningham from being washed over the side of his boat, and brought them safely back to shore. Mr Cunningham has always been generous enough to remember it.'

'And you appreciate that, don't you, Alice?' He nodded at her, as if he were sketching her character in his mind. 'I see you do. I believe you admire Mr Cunningham. He is an admirable man, I agree, but even admirable men may have their faults. Has he none, in your opinion?'

'None,' Alice replied loyally. Certainly less than you, she thought.

'Then he is a paragon indeed.'

They were silent, both gazing out over the bay. Below, on the sand, Meggy suddenly began to run, her skirts billowing about her like a landed jellyfish. Alice thought it was a silly game of catch-me and expected Jonah to chase her, but Jonah stood still upon the white sand, all the while Meggy getting further and further away from him. Cleo, tired of Ada's stick game, began to bark hysterically and bolted after Meggy.

'A tiff?' Mr Marling murmured, curious. Everything interested Mr Marling.

'It wouldn't be Meggy's fault,' Alice replied sharply, and then wished she hadn't when Mr Marling turned that look upon her again. 'I mean to say, sir, she believes her brother to be a . . . a paragon.'

'I see. And you don't agree?'

She didn't know whether he was teasing her or not, and because she was suspicious of him, felt her mouth pursing up. 'I keep my opinions to myself, sir.'

He laughed quietly.

I have your button, sir, the one you left in madam's bedroom. The words were on the tip of her tongue, but of course she didn't say them aloud. What would he do if she did? Would he beg for her silence? She rather thought he would.

Mr Marling had been commissioned to paint the opening of Parliament, and discovery of such a scandal may very well change the minds of those in power. It would certainly change Cosmo's mind. No, Mr Marling would not want her to tell.

Alice focussed again on the beach. Jonah was walking slowly after Meggy, head bent, his dark hair tousled by the wind. A cloud scudded across the sun, the sudden gloom making her shiver.

'I wonder if I might ask a favour of you, Alice.'

Alice looked up sharply, wondering if he had read her mind.

'I wonder if you would allow me to paint you. Your face is an interesting one—I would like to capture it, in my own poor fashion.'

Alice blinked in surprise. Whatever she had expected, it wasn't this. 'I . . . you're being silly, sir.'

Her own bluntness shocked her, but Mr Marling gave a merry peel of laughter. 'Indulge me, Alice. I know I have an enormous task ahead of me with the opening of Parliament, a Herculean labour. You will be my antidote, my relaxation. Will you sit for me?'

Alice felt pleasure and trepidation pulling at her equally. Her mother would tell her to agree, but she sensed her father would not be so pleased. And Bertie? Bertie would probably think it a great joke.

Mr Marling's warm eyes were pleading. 'Very well, sir.' She heard her own voice, restrained, a little nervous. 'I would be glad to have you paint my picture.'

****

After Mark's car had driven away, Rosamund wandered to the back room and tried to find some enthusiasm for her task of sorting. She felt restless. She felt like a drink—several in fact, but she resisted the temptation, instead lighting one cigarette after another.

There was no-one to distract her thoughts from herself. Kerry had returned to her cooking and Gary was with Fred Swann, working on the west wing of Colonsay. The faint strains of an old song on a radio reached her. Was that what ghosts were, faint signals from a distant past? Were only certain people receptive to those signals, or had it something to do with the surroundings? Was Colonsay an ideal receiving station, charged as it was with so many unhappy memories? Rosamund couldn't convince herself. Whatever was inhabiting Colonsay was no distant signal. It was here, now, and knew exactly what it was doing.

Restless, she moved on to the library. Sunlight shone through the windows, the rays full of dust motes. A brilliant gleam of something above the mantelpiece caught her eye, but when Rosamund looked up there was nothing, just blank wall. Ada's box was still on the floor by one of the armchairs. Rosamund sat down, carefully put aside the black photo album, and pulled out a sheaf of yellowing paper.

Old letters, bills, receipts ... A couple of letters were from Rosamund's father, complaining about lack of money and the struggle of day-to-day living. There was one from France dated 1917 and full of the sort of old-fashioned language Rosamund had always imagined was made up by movie scriptwriters. It was from Ada's husband, Adrian, and was addressed to Mrs Adrian Evans, Colonsay. He spoke about her 'hair like spun gold' and her 'wonderful smile', and their moments together in the garden at dusk, 'when I asked you, very clumsily, to marry me and you very sweetly accepted'. Despite herself, Rosamund felt her eyes fill with tears.

It was Mark's fault. His visit had made her weak and maudlin. Crossly, she wiped her face and blew her nose. She put the letters firmly aside and turned to the bills. A dozen or so were for deliveries of wood for the fires. The price seemed quite exorbitant—no wonder Colonsay had always been cold. There was a bill for the plumbing in the bathroom, with a reminder in Ada's writing to ask for a discount because of the inordinate amount of time it had taken to finish. The receipt, carefully attached, was for the discounted amount. Good old Ada.

Rosamund put the rest of these papers aside for another day, too, and returned to the box. A red-covered notebook had been poked in at the side. She drew it out, wiping off the dust on the leg of her jeans. The pages were stained and chewed at the edges, but still legible. Flicking through them, Rosamund discovered the book was a one-year appointment book but, Ada being Ada, covered many more years than one. The entries were placed each below the other, so that a page headed the 1st of May could contain appointments from 1930 to 1970.

Very confusing.

There were not a great many entries, which was just as well, and what entries there were weren't very interesting. Appointments for dentist, hair, and—as Ada grew older—glasses, cane, shoes for arthritic feet. A couple were in regard to Rosamund's school. There was one for the doctor with a question mark and, in ink beside it, in Ada's writing, 'Voices'.

Rosamund's attention was riveted. She turned forward a page or two and found another entry. 'She says she hears voices and "the lady" screaming—Doctor? Or is it better to leave be? I don't understand children.'

Rosamund laughed shakily. She wiped her palms against her blouse and found they were quite damp. There was nothing for the next two weeks, apart from accounts of solicitors who had annoyed her grandmother, tradesmen who had infuriated her, and servants who had refused to do her bidding. Then:

'She misses her parents, I suppose, although they were of little enough use to her. Bad blood. I am all she has, and must stand firm, but the thought of that tragedy being played out in this house again and again, without me being aware of it, is almost too much even for me to bear. What does she hear? I have asked her and she thinks someone is calling her name. I know differently.'

After that, Rosamund searched every word, every page, but there was only one more relevant entry. It was made some months later, and whatever had happened in between Ada had kept to herself.

'The voices have stopped. No need then for doctors and questions. And lies. No need to have the past dug up like a spade of soil, full of twisting worms and half-rotted things. What were they? Echoes of the past or restless spirits? I prefer to think the former. I will sleep well tonight, the first time in many, many weeks.'

Rosamund closed her eyes. Echoes of the past or restless spirits? The room was suddenly chill. She had asked herself the same question earlier, and she too preferred the former answer. It seemed as if the more she learned, the more questions there were to be answered. 'That tragedy'? Did Ada mean the deaths of her parents, or her young husband in the war, or her son from cancer and his wife in the mental institution . . .? God, the possibilities were endless.

Something silver glittered at the corner of Rosamund's eye. She turned sharply but, as before, there was nothing there but the old wallpaper. Perhaps it was a reflection, the light bouncing off some metal object outside. She was returning Ada's papers to the box when she noticed that the photo album had fallen open. Cosmo and Ambrosine gazed up at her, faces carefully smiling.

It was a pity they had died as they did, and yet there was a sort of rightness about it. Rosamund searched her memory for the details of the story, but could find little enough. She had never known a great deal about it, just the bare bones. Ada had never spoken of her parents' deaths, and Rosamund had found out from others.

The bare essence of it—that Ambrosine had died of influenza and Cosmo, destroyed by grief, had sailed away and never returned—was all she had. Who could argue with love like that? The very drama of it had ensured their names were remembered, while those who grew old and died in their beds were forgotten.

Was it Cosmo and Ambrosine that Ada had meant when she wrote of 'restless spirits' and 'the lady screaming'? Had Ambrosine screamed, at the end, when she knew she was dying and leaving her beloved husband behind? Rosamund closed her eyes. Ada spoke of voices. Rosamund had assumed they were calling to her, but now, like Ada, she wondered whether they weren't calling for Ambrosine. It was possible that such a formal name, beautiful as it was, would be shortened within the family to Rose. And wouldn't such a tragic circumstance be bound to leave waves on the psychic internet?

But none of that explained the brown girl.

'Mrs Markovic?'

Rosamund was on her way down the hall to the back room, avoiding various protruding boxes and bundles. Earlier, a couple of Fred Swan's crew had helped carry out a couple of trailer loads for the tip. One of them, the woman Rae, had complimented her on her staying power. 'Some of this stuff looks like it might be fixable, but as for the rest!'

Rosamund had agreed.

'You know, this place has a lot going for it,' Rae went on. 'Look at some of them old houses in Queenscliff. People pay a fortune to stay in them.' Her companion jabbed her with his elbow and she bit her lip. 'Not that you need the money, of course, Mrs Markovic.'

Mark doesn't, she thought, but didn't say it. 'That's all right. My grandmother would probably turn in her grave, if she had one, but I see your point.' Then, when they stared at her wide-eyed, she added gently, 'She was cremated.'

'Oh, right.' Rae's confident self reappeared. 'I used to drive out this way sometimes, just to take a look at Colonsay. Dad's grandmother worked here, you know.'

'Did she? For Cosmo, do you mean?'

'Yeah, she were the cook. Moved away, after they died, but some of the family came back. Really sad, weren't it, what happened? Like a movie.'

'Rae here's softer than she looks,' her companion grinned. 'Aren't you, Rae?'

Rae pulled a face, but she was laughing. 'Well, I like a bit of history. And animals, I like animals. I've been bringing a bit of food now and then for the little dog. Hope you don't mind?' This last was spoken as if it suddenly occurred to Rae she might be doing something wrong.

Rosamund shook her head, puzzled. 'It's a stray, I think,' she began hesitantly. 'If you can catch it, you can have it.'

Rae's eyes brightened. 'Are you sure? Looks like a real pet, with the ribbon and all. Bit neglected, though. Well, thanks, Mrs Markovic.'

After a few more comments on the junk in the hall, she left Rosamund to it.

Lunch had been spent arguing with Kerry, who had demanded to know why there had been no noises last night from the attic. Was it because Mr Markovic was there? Didn't that make Rosamund suspicious? Rosamund, still tired and emotionally drained from Mark's visit, and from what she had found in the library, had been in no state to draw any conclusions.

'I thought we should ask Frederick to inspect the house,' Kerry went on. She had obviously been thinking deeply about the matter. 'There must be something we've overlooked.'

'Woodworm with hammers, do you mean?'

Kerry frowned. 'You never took anything seriously, even as a child. Always a joke to divert attention, you could never cope with deeper emotions.'

'What would you know about deeper emotions, Kerry?'

Kerry's brown eyes looked hurt. She blinked and turned away. 'You know nothing about me.'

There had never seemed much to know. Rosamund wondered if she had been mistaken in this, too. Was Kerry a more complicated soul than she had imagined?

'I'm sorry,' she said. 'I'll ask him.' With a sigh, Rosamund pushed her uneaten meal away. She had a headache, probably from peering at that appointment book of Ada's.

'I'm sure you'll be glad you did,' Kerry replied, brightening. 'There has to be a rational explanation for this.'

'Mrs Markovic?'

Frederick Swann called again, and now Rosamund turned to face him. For a moment he was a black shape silhouetted against the open front door, and then he moved closer and his tanned, weathered face came into focus. His workboots made a clattery sound in the hall as he approached. The noise echoed.

'We'll be turning off the electricity for a couple of hours. Just thought I'd better let you know.'

'Have you told Kerry? She'll go mad without the oven working.'

He grinned. 'She said she could start cutting vegetables for a casserole.'

Rosamund was about to say something about inspecting the house, but Frederick seemed to be searching for other words. There was a seriousness in his face that sharpened her senses.

'I've had a few complaints from my crew,' he said at last. 'Things have been going missing.'

Rosamund nodded slowly. 'I thought a bit of

pilfering was part and parcel of a job like this?'

'Not with my crew,' he said rather sharply. 'Anyway, who'd want to steal a soup flask and a box of sandwiches?'

'I wouldn't have thought they'd need to bring their own food with Kerry on the job.'

He made an impatient movement. 'There've been other things, too. A box of nails for the nail gun, tools. Nothing expensive, but irritating nonetheless.'

'What are you saying, Fred? That I took them?'

'No.' But his uneasiness increased. 'Some of my men have been complaining about the house. They say it feels . . . uncomfortable.'

Rosamund felt chilled. 'Has Gary been talking to you?' she demanded.

Frederick shook his head, and now honest puzzlement filled his eyes. 'What should Gary be talking to me about?'

Rosamund looked away, playing for time. 'Actually, I meant to speak with you on another matter, Fred. I wondered if you might . . .' She heard her voice go on, asking for an inspection, explaining about strange noises in the night—playing it down, although Fred already knew about the visit from the police and the falling ceiling light. He nodded, serious, but his eyes were alert. He sensed she was not telling him everything and he was filling in the gaps. She wondered, with grim amusement, what Fred thought about wandering spirits.

'I can do that,' he agreed when she had finished. 'I'll get on to it tomorrow. Now, I'd better turn the electricity off, Kerry says she wants it back on by five at the latest.'

Rosamund went back to her sorting. The red

velvet couch was still in the middle of the room. She paused near the door, examining the floor. Little prints in the dust, circling the couch, around and around. They had been made since she was here yesterday. Something had been in this room. Rosamund leaned against the jamb and tried to think.

If there was a stray dog living here, how did it get in and out? The question of survival had been answered already, by Rae and her kind heart. There were no doubt places under the floorboards where a small animal could climb through, out of the weather. Well, it would probably be captured eventually, by Rae or someone else.

One question answered, then, Rosamund thought. She began to scuff the sole of her shoe over the paw marks, obliterating them. When they were gone, she sat on the couch with a sigh and reached for one of the newspaper piles she hadn't tackled yet. She flicked through the one on top. It was a *Women's Weekly* from the '40s, and the grainy illustrations and comforting articles on making do with less soothed her shaky nerves. She immersed herself in history of the less threatening kind, until an engine starting up out in the back yard brought her head up sharply. Rosamund walked over to the window—such a thing was possible now—and peered out.

A man with a petrol-driven slasher was busy cutting down the rank weeds around the old cottage, where the boxthorn hedge didn't intrude. A green snowstorm of vegetation and seedheads filled the air.

Rosamund turned back to her own work.

A collection of clippings had been folded into an old recipe book, one of those no-nonsense ones that always reminded Rosamund of fat, jolly Victorian cooks dispensing their hard-won knowledge. They were newspaper clippings, yellow and brittle with age, worn through on the fold lines, making them difficult to read. Rosamund sat hunched over them, her finger tracing the words as she read them: '. . . the most heart-rending scene . . . the casket smothered in perfumed white flowers, borne in a glass-sided funeral carriage . . . horses with black plumes at a slow walk . . . sombre mourners under a dark, rain-filled sky . . .'

It was a report of the funeral of Ambrosine Cunningham. Rosamund was aware of a constriction beginning in her chest. The words danced before her eyes. There was a sense of unreality about everything, as if she were dreaming and might any moment wake up.

Another clipping, much larger, dealt with Cosmo's state funeral, the muffled drums and the dignitaries, the public mourning for a great man, but somehow it touched Rosamund less than Ambrosine's simpler ceremony.

Underneath them both was a much more modern story, with photographs, from a weekend magazine. The article dealt with the life of one Henry Marling, a portrait painter of the late nineteenth and early twentieth centuries. There was a large reproduction of his painting of the opening of the first Federal Parliament in May 1901. A smaller black and white photograph showed Mr Marling himself, a handsome gentleman with fair hair and a stiffly twisted moustache.

Rosamund had heard of him, and the article was interesting. But as far as she could see, it did not pertain to her own family, other than that Mr

Marling had painted the opening of Parliament and had, perhaps, known the Cunninghams in a superficial way.

Outside, the slasher putted a couple of times and came to a stop. The sudden silence was immediately shattered by someone shouting. Feet came pounding down the stairs. There was such a sense of urgency in the sounds that dread gripped Rosamund. She pushed the clippings aside and ran out.

'. . . broken her arm.' She heard a voice from inside the kitchen. Kerry came out into the hall and ran to the phone.

'What's happened?' Rosamund asked.

'One of the crew fell and broke her arm,' she said shakily. 'The girl, Rae Gibbons. I'm ringing ahead to the hospital.'

'Is she all right?' Rosamund thought how stupid that sounded.

'Apart from the arm, yes. She fell quite a long way, slipped on the scaffolding, apparently. She was lucky.'

Rosamund left her to make the call and went outside. There was scaffolding all over the west wing now, in a criss-cross of metallic casing. The crew were loosely grouped about Rae as she sat hunched on a plank, one arm cradled gingerly in the other, her face white and shocked. Gary, stooped over her, caught sight of Rosamund and, with a murmured word to the others, walked over. Sweat streaked the dirt on his face and there was a new tear in his shirt.

'Kerry ringing the hospital?'

'Yes. Do you need help?'

'No, we're just bringing the car around and we'll take her straight in. Saves time.'

'Is it very bad?'

'A straight break, as far as I can tell. The doctor will know better.'

'How—?'

She didn't finish. Something in his expression stopped her. 'I suppose she slipped,' he said quietly. 'She swears she didn't, though. Says she doesn't know how it happened. She's in shock just now.'

'You mean . . .?'

But Gary was shaking his head. 'I was up there, in one of the rooms, and I could see her from the window. She cried out and then she fell. There was no reason for it, not that I could see.'

What do you mean? she wanted to shout. What are you saying to me? But this wasn't the time to ask, and she wasn't sure she wanted to hear his answers.

'Mrs Markovic.' Frederick Swann had come to join them, his face creased and worried. 'Rae was very lucky.'

'Yes, thank God.'

He smiled. 'Exactly.'

When they were gone the house seemed very quiet. Frederick had turned the electricity back on and Kerry was busy preparing the evening meal. Rosamund did not want to return to the back room. The shadows were too long now, and she kept thinking of Ambrosine's funeral moving slowly towards the cemetery, the horses draped and plumed in black, the driver wearing his black frock-coat and black top hat, all so sombre under the black sky. She shivered, and went upstairs to take a bath.

The Cunninghams had seen too much death. Of course everyone had to die, but so many of them had died before their time. It was as if they were afflicted with some curse—well, that was silly! Rosamund sank lower in her bath. The water was just warm—it had not had time to heat properly yet. The musk smell of the bath oil filled her nostrils and she thought of Mark. She sighed. His visit had not clarified anything, really.

He'll leave me. She let the thought soak into her, slowly, testing it out. Once, she would have been too afraid to live without him, but things had been different since she came to Colonsay. The house had given her a purpose which her life had previously lacked.

Rosamund stared at her toes where they rose up above the bath water. They looked white and wrinkled. Time she got out. The bathroom had grown more shadowy while she was deep in her thoughts, and the ceiling light in here was so dim she could hardly see the corners of the room. The air felt cold. Hastily Rosamund rose, splashing water and reaching for a towel. The water hadn't been hot enough to steam up the mirror, and when she stood up she was looking directly at her own naked reflection.

Only it wasn't her.

Another woman was staring at her from the mirror, her slender body superimposed upon Rosamund's larger one, her wide eyes gazing back, shocked and unblinking, from a stranger's face which was yet terrifyingly familiar. Rosamund cried out, a short sharp gasp, and the moment was gone. She was looking at herself again, dark hair damply curling, water running down her body, her face as white as death.

Somehow, her hands shaking uncontrollably, Rosamund managed to dress herself and get out of there. Once in her room she collapsed onto the bed, her legs no longer able to hold her. 'It's getting worse,' she whispered to herself.

The woman in the mirror had been alive and warm and vulnerable, not the stiffly posed figure in the photograph album. But Rosamund knew her. Ambrosine Cunningham, Cosmo's beautiful, enigmatic wife.

She hadn't been a ghost, not even the sort of living ghost the brown girl represented. Ambrosine's flesh had been warm and real, her hair soft and heavy—she had been Rosamund, and Rosamund had been her.

The sound of a car arriving shattered her concentration. She found her legs and went to look out of the window. Gary had parked in front of a large heap of broken timber and other junk waiting for a journey to the tip. He climbed out of his car and stood without moving, gazing at Colonsay as if deep in his own thoughts. Some movement Rosamund made must have attracted his attention, for he lifted his head abruptly and looked up at her window. They stared at each other without greeting, and then Gary dropped his gaze and walked slowly towards the front door.

There could be no mistaking his reluctance.

Rosamund was halfway down the stairs when she heard Kerry's questioning voice, and slowed herself to a walk. What was the point in blurting out to Gary what had happened? What could he do?

'. . . be all right,' Gary was answering.

Kerry murmured her relief. 'Dangerous, crawling around all those ladders.' Rosamund smiled despite herself.

'They'll be back in the morning. Frederick's very careful when it comes to his crew's safety, but he's had a few accidents for all that.'

He looked up as Rosamund entered the kitchen.

Something about her face must have given her away, because his eyes narrowed sharply. She spoke before he could.

'Fred is going to inspect the entire house tomorrow. Kerry thinks the answer to the noises is a structural one, and I think we should at least eliminate that theory before we go any further.'

'He inspected the entire house when he gave the quote to fix it,' Gary replied wryly.

'The simplest explanations are often the correct ones,' Kerry announced, briskly stirring mustard sauce in a small saucepan.

Rosamund didn't enter into the argument. Perhaps Fred would find something, a simple answer to this whole puzzle, but she could not begin to imagine what it might be. What could make such a noise without any visible means and produce phenomena like the brown girl and now—well, it was beyond her understanding.

'I think Colonsay caused Rae's accident today.'

Both women stopped and stared at Gary.

'I saw it happen. She didn't slip.'

'How did she fall, then?' Kerry asked softly. 'Are you trying to frighten us, Gary?'

'And succeeding,' Rosamund added. 'You're jumping too far ahead here, Gary. We've no evidence that it, whatever it is, is trying to drive us out.'

'The noise? The apparition? The voice? What else is it doing all that for?'

'I . . . I don't know. Attention-seeking? Something wants our attention, wants our help. We need to discover the problem before we can solve it.'

'What if there's another answer? What if whatever's here wants us out? We're trespassing on its property and it doesn't want to be disturbed. So it makes lots of noise and frightens us half stupid, and when that doesn't work, it begins to pick us off, one by one.'

'Don't!' Kerry gasped. She was almost grey, and Rosamund moved to take her arm.

'Gary,' she warned, 'that's enough. Really, that's quite enough.'

His mouth twisted up into a poor attempt at a smile as he turned towards the door.

'Where are you going?' Rosamund called, fear overcoming her anger. Suddenly the last thing she wanted was to be here alone.

'I'm going to see a friend.' He turned to face her and read the fear in her eyes. The expression in his own softened. 'Don't worry, I'll be back in an hour or two.'

Kerry squeezed Rosamund's hand as they listened to Gary start up his car again and drive away. 'We're better off without him,' she murmured. 'I'm rather worried about Gary, Rosamund. I think I should contact his grandfather.'

Rosamund nodded without hearing.

'Now, dinner is almost ready. Are you hungry?'

She pretended she was. Kerry lit some candles and their flame gave the meal a formal feel, despite the fact that she had left on the overhead lights. Neither of them wanted to be sitting in the dark.

They ate in silence, pretending they weren't missing Gary. Rosamund was secretly appalled that they had grown so dependent upon him so quickly, but these were extraordinary circumstances. Even several glasses of wine failed to dull her senses, and Kerry refused to join in. By the time dessert had been eaten and cleared away, Rosamund's head was swimming and she was in no fit state to read through any more of Ada's papers, even had she wanted to. Kerry, giving her a hard look, announced she was going to bed.

****

The honeysuckle vine at the front of the house was dropping its leaves, so that they were scattered all over the front garden and blew in cold gusts onto the verandah. The seasons were turning, the days drawing in, but Alice did not feel the cold. Bertie would be home soon, and for her it may as well be summer.

Cosmo and Ambrosine had taken the train and were on their way to the opening of Parliament in Melbourne. With them had gone Ada and a mountain of baggage. Ambrosine had had a new dress made for the occasion and Cosmo had insisted she take the Cunningham emeralds.

'I will feel like a king,' he announced, 'and I want my wife to look like a queen.'

Alice was glad to see them go, but only because their going meant Bertie's release from the school he hated. When they returned home, then so would he.

****

The hum of the car was loud in the stillness. There was no wind tonight, only a dark cloudy sky and the promise of rain. Rosamund held her breath, listening to the front door open and close and then his footsteps on the stairs. She sighed with relief. The wine had long ago cleared from her head, and she had gone up to bed with a book. The footsteps grew louder in the corridor as Gary approached her room, then stopped. The knock was so loud it made her jump.

'Gary?'

He opened the door and peered in. She was sitting up in bed, a cigarette in one hand, book in the other. Gary smiled and came in, leaving the door ajar.

'Sorry, I'm later than I thought I'd be. No problems?'

She knew what he meant and shook her head. 'That's two nights in a row. Is it over, do you think?'

He didn't bother to answer the question. The bed dipped as he sat down. The cold had brought colour into his face and in the lamplight his blue eyes were brilliant.

'I wanted to tell you about my friend. She's a psychic, she deals with spirits all the time. I told her what's been happening here at Colonsay and—'

'Gary! Mark doesn't want us to tell anyone. You know what would happen if the newspapers got hold of this.'

Gary frowned. 'I like his unselfish attitude.'

Rosamund stubbed out her cigarette to avoid his eyes. 'I understand it. And what use would it be to us if the story got out? We'd all look like fools. They'd *make* us look like fools.'

'Possibly.' He wasn't going to admit it. There was a stubborn jut to his chin she had never noticed before.

'Gary . . .' She sighed and lost the battle with her tongue. 'I saw Ambrosine.'

His mouth lost its tightness and hung slightly open.

'I . . . only it wasn't like the brown girl. I saw her where my reflection should have been. As if *I* were Ambrosine. And that's not all. I didn't tell you before but I've been having dreams. In them I'm dead and I'm in Ambrosine's coffin. I smell the flowers, I feel the satin lining.'

His hand closed on hers and it was very warm and very steady. Until then she hadn't realised how much she was trembling. 'You need my friend,' he murmured, leaning closer. His breath was warm on her cheek. 'You need someone to listen to you, someone who won't think you're going out of your mind.'

'That would be nice,' she managed, and cleared her throat. There were tears in her eyes but she wouldn't let them fall. 'What would this friend of yours do?'

'She'd visit the house, walk around quietly, take in the ambience, listen.'

'Listen to what?'

'To the things other people can't hear.'

Rosamund shook her head slowly. 'I don't know, Gary. I know it's scary at the moment, but it's our problem. I don't know this friend of yours, and I have a feeling that once she comes into this, becomes involved, the whole thing will slip out of our control. Before we know it we'll be starring in a Hollywood movie.'

'Zephyr's not like that.'

'Zephyr! Gary, no!'

He had the grace to blush. 'I know the name doesn't exactly inspire confidence, but she's not some airy-fairy New Age guru. Rosamund, I know her. She's helped me, and I trust her.'

'Well, I don't.'

They faced each other stubbornly. At last Gary sighed and rose to his feet. 'All right. Think about it.' He hesitated, and when she refused to answer, turned away. 'Goodnight, Rosamund.'

She still didn't answer him as he closed her door.

CHAPTER 11

It was a bleak morning. The grey sky threatened more rain and the air was moist and cold. Rosamund dressed in jeans and a sweater, pulling on her boots with an effort. It seemed pointless wearing much else when she was working up to her eyebrows in dust and dirt. Hardly a Versace situation. She had brought a couple of good outfits with her from Melbourne; she didn't know why. Had she imagined Mark would take her out and wine and dine her? Now they were pushed to the back of the wardrobe, forgotten. These days she was more interested in the past than the present.

The work crew were busy. She could hear them in the west wing, joking voices interspersed with bangs and thuds, as work progressed. Rae's accident didn't appear to have slowed them down at all. Maybe it was only Gary who believed there were forces other than natural ones at work.

Rosamund stood at her window, brushing her hair and gazing out at the view. The You Yangs were barely visible today, covered in a swathe of rain, and the bay was flat and sullen, as grey as the sky. As she picked up a clip to keep her hair back from her face, she became aware of a faint scent. Honeysuckle.

Her hand froze. She had learned by now that

there was no such plant in the garden at Colonsay, and if there ever had been it was long gone. The honeysuckle scent intensified about her, and a shudder went through Rosamund. She quelled it, using her mind over her emotions.

'You won't drive me out,' she said aloud. 'I live here, too. Do you hear me, whoever you are? I live here, too.'

The scent began to fade, was reduced to the faintest whiff. Rosamund leaned her face against the cold glass pane. 'Well, was that so hard?' she asked herself in a whisper. 'You held your ground. You beat it. You just have to keep it up.'

Downstairs, Kerry had left breakfast—pancakes—warming in the oven. She had also left a note to say she had gone grocery shopping and would be back by lunchtime. Rosamund ate a large breakfast—she was always hungry these days—and drank a strong cup of tea while she planned her day. She had already decided this morning's encounter would not reduce her to jelly.

There was still plenty to be done in the back room, and after that she had the other one to tackle. Now she came to think of it, she hadn't even looked in there yet. Well, she could do that. And there were the papers Ada had left. 'See,' she murmured, 'lots to do.'

Rosamund cleared up her dishes and went out into the hall. It was very quiet suddenly, and she came to a stop, breath held, before she realised Fred Swann's crew must be having their morning cuppa. She laughed at her nervousness and turned towards the back of the house. The door to the room she had been working in was open, the red velvet couch inviting her inside. She resisted it and turned instead to the second door.

This was closed and wouldn't budge when she tried to open it. Jammed? Rosamund surveyed it a moment, and then gave it a heave with her shoulder and hip. It opened a fraction, but still resisted. She gave a few more pushes and shoves, so that it jerked unwillingly across the wooden floor, making a horrible grating noise as it went. The air seeped out, dank and depressing.

Rosamund stuck her head cautiously inside.

With the windows covered with old sheets tied to the curtain rods, it was dark and difficult to see. But she could tell that this room was as large as the other one, though it looked smaller because of the amount of junk crammed into it. Rosamund squeezed in an arm and tried the light switch. Nothing happened. The bulb must need changing, and it wouldn't be possible to do that until she had moved some of the objects out of the room and into the hall. She heaved at the door again, giving herself more space. There appeared to be a lot more pieces of furniture in this room than the other one—a lampshade leaned drunkenly on its fitting, and a bureau as bulky as a heavyweight boxer loomed over smaller objects.

Rosamund took a deep breath and wiped a shaky hand over her forehead.

Had the other room felt like this before she started on it? She didn't think so. There was a funny smell here, too. Not honeysuckle, something sharper . . . A chill breeze wafted by her and there was a distinct scratching noise in the gloom. Panic sprang at Rosamund, and breathing loudly she tugged hard at the door, struggling to close it. She heard herself gasping as she fought with it until, with a shriek of warped wood and rusty hinges, it finally banged shut.

A trickle of perspiration ran down Rosamund's back. Now that the door was closed everything felt normal again, or as normal as was possible at Colonsay. With an enormous sense of relief, she turned back to her red velvet couch.

The newspaper clippings were where she had left them. Rosamund put them carefully aside, to be added to Ada's box of memories, and tackled the pile of newspapers.

Two hours had passed by the time she decided she had had enough. She rose, stretching her stiff joints, and wandered down to the kitchen. Kerry wasn't yet back, and Rosamund found herself missing her company.

While she was making coffee, one of the crew arrived for the tray of drinks and goodies that Kerry regularly supplied. He waited while Rosamund made tea and found some biscuits and cake to send out. Usually it was Gary who came to collect the tray, but perhaps he was avoiding her after last night.

'How's Rae's broken arm?' she asked.

'She'll be fine. She's at home with her feet up.'

'What happened, does she remember?'

She was watching him as she asked it, or she would have missed the glance he gave her.

'She slipped. Gets a bit slippery up there.'

Rosamund finished arranging the tray and he took it, thanking her, and carried it back to the west wing. Rosamund stared after him. That glance had made her uneasy. It told her things she didn't want to know, and uppermost in them was Gary's voice saying, 'I think whatever is in this house wants us out.'

Kerry was back at lunchtime, as she had promised, her car loaded to the top of the windows with supermarket bags. Rosamund raised a sardonic eyebrow at her. 'You should open a restaurant.'

Kerry pretended it was a joke and smiled, but her next words surprised Rosamund. 'Perhaps you could do that, Rosamund. Old houses make good restaurants, they have so much atmosphere. You could turn Colonsay into a guesthouse specialising in fine food.'

'I don't think Mark would appreciate sharing his weekends with half a dozen strangers.'

'No, I suppose not.' To Rosamund's surprise Kerry looked let down. She had sounded quite enthusiastic about the guesthouse idea—obviously she saw herself in the role of cook—and the drop back to reality had been a jarring one. What was going on? she asked herself. First Rae with the hotel plan, and now Kerry and her guesthouse.

'Anyway, what would Ada have thought of turning Colonsay into a guesthouse?' Rosamund went on, knowing she was baiting the other woman but unable to stop herself.

Kerry flushed bright red. 'I hadn't thought,' she whispered. 'She would have hated it, wouldn't she? How could I be so silly?'

Rosamund was instantly ashamed. 'What does it matter what she would have hated,' she murmured. 'She's dead.'

'Mrs Ada would be very proud that Mr Markovic is living here.' Kerry's colour receded. 'It would be fitting, wouldn't it? First Cosmo Cunningham, and now your husband?'

'Very fitting.'

This time Kerry seemed to notice the ironic note in her voice. 'Mr Markovic took to Colonsay from the moment he saw it. I was here and I saw the way he felt. He walked every inch of it, Rosamund, touching things, examining things. It was almost as if he had fallen in love.' She laughed as if she had made a joke, but neither of them seemed to find it very funny.

'You've confused love with the need to acquire,' Rosamund said quietly. 'Mark wants Colonsay, he doesn't love it.'

'I'm sure you're wrong.' Kerry pressed her lips together.

'Well, time will tell. And besides, Colonsay is my house. Ada left it to me.'

'But . . .' Kerry seemed uneasy, as if she might feel she was trespassing in an area not her business. 'Mr Markovic has spent so much money on the house, can you still call it yours? I don't understand legal matters very well, but I can see that he must be able to claim a part of it.'

There was that. Rosamund wondered what the point was in pretending she could tell Mark to leave. He had, as Kerry said, spent a fortune on repairs. If he left her, would he be generous enough to leave her Colonsay as part of the divorce settlement?

'Generosity has nothing to do with it,' she muttered angrily. 'I'd fight him for it.'

Kerry, puzzled, was opening her mouth to ask a question, when from outside they heard a long, shrill cry. For a second they both froze, and then one of the crew was yelling from the west wing, followed by more excited voices. Kerry gasped and ran into the hall, Rosamund close behind her.

They met Gary at the bottom of the stairs.

'An ambulance,' he managed, breathing hard. His blue eyes were wide and full of anger, or excitement, Rosamund couldn't decide which. 'One of the men has fallen off the scaffolding. Again.'

****

Mrs Gibbons was entertaining old Harry in the kitchen. Alice could hear their voices: Mrs Gibbons's high-pitched and girlish, and Harry's a deeper growl. Harry had come to the back door, bowler hat in hand, his threadbare coat brushed and his boots blacked. Meggy had giggled as she showed him in, and Mrs Gibbons had dismissed her with a frown that promised later retribution.

'At her age and all!' Meggy had exclaimed scornfully. As if age had anything to do with behaving foolishly, Alice thought with a mental sniff.

'She wouldn't have let him come if madam were here,' Meggy said now, as the two girls perched on the bottom step of the main staircase, like two disgruntled cats ejected from their place before the kitchen fire.

Alice had seen the newspaper account of the opening of Federal Parliament, and its attendant speeches and ceremonies. She imagined Cosmo's laughter and, beside him, Ambrosine smiling and smiling . . .

A strange uneven thumping began coming from the kitchen. It sounded as though Mrs Gibbons and Harry had climbed onto the furniture and were jumping off it onto the floor. The lamp on the table by the stairs shook, its crystal veil jangling. Alice and Meggy stared at each other in amazement. Then Meggy hissed, 'Come on,' and grabbed Alice's hand, pulling her out of the house and around to the side.

The small kitchen window was high on the wall, but a water barrel stood conveniently beneath it. They climbed up, skirts lifted above thick wool stockings and boots, stretching on tiptoe to see in. Alice found herself echoing Meggy's giggle, trying not to in case they were overheard.

What a sight it was! Mrs Gibbons and Harry were dancing. The cook's skirts swirled as she pranced about, her grey hair escaping from its bun and spilling like sheep's wool down her back. Harry's face was even redder than usual, his shirt sleeves rolled up, his wide mouth open and puffing.

'They're drunk as lords!' Meggy whispered, hugging Alice close, sharing the joke.

Alice tried to laugh, too, but she was thinking, Fancy making such fools of themselves. As they climbed down off the water barrel, her thoughts took another turn. Once, she had seen Ambrosine where she shouldn't, and Ambrosine had given her money. New boots had come out of that. Now she was seeing Mrs Gibbons and Harry.

Wicked, a voice whispered in her head.

'No,' retorted Alice, 'not wicked. Sagacious.'

Meggy was gawping at her as if she had lost her mind, and now Alice really did laugh.

****

The ambulance had come and gone. Work had continued in a desultory fashion but finally petered out around five o'clock. Frederick Swann's crew left in their convoy of vehicles, and Frederick himself clattered into the kitchen to speak to Rosamund. She and Kerry were huddled together over the kitchen table, too afraid to voice their fears aloud.

'Mrs Markovic?'

Rosamund stood, and Kerry jumped up to pour him some tea.

'Not good news,' he went on, shaking his head. 'I was just talking to the hospital. Head injuries, could be serious. We won't know how serious until they do X-rays and tests. His wife's up there, waiting for him to come round.'

Rosamund didn't know what to say. She felt as if she should apologise, but for what? It wasn't as if the fall had been her fault.

'How did it happen?' Kerry asked as she handed Frederick the tea.

'He slipped. Just . . . slipped. One minute he was standing on a firm broad plank, and then next thing he was in mid-air. He grabbed at part of the scaffolding as he went down, but couldn't get a good enough grip to hold him. Hit his head on it, and then the ground.' He closed his eyes, as if the memory was more than he could deal with just yet.

'So . . . he slipped.'

Frederick opened his eyes and met Rosamund's. She felt something pass between them, and clasped her arms about herself as though she needed comforting.

'Do you usually have this many accidents on a job?' she inquired.

He shook his head. 'I'm worried,' he said carefully, still watching her. 'There's an atmosphere here, Mrs Markovic. I won't pretend I understand what it is, but I know it's here. I know Gary feels it, too. He feels it worse than me, worse than any of us. This morning he had to force himself to come in here—I saw his face, I know.'

Rosamund's disbelief dried up before she could give it voice.

Kerry shifted uneasily. 'Really, Frederick, I didn't think you'd believe this nonsense.'

'I believe my own eyes and my own senses, Kerry. I don't have to have so-called scientific proof to believe. I believe in God, and that belief is an act of faith. But we should also have faith in ourselves, in what our hearts and minds tell us, not suspend our belief until it shows up on a graph or in a test-tube in a laboratory.'

Rosamund looked at him in surprise. 'So you think these accidents are caused by something at Colonsay?' she asked him baldly.

He frowned and scratched his ear. 'This is an unhappy house, Mrs Markovic.'

'And you're avoiding the question.'

He smiled wearily. 'All right. Yes, I do.'

'Then what are you going to do about the restoration? There's still so much to do.'

'I think I'll give everyone a day off, and after that we'll start afresh. In the meantime, I want to come back here tonight to say some prayers.'

'How will that help?' Rosamund couldn't keep the cynicism out of her voice.

'It can't hurt.'

'Look Fred, I don't know . . .'

He looked at her, his eyes clear and bright. 'Mrs Markovic—Rosamund, you believe in good, don't you? You believe in the finer emotions, like kindness and bravery and compassion? Do you believe a place may retain a sense of that goodness? A holy place, perhaps, where prayers have been said for centuries? A church, a temple? Well, why can't the bad emotions also prevail? If a place has seen much unhappiness, why can't those feelings be retained within its walls?'

Again, he made good sense, and much of what he said Rosamund had worked out for herself. And yet, as when Gary wanted to bring Zephyr here, Rosamund resented the need for outside assistance. This was her house, her problem, and she wanted to deal with it. Only now there had been two accidents, and she could not risk a third.

'How can a prayer hurt?' Frederick asked softly, persuasively.

Beaten, she nodded. 'All right.'

He smiled. 'Nothing to worry about, you'll see.'

She nodded again, reluctantly. Kerry saw him out.

'I hope you know what you're doing,' she said when she returned. 'Frederick's church is rather unconventional.'

'Oh?'

'It's called the Church of God's Joyful Answer.'

Rosamund groaned.

Kerry fought a smile. 'Well, it will be interesting.'

Rosamund sighed. It would be that! Why hadn't Gary told her? Where was Gary, anyway? Frederick had said he could hardly bring himself to enter the house. She hadn't realised it was so bad, although now she remembered his reluctance yesterday when he had stood by his car. She had been too caught up in her own feelings to delve into his.

Perhaps he wouldn't come back.

The pang of loss took her unawares. And made her uneasy. She didn't want to be too dependent upon Gary. She liked and trusted him, yes, but at the moment she was fully engaged in escaping the tentacles of her relationship with Mark. She wasn't ready to go diving into unknown depths again, not yet.

It was after nine when Frederick Swann and his little troop arrived. Frederick had dressed in a dark sweater and slacks, his hair was carefully brushed. He looked a different person from the man Rosamund had grown used to, in worn and stained shorts and shirt, his workman's boots splattered with cement and paint.

He introduced the three others with him. A woman with greying blonde hair called Melanie, and two men, one in his twenties called Justin and the other about sixty, Leo. Leo had a smile which seemed fixed permanently to his face, but his eyes were warm and Rosamund found herself liking him despite her prejudices. Leo closed his eyes and instantly the others were quiet. For about a minute he stood perfectly still, as if he were listening. Then he gave himself a little shake, like a dog which senses something nasty. Frederick leaned close and they spoke together in murmurs.

'I think we'll stand here, between the front door and the main staircase,' Frederick said at last.

They had brought candles, and now they set them upon the stairs and lit them. The flames flickered slightly and then burned still. Kerry hovered in the kitchen doorway, wiping her palms nervously on her skirt. Rosamund, beside her, gave her a questioning glance. Despite earlier concerns, she had hoped that Gary might come, but he hadn't even rung.

'How is the man who fell?' Kerry's question interrupted her thoughts.

Frederick's face grew even more serious. 'He hasn't regained consciousness.'

They were silent. Melanie shuddered and looked around her in a manner Rosamund found somewhat theatrical. 'Do you feel it?' she asked in a low voice. Leo smiled but didn't answer.

'Feel what?' Kerry asked in a whisper to Rosamund, but Rosamund shrugged. The house felt the same to her.

The four members of the Church of God's Joyful Answer formed themselves into a tight circle and, holding hands, began to pray. The words started as a murmur, but grew in volume until they were quite loud. Leo and Frederick were the more sure—deep and confident. Despite her own misgivings, Rosamund sensed their absolute certainty in the power of the prayers and was comforted.

'Great and powerful God, give us strength at this time. Almighty God, take pity upon those souls who cannot find peace, allow them into Your great kingdom, show them Your wonderful mercy.'

The others took up the chant. 'Show them Your mercy, oh God.'

'God, look upon those souls who cannot find peace and, according to the multitude of Your mercies, do away with their offences.'

'Amen.'

'Allow them into Your blessed paradise.'

'Amen.'

'Cast them not into the pit, oh Lord, but steer them safely through the hazards in their path to Your holy presence.'

'Amen.'

'Lord have mercy upon them.'

'Christ have mercy upon them.'

The voices continued, soothing, almost hypnotic. Beside Rosamund, Kerry had shrunk against the door jamb. The faces of the members of the Church of God's Joyful Answer were rapt; Rosamund saw the passion in them for what they were doing and what they believed. They had begun to recite the Lord's Prayer and the words saturated the air, each one like a drum, beating against the darkness. Beyond the burning candles, Colonsay was quiet, Colonsay was at peace.

But something was stirring.

Rosamund didn't know how she knew, only that she did. There was movement in the air around them. A silent thing, passing among them, watching, laughing at them, jeering . . . Rosamund cried out sharply, just as the candles began to duck and dive, smoking sourly.

Frederick and his friends kept up the chant, their voices rising. It was as if the disturbance had spurred them on to greater heights, turning their pleas into demands. Frederick lifted his bible above his head, his arm rigid, his face as if lit from within.

Quite suddenly Rosamund was afraid for him.

'Oh God, cleanse this house, Colonsay. Shine Your love and goodness upon Colonsay. Cast out all darkness and evil.'

'Oh God, cleanse this house—'

The thud was like a boulder falling from a great height. The whole house shook with it. Kerry jumped and screamed. The voices faltered but Frederick's continued, forcing them by sheer power of will to continue in the wake of his words. Another thud, a giant's footstep, and something upstairs fell over with a bang and a rattle.

'Fred,' Rosamund managed breathlessly. 'I think you should stop.'

But he wouldn't. The words were coming quicker and louder, so that the others could hardly keep up with him. The noises from the attic were so loud and came so close together it seemed like one long thunderous rumbling. Kerry had covered her face with her hands and Rosamund shouted again for them to stop. Melanie, white-faced and terrified, wrenched open the front door and ran. Justin hesitated in the doorway, plainly wanting to follow. Only Fred and Leo remained, still praying, still waving the bible, their faces shining with sweat..

Rosamund knew what it cost them. She too had lived through this, but she had never tried to stand against it.

Suddenly she was aware of a darkness at the top of the stairs which had nothing to do with night shadows. She sensed something cold and violent that left her shaken to her very core.

She ran to Frederick and caught his arm. He looked at her but didn't see her. He was vibrating with a force she could barely imagine, pitting himself against whatever inhabited Colonsay.

Abruptly the noise from upstairs stopped, and a heartbeat later Frederick stopped too. He cocked his head to the side, listening, but all was still. It was the tangible stillness that always came after the terrible noise. Rosamund heard Frederick's quick breathing, saw his chest rising and falling, and realised she was still clinging to his arm. She released him and stepped back on shaky legs. Justin crept closer. Leo was looking up the stairs into the silence of the upper floor. Melanie had not returned. Rosamund wondered, with black humour, whether she had reached the bay yet.

'We've banished it,' Leo murmured, the beginnings of triumph in his face.

'Of course we have,' Frederick replied, his voice soaring. 'God's will be done!'

The small table at the top of the landing rose grandly into the air, pausing until it had their full, open-mouthed attention, and then came hurtling down the stairs towards them. Rosamund screamed and jumped out of the way, but the table wasn't aimed at her. It struck Fred in the chest, sending him catapulting backwards through the front door and out into the front yard.

Leo and Justin ran after him. As Rosamund reached the front door, she saw that they were helping him up. 'Are you all right?' she managed, the words husky in her dry throat.

'Only bruised, I think.'

She could see his white face in the light from the hall behind her, he seemed to have aged ten years. For the first time he looked truly afraid, and it made her heart shrivel inside her with fear and pity.

'I need more people,' he said. 'More prayers. Stronger prayers.'

'No.'

'But you saw, you heard!'

'It didn't work.'

'Sometimes it takes weeks before it works. Months!'

Rosamund's eyes grew wider. 'You've seen something like this before?'

He looked uneasy. 'Not me. But I've spoken to others. I know what to do.'

'I should never have allowed you to come,' she whispered. 'You're an amateur, Fred. This . . . thing, whatever it is, doesn't want to be banished.'

'Don't listen to it,' he cried, his eyes wide. 'There's evil here, and you mustn't listen—'

Rosamund slammed the front door on him, and stood shaking. 'You don't understand,' she whispered. After a moment she wiped her face with her hands, feeling its cold dampness, and turned to find Kerry's eyes watching her out of a drawn and white face.

'Is he right? Is Colonsay evil?'

'I don't know.'

'You should leave, Rosamund. It started when you came, and if you go it will stop.'

'And what then?' she cried, her voice harsh. 'I don't want to be banished forever from my own house. Besides, how do you know it won't follow me?'

The phone began to ring, shrill and sharp, making them both jump. Kerry didn't move, she appeared to be riveted to the spot. It was Rosamund who picked her way through the wreckage of the table to answer it.

'Rosamund?'

'Gary—'

'Did it work?'

She laughed angrily. 'We've had the giant from Jack's beanstalk in the attic, and then Fred was hit by a flying table. No, it didn't work.'

A pause. 'Do you want me to come back tonight?'

'Can you?'

'Do you remember what I told you about the feeling I used to get when I visited Colonsay?'

'I remember.'

'It's worse now. It's like a wall . . . a barrier. Soon I won't be able to get through it at all.'

'You must stay away, then.'

'Maybe I will, just for tonight. I'll save myself for tomorrow. We've got the day off, anyway. I want Zephyr to come with me.'

'Gary, no. I don't want a repetition of tonight!'

'It won't be. She won't try and do anything you don't want her to. She'll just explore, listen. We have to know what we're up against if we're going to solve the mystery. Isn't that what you want?'

In the silence she could hear him breathing, waiting.

'Yes.' She was reluctant, but she just didn't know what else to do.

He sighed with relief. 'Tomorrow, then. Be careful.'

Be careful, she repeated to herself, as she hung up.

'He's bringing Zephyr.'

Kerry closed her eyes. 'Good heavens, has it come to that!'

Somehow, Rosamund managed to laugh.

CHAPTER 12

Despite everything, Rosamund slept well. Not so, it appeared, for Kerry. In the morning she looked haggard and showed a most uncharacteristic lack of interest in the stove.

'I might go back upstairs and have a lie down,' she said at last. 'If that's all right, Rosamund?'

'Of course it's all right! Sleep all day if you want to.'

'Oh no, I won't do that. I was planning to do something with a chicken for dinner.'

Rosamund sighed and sipped her coffee. When Kerry had gone and the house was quiet again, she went out into the back yard and lit a cigarette. The slasher had cleared most of the area around the old cottage and almost half of the rest of the yard. Rosamund wondered what irreplaceable old plants had been destroyed with the thistle and nettle. Well, no use worrying now.

The air was chill and damp but fresh against her skin. She walked over to the cottage, edging through the gap in the boxthorn, and peered through the window. It was very dark in there but she could see the shovels standing to attention. Who had lived there? Some old family retainer? If Ada had ever told Rosamund, she had now forgotten.

Something moved in the corner and Rosamund blinked in amazement. A small, pointed face peered out at her from the folds of the tennis net. Tan-coloured hair was matted around the black button-nosed snout, and a narrow ribbon hung forlornly over one ear.

'Oh, you poor thing,' she breathed.

The terrier fixed her with big brown begging eyes. Rosamund moved towards the door and creaked it open. The cottage hummed with trapped flies, and dust settled gently on the crowded shelves. Rosamund knelt, calling softly, her hand outstretched. But the dog had gone, either back into the piles of cottage junk or outside through one of the many gaps in the walls.

She was in the kitchen making up a plate of tempting leftovers when the sound of a car engine brought her hurrying to the front door. Gary's car pulled up in the muddy quagmire at the front. There were two of them in it, Gary and a woman with fair hair. For a second Rosamund thought it was Melanie returned from wherever she had gone last night, but when the car door opened and the woman climbed out she realised that this was someone different.

She was on the short and stout side and wore a tweed skirt and a navy blazer with a pale mauve scarf loosely knotted about her throat. Her hair wasn't blonde after all but silver, cut to her shoulders in a thick, gleaming bob. Gary took her arm as they started towards the house. He looked as pale and drawn as Kerry, and as he came nearer she saw his steps grow more uncertain.

The woman—Zephyr?—turned towards him, placing both her hands on his shoulders and speaking softly. Gary straightened and, with his face still grey but his eyes fixed on Rosamund's, he walked forward.

'How are you?' she asked with concern. 'Is it . . . is it very bad?'

'In a word, yes.'

He brushed by her into the hall and then Zephyr stood before Rosamund, smiling. Her face was round and fleshy, skin taut as a baby's, her eyes dark and sympathetic. The hand that clasped Rosamund's was warm and strong.

'Mrs Markovic, it's a pleasure to meet you. I've never visited Colonsay, but I've always been very interested.'

Disarmed, Rosamund stepped back to allow Zephyr in and closed the door. This wasn't quite what she had expected and she tried to gather her wits, preparing her defences for the New Age assault. Zephyr was giving Gary her sympathetic look. He responded with a wobbly smile before turning to Rosamund.

'Do you mind if I have a cup of coffee? Caffeine seems to help.'

'I'll make instant, it's quicker.' Rosamund led the way into the kitchen and put the kettle on to boil. Behind her Gary slumped into a chair at the table, while Zephyr walked about the room smiling to herself, appearing to examine the decor, and yet . . . She was listening, Rosamund realised with a chill. That was what Gary had said she did, wasn't it? Listen for things that other people couldn't hear?

'I understand Frederick Swann was here last night,' she said pleasantly.

Rosamund poured hot water into a mug and stirred in milk and sugar. 'Yes.'

The one grim word seemed to amuse Gary. 'You

said over the phone it wasn't very successful.'

'An understatement. One to Colonsay, nil to Fred Swann, I'd say.'

'Frederick is a good man but he lacks experience in these matters.'

Rosamund glanced at Zephyr uneasily, wondering if she expected an answer to that pronouncement. She didn't seem to, so Rosamund went to sit with Gary. His hand rested on the table, and on impulse she reached over and clasped it in her own. His fingers felt cold and stiff but closed eagerly enough over hers. He smiled wryly.

'I was supposed to be looking after you and Kerry. I'm sorry.'

Behind them Zephyr said, 'You need to listen to what your inner self is telling you. Ignoring that voice can be very dangerous.'

Another pronouncement? Rosamund rolled her eyes. Gary frowned at her, but there was a lurking smile in his blue eyes.

'How's Fred's man, the one who fell?' she asked.

'He regained consciousness late last night. They've still got tests to run. It's a wait and see thing.' He squeezed Rosamund's fingers hard, then released them, swallowing his coffee.

'Are you ready to look over the rest of the house now, Zephyr?'

She nodded.

'Will I show you?'

'No, Rosamund can show me. You stay here, Gary. The kitchen seems to be relatively clear.' She smiled at Rosamund and waited for her to precede her into the hall.

'Kerry . . . Mrs Scott, is in her room resting. She didn't sleep well last night.'

'There will be no need to disturb Mrs Scott.' Zephyr's dark eyes were so dark that the pupil was hardly discernible from the iris. They looked into Rosamund's and widened slightly, but she said nothing, patiently waiting for Rosamund to lead the way down the hall.

'This is the library.' Rosamund opened the door and Zephyr stepped in, strolling to the window. Rosamund wondered whether she was supposed to provide a running commentary, like a tour guide. Well, she wasn't going to. She stood and waited in silence while Zephyr did her thing, which appeared to be inspecting the worn furniture and the wall near the mantelpiece, before moving on to the next room. They did this all the way down the hall to the back of the house, where Zephyr peered into the room Rosamund had been clearing.

'I sense great violence.'

'What?'

Abruptly, Zephyr turned and looked at the second room, the one with the warped door. 'There is violence here.'

Rosamund tried to ignore the shiver that was squirming down her back. 'The door's jammed,' she murmured. 'I can try and open it.'

Zephyr nodded, and waited while Rosamund heaved with hip and shoulder. The door opened a mere fraction and no more—as if Godzilla was leaning on it from the other side. After a short struggle, Rosamund stood back and took a deep breath.

'I'm sorry. It won't open today. I . . . I don't like that room.'

The last bit just popped out. Zephyr gave her one of those searching looks, then stepped forward to place her palms on the door. 'No,' she said quietly, 'it's not a pleasant room. There's a man here. He's suffering. He's looking for someone. He's calling out to them . . . a name.'

'Rosie.' Rosamund hardly recognised her own voice.

'Yes, I think you're right.' Zephyr sighed. 'At the moment Colonsay is very active, psychically, and this room is one of the main hot spots. Violence, Rosamund. Trapped here.' She took a handkerchief out of her pocket and wiped her hands as if they were soiled. 'Lead on.'

They went upstairs. The corridor was cool and silent, their echoing footsteps almost an intrusion. Rosamund did not speak. She just followed behind, allowing Zephyr to go where she willed. She willed to go into Rosamund's bedroom, then to the end of the corridor, to the stained-glass window.

'Do you feel very tired sometimes, Rosamund?'

'Well, yes, I do. Did Gary tell you about—?'

'No. I don't want to know what's happened and what you've seen. That's not how I do my job. So you feel tired? Exhausted?'

'Yes.'

'The spirits have little energy of their own. They must use what is available to them. If you feel tired, it's because they are using your energy to manifest or create some disturbance. You must get out of here as much as possible, or you could become ill.'

Zephyr wandered into the west wing, peering through the gaps where Frederick Swann had removed the windows, and then up the narrow enclosed stairs to the attic.

Not once did she flinch or cry out. Not once did

she point and say in strangled tones, 'Can't you see it?' as Rosamund had expected her to. The fact that she was so quiet, so controlled should have been an anticlimax, but it was not. It made the whole episode even more frightening.

They returned to the foot of the main staircase, where Frederick had set his candles last night. There were still drops of wax on the treads.

'There's someone here who is very unhappy,' Zephyr pronounced. 'I feel there has been a wrong done, and until that wrong is put right this spirit cannot leave Colonsay.'

It sounded like the standard haunted house explanation but Rosamund felt compelled to ask, 'Do you know who the spirit is?'

'This spirit is showing herself as young but she might not have died young.'

'She?'

'Oh, it's a woman.'

For some reason Rosamund immediately thought of Ada. Her imagination, fuelled by all that had happened, went into overdrive. How could she live here if Ada was haunting the house, tapping along the corridor with her cane, the photograph of her dead husband clutched in her liver-spotted hand?

'There's a connection between you and this spirit,' Zephyr went on. 'It's as if she's using you to bring the past alive.'

'Can you tell me more?'

But Zephyr was listening again and it was not to Rosamund. 'I don't know if much can be done here,' she said quietly. 'I sense violence, great violence. Someone is very unhappy. I think that is enough for now.' She shook her head slightly, and smiled at Rosamund as if she had never spoken those words. 'I'll walk in the front garden for a little while. Call me when Gary is ready to take me home.'

Front garden? Rosamund repeated to herself sarcastically, but she opened the front door for Zephyr and went back to the kitchen and Gary. He looked up at her, his mouth hard and straight. Whatever it was that lived in Colonsay was draining the life out of him, just as Zephyr had warned.

'There's been no violence here, Gary, has there?'

'Depends what sort. Emotional violence? Is there such a thing?'

'Yes, I suppose there is. But I think Zephyr means the usual sort of violence.' Rosamund shivered. 'She says there's a man calling for Rosie and a girl who wants to bring back the dead.' She went on to explain more fully what Zephyr had said, and they puzzled over it in silence.

'Do you want another cup of coffee?' Rosamund asked at last.

'No, I'd better be going. Rosamund?'

She looked up, worry pinching her face. He touched her cheek gently with his finger. 'I'm going out in the boat this afternoon. It'll be calm enough. Will you come?'

Rosamund thought of herself under a wide, endless sky, free of restrictions, physical or emotional, and smiled. 'Thank you, I'd love to.'

Something in his face relaxed. 'I'll pick you up after lunch. Wear warm clothes. I have some waterproofs if we need them.'

Her voice stopped him at the door. 'Gary? Thank you.'

He nodded, and then she heard the front door close behind him. Shortly afterwards the car drove away. Rosamund stayed where she was, full of questions without answers. Zephyr had not really provided any. And the violence, well that made no sense at all. Colonsay had always been an unhappy house, the Cunninghams were an unhappy family. But, as far as she knew, they were not prone to homicidal mania. Perhaps even Zephyr could be wrong sometimes.

****

The train was due in and the carriage had been sent to the station to collect Cosmo and Ambrosine. And Bertie.

Alice could hardly contain herself. Her excitement was like a living thing, jumping and skipping inside her chest, bruising her ribs in its eagerness to get out. Bertie would be home. At last.

For days Mrs Gibbons had been busy baking, preparing Colonsay for the flood of guests she expected to follow Cosmo. Presently she was chopping onions and, in between sniffs, singing, 'If I were the only girl in the world,' to Meggy's sour amusement.

Meggy had been full of smiles while the Cunninghams were away, but today her face was glum and her humour had taken on a sarcastic bent. Jonah's doing, probably, thought Alice.

'Go and open the door, Alice!'

Alice jumped up automatically at the cook's excited cry. The clomp and rattle of a horse and vehicle drew closer and it was all she could do to stop herself running to the door and throwing it open. She waited, legs trembling, as the carriage drew to a halt, and heard the murmur of the driver and Jonah and then Cosmo's louder voice.

'Glad to be back!'

Alice smoothed her starched apron yet again. Her throat was dry. She moved to open the door, her palm slippery on the polished brass knob, and stood with the chill wind stirring the ruffles at her breast and the tendrils of hair escaping her white cap.

'Alice!' Cosmo beamed at her as he stamped his feet on the verandah before entering the house. 'How are your father and mother? Well, I trust?'

'Very well, sir.' Her voice trembled but he didn't notice.

Ambrosine looked pale and tired and held a hand to her eyes. She murmured, 'Tell Mrs Gibbons I require something for my headache,' before climbing the stairs to her bedroom. Behind Ambrosine skipped Ada, who shook off her nursemaid's hand and poked out her tongue. Bertie was last of all, an afterthought.

Alice would hardly have known him.

His round face was still round, but the eyes behind the spectacles were sunken and shadowed. His skin was pale and colourless, and his smile so tentative it squeezed her heart.

'I'm home, Alice,' he said. But he said it as if he didn't really believe it.

****

The bay was a calm steely grey. Gary's boat cut through the water, making what she could of the breeze. There wasn't much to puff out the sails, and more often than not he had to resort to the engine. Rosamund didn't mind. She sat back in the cockpit and let Gary run things.

The smell of salt and sea turned her head inside out, scouring it clean of everything that had been clogging her thoughts. She felt wonderfully new and alive.

'We'll head towards Queenscliff.' Gary pointed as he shouted above the engine.

Rosamund nodded, but she didn't really care where they were going. Her thick sweater kept her warm, and Gary had lent her a yellow waterproof jacket with a hood. She was snug and cosy, and if she wanted more, he had offered to make her a hot cuppa in the little galley below decks. There was even a single bunk down there, tucked away between a narrow table and lockers.

It certainly wasn't a state-of-the-art racing yacht, but Gary obviously loved it.

They watched as a huge tanker ploughed its way through the deeper channel towards the Rip and the sea. Gary's boat seemed like a tiny cork in comparison, and as they passed in the tanker's wake Rosamund looked up in awe at the rusting metal.

He was laughing at her. 'Don't worry, I know what I'm doing.'

Once they were out of the shelter of the land, a breeze sprang up and Gary took advantage of it. The ropes were wet and cold in Rosamund's hands as she held them and loosened them off when he told her to. The little boat heeled, racing with the wind, and one of the larger waves washed across the deck and into the cockpit, soaking Rosamund's shoes before it trickled out again.

'Haven't you ever been sailing before?' he shouted.

'Not like this. I once attended a dinner party on a yacht but it was done out like somebody's town house. You'd never have known you were afloat.'

'I prefer to be a little closer to the elements!'

She laughed and the cold wind carried the sound away. Her hood had fallen back and her hair was blowing wildly. Her eyes shone and her skin glowed.

'You look sixteen years old.'

There was something in his eyes—Rosamund knew she should look away but didn't. 'I'm far from that,' she murmured, and didn't know if he had heard her. And then he was pulling on the sail again as the wind gusted and flapped the canvas and a hard, cold rainshower pelted them briefly before passing on.

All too soon he returned them to shore at Portarlington and tied up at his mooring. Rosamund helped to tidy up and stow things away, working silently but companionably. She didn't need to speak, there was nothing just now she wanted to talk about. Colonsay would be there when she got home, time enough then to worry about what she must or must not do.

'Thank you,' she said, looking up at last.

Gary smiled, puzzled. 'Thank you for what?'

She shrugged. 'Just thank you.'

'Will you come and have a drink with me before we go back?'

Rosamund was tempted, but a flicker of alarm sounded far back in her mind, making her uncomfortably aware of how long they had been gone. Kerry would be waiting.

'I'd better get back. Do you mind?'

His turn to shrug. They walked together up the wooden jetty towards the car park, and Rosamund didn't pull her hand away when he took it.

It was getting dark. Gary stopped the car and sat staring ahead at Colonsay. It's just a house, Rosamund reminded herself. What's to be afraid of? But with every mile they had travelled on the way home her spirits had slipped lower, and soon it had been almost as though the afternoon of freedom had never happened.

It began to rain as they pulled off the road onto the driveway. Rosamund glanced at the tall shape of the column that was Cosmo Cunningham's memorial. A flash of crimson caught her eye, disappearing behind the shadowy stones as soon as she had seen it. The old man from the historical society? What an afternoon to be doing maintenance work. Well, she supposed some people were more dedicated than others.

The rain pelted the windscreen, turning their view of Colonsay into a blurred watercolour. All greys and browns, with a touch of silver at the top where the attic windows reflected the sky.

'There are no lights on!'

Gary was out of the car and running before Rosamund realised what he meant. It was a dull afternoon swiftly turning to evening. Why weren't the lights on?

Gary had stopped at the front door when Rosamund reached him. Even in the fading light she could see his skin had a greenish pallor and he looked like he was going to be sick. 'Go in,' he gasped. 'I'll follow in a minute.'

The door was unlocked and Rosamund took a

step into the hallway, blinking in the thick gloom. From the direction of the kitchen the refrigerator clicked into life, but that was the only sound. She flicked on the hallway light.

'Kerry?'

Silence. She walked down the hall and put her head around the kitchen door, but the room was empty. There was a plate and cup on the sink, draining, but no other sign of activity. Everything was clean, wiped down. By now Kerry should have been well into dinner preparations.

Rosamund ran up the stairs. Kerry's room was empty, the bed slightly rumpled. There was a book tossed on the bedspread, its bright cover displaying a taste in fiction Rosamund found amusing, if a little surprising. Kerry a cupboard romantic?

'Kerry! Are you here?'

This time there was a reply, muffled, as though the voice came from inside a closed chest. As though Kerry had been swallowed whole into the walls of Colonsay. A bizarre picture flashed into Rosamund's mind—Kerry huddled in the wall cavity, face and palms pressed to the stone and plaster, mouth wide . . .

'Stop it,' Rosamund muttered to herself. They should never have left her here alone. She reached the head of the stairs and called again.

The reply was still muffled, but closer now.

'Here!' Gary called as she clattered down the stairs. He was standing by the cellar door, still looking ill but also grimly determined. 'She's in here. It's locked. Do you have a key?'

'There is no key,' she said in surprise. She reached past him and closed her hand on the knob. The door opened for her instantly. She looked at Gary.

'It *was* locked,' he said dully.

Rosamund stepped onto the cellar landing. 'Kerry?' she called in a voice striving to be courageous. 'Kerry?' She flicked on the light switch and the bulb blinked into life, illuminating the cellar. A smell of damp earth rose up, mingling with the well water. Kerry was huddled at the bottom of the wooden ladder, her knees tucked up to her chest, arms clasped over her head.

Somehow, without remembering moving, Rosamund was down the ladder and by her side. 'Kerry! What happened?'

The older woman clung to Rosamund as if she were drowning and Rosamund a life raft. Her body was shaking violently, even her teeth were chattering, and her hands were icy claws. 'There was someone . . . someone . . .' she gasped. 'I heard someone . . . but when I came down the light went out and the door shut and I couldn't get out!' She ended on a thin wail that broke into a sob.

Gary touched Rosamund's shoulder. 'Let me carry her,' he suggested.

They got Kerry up the ladder and out into the hall. She was still shaking, even when they set her down in the kitchen and Rosamund had made her a strong, sweet cup of tea with a decent slug of brandy in it. Gary had to hold the cup to her lips, and more slopped down the front of her than went into her mouth.

'Who did you hear?' Rosamund asked at last, knowing she shouldn't but unable to help herself.

Kerry swallowed convulsively, and then choked on the tea. When she had stopped coughing, she seemed a little better. There was certainly more colour in her face. She looked about her, eyes shining with tears.

'Who did you hear in the cellar?' Gary repeated, his arm around her shoulders.

Kerry looked up at Rosamund, her lips trembling. 'It was you, Rosamund. I wouldn't have gone down there for anybody else. I heard *you*.'

CHAPTER 13

The thud was so soft that at first Rosamund took it to be the brush of a branch against the house. Only there were no trees that close to Colonsay. She sat up, blinking into the darkness, holding her breath. She had no idea how long she'd been asleep. They had had tinned soup for dinner, with plenty of bread and butter. Rosamund had helped Kerry into bed after that, offering comfort with words and kindness when there was really none to offer. Gary had suggested they go to a hotel for the night, but Kerry had refused and Rosamund had also been reluctant.

She had the feeling that once she left Colonsay she would never return.

'I must have imagined it,' Kerry kept saying. 'How could you have been there? I knew it couldn't be you, and yet it sounded like you and I thought . . . I couldn't not go and look, could I? Just to be sure?'

'No, you couldn't,' murmured Rosamund as she pulled the quilt up about Kerry's ears. She looked small beneath it, like a grey-haired child.

'I must have been mistaken, mustn't I?'

But there was no answer Rosamund could give her.

Kerry fell asleep immediately and Rosamund

went to her own room for an early night, tired after her afternoon on the boat. Gary had wanted to stay but Rosamund persuaded him against it. She saw what being in the vicinity of Colonsay did to him, and she didn't want to be responsible for him as well as Kerry. They would manage.

The thud came again, louder this time. There was now no mistaking what it portended. Rosamund climbed out of bed and quickly pulled on her jeans and sweater. As she reached her bedroom door an especially loud crash shook the whole house. A scream came from Kerry's room.

Rosamund flung open her door. The corridor was lit—she had left on the overhead light. The bulb flickered violently, and went out. Rosamund stood, her heart pounding in her ears. She almost turned and bolted downstairs, leaving Kerry to her fate, but even as she thought it, Kerry screamed again and she knew she couldn't.

Rosamund could find her way without light. Only a few more steps and she would be at Kerry's door. Her feet scuffed the worn runner and she trailed her hand along the wall, feeling the rough edges of torn wallpaper and a sticky place where a strip had peeled off altogether. The painted wood of the door was contrastingly smooth under her fingertips. She found the knob and turned it.

Kerry's warm, angular body crashed into her and sent her flying backwards. She was briefly aware of a cacophony consisting of ghostly thumps and Kerry's wails, and then the air was knocked out of her and she lay breathless.

Kerry crawled across the floor and found her, her nails scratching Rosamund's face and tangling her hair. 'Oh no, oh no,' she was moaning.

Rosamund managed to catch her breath at last. 'It's all right,' she said, her voice oddly calm. There was something stirring inside her—a rarely used emotion. 'Help me up and we'll go downstairs.'

Kerry heaved at her arm and Rosamund got to her feet. The noise about them rose and fell. They staggered together down the stairs and into the kitchen. The light wasn't working there either, but at least it felt safer. Kerry rummaged in one of the cupboards and found a candle. She lit it, the shadows dancing on her face as the flame flared and waned.

Their eyes met. 'Are you all right?' asked Rosamund.

Kerry nodded jerkily. 'And you?'

Slowly Rosamund shook her head. 'I'm not hurt. I feel . . . this seems strange, but I feel angry.'

Kerry almost laughed.

It was true. The feeling had come upon her slowly, slipping past terror, past fear, until now it swelled like a bellows within her, supplying her with much-needed courage. Rosamund went to the door and flung it open. The deep booming noise from the attic was continuing, interspersed with staccato blows. Rosamund ran to the bottom of the staircase.

'*Go away!*' she screamed. There was something very liberating in letting it all out. 'Leave us alone! You can't drive us out! Do you hear me! You can't drive us out.'

The racket suddenly stopped.

Behind her, Kerry's breathing sounded very loud. She had come up without Rosamund even hearing her. 'I have this fear,' she whispered, and swallowed. 'I have this fear, Rosamund, that whatever is up there will one day come down.'

Rosamund turned and looked at her. The candle flame flickered between them. 'But it is down here, Kerry. It's here, all around us.'

'*Rosie.*'

The word ended on a low, moaning sob. Rosamund shuddered violently. 'Did you hear?'

Kerry was staring at her, eyes huge. 'Yes.'

'This house wants something from me, Kerry.'

'How can you find out what that is?'

Rosamund smiled wryly. 'We'll have to call in the spirit counsellor. I'll ring Gary in the morning and ask him to find out if Zephyr will make another house call. I wonder what she charges?'

'I thought those sort of people didn't take money,' Kerry replied primly. 'I'm sure Doris Stokes never did.'

'They call it a donation.'

Kerry was still holding the candle and now she carried it carefully back into the kitchen. As she set it down on the table, the refrigerator began to hum and the kitchen was flooded with bright, fluorescent light.

They both breathed a sigh of relief. Kerry blew out the candle and proceeded to put on the kettle. 'It's strange,' she said thoughtfully, 'but I don't feel too bad. I mean, with the noise and everything. I'm almost getting used to it.'

'What an admission!'

Kerry didn't smile. 'The first time it happened I was terrified, but now—I won't say I enjoy it, but I can cope.' Her lips trembled and she bit them to steady herself. 'I didn't like the cellar. You know I . . . I can't stand to be in enclosed spaces, Rosamund.'

Rosamund patted her shoulder. 'Our noisy spirit is a mimic, and an intelligent one. It knew you wouldn't go down there for just anyone, that you'd feel a responsibility for me. So it became me.'

'Do you think that was it?'

'Yes, I do.' Rosamund yawned and stretched. 'I saw that dog this morning. I put some scraps out for it. Did you notice if they were gone?'

Kerry looked puzzled. 'No, I didn't. Are you sure it was a dog?'

'Yes. A little terrier, the hairy sort. Had a bow in its hair. Poor creature. I'll have to catch it before it dies, or turns feral.'

Kerry opened her mouth to reply, but the phone rang shrilly, interrupting them.

'Bit late, isn't it?' Rosamund murmured, but when she looked at the clock above the stove it was only ten past ten. Kerry hurried out to answer the phone. When she came back she pulled a face.

'That was Frederick Swann. He won't be over tomorrow. He says the weather doesn't look good and he has another job to do. He'll probably be back again next week. Do you want to talk to him?'

Rosamund went out and picked up the phone. 'You can't just stop work, Fred,' she said without preamble.

'I'm not.' His voice sounded solid and soothing—the typical tradesman in a corner. 'I'll be back next week.'

'But why?' As if she didn't know.

'I think we could do with a break from Colonsay. The accidents ... some of the crew are nervous. Give them a few days away and they'll be okay again.'

'Fred, about what happened—'

'No,' he cut in on her. 'I'm not upset about that.

I understand why you were angry. It got worse when we prayed, but that's usual. You don't understand these things, Mrs Markovic.'

'Neither do you.'

'Maybe not, but I've been around them and I've listened to those who do. It always gets worse before it gets better. Evil fights for survival and it'll throw every trick it has at you before it finally goes under. It's never as easy as one prayer. I should have told you that before I started, but I didn't think you'd let me in.'

Rosamund was silent, annoyed at his deception but impressed by his sincerity.

'Gary tells me you've had a visit from Zephyr.'

He made it sound like a pest-control firm. 'Yes. She didn't give me any real answers either.'

'You shouldn't try and reason with these things, Rosamund. You shouldn't argue with them or communicate with them.'

'I think communication is the only way we're going to find out what it wants.'

'It wants your immortal soul.'

She couldn't think of anything to say to that, and there was a long silence. She could hear him breathing down the telephone line.

'Call me if you need me,' he said at last. 'God bless you, Rosamund.'

She stood holding the telephone a long while after it had gone dead.

As soon as she replaced it, it rang again.

'Mrs Markovic?' A man's voice, a 'good school' voice, with authority.

'Yes?' She was slightly breathless.

'This is Graham Peel-Johnson. From Johnson, Mitchell and Williams.'

'Yes?'

'Your husband has asked me to act for him in a rather delicate matter. I'm sorry for ringing you so late, but I only received his instructions an hour ago. I'd like to visit you tomorrow, Mrs Markovic.'

She couldn't think. Nothing whatsoever occurred to her.

'Mrs Markovic?'

'I'm sorry. Tomorrow. Yes, all right.'

'I'll be there in the afternoon, after one. If there's a change in plan, I'll ring and let you know.'

'Can you tell me what you want to talk about, Mr Peel-Johnson?'

But he couldn't, or wouldn't. Politely deflecting her question, he hung up. Rosamund set the phone down for the second time and turned to find Kerry watching her from the kitchen doorway.

'Fred isn't coming until next week, assuming I haven't lost my immortal soul by then, and Mr Peel-Johnson, a solicitor acting for Mark, will be calling after one.'

Kerry opened her mouth to ask the inevitable question, but Rosamund couldn't face it. She turned abruptly to the stairs.

'I'm going to bed,' she said.

'But your hot drink—'

'You have it.' She stopped, and looked back over the banister rail, ashamed of her bad temper. It wasn't Kerry's fault; Kerry had given more tonight than any employer, or friend, had a right to expect. 'Sorry. I need to go to bed. Will you be all right?'

'I'll sit up a little while. I might make a batch of biscuits.'

Rosamund laughed. What a woman. 'Goodnight.'

Kerry's reply echoed up the stairs after her as Rosamund took her tired body and bitter thoughts to bed.

****

'You must be glad to be home, Master Bertie!' Mrs Gibbons beamed at the boy, her plump face puffed out even more by her smiling cheeks.

Wanly, Bertie smiled back. 'Yes, Cook. Very glad.'

'I've some humbugs put by. I'll fetch them out, shall I?'

'Thank you.'

She handed him the sweets, patting his head as if he were still a little child. Alice winced but Bertie didn't appear to mind; he just smiled again and wandered off on his own business. He had been like that ever since he returned. He smiled and spoke and did all the things required of him by others, but he wasn't really there. It was as if he had suffered a terrible bereavement and had withdrawn some vital part of himself.

'Why can't I have one?' Ada's small face was twisted into a furious frown.

Mrs Gibbons laughed and found some more humbugs. 'Now, now, my poppet,' she crooned as she handed them over. 'What do you say?'

'I say that isn't enough,' Ada rejoined.

The cook found that even funnier and doubled over with laughter. Ada smirked at Alice and ran out the back door, across the yard towards the stables.

'She's a trick, that one,' Mrs Gibbons sighed, wiping her streaming eyes. 'We'll have our hands full when her hair is up.'

Alice tightened her lips and bent to her task without replying. What she thought of Ada Cunningham was her own business and best not repeated.

'And what lemon have you been sucking, Alice Parkin?' the cook demanded.

'I was thinking how some people seem to have no qualms about taking advantage of others, Mrs Gibbons.' The words came easily from Alice's mouth. She had been practising them now for a week but had not really believed she would say them. And now here they were, smooth as butter, sliding over her tongue.

Mrs Gibbons's eyes narrowed. 'I hope you don't mean Miss Ada, Alice.'

'No, not Miss Ada. I was thinking of others. I was thinking of servants who take advantage of their employers. Who betray their trust.'

Now she had the cook's attention. Mrs Gibbons came closer, until she was standing over Alice, her dark rustling skirt brushing Alice's arm. She smelled of onion, but beneath that was the strong herbal scent of her special tonic. The more tonic Mrs Gibbons drank, the more unsteady on her feet she became, but it was still early in the day and she seemed to be having no trouble with her balance.

'Betray their trust?' she repeated loudly. 'What are you on about, girl!'

'Servants who invite their . . . friends inside to eat and drink and dance.'

She paused there, glancing up at Mrs Gibbons. The cook seemed to freeze. 'They invite them in when their employers are away. I'm sure that's not right, is it, Mrs Gibbons? What would Mrs Cunningham say if she had a servant like that? How would she feel to know such things were going on?'

'What indeed,' the cook murmured, but she sounded as if she were choking. She struck out, catching Alice across the cheek with the flat of her hand. Alice cried out and fell back, covering the reddening mark with her cool palm. Mrs Gibbons loomed over her again, obscuring the light.

'You have a sly and wicked tongue, girl.'

'I have an honest tongue,' Alice managed through stiff lips.

She expected it to earn her another blow, but with difficulty Mrs Gibbons regained control. She took a step back, her fat face as mottled as a cherry clafouti.

'Mrs Cunningham's very fond of me. She understands my ways.' Mrs Gibbons's voice was hearty, but her eyes told the lie. 'She'd never turn out her old cook for such a little thing!'

'*Mr* Cunningham is very fond of *me*,' Alice countered slowly. 'My father saved his life, remember. And he might not understand your ways as well as his wife does.'

'He wouldn't believe you!'

'Well, then,' Alice managed to smile, though it hurt the bruised side of her face, 'I'm glad you don't mind me telling him the truth, Mrs Gibbons, because I'm an honest girl and I don't enjoy lying.'

'An honest girl!' Cook snorted furiously.

'I'm good at keeping secrets, too,' Alice went on, as if she hadn't heard. 'I can keep a secret like an oyster its pearl if I'm given a good enough reason to keep it.'

They stared at each other in silence. Slowly the cook relaxed, the outraged stiffness leaving her back and shoulders, so that she slumped into something more like her usual posture. 'I see your game now,' she muttered, and clenched her teeth in a vicious smile. 'What is it you want, Alice?'

****

Zephyr arrived mid-morning. Gary brought her in his car and they both reached the door breathless from their dash through the rain. Frederick had been right about the weather.

Zephyr was wearing dark slacks and a mustard-coloured sweater, her silver hair tied back with a scarf of similar colour. She smiled at Rosamund in a friendly fashion, as if she were a long-awaited relative rather than a psychic come to raise spirits.

Gary was pale but determined. Once inside he headed straight for the kitchen, where Kerry was already pouring his coffee. Rosamund and Zephyr paused in the hall near the stairs and Rosamund explained what had happened the afternoon and the night before.

'This sounds like poltergeist activity,' Zephyr murmured thoughtfully, 'and yet there are factors which don't fit. Not that we should ever try and categorise ghosts,' she added with another smile. 'But Kerry being locked in the cellar, that isn't very nice, is it?'

Rosamund gave a nervous laugh. 'No, it isn't.'

'Some people believe poltergeist activity is caused by humans themselves—that the human brain has an ability to create havoc. Particularly children reaching puberty, who give off an enormous amount of energy. This can have very disturbing effects on the world around them. Others believe the poltergeist is a separate entity which taps into that energy for its own mischievous uses. Either way, you will find many famous cases of poltergeists involving teenagers. My personal view is that poltergeists are a separate entity and are not confined to houses where there are pubescent children. I believe they are a type of elemental being—animal or nature spirits—rather like cats and dogs. They're prone to mischief and they enjoy upsetting humans, throwing objects about, making lots of noise, that sort of thing. They can be terribly frustrating and destructive, but thankfully their visits are usually brief and they don't actually seriously hurt anyone.'

She raised her eyebrows at the sceptical look on Rosamund's face. 'A great number of people have experienced the sorts of things you're going through—seen a "ghost". Ask around for yourself. It can't all be nervous hysteria and charlatans, surely?'

Rosamund sighed. 'I don't know. I don't know what it is. That's why *you're* here, isn't it?'

Zephyr smiled her imperturbable smile and said nothing.

'So you think we have a poltergeist here at Colonsay? Is that what you're saying?'

'Not entirely, no. Your spirit is too clever. As I said, poltergeists are lower elementals, and they tend to learn their mischief as they go along. Your spirit appears to have some set agenda. What I'll do today is attempt to communicate directly with it. If we can learn a little about it, you may be able to discover why it's refusing to leave Colonsay.'

'Do you mean the spirit could leave if it wanted to?'

Zephyr smiled. 'Sometimes a spirit is simply stuck. They may have lessons to learn which have not yet been learned, or they may be held to this earth by a sense of something unfinished, or a message they want to pass on, or it may be that their death was violent and unpleasant and they are trapped and confused. I've even known of spirits refusing to believe they are dead!'

'Yesterday you said there was violence here, but as far as I know there have never been any violent deaths at Colonsay.'

'Perhaps you should look harder.'

Rosamund resented her assumption that she was right and Rosamund wrong, but held her tongue.

They decided upon the library, and Gary helped pull the chairs together in a semicircle. He drew the curtains on Zephyr's instructions and flipped on a lamp to one side of her. The room became dim, the shadows thicker on the outer edges of it, and softly lit in the centre where they were seated.

'Sometimes nothing happens,' she warned them. 'Calling up spirits isn't like ordering a pizza. And one thing more. Spirits, in my experience, are often unreliable. In short, they lie.'

Hardly seems worth it then, Rosamund thought as Zephyr leaned back and closed her eyes, consciously relaxing herself. She began to take deep breaths. Rosamund had seen enough portrayals of mediums on television and in the movies to know she was sending herself into a trance. They sat and waited. Kerry glanced at her and gave a shaky smile. Gary reached out and touched her hand, as if to comfort. But her mind wasn't with them. She was thinking of Mr Peel-Johnson, who would be arriving after one, and wondering what Mark had instructed him to say to her.

Best not to think of that now, warned a voice in her head, but she couldn't help but think of it. What if he arrived early and found them gathered together like this, holding a seance? He'd tell Mark to have her committed as soon as possible. Perhaps they should all be committed, Kerry and Gary and Zephyr, Fred Swann ... But they couldn't all be hallucinating. They couldn't all be mad—

'Help me!'

It was so still in the library. Rosamund looked around her, uncertain at first who had spoken.

'You must help me ...'

Zephyr was speaking but she sounded different, her voice lighter and pitched higher. Rosamund watched, fascinated, wondering if she was seeing a clever performance or a genuine phenomenon.

'Help me!'

There was silence again. The rain pattered softly outside the window. The room felt chill and Rosamund wished they had lit the fire before they sat down. The crackling flames would have been cheering to look at, even if the warmth didn't reach very far into the room.

Gary leaned forward. Evidently he knew the format. 'Who is this?' he asked in a firm voice. 'Who are we speaking to?'

'Falling rain ...'

'Please, who are you?'

'... grey skies ...'

Rosamund froze. It was the opening line to her song, the band's one big hit, 'Grey Skies'.

Falling rain, grey skies
I'm walking away
Leaving you behind
And the grey skies

She felt Gary's eyes on her. Zephyr began to hum, the sound fading eerily into silence. A long silence.

'Who are you, can you tell us?' Gary again.

'Who are *you*?' the voice replied.

'My name is Gary Munro and I want to help you. Tell us what to do so that we can help you.' Gary spoke earnestly.

'Gary, I know you . . . watched you.'

'Is Colonsay your home?'

'I live here.'

'Yes, but who are you? Are you a Cunningham?'

Zephyr gave a gasp which sounded like a laugh. 'I'm walking away, leaving you behind.'

Rosamund couldn't help it. 'How do you know that song?' she burst out. 'How *can* you know it?'

Gary reached over and caught her hand in his, squeezing it tightly. But Zephyr was already speaking again, her words bumping into each other in their effort to get out.

'Blood . . . there was blood. Blood on the floor and the rug, blood on my hand . . . The smell of blood in my hair stayed and stayed, though I washed and washed . . .' Zephyr's breathing quickened. She opened her eyes, staring straight at Rosamund. They were so dark it was like looking into two tunnels in her face. 'Never meant,' she whispered. 'Never meant . . .'

'Who is this?' Gary repeated patiently. 'Who are we speaking to?'

'Forgive . . .'

Zephyr closed her eyes, her head falling back onto the leather chair, her mouth slightly open. She took her time, slowing her breathing, blinking like an owl in torchlight. Whatever had been inside her, for a time, was gone.

'Who was it?' Kerry whispered.

Zephyr seemed tired but she managed a smile. 'I sensed she was female. Not old. She is very distressed. I think some unfinished business is keeping her here at Colonsay.' She looked at Rosamund. 'Did any of it make sense to you?'

'Only the song, my song. How could she know that?'

Gary answered her. 'Sometimes they pick up information from whoever's present. Mind-reading, if you like.'

Rosamund tried to take this in.

'A pity the rest of it didn't make sense to you,' Zephyr said wearily. 'You might find it will eventually. You just haven't found the right lock yet, in which to fit the key.'

That was easy to say. A shiver was still running up and down Rosamund's spine. Forgive? Did that mean forgive *her*?

Zephyr was speaking to Kerry now, and Rosamund tried to concentrate. 'Gary has a very strong gift but he finds it difficult to control it. At the moment he's rather like a sponge, soaking up all the emotions trapped in this house, but with time he could learn to shield himself. Filter out what he wants to know and let the rest pass him by.' She gave Gary a sympathetic and, Rosamund thought, rather disappointed smile. 'Unfortunately, I don't think he enjoys making contact with the spirit world. Do you, Gary?'

'No, Zephyr. If you're looking for an apprentice, count me out.'

They had tea and cake, and the colour began to return to Zephyr's face. It struck Rosamund that Zephyr looked just like she felt after her own encounters with the spirit world. As Zephyr was leaving, she paused at the front door to take Rosamund's hand. Her fingers were cool and strong, and sent a tingle of shock up Rosamund's arm.

'Don't concern yourself with the man who is coming to see you,' she said firmly. 'He can't harm you. You're already too strong for him.' And before Rosamund could answer, she had gone, hurrying back through the rain to Gary's car.

Gary hesitated. 'I'll be back later,' he said. 'Will you be okay?'

'I think so. I'm beginning to think I can handle anything. Not bad for a failed wife.' Tears stung her eyes and she felt suddenly vulnerable.

Gary looked at her intently. 'You're not a failure, Rose. You're the most courageous woman I know.' He bent and kissed her lips, very gently, and then turned and followed Zephyr.

'We have time for a quick lunch before your visitor,' Kerry called from the kitchen.

'Better make it a hearty one,' said Rosamund, and closed the door.

****

Colonsay was dark. Alice had been sitting on the attic steps for a long time, hoping that Bertie might come. He hadn't. She longed to speak with him but he didn't make the effort to speak to her. Not properly. He'd withdrawn from her, tucked all that made him special into a tiny box inside him, and it was closed tight.

Someone in the nursery was crying, a loud, gasping cry that could only be Ada.

'Stomach-ache from all those humbugs,' Alice muttered to herself.

Ada had been in disgrace this afternoon, sent to her room by her father for sneaking away from lessons and then nearly being kicked by a horse in the stables. Ambrosine had come running in from her ride, wild-eyed and dishevelled, gripping Ada's hand tightly in her own gloved one. There was blood on the child's knee, but it was from her fall to the ground, the fall which had saved her from the horse's sharp hooves. Her mother's distress had not saved Ada from her father's anger and, as she passed Alice in the hall, her small pale face was bowed and her lower lip stuck out. She hadn't even taken the opportunity to say something nasty to Alice, or pinch her, as she usually did.

Now Alice could hear the murmur of the nursemaid, and gradually Ada's sobs quietened. The clock downstairs struck the hour. One o'clock. Bertie would not come now. With a sigh, Alice rose and stretched, her body stiff from the cold. She had found a shell two weeks ago on a trip to Portarlington with her parents. She had kept it to ask Bertie what it was. It would be an excuse to speak with him. These days, it seemed, she needed an excuse.

Alice slipped into the east wing and paused, listening. Nothing. Ambrosine was not about tonight, but then Mr Marling was away in Melbourne, so she would have no reason to be creeping about the house in the dark, would she? Alice continued on her way to the head of the stairs.

She had an extra blanket on her bed tonight. Mrs Gibbons had expressed concern that these cold nights must turn Alice and Meggy's little room into an ice box. She would find two extra blankets for them, she said, her round face pulled into an expression of concern and benevolence.

Meggy had been touched. 'Who'd have thought it? There's good in everyone, isn't there, Alice?'

CHAPTER 14

Graham Peel-Johnson arrived slightly after one o'clock. He was much as he had sounded on the phone, neat and well pressed with thinning fair hair. He carried a brown leather briefcase. Rosamund led the way into the library, trying not to remember what had so recently taken place in there, and offered him tea or coffee.

'Thank you. Tea would be fine.'

Rosamund went out to fetch it, leaving him alone. She wondered if the ghost girl was watching him and thought it would serve him right if she gave him a fright, but when she returned with a tray Graham Peel-Johnson seemed just as calm and businesslike as before.

'You're very kind,' he said when he saw Kerry's efforts. As well as tea, the tray held a plate of sandwiches and a newly baked carrot cake.

'You said on the phone that you spoke with my husband late last night?'

He nodded, hastily swallowing a ham and mustard sandwich, and reached for his briefcase. 'Yes. I'm sorry to put you to the inconvenience.'

'And Mark couldn't tell me himself?' Of course he couldn't, he was far too busy.

'You should take that up with Mr Markovic.'

Rosamund nodded as if she intended to, and waited.

Peel-Johnson removed some papers from his briefcase, smearing them with mustard. He clicked his tongue and dabbed at the mark with his spotless handkerchief while Rosamund pretended not to notice.

'You and Mr Markovic didn't have any documents drawn up before you got married, is that right, Mrs Markovic? I mean, of course, a prenuptial agreement.'

Stunned, for a moment Rosamund couldn't think of anything to say. 'No.' She cleared her throat. 'Prenuptial agreements weren't the fashion in those days. But I doubt we would have, even if they were.'

'Well, of course, we're all optimistic when we marry, aren't we?' His look was a combination of the sympathetic and the humorous.

Rosamund leaned forward. 'I don't quite understand what this is about. Do you mean to tell me that Mark wants a prenuptial agreement? Now? Isn't it a little late?'

'Well, something similar. He feels rather vulnerable in his present position. Mr Markovic wants to clarify that position in the unfortunate event that you, or he, should decide to bring your relationship to a mutually acceptable conclusion.'

Was that a roundabout way of saying divorce? Rosamund mulled over what she had just heard. Her heart felt numb, but her mind was working remarkably well.

'He wants me to make promises in the event of our divorce,' she said evenly. 'Well, I won't.'

'Mrs Markovic—'

'That's enough. I want you to leave.'

'Please, at least read what I've drawn up. You will find it very fair. Indeed, Mr Markovic has been more than fair.'

'And Colonsay, what about that?'

His eyes, a warm sherry colour, gazed earnestly into Rosamund's. She felt the urge to trust him but resisted. 'Mrs Markovic, you can't deny that your husband is paying a substantial amount of money to have the house restored to its original glory, and that maintenance will be an ongoing, and costly, expense?'

'I don't deny that, no.' Rosamund was pleased to see he was slightly taken aback. What had he expected? Tears and pleas? The ranting of a mad woman? God knows what Mark had told him about her.

'If necessary, I am prepared to pay him back every cent,' she went on. 'Colonsay would make an excellent up-market guesthouse. Fine surroundings, fine food—I have an excellent cook. An historic weekend away for those bored with skiing and wine-tasting. I could name my price, Mr Peel-Johnson.' She smiled blandly at him.

'I'm not in a position to agree or disagree with that, Mrs Markovic.' His voice was as smooth and calm as ever. 'I am here on behalf of your husband, and he wants your assurance that in the event of a split between you, Colonsay will be handed over to him without any undue ... fuss.'

The breath went out of her. She had expected it, known it, but it was still a shock to hear it said so baldly. Mark was desperate to have Colonsay. So desperate that he would sacrifice her for it. In fact he would sacrifice just about anything.

'No,' she whispered, and heard the quaver in

her voice. She waited a moment, until it was gone. 'No, he can't have Colonsay. As you probably know, Colonsay was left to me in the will of my grandmother.'

'Yes, Mr Markovic mentioned it. A very old woman, wandering, perhaps, in her mind? You ran away from her when you were seventeen, I believe. And you stated a desire not to have the house, and certainly not to reside in it. It seems odd, to say the least, that she would have left the house to you if she had been clear in her mind, Mrs Markovic.'

Rosamund laughed in disbelief. 'Grandma Ada? She was as sharp as two pins. She left it to me because she wanted me to have it. I am the last of the Cunninghams, Mr Peel-Johnson. There are no more. And the family name meant more to her than any grudge she held against me. I think you'd have some difficulty making any court believe Ada would have preferred Colonsay to go to Mark in those circumstances.'

Carefully he smoothed what hair he had left. It gave him time to think. Evidently, Rosamund thought, Mark had not told him everything.

'You wish me to repeat what you have said to your husband?'

'Yes, you do that. Repeat what I've said. And tell him that next time he wants something from me, he should have the guts to come and ask me himself.'

'Mrs Markovic, I know you're upset. These sorts of situations can quickly degenerate into unpleasantness. That was one of the reasons your husband asked me to come.'

'Oh? So he wouldn't have to face the "unpleasantness" himself? Please, just go.'

He gave one longing glance at the plate of sandwiches and returned the papers to his briefcase. 'Very well. I'm sorry this meeting wasn't more productive.'

'I'm sorry you wasted your time.'

'Oh, it wasn't wasted.' He looked at her. 'One step at a time, Mrs Markovic. And today you and your husband have taken the first step in this very delicate matter.'

The first step? The first step to where, to what? To ending it? Rosamund didn't know what to reply. Graham Peel-Johnson had in fact clarified very little. Mark wanted an agreement between them in the event they were to divorce, and yet he had not asked for a divorce. He had sent Peel-Johnson down to test her out on the matter before he made his next move.

How dare Mark send his lackey! There was no excuse for it. And yet, as always, on some level she understood it. Last time he had come himself, and whatever was still between them had got in the way of his intention to rid himself of an unsuitable wife. So this time he had sent someone neutral.

I won't let him have Colonsay, she told herself angrily once Peel-Johnson had left. He can try and destroy me, if that's what he wants, but I'll fight him for this house.

****

'Do you know what sort of shell it is?'

Bertie bent close, turning it in his hand,

studying it with unblinking eyes. 'A type of ear-shell. Where did you find it?'

'On the beach at Portarlington.'

Alice had finally had her chance to produce the shell for Bertie. He had been wandering in the front garden with a book and Alice had been picking flowers for Ambrosine's room—madam had another of her headaches and Cook thought it would cheer her. Their paths had collided, accidentally on Bertie's part, on purpose on Alice's.

'Bertie?' Alice bit her lip as he looked up at her. He was so pale and his smile wasn't his at all. He looked like he expected her to strike him, and not only that. He looked like he wouldn't mind it if she did.

'Will you meet me in the attic tonight? I still go there, sometimes. I like to go there. It'd be fun. I could sneak some food up and we could have a midnight picnic, like we used to.'

He glanced over his shoulder.

'No-one'll know. Please?'

Bertie sighed, so easily coerced. 'All right, Alice.'

A bird darted over them, its dark feathers ruffled by the wind. It fluttered with rapidly moving wings like an arrow in the cloudy sky. Bertie squinted up at it and briefly his face lit up. 'A storm petrel,' he said. 'But it has a dark face instead of the usual white. And the season is wrong. Perhaps it's been blown off course.' Suddenly he looked sad, as if he understood such things very well.

****

Rosamund had slept surprisingly well, despite tangled thoughts of Mark and Graham Peel-Johnson. The noisy ghost had been on holiday somewhere else and the phantom who called for Rosie had also packed up and gone. Kerry met her over breakfast looking almost as she used to. 'Perhaps it's stopped,' she said, ever the optimist, and Rosamund didn't like to spoil it for her.

The day was a sunny one, but cold. The house had a chill about it which resisted any amount of lit fires and warm clothes. Apart from the kitchen. The kitchen was always warm and cosy. No wonder Kerry spent so much of her time in it.

After breakfast, Rosamund took a plate of left-overs into the back garden, near the old cottage. Last night's offering had been licked clean. 'Well, something's eating it,' she declared to Kerry.

Kerry seemed dubious. 'Yes, but how can you be sure it's the dog?' Rosamund sensed that Kerry only half believed there was a dog. But then, she hadn't seen it.

Rosamund retired to the room at the back of the house to continue her delving into the Cunningham past. Her first find was a rusted bugle, but she baulked at placing her mouth on it. There was a thick wad of webs inside, and the thought of breathing in a nice fat spider was enough to curb her enthusiasm for the Last Post.

Why couldn't it have been a Stradivarius? she thought. Then I could pay Mark back and he'd have to call Peel-Johnson off.

A set of encyclopaedias was covered in dust and more spiderwebs. The books were old and out of date, and must have been relegated to the attic after being superseded by the newer set in the library. Thoughts of the library stirred another idea in Rosamund's head. She should sort through the books, catalogue them. Perhaps there were some first editions in there. She had heard of first editions going for a fortune at Sotheby's auctions. Well, time for that when she had finished in here.

A water-sodden cardboard box contained some equally sodden games—Snakes and Ladders, Tiddlywinks . . . Rosamund dragged them as carefully as she could into the junk pile in the hall, pulling a face at the feel of the mushy cardboard.

Back in the room, she made herself comfortable on the red velvet couch and lit a cigarette, tucking her legs up under her, and looked about. She had almost finished. There only remained a couple of piles against the far wall, which contained, among other things, a broken chair, another stack of yellow newspapers and a Victorian glass dome which must once have covered a dried flower arrangement and was now cracked almost in half. After she had sorted that lot she would have to begin work on the other room. And she wasn't looking forward to that at all.

She squashed the butt of her cigarette in the cheap china ashtray she had found amongst the junk. It was decorated with an amateur-looking painting of an impossibly angelic child holding a bucket and spade. Some souvenir from a long-ago holiday, perhaps.

I've let Zephyr frighten me, Rosamund told herself. If I mean to keep Colonsay, to live here permanently, then I have to face whatever there is to face. But there was another voice in her head, faint but persistent, saying, No, that's not true. You know that's not true. Ignoring it, feeling suddenly resolute, Rosamund rose and walked down the hall to stand in front of the warped door.

Shadows had crept into the hall. The sun was lower these days, and this part of the house darker. Rosamund tried to shift her thoughts from foreboding to cheerful. Purposely she glanced about, wondering what could be done to brighten up the place. A pretty lamp, perhaps, and cream-coloured paint on the walls. A large plant or two, with glossy shining leaves, in heavy white ceramic pots. That would be in character, surely? For without really having decided upon it, she knew she meant to decorate and furnish Colonsay in the style of the Federation era. Colonsay's heyday.

Trying not to think about what she was doing, Rosamund closed her hand over the smooth porcelain doorknob and pushed hard. The door opened easily. It took her by surprise and she half fell inside the room. Dank, depressing air poured out over her like oil.

Rosamund choked and instinctively moved to pull the door closed again. Coward! The thought stopped her dead. When did you become such a coward, Rosamund Cunningham? Or have you always been one? Gary had called her courageous. Perhaps it was that memory which supplied the impetus she needed. With forced bravado, Rosamund stepped into the room.

Slowly, she turned her head from side to side. The shadows were deeper in here, the windows where the sheets hung were the colour of wet sand. The walls appeared to be streaked with something—perhaps the rain had got in from upstairs. The bureau seemed larger and more bullying than last time. 'That must be Cosmo's,' she said to herself, and then laughed uneasily, wondering why she should think so. Had Cosmo been such a bully? Was Cosmo the man Zephyr had sensed?

Her voice jarred in the quiet room and she wished she'd stayed silent. Suddenly it was as if there was something sleeping in here, waiting in here. And Rosamund did not want it to wake. She turned to go.

A small, pale object on the bureau caught the stream of light from the doorway. It winked and blinked, beckoning her. 'So this is where you've been hiding,' Rosamund whispered. Her voice echoed, hissing back and forth. She picked her way awkwardly closer and nervously stretched out her arm. With a grunt of satisfaction she closed her fingers tightly over the hard round shape.

The button.

Rosamund edged back from the bureau and pocketed the ivory button, keeping her fist clenched about it. This time she wouldn't let it out of her sight.

She took another look at her surroundings. Her skin felt gritty and she had the urge to sneeze, but apart from that the air seemed to have cleared slightly. Perhaps all this room really needed was for the door to be left open.

And then another smell came drifting into her senses like an afterthought. Sharp. Metallic. It was familiar and yet for a moment she had trouble placing it. The dank odour had almost gone, or perhaps it was just that this new smell had covered it.

Rosamund suddenly felt her heart begin to bump in her chest and her hand was shaking as she reached out to grasp the door jamb. She knew now what that smell was. Blood. And not the small amount she was used to dealing with each month. A great deal of blood. Overwhelming, nauseating ... The streaky shadows on the walls wavered, appearing to run and drip. Rosamund's knees buckled and she pushed hard on the jamb, trying to right herself. Her hand came away with a sticky squelch. Slowly, unbelievingly, Rosamund lifted her hand up to her eyes. The blood on it looked black, thick and gleaming.

She cried out but her voice was tiny compared to the roaring in her head. All her strength had gone and she stumbled and fell to her knees. The shadows were whirling sickeningly around her. Rosamund bowed her head and closed her eyes. The hot, prickly darkness of unconsciousness danced about the edges of her vision, but she fought desperately to hold on. The idea of lying here, defenceless, was even worse than what she was now experiencing.

With excruciating slowness, the moment passed. Like an old crippled woman whose each movement was an effort, Rosamund straightened and opened her eyes. The blood was gone. The room now smelled of nothing but the usual damp, mould and dust, was full of nothing but old junk. Trembling, she raised her hand, spreading her fingers wide. No blood. There never had been. Whatever she had seen was from another time, now long past. It could not hurt her.

The phone began to ring. Her heartbeat, which had just begun to return to normal, picked up again. Rosamund managed to struggle to her feet. Her legs were like overcooked spaghetti, but she took some deep breaths and felt better. She heard Kerry's quick footsteps and then the murmur of her voice.

Rosamund grasped the doorknob and went to

close the door. The base of it dragged against the floor like a soul in torment, but she kept pulling until it was shut.

'Rosamund?' Kerry peered at her down the length of the hall. 'Mr Markovic wants to speak with you.'

Rosamund wiped her palms on her jeans and found they were suddenly remarkably steady. 'No.'

'But—'

'Tell him I don't want to speak to him.'

Kerry opened her mouth again, as if to remonstrate, then thought better of it and turned back to the telephone. The conversation was, Rosamund thought, overly long for such a short message, but eventually Kerry put the receiver down. Rosamund resisted the urge to ask her what he had said.

'He'll ring again tonight.'

'Wonderful.'

Kerry gave up and went back to the kitchen. Rosamund closed her eyes and leaned against the wall. Blood . . . there was blood on my hand. That was what Zephyr's spirit had said. And now, hey-presto, Rosamund was seeing and smelling blood. She wished she could convince herself it was auto-suggestion—the cynic was strong in her—but she was having a hard job of it.

'Help me,' she whispered. 'Whoever you are, help me to understand.'

Was it her imagination, or was there a brief, tantalising whiff of honeysuckle?

It was a cold clear night, the moonlight shone through the diamond-paned windows and across the cluttered attic in distorted strips. Alice and Bertie huddled in their usual place, the stuffed peacock standing guard. Bertie had been looking through his treasure box, turning each object over in his fingers as if it belonged to somebody else. Alice had brought a napkin wrapped about two pieces of fruit cake and a hard slab of toffee she had found in a jar in the pantry. They ate the cake and then broke up the toffee with a blow from an old iron kettle. The noise seemed very loud in the silence but it was mercifully brief. The toffee shattered into pieces and they shared them out, popping several at once into their mouths.

'Do you do this at school?' Alice asked, rearranging her bulging cheek so that she could speak.

Bertie stopped smiling. 'No.'

'I wish—'

'Don't talk about school,' he begged her. 'I want to pretend it doesn't exist.'

Alice, who desperately wanted to know what was wrong, longed to pursue the subject, but the pleading in his short-sighted eyes stopped her. 'All right, Bertie. I won't ask.'

They fell silent, the only sounds the toffee against their teeth and the creaking of the old house.

****

Gary was waiting in the kitchen when Rosamund came downstairs from her bath. She was glad, as he rose from the chair, that she had decided to dress in a black wool skirt and red blouse. The dramatic colours suited her and she had felt the need to look good after the news from Graham Peel-Johnson.

Gary was dressed up, too, in beige slacks and a long-sleeved, blue-checked shirt which accentuated his blue eyes. He looked a bit pale under his tan but, whatever he was feeling about being here at Colonsay, he was inclined to be reticent about it.

'Some days it's worse than others,' he said, in answer to her unspoken question. 'Some days it starts off okay and gets more difficult. It's not too bad tonight.'

'Is it a physical thing?' Rosamund asked curiously. 'I mean, do you feel an actual physical barrier?'

'An invisible brick wall? No. It's not like something actually touching me. More emotional.' He shrugged. 'Intellectual. A sense of overwhelming despair. It covers me like a wave. Have you ever been under a big breaking wave? Gasping for air, wondering if you'll ever reach the surface? I feel anger, too, but the despair is worse. And I think if I stayed here too long I might begin to feel suicidal.'

He laughed offhandedly when he said it, but he was serious. Rosamund was shocked by this revelation. Kerry, too, looked up in sharp surprise. 'You should go,' she said.

'No, it's all right now. I told you, sometimes it's better than others, and just now I can handle it. Don't worry, if I can't I'll get up and run for it. Just stand clear.'

They all laughed uneasily.

'Zephyr seems to think she can help you cope,' Rosamund said at last.

He half smiled. 'She sees me following in her footsteps. I've always seen things, heard things. Felt things. I came to accept it long ago. Though it's never been as bad as it is here at Colonsay. This is a special case.'

'I wish we'd talked about this before.' Rosamund was thoughtful. 'I mean, when we were young.'

'You'd have run a mile, Rose.'

She didn't want to believe it.

'Even now you find it hard to take. Don't you?'

Rosamund shook her head, her throat constricting. 'Have you ever seen blood running down the walls, Gary?'

Kerry and Gary both gaped at her, open-mouthed.

'I'm sorry,' she mumbled. 'I didn't mean to say it like that. But I did see it. Blood. Violence. I think Zephyr was right. Something has happened here. I don't know what. I wish I did.'

Gary nodded slowly. 'Maybe it's time you spoke to Enderby,' he said. 'If there's something to find out, my grandfather will have found it. He's obsessed with the Cunninghams.'

'Will he ... I mean, can he ...?' Rosamund broke off awkwardly.

Gary laughed. 'Yes to both. He can and he will. Enderby still has all his marbles.' He pulled a wry face. 'Sometimes I think he's doing better than me in that department.'

Rosamund didn't answer. Seeing Enderby again would be like seeing Grandma Ada, and it was only desperation that was driving her.

CHAPTER 15

They didn't hear her coming, her bare feet so light on the dusty wood of the floor. They didn't know she was there until she stood in front of them, pale nightgown shining in the moonlight, fair hair twisted in curling-rags about her shoulders. Smiling triumphantly.

'I knew you'd be here,' she said, her voice rising on the last word.

Alice jumped up. 'Miss Ada!'

'Miss Ada,' she mocked, and laughed. 'I saw you sneaking up here, Alice Parkin. Mooning about, looking for Bertie. What would Bertie want with ugly old you? He only comes here 'cause you bring him cake to eat.'

Alice disregarded the hurtful remarks—Ada specialised in being hurtful—she had already seen the little girl eyeing the napkin on the floor by Bertie. 'Do you want some toffee?' she asked. 'You can have some if you don't tell.'

'Take some, Ada, and be quiet,' Bertie broke in impatiently. He was looking at his sister with real dislike. 'They'll break your teeth.'

Ada snatched a hard sliver of toffee from his hand. She licked it thoughtfully, then popped it into her cheek and smiled. 'I'm going to tell anyway,' she announced, and turned for the stairs.

Bertie stood up. 'You'd better not,' he called softly after her, but his anger was tempered by a note of fear.

Ada heard it and seized upon it. She hovered in the shadows, her voluminous white nightgown and fair hair making her look angelic. 'Will so,' she hissed. 'I know lots of secrets, Bertie, so there. Secrets so bad they hurt my heart. I can't tell, because Mama says ... Mama says ...' But she bit her lip on whatever Ambrosine had said, and tears shone in her eyes from the effort of her silence. 'I hope Father hits you hard,' she managed at last in a choked and angry little voice. 'Alice is a servant, she can't be your friend. We Cunninghams are far too good for her.'

'You horrid little snob!' Bertie gasped, but his sister was already gone, silent as she had come.

Alice watched him, holding her breath, pain and anger twisting inside her stomach until it felt like she had eaten too many green plums. Slowly Bertie wiped his hands on the empty napkin, slipping it into his pocket.

'She doesn't mean it,' he said, but he sounded weak, ineffectual. 'She's only saying it to frighten us.'

'What will your father do?' Alice asked breathlessly. She didn't believe him for a moment.

'Send me back to school early, I expect.' His voice was hollow.

'It was my fault. I'll say it was my fault. I'll make them listen to me, Bertie. I'll make them.'

He smiled kindly but she could see he didn't believe her. He saw his fate before him and accepted it without a struggle. Bertie was not the sort to fight. Well, Alice would fight for him. She felt the power swell within her. In her way, she was like Ada. She had secrets and she had kept them safe. Now she would use them to get what she wanted.

****

It was the silence that woke Rosamund. Not a sound stirred outside or inside. She lay staring into the dark, wondering if the attic was about to erupt. Perhaps, if the noise they had been plagued with since she arrived was a form of attention-seeking, then it had served its purpose.

Gary had left early and, it seemed to Rosamund, regretfully. She had wanted to tell him about the visit from Mark's solicitor, but the right moment hadn't presented itself. She could talk to him when they went together to see Enderby. Maybe Gary would have some ideas on what she could do to fight Mark's attempt to wrest Colonsay from her.

Rosamund turned over and stared at the lighter shape of the windows behind the curtains. She felt wide awake. After a moment she rose and, shivering, pulled on some clothes.

At the far end of the corridor, the stained-glass window glowed softly. Rosamund remembered that Frederick was supposed to have arranged for it to be taken away and repaired. She supposed she should follow that up, though how she was to pay if Mark decided to withdraw financial support was anyone's guess.

The stairs creaked as Rosamund descended them. In the library the open fire still glowed with red coals. It took her a few minutes to stir it back to life, adding bits and pieces of wood until the flames crackled greedily. She sat for a time and held her hands towards it, warming her cold fingers, before turning to Ada's box of papers.

Rosamund knew she had been neglecting the box, when it possibly contained more of the secrets she needed to unlock if she was to sort out the puzzle of Colonsay. She settled herself into a more comfortable position, back resting against the soft leather arm of one of the chairs, legs curled beneath her. She put aside the photo album, appointment book and the various papers she had already looked through. A bundle of letters, bound tightly together with rough string, caught her eye. It took her several moments to unpick the knot.

A couple of the letters, dated in the 1950s, were from Rosamund's father, asking obliquely if Ada was able to lend him some money. Going by the return addresses, he was travelling. There was another note from her father from the time he'd been in the war. He was joking about the food the army served up and sounding like an over-excited schoolboy. Rosamund found his excitement rather poignant.

Next she picked up a rather grubby sheet of unlined paper dated 2nd April 1920, from a place called Tinyutin. 'Dear Miss Ada,' it began, 'Do you remember me?'

> *I ask 'cause I will always remember you and your family. Things have been hard. You always said you hoped I'd starve but I don't think you meant it. I could have made a few bob by going to one of them Bolshie newspapers, but I never did. Not that I didn't need the money, but I knew Jonah wouldn't have*

liked it. He wouldn't have liked me asking for help from you, either, but as I said things have been hard. You know where he is, don't you? Of course you do. You know everything.'

The letter rambled on for another couple of lines, diverging incongruously to the state of the weather and the crops currently being grown up on the Murray. It was signed 'Meggy', in a childlike hand.

Rosamund read it again. It was the 'Miss Ada' that teased at her mind. Surely only someone who had known Ada before her marriage would call her Miss. It was an old-fashioned way of addressing someone, a servant's respectful title for a young mistress. Was Meggy a former Colonsay servant?

Perhaps Enderby would know.

The bit about hoping Meggy would starve sounded uncomfortably like Ada. She had had no time for the poor and unfortunate. The rest was beyond Rosamund's comprehension. How could Meggy have made money from the 'Bolshie' newspapers? Was there something she could tell them, that they would pay her for? Some government plot afoot? Some secret of Ada's that was a possible blackmail tool? And what had prevented her from telling, apart from Jonah's squeamishness? Then there was the assertion that Ada knew where the person called Jonah was. None of it made sense.

Rosamund yawned. She was tired now. She could sleep. She repacked the box, set the safety screen across the hearth and returned to her bed. Just as she was dozing off, another unanswerable question popped into her head.

Who was Jonah?

Enderby Munro lived in a nursing home at Queenscliff, a small town across the Bellarine Peninsula from Colonsay. In the 1880s its proximity to the Rip, the entrance to Port Phillip Bay, had made it a strategic position in the event of a Russian invasion, and a fort had been built on the foreshore. Cosmo had been among the volunteers who drilled there and it was this period in his life which had strengthened his resolve to make Australia a single nation, with a single defence force.

Queenscliff had a number of beautiful old hotels, leftovers from a Victorian boom time when visits to the seaside were *de rigueur*. There was still a ferry terminus but these days the ferries that docked there were sleek and modern, not the steam-powered vessels of Cosmo's time.

The nursing home was expensive, Gary said, but Enderby could afford it. 'He's been there nearly ten years. Sometimes I think he runs the place, the way he orders the staff around. They're kind enough to let him believe it, anyway.'

It was lightly raining. From the comfort of the car Rosamund watched a few tourists, huddled in their parkas and boots outside the shop fronts. The locals had more sense.

Neither Rosamund nor Gary had said much during the journey. Gary seemed full of his own thoughts, and Rosamund kept remembering Graham Peel-Johnson's words to her. If Mark took Colonsay, what would she have left?

Gary turned the car into a quiet street and drew up before a large, verandahed house with a pastel noticeboard out the front. WATERSIDE HOME, it said.

Gary was watching her. 'Are you all right?'

She didn't meet his eyes. 'Mark sent someone to

see me yesterday. A solicitor. He wants me to sign an agreement.'

'What sort of agreement?'

'A precursor to divorce. To protect his assets.'

Gary laughed in disbelief. 'Is that legal?'

'I don't know. He wants Colonsay.'

'Will you let him have it?'

Now she did look at him. 'What do you think?'

He grinned. 'Yeah, well . . . I wondered if you might think yourself well rid of it, after what's happened.'

She shook her head slowly. 'No, I don't feel like that at all. And it's not just that I've nowhere else to go. I feel like I'm changing, Gary. You don't know what my life's been like these past years with Mark. I've felt as if I were a nothing person. Colonsay has given me a purpose—I'm alive again.'

'Then you have to fight him. Stop him. I'll help you.'

She turned to him. 'Will you? Really?'

'You know I will, Rose.' He touched her shoulder. 'Now come on. Forget about Mark. Let's see what Enderby has to say.'

The nurse who opened the door to them directed them into the sun room, a glassed-in area which had once been a side verandah and was designed to hoard the warmth in winter. But today the only warmth was blasting out from a central heater. The occupants sat about in deck-chairs, as if they were voyagers on an ocean liner.

An old lady with carefully permed hair nodded at them as they passed. 'Pity about the weather,' she said. 'Still, must make the most of it, I suppose.'

As if, thought Rosamund, she were on holiday rather than a patient.

Enderby was closest to the window, his chair placed in a space between the glass and a large fern. He was wearing a green sweater and his back was permanently hunched over, so that when he peered up at them, a green frond brushing his shoulder, he reminded Rosamund of a black-eyed caterpillar.

She felt her nerve ends quiver. Enderby may be more wrinkled and stooped, but she would have known those bright button eyes anywhere. They stared unwinking out of his aged face as she and Gary approached.

'Rosie!' he cried, and smiled, showing surprisingly big white false teeth.

'Enderby.' She bent and kissed his cheek.

'Gary.' The black eyes creased up to nothing at the sight of his grandson.

'You're looking in top shape,' Gary said, and pulled two chairs up, arranging them in front of the old man. Outside the window pane, the rain trickled drearily onto a lush green garden.

'Can't complain,' replied Enderby. Pleasantries over, he turned his attention back to Rosamund. 'You're very like your grandmother, Rosie. Same mouth, same eyes. Hair's different, of course. Beautiful woman, Ada, in her younger days. Pity she never went anywhere or did anything. All wasted.' He shook his head.

'She didn't seem to think so,' Rosamund replied carefully. 'Colonsay, and the Cunninghams, were her entire life.'

'And you,' Enderby corrected her.

'I came a very distant third.'

'She was very fond of you, Rosie. Did her best for you. I don't say her best was all that good—she was never a motherly sort of woman, and she'd suffered herself. She was damaged, isn't that what they say these days? A bit unlikely she could turn around and become the perfect grandmother. And you were a difficult child to love, little Rosie. Sullen and secretive. Sometimes I think you frightened her.'

It sounded as if he were discussing someone else. Rosamund tried to put herself into the shoes of this allegedly sullen and secretive child, and couldn't. It was too long ago, and she had changed.

'Did you know about the voices I heard when I was a child?' she asked suddenly.

The black eyes didn't even flicker. 'I don't believe in that rot, so it's no use asking me.'

One goal to Enderby, Rosamund nil.

'She didn't die of the flu, you know,' he told her.

'Oh?' She didn't have a clue what he was talking about, and put on a fake smile.

'Ambrosine,' Gary murmured helpfully in her ear.

'It was all hushed up, of course,' Enderby went on. 'Had to be. Important man like that, a national hero. He had plenty of important friends, too, willing to see his name was kept spotless. The truth never leaked out. Ada knew. That was part of what kept her there at Colonsay, that secret. She was bound to Colonsay and it was bound to her.'

Rosamund leaned closer. 'I don't understand,' she said plaintively. 'What was hushed up?'

Enderby gave her his big white smile. 'Gary knows, don't you, Gary?'

Gary gave him a sideways glance. 'I know what you say about it, but I never really believed—'

'Never wanted to, you mean. Tell her.' His voice grew louder. 'Go on, tell her!'

Several of the other residents glared at Enderby but he ignored them. If he had been capable of jumping up and down in his chair with excitement, he would have done it now. As it was, he was twitching all over.

Gary sighed and gave Rosamund an apologetic look. 'Enderby believes Cosmo murdered Ambrosine and then killed himself. A murder-suicide.'

Rosamund didn't know whether to laugh or cry. To have built her hopes up so much, and then this! A ludicrously contrived piece of nonsense.

'It's true,' Enderby said mildly. He was watching her closely, his black eyes gleaming. 'It was all hushed up. Just imagine what it would have done to the Cunningham name, a scandal like that. Your grandmother never disputed the reasons for the cover-up. Anything to keep the family name out of the muck.'

'But how could Grandma Ada know such a thing?' Rosamund asked in angry disbelief. 'She was only a child when her parents died.'

Enderby hunched down even further. 'She was there. She was only a child, but she was there. Children see and hear more than adults realise. It wasn't something Ada was likely to forget, her father murdering her mother and then him killing himself. She was suddenly an orphan, alone, thrust into the care of near-strangers. No, it wasn't something Ada was ever likely to forget.'

He waited while Rosamund took that in before continuing. 'She went through a stage where she wanted the propaganda to be true. The lies were kinder. A love story, tragic but inspiring. Better than the truth. I think she hoped that as a child she had somehow been mistaken, misunderstood. She asked me to look into the matter for her—she knew she could trust me. I searched about, asked some people I knew. I found out enough to be able to confirm her memories.'

Enderby looked briefly sad. 'I could have pretended otherwise, I suppose. Eased her mind. But Ada wouldn't have wanted that. She was strong enough to face the truth and that was what I gave her. Stark and unadorned. And that's what I have given you, Rosie. Are you in the same mould as your grandmother? Or are you one of these weak young women who can't face anything the slightest bit unpleasant?'

Rosamund waved away the last bit. 'But the story's famous! Ambrosine died of influenza in her husband's arms and then Cosmo sailed to his own death. Everyone knows it.'

Enderby gave her a look that was almost pitying. 'Exactly.'

'I can't believe this,' Rosamund repeated, shaking her head. 'It's so ... so monstrous. Enderby, do you know what you're saying? Can you prove any of this?'

'Of course.' He gave his grandson an amused glance. 'Go and get my scrapbook from my room. Book number two.'

Gary got obediently to his feet.

'How many scrapbooks are there?' Rosamund asked, trying for a sense of normality. Her world was teetering dangerously around her.

'Fifteen, at last count. Of course, your husband's filled a few pages lately, although he's not a real Cunningham, is he? Only married to one.'

She didn't like the speculative look in his eyes and made no reply. The state of her marriage was none of Enderby's business.

'I don't understand,' she said, more to herself

than him. 'If there's any truth in what you say, how could such a thing be kept secret for so long?'

'Why not? How many people were there to bribe? Ada was a child, so she didn't count. Children were seen and not heard in those days. The servants? They could be paid off and moved away, and if they talked later on, who would listen to them? Anyway, they were probably too shocked to talk, and too frightened. It was a matter of national importance, and in those days people did what they were told. They didn't gossip to the first journalist who came along.'

Rosamund looked at him sharply. 'Would the Bolsheviks have been interested? Later on, I mean. 1920 or so.'

Enderby gave a cackling laugh. 'What do you think?'

Gary was weaving his way through the deckchairs towards her. He gave her a questioning look as he sat down. 'Here we are. Number two.'

Enderby took the bulging scrapbook. It was actually a binder, full of plastic envelopes. When Enderby opened the cover, Rosamund saw that the envelopes contained newspaper cuttings, photocopies and letters, and in one a moth-eaten invitation to a celebratory dinner at Colonsay. It was Enderby's own record of the Cunningham family.

Enderby turned the pages awkwardly, his fingers stiff with arthritis. Progress was slow but no-one spoke. About halfway through he stopped and read something silently and very carefully, before a smile spread across his face. He turned the binder around towards Rosamund.

'What do you make of this?'

The letter was imprinted with a Federal Government letterhead and the signature at the bottom was well known to Rosamund, an important name from politics in the 1950s.

It said that the details Enderby was requesting on behalf of Ada had been sealed as top secret and were not to be opened until 2050. Even Ada Cunningham, daughter of Cosmo, was denied access.

'It could mean anything,' Rosamund said stubbornly. 'A matter of national security ... some deal Cosmo was involved in ... or ... or ... talks with a foreign government. How can you use this as proof?'

But at the same time as she was protesting so vigorously, her stomach was churning. Flashes of memory and disjointed sentences popped into her mind. The blood in the back room, Zephyr speaking of violence, the spirit talking through her. And the letter she had read last night, from the mysterious Meggy.

'I agree,' said Gary, handing back the Federal Government letter. 'It's far too vague for us to know what's being discussed. Could be a new septic system.'

'Don't be fatuous,' Enderby growled.

'And why would Cosmo murder his wife?' Gary went on. 'She was the light of his life, wasn't she? Beautiful and elegant. Why would he kill her and then himself? Are you trying to tell us he was mentally deranged all the time he was helping to draw up the Constitution? Is that why it was hushed up, because people would believe the Federation had been inspired by a homicidal maniac?'

Enderby looked impressed. 'Yes, I imagine so. The scandal could have destabilised the government, and it was a very new government, only months old, remember. You were wasted on that newspaper, boy.'

Gary flushed. 'You haven't answered the first question,' he said in annoyance.

'Haven't I? What was it? Oh, yes, why did Cosmo kill his wife? The usual reasons, I imagine. She was having an affair.'

It was possible. Ambrosine, young and beautiful, and Cosmo, the adoring older husband. The jealous older husband. He discovers she's been unfaithful, and wallop . . . Rosamund shuddered.

'I'm actually starting to believe it,' she said shakily.

'Enderby has that effect,' was Gary's grim reply.

The old man snatched the scrapbook back and closed it with a snap. 'It's true. Believe it. I worked for the government and I've heard things. I know people and they've spoken to me, though they wouldn't put anything in writing. But I am satisfied in my own mind that what I've told you is the truth. Your grandmother spoke to me, she trusted me. I was the only one she did trust. As the last of the Cunninghams, I think you also have a right to know the truth.'

Rosamund took a deep breath. 'Look, I'll need to think about all this.'

Gary stood up. 'We'd better go.' He gave Enderby a mock-stern look. 'My grandfather needs his rest.'

Enderby chuckled. 'Euchre this afternoon,' he announced. 'Yesterday I won five dollars from Mrs Bowen. She has Alzheimer's. Keeps forgetting what's trumps.'

God, he's a monster, thought Rosamund.

Enderby peered up at her intently as she said her goodbyes. 'You might like to take a look at the portrait of Ambrosine in the National Gallery,' he said. 'You won't understand anything until you've seen that.'

'I have photographs of her—'

'Photographs!' was his scathing reply. 'Take a look at the portrait. It's by Henry Marling, important man in those days. You'll understand then, Rosie.'

They found their way back to the front door. A television was on in one of the other rooms, blaring out the theme tune of a well-known daytime soapie. Gary took her arm as they walked down the path, its cement darkened by rain. The soft droplets felt refreshing against Rosamund's skin, and like a child she lifted her face to the sky and stuck out her tongue.

Gary laughed. 'Is that the effect Enderby has on you?'

Rosamund smiled but more serious matters prevented her from joking along with him. 'Did you really know about this? Why didn't you tell me?'

He shifted his shoulders uncomfortably. 'Enderby had mentioned it, but I couldn't bring myself to believe it. I didn't want to believe it. You know how I felt about Colonsay. And anyway, after all that's happened there, I didn't want to fill your head with wild stories which may not be true. You needed to hear them for yourself.'

'What was Enderby in the government? I've never seen his name mentioned in the history books.'

'I don't know exactly. He's dropped hints that he was some sort of top-security man. He says he's still bound by an oath of secrecy.'

'What, ASIO? Come on. Enderby?'

'Well, maybe an early form of it.'

They exchanged uneasy laughter.

'You're a journalist,' Rosamund continued when they reached the car. 'If you were still working for a newspaper, would you follow up on this story?'

Gary had unlocked the car and they climbed in. He didn't answer until he had turned on the heater full blast. 'I'd check it out. I have a few government contacts, too. Yes, I'd follow it.'

Rosamund let out her breath on a long sigh. 'Then that's what we'd better do.'

****

Alice stood outside the door of the library. Inside, she could hear the rhythmic, sickening *womp* of a belt against unprotected flesh. With each blow her skin crawled and her breath grew shakier in her throat. She wasn't afraid for herself; she had been beaten before. She was afraid for Bertie and what would happen to him now.

The door opened and Cosmo filled the space. His flushed, angry face was made brighter by his grey hair, his eyes gleamed like swords. Bertie crept past him, head bowed, but Alice could see the dirty streaks where the tears had run. He didn't glance at her as he passed by; he seemed to have shrunk even further inside himself.

'Tomorrow you will return to school,' Cosmo's voice boomed down the hallway. 'And there you will stay until Christmas.'

Alice had meant to speak up, to beg Cosmo, to

take the blame. But her fear betrayed her. It was as if her throat had closed over, preventing the escape of even the smallest sound.

'Alice!'

She stepped into the room at his command and the door closed behind her. Ambrosine was seated on one of the leather chairs by the hearth, her face a white oval, her eyes teary and wild. Her long-fingered hands twisted on her lap as if she were trying to tie them into knots.

Alice took her eyes from Ambrosine and lifted them to Cosmo. He was staring down at her like an eagle at its prey, and yet—was there a glimmer of humour there?

'What were you thinking of, making assignations with my son?'

Assignations were things lovers had, Alice thought, her mind disputing instantly what was in his. We are friends, that's all. But again her fear betrayed her, and she remained silent.

'Bertie is a Cunningham and must learn to behave like one. Cunninghams do not consort with servants in the attic, Alice. Do they?'

She shook her head.

Cosmo walked to the hearth, his hands behind his back. His profile appeared very dramatic against the dark wood of the mantel, the veteran's sword on the wall to one side giving him a martial air. Ambrosine looked up and her eyes met Alice's. The girl saw the woman swallow, as though the same obstruction that blocked Alice's throat also choked hers.

'Cosmo, I'm sure Alice did not know—'

Cosmo glanced down at her, and whatever it was she saw in his face brought her to a halt. 'You've turned Bertie into a milksop,' he said softly, dangerously. 'Don't defend him now, for God's sake.'

'I'm not defending him, I . . . Alice is a good girl, a good servant. I don't believe there was anything about their meeting that should cause you concern, Cosmo. Ada is a child, and sometimes children misunderstand these matters.'

Her hands were shaking as she grasped them rigidly in her lap. Alice told herself that Ambrosine was only defending her because she felt she had no choice. She thought that Alice would tell, if she did not.

'A good girl, is she?' Cosmo reached out and caught Alice's chin in his hand, pulling her head up so that he could peer down into her face. Her neck was stretched out so far it ached, but Alice did not make a sound.

'Yes, I see she is a good girl. But she is not to play bloody milksop games with my son in the attic! He'll never be a man while he refuses to do manly things.' He released Alice and, thankfully, she bowed her head again. 'Alice, I won't dismiss you. I owe your father too much. But I will order you not to speak to my son again.'

'Yes, sir.' Even as she accepted it, she was denying it. She would not fail Bertie, not if it cost her everything she had.

Ambrosine said nothing, staring at her hands and biting her lip. She was worse than useless. People such as Ambrosine were like dumb beasts, and needed to be driven to do as they ought. Well, Alice had the means to drive her.

CHAPTER 16

Rosamund sipped her tea and began to unpack Ada's box of papers. She had set up on the library table as soon as she returned from seeing Enderby. Gary had dropped her off at the front door of Colonsay, after extracting a promise from her that she would come out with him that night for a meal.

'If Kerry doesn't mind,' she added, as a qualifier.

Kerry hadn't minded. In fact she was taking the opportunity to visit her sister in Geelong. Relieved by this news, Rosamund was able to genuinely look forward to her evening out.

'You need some fun,' Kerry announced, her face carefully blank.

'Fun?'

'I mean, to take your mind off things.'

'Yes, I suppose I do.'

'Mr Markovic rang again.' The way she said it made Rosamund wonder just what Mark had said to her. There was a repressive quality to her voice that had never been there before when Kerry spoke of Mark. What had he done to cause this topple from his Godlike throne?

'Did you tell him I was out?'

'Yes. He wants you to ring him. He says he needs to talk to you urgently.'

Rosamund's smile was grim. 'I can imagine. Well, you may as well know, Kerry, I have no intention of speaking to him. He wants to take Colonsay from me. He sees himself living here as a sort of 21st-century Cosmo Cunningham. I'll turn the place into a brothel before I let that happen.'

Kerry gave a surprised laugh. 'You'd better not say that to Frederick Swann. He may never come back.'

Rosamund blinked at her. Was Kerry on her side, after all? A sense of warm gratitude filled her. She had never had many people on her side. Her 'friends' were mainly faces from the old days, or just new acquaintances. No-one to rely on, no-one to trust. This felt nice, very nice.

'Thank you,' she said with sincerity.

Kerry looked uncomfortable and went on folding the towels. The moment passed.

'Do you know it was Mark who told me a brothel was a good investment?'

'Indeed!' Kerry folded more vigorously.

Time to change the subject. 'Has that dog turned up?' Rosamund asked neutrally.

'The food was gone again this morning, but I haven't seen anything eating it.'

'We're probably feeding the local rat population,' Rosamund said. She hesitated—she was longing to ask Kerry if she knew anything about the murder-suicide. Well, no point in beating about the bush.

'Did my grandmother ever mention anything about a murder at Colonsay?'

Kerry's eyes widened. 'Goodness, no. A murder at Colonsay? Whoever told you that?' Her eyes narrowed again. 'Not that Enderby Munro? Oh,

Rosamund, I've heard he's gone very strange in the last few years. I wouldn't listen to what he tells you.'

'I wish I didn't have to,' Rosamund sighed.

She had taken a cup of tea into the library, prepared to spend what was left of the day exploring Ada's papers in the light of Enderby's revelations. She was still inclined to treat the whole thing as a lunatic's ramblings, as Kerry suggested, but maybe that was just wishful thinking. Rosamund knew she must follow up what Enderby had said, however unpalatable it might be.

The photographs seemed suddenly much more poignant. Ambrosine, elegant in her fashionable Edwardian clothing—had she really died so violent a death?—and Cosmo, chin pushed out pugnaciously as he smiled. Was he a murderer? How had he done it? She hadn't asked Enderby. Did he shoot her or stab her? Or in the heat of the moment use his fists to beat her to death? Rosamund shut the album with a slam. Her hands shaking, she swallowed the rest of her tea.

Her eye caught sight of the red appointment book and she picked it up to read again. Her skin crawled. 'She says she hears voices and "the lady" screaming . . . the thought of that tragedy being played out in this house again and again, without me being aware of it, is almost too much even for me to bear . . . she thinks someone is calling her name. I know differently. No need to have the past dug up like a spade of soil, full of twisting worms and half-rotted things.'

So easy, thought Rosamund, to twist those words to support Enderby's theory.

In this new light the letter from Meggy also became more sinister, with its references to things remembered and hints of stories untold. There was also something about it that Rosamund hadn't noticed before. Meggy had written to Ada as a servant writes to her mistress, but there was a quiet menace beneath the self-effaciveness.

There was little else of immediate interest. A couple of bills for long-discarded items of clothing, and a letter from the Historical Society about a remembrance service fifty years after Cosmo's death. A prayer book with the favourite passages marked in purple ink. A receipt for a pair of hand-sewn men's brown leather riding-boots, ten guineas, made out to Mrs Ambrosine Cunningham and dated December 1900.

Rosamund smiled as she smoothed it out. A Christmas present for Cosmo? Maybe they were the boots he was wearing as he rode away from Colonsay after beating his wife to death ... Hastily, she put it to one side, and picked up the last item in the box. It was a birthday card which Rosamund herself had made out of pink cardboard and pressed flowers. 'To Grandma Ada, Happiest birthday. Love Rosamund'.

A little jolt of feeling caught her unawares. A vague sense of pleasure. It hadn't been all misery then, her childhood at Colonsay. There had been some good moments. Rosamund sat on in the growing darkness, lost in the past, until she remembered the time and ran upstairs to get ready.

Gary took her to one of the local hotels. Rosamund, in dark slacks and a midnight-blue satin blouse, her hair washed and glossy and pinned up, felt slightly overdressed, but Gary's smile told her otherwise. The room was full of smoke and noise, but Gary managed to find them a table in a corner, a little away from the crowd. They ordered steak, and it came quickly. It was big enough to cover all but a tiny segment of the plate, and that was crammed with fried chips and salad.

'There goes my cholesterol-free diet,' Rosamund said.

Most of the crowd in the bar seemed to know Gary, and several of them had stopped him with good-natured chat. He had side-stepped them, refusing to be drawn into any long conversations. Rosamund realised, with a feeling of pleased confusion, that it was because he wanted to spend the time exclusively with her.

Tonight he was wearing jeans, a white shirt with a jacket over the top. Rosamund reaffirmed to herself what an attractive man he was, his face full of good humour. He was so different from the Gary she remembered from her childhood that she found it hard to believe they were the same person. He could almost be classed as a local. Unlike her. Rosamund, though brought up here, had never been a local. She had kept her distance, partly through her own inclination and partly through Ada's. If the murder story was true, it might have been more than snobbery that had given Ada her taste for isolation.

'Food okay?'

Rosamund looked up and smiled, making a conscious effort to set aside her grim thoughts. 'Yes, thank you.'

'I was thinking I might go up to Melbourne tomorrow. Frederick's not working on Colonsay and he doesn't need me on the other job. It would be a good opportunity to approach some of my old contacts, get the answers to a few questions.'

'Can I come? I'd like to see the portrait your grandfather mentioned.'

Gary was watching her over his fork. 'The Marling?'

'Yes. I found a clipping on Henry Marling among some of the Cunningham junk. I couldn't see the connection then. I suppose he must have come down here to Colonsay to paint Ambrosine.'

'I suppose he must have.'

The black and white photograph of the handsome man with the moustache popped into Rosamund's head. She made a mental note to find out more about Henry Marling.

'Rosamund?'

'I'm all right. I'm just finding it difficult to accept that anything so horrible could have happened at Colonsay and I never knew about it.'

'But you might have known about it. What about the voices, when you were very young?'

'So, you think what Enderby said is true? You do accept it, Gary?'

He smiled without humour. 'I think I knew it all along. An event like that would leave a big wave of emotion behind, don't you think? Pain and fear, anger and despair. It'd explain what I feel every time I walk into Colonsay.'

'Do you believe that's it? That everything we've experienced at Colonsay has been tied up with the deaths of Ambrosine and Cosmo? That the house has somehow soaked up the intensity of those last moments and retained them, like a giant video recorder, to replay over and over?'

'Could be. Why can't emotion leave an imprint, if it's intense enough?'

Ever since the disturbances started, they had thrown around any number of wild theories. This one was just as likely as some of the others.

'Zephyr knew there was violence at Colonsay. And she couldn't have read my mind because I didn't know it then. Or looked it up in the histories—there's nothing in them. Yet she really did feel it, didn't she?'

That thought kept them both silent for a while.

When Rosamund looked about the room again, she sensed a change in the atmosphere. The meals were being cleared away and some spotlights had come on over a small stage, which was set against the wall adjacent to the bar. A keyboard player was in the process of setting up, uncoiling cords and plugging them in. He was dressed in black jeans, black T-shirt and black boots. His long hair was tied back and he wore a brightly coloured scarf around his head in the style of a buccaneer.

'Not hungry?'

Rosamund looked down at her plate and realised she had hardly eaten. She smiled weakly at Gary.

'Sorry.'

'Don't worry, neither am I. Let's watch the show instead.' Suddenly Rosamund felt awkward. Don't be ridiculous, she chided herself. This is Gary, Gary from the old days, who saw you at your very worst. He's a friend, that's all, just a friend.

A man in a sheepskin coat had come up from the audience and taken the microphone. He now launched into a rendition of 'I Honestly Love You', with accompanying cat-calls from the crowd. Rosamund felt her blood cool.

This must be the contest Gary had told her about, where people sang and won prizes. He must have known when he brought her here. Had he brought her because . . .? Rosamund turned and found him watching her, reading her thoughts, a mixture of guilt and humour gleaming in his eyes.

'No,' she said firmly.

'I won't make you,' he replied gently. 'It just seems a waste for a woman with your talent not to share it.'

'I'm too old to make a comeback,' she quipped stiffly, her standard line when someone reminded her of her brief glory days.

Gary was unimpressed. 'Oh, right,' he mocked.

Sheepskin-coat was finished and a young girl stepped into his place. Nervous, her jeans far too tight, she nevertheless made a fair attempt at 'Wannabe'. The crowd were generous in their applause. The next performer was a woman with a big professional smile. She belted out her song in a way which made all the others appear very amateurish, but the audience didn't appreciate it and the applause for her was half-hearted.

Gary leaned across the table to Rosamund. 'Go on,' he murmured. 'I won't laugh. No-one will. You've done it before. Sing for me, Rose.'

She wondered if he knew what it would cost her to stand up and try to recreate her past.

'I can't,' she said, and tried to laugh. 'I'd make a fool of myself.'

'No, you won't, and even if you did no-one would care.'

'I'd care.'

'Rosie,' he said. 'I think you should, I think you have to.'

An ache was growing in her throat and she swallowed. She felt light-headed, as though she had drunk too much. In all the years since she had met Mark and given up singing, she had not once returned to it. The thought of doing so now was like throwing herself at a solid wall. She didn't know if she could take that first step, let alone break through to the other side.

'Gary—'

'Go on.'

His hand was on hers, urging her up, and somehow she was on her feet, moving towards the stage. People stood back to let her through and she climbed up the single step to stand beside the keyboard player. He glanced at her, bleary-eyed from too many late nights, and then smiled.

'Rose Cunningham, right? Gary said you'd do "Grey Skies", that right? Great to meet you. Been a fan for years.'

She must have said yes, because suddenly the keyboard player was talking over the microphone, saying they were very privileged tonight to have her as their guest singer, and then the microphone was in her hands, so familiar and yet so strange. Rosamund had sung in places like this a hundred times, but that was long ago. Another time, another life.

This is a mistake, she thought. I'll tell them it's a joke and step down. But it was too late. The music had already started, the slow introduction to 'Grey Skies' like soft, soft rain on a tin roof.

Somehow, across the smoky room, she found the outline of Gary's blond head and focussed on it. The music curled about her and she took that first breath. Her voice came out low and husky, and after the first familiar lines the room seemed to hush. Rosamund knew, sometimes, it really did go quiet, and at others it was just her withdrawing into herself. Either way it didn't matter.

One verse into the song and it was as if she had

rediscovered someone she had thought long dead. Two verses and she might have never stopped singing. The closed part inside her opened wide, the magic of it bringing tears to burn her eyes. She closed them, shutting out the rapt faces and the beery smiles. Now it was just her and the music, just as it had always been.

All too soon the moment had passed and the song ended. The audience clapped with wild enthusiasm. She couldn't have asked for more.

'Bloody good!' The keyboard player's whisky voice rose above the noise.

Rosamund, still lost in her dream, climbed down off the stage and wound her way through chairs, tables and protruding feet back to Gary. Hands reached out for hers and voices yelled congratulations, and then she heard the music start up again and a man's deep voice growling out a rocky country-and-western number. The crowd hooted and began to clap along.

Rosamund sat down and Gary reached over and gripped her hand hard in his. 'You were wonderful,' he breathed. 'God, what a voice.' He glanced about him at the surging crowd. 'This lot don't know what they've just been privileged enough to hear.'

She realised that he thought she might be disappointed with her reception and was trying to comfort her. Didn't he know that it wasn't the crowd that made her sing? It was what happened inside.

'You're beautiful,' he said, as if he couldn't help himself. 'I thought I must have dreamed it, that time I heard you sing in Melbourne, I thought no-one could sing like that. But it wasn't a dream.'

Rosamund felt the dislocation begin to leave

her, and for an instant reality swung back in like a slam from a gloved fist. She had stood up and sung, she had turned back the clock, she had done something Mark would hate—again. Rosamund gasped and began to shake. Gary's grip tightened and she held on to his hand as if it were a bungee rope and she had just jumped thirty metres.

'I can't believe I did it.'

'You did. You did do it. And you did it *well*. God, Rosie, you've got a wonderful voice. It sends shivers up and down my spine.'

His face was alight, his eyes were shining. He meant it, every word, and Rosamund felt the self-confidence soar up again inside her. 'If you keep that up I'll become a real pain in the arse.'

'I want you to.'

Something in his face gave it away, what she had begun to suspect he felt for her. Embarrassed, Rosamund turned to stare at the stage. Gary had bought her another drink and she swallowed it down. The alcohol should have blurred what she was feeling, but it didn't. She was too high for anything to touch her. She was like a dog let off her leash, running with the wind in her face, not caring where her legs were taking her, just running.

They waited for the show to finish before they left. The air outside was cold and sharp, their breath milky white. When Gary put his arm about her shoulders, Rosamund didn't pull away. The other patrons were going their own ways, laughing and talking. A car revved loudly, doors slammed, but it all passed Rosamund by. She and Gary walked in a silence of their own making.

He unlocked her door first and, as he opened it for her to climb in, he leaned closer. 'Rosie . . .'

His lips were warm in the cold, meeting hers. Her insides, which had begun to melt as she sang, flowed down into her belly and groin. She slipped her arms under his jacket, around his waist, pressing against him, feeling the hard warmth of his body through his clothes.

'Come home with me,' he whispered. His breath tickled her ear.

Rosamund shook her head. 'I can't leave Kerry alone.'

He sighed, rubbing his cheek gently against hers. 'You know what that means? It means I'll have to come home with you.'

She understood why he wasn't keen. 'Maybe you shouldn't,' she murmured, and began to nibble on his earlobe.

He groaned, half-pretence and half-real. 'God, Rosie, I'll just have to risk it.'

****

Bertie had gone. Alice hadn't even seen him leave, but Meggy had. She said he looked as if he were still half asleep, the way he stumbled down the stairs and out to the gig which was to take him to the station.

Meggy eyed Alice uncertainly, as if she wasn't sure how the other girl might react. Alice had been so silent since it happened. Meggy was afraid for her. Meggy was afraid of her. She just wished that things could go back to the way they were before.

'I have to get him back,' Alice whispered.

Meggy tried to laugh but it didn't come out

right. 'How can you do that?' she blustered. 'Jonah says the master is set on making a man out of Bertie and can't see that he'll never be that sort of man. Can't or won't, Jonah says ...'

Her voice drifted off and Meggy shrugged. Best leave Alice to herself, she thought. She'd come around.

Alice had no intention of coming around. She had her plans, and one of them she could put into motion right now. Ignoring Meggy's curious stare, she left the kitchen and went to her room.

The air was cold in here, with a damp feel to it. The cook had allowed her and Meggy to make a small fire but it gave off very little heat, barely enough to dry their underwear. Alice reached for the top right-hand drawer of the dresser she and Meggy shared, and pulled it open. Her eyes slid over the contents, the handkerchiefs and the cairngorm. The button was there, hidden beneath Bertie's letter.

She held it in her open palm. The ivory, with its carved rose, was the same pale colour as Bertie's face the last time she saw him. Her fingers closed hard into a fist with the button at its core, and Alice set her mouth into a straight, determined line.

Yesterday, in the library, Cosmo had frightened her very much, more than she had shown. She had felt the ground she had thought so solid shift a little beneath her feet. Perhaps she was not so secure here at Colonsay as she had thought but, whatever the consequences might be, she must do this thing.

For Bertie.

****

Colonsay was a dark shadow against the cloud-filled sky. The only light came from the kitchen window at the side. Rosamund turned her key in the lock and heard the click. Kerry must be home: a pleasant smell of cooking wafted out from the kitchen. There she found a plate of coconut macaroons on the table, with a note to say Kerry had gone to bed and would see Rosamund in the morning.

Rosamund smiled over her shoulder at Gary. 'Coffee?'

He shook his head. 'I can manage without it.'

'You feel all right then?'

'Perhaps I've got something else on my mind.'

She put the note down and held out the plate. Gary came towards her but he didn't take a macaroon. He gently removed the plate from her hand and returned it to the table. He placed his hands on her shoulders, his eyes watchful. He gave her plenty of time to turn away, but Rosamund didn't want to. The kiss started as an exploration, but changed about halfway through into something passionate and unstoppable.

Gary put one arm about her waist and bent, slipping the other under her knees. Realising what he meant to do, Rosamund began to protest. 'You'll break your back!' she wailed, trying not to laugh. But he lifted her up, holding her firmly in his arms. Rosamund put her own arms about his neck and gave up the struggle. He grinned back at her.

'You're beautiful,' he said.

It was the second time he had said that tonight. She touched his lips with one fingertip, tracing their contours. 'Gary,' she began. What could she say? I'm a bad bet. I'm Mark's wife. I have so many problems to sort out. I'm only just beginning to find my feet again . . . The last struck her as funny, considering her current position, and she began to laugh again.

'Stop that,' he warned, 'or I'll drop you.'

He carried her to the bottom of the stairs and looked up them. His expression grew slightly tortured, and still laughing Rosamund struggled out of his grip. 'It's all right, Mr Butler,' she whispered. 'I'll walk.' Taking his hand, she drew him after her.

****

Ambrosine was in her bedroom. Alice knocked and opened the door. There was no light in the room, and no air. White flowers, like ghostly moths, seemed to hover above a side table. Ambrosine lay on the day-bed, a lavender-soaked handkerchief across her eyes and Cleo huddled at her feet.

'Mrs Gibbons?' she murmured, her voice drowsy with sleep and laudanum.

'No, madam.'

'Alice?' She sat up awkwardly, her usual grace deserting her. The handkerchief slipped onto the floor but she ignored it, blinking as she tried to focus on the silhouette in the doorway. 'What are you doing here, Alice?'

'I've come to speak with you, madam.'

Ambrosine blinked again, and Alice could see her struggling to clear her mind, to understand. Hatred filled her, and scorn for such weakness. Instead of fighting for her son, she had come up here to hide in her room and send herself to sleep with poppy juice. Well then, if she would not fight then Alice would make her fight.

'I think you take too much upon yourself,' Ambrosine began, her voice sounding rusty.

Alice closed the door behind her without being asked and walked towards the day-bed. Cleo lifted her head and growled. Ambrosine sat up straighter, swinging her legs around so that her stockinged feet rested on the rug on the floor. Her beautiful face was drawn and still, like a sculpture. Call it *The Ravaged Mother*, Alice thought with scorn. Ambrosine was a fine actress. If she had truly cared about Bertie she would have done something.

'What do you want?' This time there was no pretence at keeping the distance of mistress and servant between them. Ambrosine sounded bitter and defeated.

Now that Alice was closer, she could see the woman's eyes were swollen and red from weeping. Good, she thought. I'm glad. She stuck out her hand so that it was right under Ambrosine's nose, and Cleo growled again. Ambrosine started back slightly, as if expecting to be struck, and then stopped herself. She gazed down at the button as if she had never seen it before. 'What is that?' she croaked.

'Mr Marling's button, madam. I found it in here. *In here*. How could it be in here, I wonder?'

'I, I don't know.' She was shaking her head, but as if to clear it rather than in denial.

'But you do, madam. You do know. You and Mr Marling are more than friends. I'll show this to Mr Cunningham and see what he makes of it. He'll know what to do. I'll show him, I will, unless you get Bertie home again.'

Silence, and then Ambrosine began to laugh. Startled, Cleo sprang down from the day-bed and crept under it.

'I mean it, madam,' Alice whispered furiously. Her hand was shaking so much she had to pull it back, fingers closing tightly upon the ivory button, forcing it into her skin.

Ambrosine bowed her head and covered her face with her hands. Her shoulders shook with laughter; she couldn't seem to stop. Alice, hot and trembling with her anger, stood watching. Of all the things she had expected and planned for, she could never have imagined this.

At last Ambrosine lifted her head. Her white face was flushed and there were tears spilling down her cheeks. Her lips shook. 'Go away, Alice,' she said, her voice sliding up and down the scale like an old woman's. 'You don't know what you're talking about. Go away, and next time you come to me with your tales and your threats I'll go to your father and tell him what you are. I'm sure he'll listen to me, even if my husband won't.' Alice had no doubt she meant it.

Ambrosine had already turned away. Alice left her, almost running down the corridor and then down the main staircase. The hallstand by the door was heavy with coats and hats, and she caught a glimpse of Bertie's straw boater.

The sudden sight of it was like a spear in her heart and she cried out. Her foot caught on a fold in the carpet, and Alice let herself fall.

****

Rosamund cried out in the darkness, her body pressing against other flesh and sinew, her mouth finding other lips, her breath and his mingling. Gradually her heartbeat slowed, the perspiration dried on her skin. She felt his finger stroking her shoulder, where the collarbone curved.

'Rosie,' he whispered. It seemed enough. She smiled and closed her eyes. She felt more at peace than she had been for years, and that was very strange considering the present state of her life. Gary slipped his arm about her waist, holding her warm against him, and sighed contentedly.

Rosamund snuggled in against him, ignoring the tiny doubts, like slivers of glass in her heart. This relationship was new, she must give it time. Gary was so different from Mark, and he held her as if the holding itself were enough.

As sleep claimed her, she was aware of a scratching noise near her door. The mice again. 'Go away, mice,' she murmured drowsily. Gary tightened his arm, his breath warm on her shoulder. This is nice, she thought. And thinking it, she fell asleep.

CHAPTER 17

Alice's head hurt.

She tried to open her eyes but there was too much light and she closed them again. 'Alice? Oh, Alice, you did give us a fright!'

The voice was familiar. Gradually she became aware of the button-back sofa beneath her, and the clean smells of polish and flowers. Someone had carried her to Ambrosine's sitting room.

'We've sent for the doctor,' the same voice went on—she realised now that it was Ada's nurse. 'You just lie still until he comes.'

Alice vaguely remembered falling, but it was all mixed up with other things, and it hurt her head too much to think about them. She let herself drift, soaking in the rare luxury of lying doing nothing while others fussed about her. Was this how Ambrosine felt when she took to her room with one of her frequent headaches?

There was a tap on the door and soft voices rolled across the room, a small wave of sound. All about her was the usual ebb and flow of the house, but Alice had stepped out of the tidal pull for a time, into her own private rockpool.

She must have slept. When she woke the doctor was bending over her. He lifted her eyelids and peered into her eyes, and then examined the bump on the side of her head. 'Doesn't appear to be any lasting damage,' he said to someone whom Alice couldn't see, standing behind him. 'However, best to take no chances. I'll leave some medicine, and she should remain on a restricted diet for a day or two. Nothing hot or spicy, nothing to excite the blood.'

'Yes, doctor.'

It was Mrs Gibbons. She peered over the doctor's shoulder, her moon face flushed and agitated. Surprised, Alice wondered that her small accident had caused such an upheaval of emotion in the other woman. And could not quite believe it.

'She can perform light duties. You may feel the need of her help, after what has happened today.'

'Yes, sir.' Cook's eyes watered and she mopped at them with her sleeve, snivelling a little. 'Poor boy, oh poor dear boy.'

'Now, Mrs Gibbons, don't upset yourself. Your mistress needs you and you must rise to the occasion.'

She nodded and gave a last determined sniff. 'I know that, sir. I'll do all I can.'

'Good woman.' The doctor turned back to Alice. 'Very well, young Alice. You've taken a nasty knock, but you'll recover. Rest today. I'll give you a draught now, to help you sleep. Open up. That's it.'

The medicine was too sweet but Alice swallowed it. She was trying to understand what was happening, but all her thoughts kept breaking up, fragmenting like worms beneath a sharp-edged spade.

'What is it?' she whispered, and was appalled to hear her words slurred, like Mrs Gibbons when she had taken too much of her herbal tonic.

Cook shot her a malicious look. 'This is your fault, Alice! If he hadn't been sent back to school this morning, he'd still be alive now.'

Terror gripped her. The room began to whirl about her.

'Mrs Gibbons!' The doctor was sharp, but his eyes on Alice were warm with sympathy. 'That is quite uncalled for, and quite untrue. Alice, we have had some bad news. I know you will be as saddened by it as all of us. Young Bertie was killed. He climbed off the train while it was stopped briefly, and stepped in front of another train.'

But Alice was whirling and whirling into a blackness that had no sound and no light, into nothing, as the medicine took effect.

****

Rosamund stirred uneasily. It was cold. Gary's arm still lay heavily about her waist and she slipped out from under it. He murmured in his sleep and rolled over. She wondered if she should wake him and send him home. The thought of Kerry's face in the morning tussled in her mind with her own reluctance.

The scratching at the door distracted her, and she sat up. Was it mice? The sound was very loud in the silence. After a brief hesitation, Rosamund climbed out of bed. The room was quite light, moonlight filling the window and making broad strokes across the floor. The scratching continued, soft and insistent. It didn't sound like mice—surely this was a larger animal?

Rosamund tiptoed across the cold bare boards towards the door. Her breathing sounded inordinately loud, and as she reached out to grasp the doorknob she steadied it. And opened the door with a swift tug.

The little dog looked up at her, moist eyes gleaming in the light from the window. Its tan-coloured coat was matted and unkempt, the ribbon trailing over one ear. Rosamund gasped loudly. Her sudden opening of the door had frightened the creature. With a skitter of claws on the wood floor, it turned and ran for the stairs. With a soft cry, Rosamund gave chase.

More moonlight shone through the coloured panes of glass either side of the front door, illuminating the entrance hall. As Rosamund descended the stairs, she could see the dog reach the bottom and turn, skidding, fighting to keep its grip, and then bolt towards the back of the house.

'Come here,' she said, heart thudding, her breath coming hard. 'Come here, damn you!'

She reached the entrance hall and spun around, grasping the newel post to keep her balance. The hall stretched before her, shadows gathering, silent, and as far as she could tell, empty.

Rosamund hesitated, but only for a moment. The air was colder here and the moonlight didn't reach very far into the darkness. A warning sounded in her mind but she ignored it. The dog was down there. It was hiding, frightened and alone, and she would find it if it was the last thing she did.

She flicked on the light, its dull gleam chasing away some of the shadows. She could plainly see the dog's paw prints in the dust, making a direct line down the hall. Rosamund quickly followed them. 'Here, dog,' she called gently. 'Come on, dog. Here, dog.'

No answering sound. Her steps grew hesitant. She had reached the door of the second junkroom before she realised it was ajar. Shocked, she stopped and stared. How could it be ajar? She knew she had closed it. Had someone else left it open? She moved slightly closer. The darkness inside the room was gritty, like loosely packed soil. Had the dog gone in there? Was that where it had been hiding? It made sense. No-one went in there, and it would be safe and undisturbed. Well, she could just take a peep.

Now her heart really was racing, filling the silence all about her. She was hesitating on the threshold when a tiny sound came from inside the room. A scratching sound, like a dog's claws. Rosamund almost laughed with relief.

'Come here,' she called, striving for kindness. 'Dog, come here!'

Rosamund took a step into the close and cluttered darkness, into the dank smell that was frighteningly familiar. And then another. Then the door closed behind her.

A surge of adrenalin sent her scrambling backwards, half falling and bruising her hip on the corner of something sharp. The heavy bureau loomed to one side. Panicking, she crashed into something hard at knee level, and tears burned her eyes. She stretched her hands out, finding the wood of the door, and then the knob. It turned under her grasping fingers but the door itself didn't budge. Rosamund braced her feet, and leaning back pulled with all her might.

The door was stuck fast. Immoveable.

Behind her the musty air stirred. She froze, her

fear as much as the closed door holding her prisoner. With a soft, choked cry, she pressed her face to the hard wooden surface of the door. She could smell the blood now, so strong it made her want to gag. There were weird sounds, a rustling further down the room, near the window. A whispering. Then an echoing thud, as if some piece of furniture had been overturned. A slap, the blow from an open hand. A frightened woman's voice growing louder, then falling away, and a man groaning out her name in anger and pain. '*Rosie* . . .'

Silence, but a silence pregnant with horror. There was something in the room behind her. She knew it with every pore of her being. Her senses were screaming it out to her. Perspiration trickled down her back, cold as thawing snow. The sickly metallic smell of blood was replaced by something just as bad, the oversweet smell of roses.

Rosamund felt a terrible compulsion to turn, to look for herself, but she knew that if she did she might very well lose her mind. She raised her hands, the muscles stiff and creaking, forcing them to work, bringing her palm down hard against the door. The noise was ineffectual. She did it again. And again. She began to scream out words that had no meaning, driven only by her desperate need to escape.

It seemed like hours that she waited but Rosamund knew it must have been mere moments. She felt the door being shoved from the other side and then Kerry's voice calling to her, and Gary's deeper one. The door opened, suddenly and violently, knocking Rosamund backwards. She fell, screaming, into the piles of musty books and dusty furniture, her outflung hand striking the side of the bureau.

The pain was nothing. She was scrambling, sobbing, trying to get to her feet. Beyond the now open door, in the hall, were two frightened familiar faces.

'Oh God, Rosie . . .' Gary was helping her up, holding her hard against his chest.

'Rosamund.' Kerry sounded shocked.

'The dog,' she gasped. 'The blood.' She made a whimpering sound and bit her lip to stop it. Gary held her so hard she could hardly breathe, but it still wasn't hard enough. It didn't make the memory of what she had experienced go away. And while she revelled in his closeness and comfort, she knew he could not save her from what was happening here at Colonsay.

No-one could save her but herself.

****

When Alice awoke it was dark. Night dark. She lay for a long time, sorting out her thoughts. They were disarranged and disordered, as though someone had lain them out on the floor like cards and then proceeded to shuffle them.

In the next bed, Alice could hear Meggy's soft breathing, broken by the occasional snort. The chest of drawers was a darker shadow at the bottom of the bed, and there was still a faint glow of coals in the tiny hearth. Alice could smell the ashes, they made her feel slightly sick.

Bertie's dead.

The thought popped into her head, but she pushed it violently away. It was very still outside, as though the whole world had stopped. Alice tried to visualise the garden and the trees, but instead a picture came to her of Bertie, lying on the railway tracks, all bloody and torn. A gasping sob rose into her throat but she choked it down.

Far away, out in the bay, a bell sounded. There must be fog. Thick, creeping fog. *Bertie's dead.* The sob came again and this time she couldn't stop it. The sound was wrenched out of her so violently she doubled up.

Meggy turned over, her bed creaking noisily.

'Bertie's dead,' Alice whispered to herself.

It seemed impossible. What had Mrs Gibbons said? If Alice hadn't caused him to return to school so soon ... No! She couldn't go down that path. If Bertie's death was anybody's fault, then it was his mother's. Alice had tried so hard to make her see, to force her to act and keep Bertie at home. It had all been in vain. Ambrosine had laughed. Laughed!

Alice felt the cold floor beneath her bare feet and realised she was standing by the door. The depth of her anger and despair forced her to act, to move, to do *something*. If she lay in her bed, then she would die of grief. Like Bertie.

The stairs were lit by the lamp on the landing, and Alice climbed beyond the point where she had earlier fallen and hit her head. It didn't matter now, none of it mattered. Bertie was dead.

The west wing was quiet, Ada sleeping. Did she know and understand what had happened to her brother? Did she know where her tale-telling had led? The question came and went without pausing for an answer, a train speeding through the half-dawn darkness.

How had he not seen it or heard it? Why had

he climbed down onto the tracks? She pictured him, a small, plump figure, blinking through his glasses. Perhaps he had been crying, thinking of the long months ahead without promise of returning home. Perhaps he had simply wanted some fresh air.

The attic stairs had a slight concave in their centre, worn down from long years of use. At the top of them Alice stood and gazed around.

There the stuffed peacock, and there Bertie's secret place, and there his treasure box and his book on birds. He must have left it here. He must have known he would not need it again. But—how had he known that he would die?

And then suddenly it came to her, as if Bertie stood before her and spoke to her from his own dead lips. Bertie had known he would die because he had planned to die. Rather than return to the place in which he was so unhappy, rather than cause any more trouble and disappointment for his family, he had brought about his own death.

In his letter he had seen himself as something small and inconspicuous, something of little worth. Such was Bertie's place in the world of the Cunninghams.

In her grief and fury, Alice picked up the book and flung it as hard as she could across the long, low room. It smacked into the wall. The sound spurred her on. Wildly, she picked up a broken chair and threw it, sending it crashing and somersaulting. There were so many things to throw and break, but with each one her feelings swelled rather than subsided, like yeast on a warm hearth. She was almost glad when they came up to see what was making the shocking noise, and to stop her. Because she could never have stopped herself.

****

'Feeling better?'

Rosamund nodded. She was sitting up in bed, her hands clasped around a hot cup of sweet tea, a quilt draped about her shoulders, and several pillows behind her back. Kerry had brought the tea and watched, deeply concerned, while Rosamund sipped it. Gary had arranged the quilt and the pillows, and supplied the hand-holding and stroking when required. Rosamund found she required both constantly.

'I shouldn't have gone down there,' she said, trying to look at things calmly and practically, and not to remember ... She shuddered and Gary patted her knee.

Kerry cleared her throat loudly. 'Perhaps you were sleepwalking,' she said. 'Perhaps it was all a dream. You used to sleepwalk as a child. Do you remember? We were always finding you down there.'

Rosamund and Gary gaped at her. Kerry looked defensive. 'That's not so unusual. People do.'

'But ... *that* room?' Rosamund whispered.

'Yes, I'm sure it was that room. Mrs Ada called it the sitting room, but she never used it. It was her mother's room.'

'Her mother's room? Ambrosine's room? Then that was where it happened.' Rosamund shook her head in disbelief. 'That was where he killed her.'

She looked up and met Gary's eyes. She didn't need to tell him she had finally surrendered the last of her doubts.

'Do you still want to go to Melbourne tomorrow?' he asked softly.

She nodded. 'More than ever. I need to know what happened. It's the only way I'll ever be able to live here. And I want to live here, Gary. Not like Ada did, not wallowing in the past, drowning in it. I need Colonsay to be at peace, and I think that's what Colonsay wants, too.'

****

Mr Parkin was very angry. Mira Parkin had warned her daughter this was so, but Alice could see it well enough for herself. When her father was angry he went pale and silent, and his eyes turned as hard as agates.

She did not know what Cosmo had told him but it must have been close to the truth. She had fallen down the stairs and then run amok in the attic. They had blamed the one on the other, assuming she was temporarily out of her wits, but in her father's eyes it was still inexcusable for a servant to act in such an ungrateful and undisciplined manner.

Mira was more sympathetic. 'How is your head today, Alice? More lemon barley to drink, love? There now, there.'

Overshadowing Alice's misdemeanour was Bertie's death. It overshadowed everything, literally. The light had gone out of the sun, so that Alice was positive the world was hung in black mourning. The town was as shocked at the tragedy as the family, and the funeral had been a sight to behold, with so many mourners and flowers they spilled over the road into the next paddock. The only sour note, according to Mira, had been that none of them were invited back to Colonsay to partake of the cold meats. That privilege had been reserved for the guests from Melbourne, the politicians and the like.

Alice had not gone, had not wanted to go. For her, Bertie had died long ago, and the boy who had returned to Colonsay in May was not Bertie, not the Bertie she knew and loved. Her friend. Ambrosine had killed Bertie, not the train. She had done nothing to prevent him going away, too caught up in her own selfishness to see or understand his anguish. Too selfish to care.

Sometimes the anger raged inside Alice, just as it had that night in the attic, though now she could better control it. These feelings she kept to herself. To her parents she was Alice, unchanged, if a little pale.

You'll be sorry, she thought, every morning when she woke up. I'll make you sorry.

She already knew how she was going to do it, she just didn't know when.

****

The highway was busy and they didn't have much to say. Gary concentrated on his driving and Rosamund watched the scenery go by.

They crossed over the West Gate Bridge about ten and headed into the centre of the city. Gary parked in a multi-storey car park in Bourke Street.

Rosamund felt strangely bemused by the noise and roar of the traffic, and the pushing, thrusting crowd. She had been at Colonsay only a short time, but already she had grown used to the slower pace and lack of urgency. The desire to keep up with everyone else had all but disappeared.

'I've got a couple of people to see,' Gary had told her. He would leave her in the city and meet up with her again about four. That would give her plenty of time to go to the National Gallery and find the Marling portrait.

'Markovic Constructions is just up the road from here,' Gary said as they crossed at the lights.

Rosamund gave him a blank look.

'I thought you might want to visit your husband.'

'Visit Mark?' she repeated. Was he joking or was this some kind of test of her feelings? 'No, I don't think so.'

He glanced at her sideways. She knew her face was closed, her lips pressed tightly together. She wasn't going to discuss Mark with him, not now, not even after last night.

'Look, it was a bad joke. I didn't mean . . .'

They'd stopped in front of a book store. He gazed unseeingly into the window. The suit and tie he was wearing made him look like a stranger, and Rosamund knew she was just as unfamiliar in her short dark skirt and jacket. Odd, how once away from Colonsay they became different people. Was she beginning to have regrets? Was he? Surreptitiously, they inspected each other in the expanse of glass, pretending to examine the book display.

'Do you think that'll be you one day?' she asked, trying to lighten the atmosphere. 'Gary Munro's latest blockbuster.'

'Yeah, sure.' He half smiled, but his eyes were serious. Rosamund found it difficult to believe she had spent last night in bed with this man, that they had held each other in the most intimate of all embraces. Today he was someone else.

'What's your book about?'

'Life and death, the struggle for power. The usual.'

Another awkward pause.

'I'll meet you here at four,' Gary said.

'Okay.'

Still he hesitated.

'Thank you for last night,' she said quickly, before she lost the courage to. 'The singing, I mean. And for caring enough to make me do it.'

'You mean something to me.' Gary was smiling properly now, more like his easy, relaxed self. 'You mean a lot to me.'

'You mean a lot to me, too.'

They grinned at each other in the window like idiots. He bent and kissed her quickly on her carefully painted lips and walked away. She watched him go, admiring the look of him, until he was lost from sight among the crowd and the cars.

****

Alice glared at Petersham's red-coated back as the old soldier stumped down the road towards Colonsay. He held the usual pathetic bunch of flowers in his horny hand. Alice wondered at the man's stupidity. What did Ambrosine care for him, for anyone, other than herself? They said she had taken ill after the death of her son but Alice doubted that. Cosmo, said to be equally devastated, had returned to the Parliament in Melbourne, leaving his wife at Colonsay. Alone. Probably that had always been her aim. For now Mr Marling was there, visiting.

Yesterday he had come into town to see Alice. He'd charmed Mira and even surprised Mr Parkin with his good sense. It seemed that even men in exuberant waistcoats could be sensible at times. He said he still wanted to paint Alice and she had allowed herself to be persuaded. He made a few sketches, his hand moving quickly, although he never stopped talking for even a moment.

'You must be very sad about Bertie,' he ventured when he had her all relaxed and unsuspecting.

'I am,' Alice replied, on her guard again.

He eyed her curiously, as if he knew very well what she was feeling, although she doubted that he did. No-one did.

'Mrs Cunningham commissioned me to enquire after your health,' he went on. 'Don't look so surprised, Alice! Do you imagine you aren't missed?'

She wondered if he knew what she had done the night she heard of Bertie's death. She suspected he did. Mr Marling knew everything, and if he didn't know, he had the lucky knack of finding out.

Now he changed the subject slightly. 'Every time I visit, Mr Cunningham tells me the story of how your father saved his life.'

'I didn't think Mr Cunningham was at Colonsay every time you visited, sir.'

He let his eyes rest on her, and although he was still smiling she knew he had taken her point. 'Of course. I stand corrected. When he's at Colonsay he tells me the story. When he's not, he cannot.'

'Why do you want to paint me, Mr Marling? I'm not pretty or unusual. I'm a servant and I can't pay you lots of money. I don't understand it.'

'You *are* unusual, Alice. I find you very unusual. That's why I want to paint you. Aren't you flattered? I would have thought you would be. I imagine Meggy or Mrs Gibbons would be very flattered if I asked them.'

She managed a smile. 'Perhaps you should then, sir.'

He laughed. 'I don't think so. They will live and die and, although their lives may be all very interesting to themselves, they will never interest me. You are different, Alice. You are a conundrum.'

She didn't answer him. She didn't know the word and now had no chance to look it up in the big dictionary at Colonsay. Instead, she closed her lips very firmly, as if daring him to say more.

Henry Marling smiled and continued with his sketches.

The National Gallery of Victoria was in St Kilda Road. Rosamund decided to walk. She couldn't remember the last time she had visited the gallery, although she came to town shopping often enough. Mark liked beautiful things but he preferred to let someone else do the buying. He didn't trust his own judgment. He had not been trained in sorting the kitsch from the acceptable, and was afraid of laying himself open to ridicule and laughter. Mark was quite happy to use his humble origins as a tool in his campaign but was also very vulnerable about them.

The open spire of the Arts Centre was visible across the Yarra. The river was busy today with tourist cruise boats and floating restaurants. As Rosamund crossed Princess Bridge, with its Victorian-era lampposts, a man in black with long grey hair began to play his saxophone. She found a couple of coins in her purse to drop into his waiting hat. The cafes and restaurants at Southbank were filling up for lunch, but Rosamund walked on to the gallery.

She collected a guidebook at the door. The rooms of Australian art were on the ground floor, beyond the gallery shop, opening into each other. Some of their canvases Rosamund felt an instant familiarity with: Roberts, Streeton, McCubbin. Here was the stuff of Victorian and Edwardian Australia, their images hidden deep in modern hearts, which had been convinced such feelings were too sentimental. But today Rosamund spared them little more than a glance. The room she wanted was in the centre of the Australian section, the one housing the Marling collection.

She saw it from the moment she entered the wide carpeted space. A huge dark canvas, its central character depicted in a luminous and ghostly white. Ambrosine Cunningham, living and breathing again, in paint.

Slowly, Rosamund approached the portrait, then halted. Her head felt oddly light, as if it were floating, as if she were floating. As if she weren't really there at all. Ambrosine was seated but leaning forward from the waist, so that she appeared to be on the point of sharing some confidence with the observer. The pale sheer material of her blouse disclosed more than it concealed, and her parted lips were moist and sensuous. Her dark hair, coiled on top of her head, ringlets arranged artfully about her face, would surely be soft and lustrous to the touch.

But it was her eyes which held Rosamund spellbound. They gazed into hers, willing her to understand. There was a whole landscape of expression in them. Rosamund took a step closer, unable to decide which was uppermost, warmth or hauteur. Laughter or sadness. Pride or sensuality. And then, with a shiver of surprise, she knew. Ambrosine was saying none of those things. She was pleading for help. Help me, she cried. I am trapped. I am afraid . . . The words seemed to whisper in Rosamund's head.

As her emotional reaction dissipated, Rosamund began to notice the more prosaic things. The strong resemblance to Ada in the shape of Ambrosine's face and nose. There, too, was Rosamund's father, in Ambrosine's eyes and the colour of her hair. And, of course, Rosamund herself.

'Marvellous, isn't it?'

Rosamund jumped, turning sharply. A middle-aged man stood beside her. He had the lonely, hungry look of a man on his own and desperate for conversation. She forced herself to smile.

'Yes, wonderful.'

'My wife always thought it was one of Marling's best. We used to come quite often to look at it. Now I come alone.' He cleared his throat and gestured towards the portrait. 'In my opinion, he was never as well known as he should have been, despite the portrait he did of the opening of Federal Parliament. That hangs in Parliament House, in Canberra, more's the pity.'

'I see.'

'He went off the rails a bit, towards the end of his life. Witnessed some sort of accident and took to the drink.'

Rosamund made an appropriate face and was relieved when the man moved on. She turned back to the portrait. For the first time she noticed the brass plaque on the wall beside it: 'Ambrosine Cunningham, wife of Cosmo, 1872–1901. This portrait painted 1900–01. Henry Marling, Australian artist. Donated by Mrs Ada Evans, 1930.'

Rosamund hadn't expected that. She hadn't known that this portrait had ever hung at Colonsay. Now she realised nothing could be more natural. Cosmo must have commissioned it, a portrait of his beloved and beautiful young wife. And dutifully, Ambrosine would have posed.

What could have happened to make him kill her and then take his own life?

If Rosamund still doubted such an event took place, the portrait convinced her. There was a disturbing sense of tragedy about Ambrosine. Despair curved her lips, despite their seductive quality, and sorrow glowed deep within those dark eyes. It was as if she had never been meant to be happy.

With an effort Rosamund turned away from the magnetic Ambrosine. Portraiture was Marling's specialty and there were quite a few others in the collection, though none as wonderfully gripping as Ambrosine's. Rosamund dutifully examined each one, noting the use of colour and the sure brushstrokes. There was one of a group picnicking by the water, and Rosamund rather thought the location was the Bellarine Peninsula. She returned to Ambrosine and stood before her once more, taking her fill.

The painting was more than magnetic, it was mesmerising. Rosamund knew she had to have a copy, and wondered if there was one in the gallery shop. Eventually, if things at Colonsay turned out as she planned, she hoped to have a replica of this portrait in one of the rooms.

It was on her way out that Rosamund found she had missed one of Marling's portraits. A smaller canvas hung to one side of a piece of early Australian furniture, half hidden by it.

The background of this canvas was brown rather than the rich black of Ambrosine's. The subject, a girl, was standing. She had long straight hair which framed her narrow face, and her eyes were clear and unflinching. It was her mouth that spoiled the depiction of innocent girlhood. Thin and straight, it was far too old for her.

Rosamund's breath quickened and she stood perfectly still. It was the brown girl. She knew her at once. Heart thudding, she bent to read the small brass plaque. '*Alice*, by Henry Marling. Purchased for the Marling collection in 1950.'

'Alice,' she whispered jubilantly. 'I have you now.'

****

Meggy was thinner, her brown eyes larger. It was her morning off. Normally she and Jonah would be together, she said, but Ambrosine had taken a sudden urge to go riding and Jonah had had to go with her.

'He says if he says no then they'll think he's a poor sort of servant, and if he says yes then I'll think he's a poor sort of brother.' Meggy smiled but Alice thought it was a strain. As though smiling were something Meggy had got out of the way of lately.

'Cosmo's had to go back to Melbourne and see to his work there,' she went on after a moment, when it seemed clear Alice wasn't going to comment. 'The house is so quiet, Alice. I can hear my own breath. Mrs Gibbons fell over yesterday and when I tried to help her up she swore at me and called me names. Ada has nightmares nearly every night. She had a tantrum on the stairs and screamed so loud her mother woke and came to see what was wrong. And then Ada pushed her away and said she hated her, and madam went the colour of bad cheese. Oh Alice, you don't know what it's like. Be glad you're not there. I want to leave. I want to go home with Jonah. But he says he can't, not yet.'

'What good is he? Go without him,' Alice whispered, but it was the wrong thing to say.

Meggy turned pink. 'Jonah is my brother,' she said, clenching her rough red hands. 'You don't know him.'

Didn't she? Alice remembered the night in the garden when Jonah had stood smoking and saying nothing. She had sensed something in him then, a kind of reckless danger. Was that what attracted girls, that dangerous quality?

'When does the master come back?' she asked.

Meggy blinked at her, thrown by the change of subject. 'Next Wednesday. He's bringing guests with him.'

Alice nodded and turned away. She had the

information she wanted, and there was no more to say. In a moment, she heard the door close.

****

'Are you hungry?'

Rosamund had spent the last hour browsing in the book store and drinking coffee. The latter had made her feel jittery and slightly sick. 'No, I'm not hungry.'

'We may as well get going then.'

Gary wound his way down out of the car park while Rosamund closed her eyes and tried to ignore the feeling of being on a joyride at a fair.

'What did you find out?'

He hadn't offered her any information and now she was forced to ask.

'Nothing really. Just a few hints. I'm hoping to hear more in a day or two. I have someone looking up a file for me. I did them a favour once and I've called it in today.'

Rosamund was disappointed. Despite the unlikeliness of it, she had hoped to be presented with the whole truth. Immediately.

'What about you?' Braking at the lights, Gary glanced at her.

'I saw the portrait.' Her voice filled with excitement. 'It really is amazing. Did you know that Ada donated it to the gallery in 1930? I didn't think she'd ever donated anything to anyone in her life. I suppose she had no choice. She wouldn't have been able to bring herself to sell it, her own murdered mother's portrait, and she wouldn't have wanted it in the house. I suppose until she gave it away it was tucked up in the attic somewhere.'

'But why not? Why wouldn't she have wanted Ambrosine's portrait in the house?'

She looked at him in surprise. 'Well, it would have reminded her, wouldn't it, of what happened, of the secret she was keeping. No, she'd have had to get rid of it, one way or another.'

'Why wait until 1930?'

'Maybe 1930 was the year she began to search out any saleable items, the year she realised she couldn't survive at Colonsay without more money.' Rosamund paused, took a breath. 'There's something else, Gary. There was another portrait by Marling. Called *Alice*. It's her, Gary. It's the ghost. The brown girl. Her name was . . . *is* Alice.'

'Shit.'

Rosamund reached over into the back seat and found the bag from the gallery book store. 'I bought this. It's a book on Marling. There are copies of all his paintings in it. I read some of it while I was waiting for you. Did you know he was very good friends with Cosmo Cunningham? It was probably the reason why he got the job of painting the opening of the Federal Parliament. He spent a lot of time at Colonsay. He painted the portrait of Ambrosine in one of the upstairs rooms. I suppose he must have painted Alice at the same time.'

'Hang on,' Gary interrupted. 'Who was Alice? Another daughter?'

'No,' Rosamund replied thoughtfully, 'not a daughter. A servant, I would think. Yes, a servant. He must have seen her at Colonsay and thought her interesting enough to paint. And she does look interesting. Different.' She found the page and turned it towards him. 'Here.' Gary glanced from the road and back.

'Doesn't look very interesting to me. Sour little puss. God, no wonder you fainted when you turned around and found her behind you.'

Rosamund stared down at the painting. She remembered that night very well. The silence of the west wing and the sense of a watching presence behind her, the rustle of clothing, the tap of a shoe. Alice, her brown hair loose, her composed young-old face, her eyes brilliantly alive.

Rosamund shivered.

'She wasn't like that when I saw her,' she said. 'I don't mean it wasn't her, because it was. But she was alive, just as a real person is alive. Not like a painting.'

'You're giving me the heebie-jeebies.'

Rosamund laughed, and it was a relief to do so. 'Sorry.'

He was silent a moment, concentrating on the traffic. The Melbourne winter sky was darkening and lights already shone from buildings and neon signs. Traffic exhausts puffed like hot breath into the cold air. A tram rumbled by.

'There's definitely something to what Enderby told us,' Gary said at last. 'Even though my contacts weren't saying much, I smelled it.'

'You smelled it with your long journalist's nose, do you mean?' she mocked gently.

He grinned. 'Yeah, that's it. A bad smell. But it's not a secret I'm going to get out of them easily. Maybe you should have a go. Remind them who your great-grandfather was, that you have a right to know.'

'I don't know anyone influential enough to ask.'

'You know Mark Markovic.'

She was stunned. Ask Mark for a favour? That would surprise him. He'd wonder what she was up to. It might be worth it, just to see the look on his face.

'It was a joke,' Gary said drily. 'Just leave it to me for now. If I don't come up with any hard evidence, then we can explore other avenues.'

He even talks like a journalist, Rosamund thought, and then was annoyed with herself for thinking it. Gary had been good to her. He deserved more. Perhaps she should tell him now that last night was a mistake, that she wanted to cool it. Instead, she turned and deliberately placed her hand on his thigh. She felt his muscles tense and then relax, as if he were making a conscious effort. He turned to look at her and smiled.

'Do you want to stop for a while? There's no hurry to get back, is there?'

Was there? Rosamund couldn't think of one. Gazing into his warm blue eyes, the old recklessness that Mark abhorred seized her.

'No hurry at all.'

CHAPTER 18

'She was a very striking woman.' Next morning, Kerry was looking at the reproduction of Ambrosine's portrait in the Marling book. 'She looks like you,' she added, glancing up.

'I'm not quite in her league.' But the possibility of it gave Rosamund a frisson of pleasure, and fear.

'I don't recognise Alice.' Kerry frowned at the smaller painting. It did not fully capture what Rosamund had seen in the 'real' thing, but Marling had certainly managed a decent hint at a feeling of repressed emotion, of hidden depths.

'Was she a servant, do you think?'

'I think so. It would have helped if Marling had given us a surname.'

'Yes. There used to be some old household accounts books, but Mrs Ada gave them to the Historical Society.'

Rosamund lit a cigarette and almost immediately put it out. 'Do you know anyone who works for them? I don't think I want to march up and explain myself to a stranger.'

Kerry looked amused. 'You sound like your grandmother.'

'Oh, *please.*'

'Now I come to think of it, there's Mrs Gibbons.

She helps out there. That's Rae's mother—the girl who fell and broke her arm.'

Rosamund remembered something. 'Rae told me her great-grandmother was Cosmo's cook!'

'Yes, that's right. The family moved away after . . . afterwards. Oddly enough, all of the servants left the district.'

Rosamund looked thoughtful.

'Mrs Gibbons and Rae live not far from Colonsay, on the housing estate that was built after the swamp was drained and filled. They did that in the '60s. There was that nasty business, do you remember?'

'Refresh my memory,' Rosamund said, only half listening.

'Well,' Kerry settled herself, 'they found a man's body in the swamp. It had lain there for years and no-one knew. Quite well preserved, I believe, something to do with the moisture and the mud. Your grandmother took an interest in the details. Always on the phone, she was. Anyway, no-one claimed him, and eventually the housing estate went ahead.'

'How long had he been in the swamp?'

'A long time. Since the end of last century, I think. Mrs Ada knew of a man who lived there when her parents were alive. An old man who had been a performer, a showman. Harry Simmons. She was certain it must have been him.'

Rosamund smiled. 'You really are a fount of information, Kerry. Do you think Mrs Gibbons would talk to me? I'd like to see how Rae is, too.'

Kerry stood up. 'I'll call her now.'

Rosamund listened to the sound of the phone being dialled, and then Kerry's voice. Her thoughts drifted back through yesterday to the gallery and the paintings, and the discoveries she had made. On their way home she and Gary had stopped at a little hotel and taken a room for the 'night'. The place was old, built of bluestone, and had been restored to its former glory by the owner's loving hands. She had called Kerry to tell her they'd be late, and made some excuse. If Kerry knew the truth, she had been generous enough not to let on.

While the evening shadows had deepened in their room, they had lain together in the reproduction four-poster bed with its faded patchwork quilt, and made love long and hungrily. Rosamund felt sixteen years old, but much happier. It was worrying. She was not used to being happy.

'Rosamund?' Kerry's voice brought her back to reality. 'She'll be there tomorrow, if you want to go around. I told her about the Colonsay household accounts books, so she may look them up for you. She says she has one or two things from the Gibbons side of the family, and a family tree, of course.'

'Of course.'

'Rae will be there, too.'

'Thank you, Kerry.' Rosamund stood up with sudden decision. 'I think I'll go and visit the graves.' She laughed at Kerry's startled look. 'I want to stretch my legs, that's all. By the sound of the weather report, we'll be housebound for the next few days.'

'Better put on your coat,' Kerry called after her. 'It's freezing out there.'

Colonsay had a watchful feel. Upstairs in the west wing, where the windows had been, tarpaulins flapped against their fastenings. There was supposed to be some bad weather coming in. Rosamund hoped everything was watertight.

The air was cold enough already, stinging her lips and eyes, the wind pulling at her hair with a random cruelty. The pine trees creaked and groaned like a senior citizen's aerobics class. Rosamund jammed her hands in her pockets and followed the muddy driveway that led towards the family plot.

She saw Cosmo's monument first. It rose above the rest, a suitable memorial for the great man. Gradually, the remainder of the stones began to appear over the brow of the hill, silent disciples. They stood within their white picket fence, stark against a now black and thunderous sky.

The wind gusted, blowing the grass almost flat. Rosamund cut across the paddock and it caught her breath, making her gasp. She almost turned back then, and indeed had paused, when she caught sight of a crimson coat moving among the grey stones.

Today, Rosamund wasn't averse to some conversation about the past. Surely someone like the man in the red coat, so dedicated, would know all about the Cunninghams? Rosamund picked up her pace again, striding out.

The man was stooped low over one of the graves and appeared to be tidying away the dead flowers. She watched his slow, awkward movements and decided he was probably cold. The sound of a passing car startled her and she glanced over her shoulder in time to see a black, shiny BMW make a sharp turn from the road onto the driveway. It didn't pause, but continued towards the house.

She stared after it, forgetting the cold sting of the wind. Mark. What now? Had he decided to come himself after all, as she had dared him? Had he armoured himself against her so successfully that he was no longer afraid of her upsetting his plans? Or was he intending to evict her?

Shivering, she turned back to the graveyard. The old man in the crimson coat had gone. She turned from side to side, searching. There was no sign of him, no glimpse of his sturdy figure walking across the paddock or along the road, or even towards the cliffs and the bay. He had simply vanished, and the certain knowledge of it shocked her.

I shouldn't be shocked, she thought. She had seen and heard so much lately, this should not have been a surprise. And yet it was. He had seemed so solid, so real. She had had no inkling he might not be there at all, might be something left over from another time.

Slowly, stumbling a little, Rosamund continued on her way, but now she approached the stones warily.

There was something on one of the graves. Rosamund drew closer, until she reached Ambrosine's resting place. A bunch of flowers lay across the pink stone. White flowers, roses and daisies, and among them the bright red of cotoneaster berries. Like blood on snow. Rosamund shivered and, despite her unease, moved closer. She stretched out her hand to touch them, to feel if they were as real as they looked. But she could not bring herself to do it. Quickly, she turned and walked away.

The wind was behind her now, tangling her hair over her face and into her eyes. Impatiently, she reached up to push it back. Where could she go? In one direction the road led to town, and in the other, Geelong. Otherwise there were only the cliffs and the bay, grey and rough, where Cosmo had drowned. Where could she go?

I have nowhere to go but Colonsay, she thought. And wondered if Ambrosine had felt the same sense of trapped desperation.

A rattle of rain struck Rosamund's back, and then another, blown by the wind. Soon it would begin to pour. Forcing her legs into motion, she set off back the way she had come.

The black car was parked outside the house, its glossy sheen speckled by the rain. Rosamund rested her hand on the bonnet and found it still warm.

Inside the front door she paused. The warm smells from the kitchen tantalised and at the same time made her feel slightly sick. She could hear voices, Kerry's falsely bright and Mark's softer, deeper murmur. With a conscious relaxing of tense muscles, Rosamund walked into the kitchen.

He had his back to her but Kerry's glance brought his head around. He looked drawn and pale, the lines on his face deeper, more prominent than Rosamund had ever seen them. Mark was, today, every bit his age.

'Mr Markovic is here,' Kerry said unnecessarily, filling the silence.

Mark turned away again and Rosamund moved further into the room. The warmth was making her feel too hot and she knew her face was flushed. 'It's starting to rain,' she announced.

'Did you have to turn back?' Kerry asked.

'No. No, I only stayed a minute.'

She reached the table and stood behind one of the chairs. Mark was looking down at his hands, clasped about a mug of black coffee. He was wearing a black suit, black shirt and black tie. The starkness of the outfit suited his rather austere handsomeness.

'Where's Peel-Johnson?' She heard her voice hard and cold, like the rain which had begun to strike against the window.

'In Melbourne.'

'I thought you might have brought him and his briefcase with you.'

'Why don't you both go into the library?' Kerry suggested nervously. 'I can light the fire in there.'

They both ignored her.

'Colonsay is my house, Mark. I told Peel-Johnson that, and now I'm telling you. Ada left it to me, and I want it. Now, I think you should get back into your car and leave. You don't belong here.'

Throughout her speech, he had continued to stare down into his cup. Now he laughed, cheerlessly, his shoulders jerking. He nodded towards a thick wad of newsprint on the table beside him. 'Have you seen the newspapers today?'

Angrily, Rosamund shook her head, preparing to launch another attack. But he looked up and she saw something in his eyes that stopped her.

'You should take a look, Rose. Everyone else has read it. If you go by what it says here, I'm finished. Over. That's why I'm here, not because I want to take anything from you, but because I've got nowhere else to go.'

Cautiously, Rosamund reached across and lifted the uppermost newspaper. The story took up the full front page. There was a picture of Mark, smiling and urbane, at his most trustworthy, and next to him a grainy shot of a two-storey house. The headline screamed, 'Mark Markovic involved in risky business—construction company brothel'.

Hand shaking, Rosamund reached for the other papers, each headline was more shocking than the last. 'Markovic, brothel-owner?' and 'Mark and the girls!' The photos were garish, the text lurid.

Rosamund looked at him, the colour gone from her face. 'God, Mark, what's this all about?'

'Someone's set me up,' he said, and then his mouth twisted. 'The idea is to destroy me, and whoever it was has done a good job. No-one will vote for me now. Who wants an M.P. with this sort of dirt sticking to him? I'll sue, of course.'

'Tell me,' she said sharply.

'Go into the library.' Kerry had tears in her eyes. 'I'll bring some sandwiches and freshen the coffee.'

Mark pushed back his chair and stood up. He glanced in Kerry's direction and left the room. Rosamund stared after him. 'I don't understand.'

Kerry was bustling about with bread and butter. 'You must comfort your husband,' she said in her best 'Dear Kerry' voice. 'He needs you now.'

'Oh, does he?' Rosamund snapped. There was a sour taste in her mouth. 'God, Kerry, have you seen this stuff?'

'He says someone's set him up. Now, there are matches in on the mantelpiece. Light the fire. I'll bring in a tray in a minute.'

There didn't seem any point arguing further, but Rosamund hesitated at the door. 'I'll listen to him,' she said quietly, 'but I can't do any more than that. I have my own life now. I'm just starting to put it together again.'

'Oh, are you?'

'You don't understand—'

'Don't I?' Kerry's eyes were hard and accusing. 'I'm aware of what's going on between you and Gary. I warned you not to trust him, but you think you can see depths in him that other people can't. Rosamund, your husband is here now, and—'

'And therefore I must drop everything, give up my hopes and dreams, and turn back into the thing I despised. I won't, Kerry. I'm different, and I'm never going back.'

'Then don't. But he needs you. He's come here because he needs you.'

'He's come here because he has nowhere else to go,' Rosamund mocked, but in saying it she realised she had said the very same thing to herself. She had nowhere else to go, and now Mark was in the same situation. Colonsay had become their refuge.

When Rosamund opened the library door she found Mark sitting in one of the leather chairs. He was leaning forward, staring into the blackened leftovers of the fireplace. With an impatient sigh, Rosamund raked out the ashes onto a sheet of newspaper and started a new fire. It soon caught and spread.

For a long moment she gazed at it, saying nothing. She was remembering, despite herself, the last time they had been here together, how Mark had put his arms about her. Rosamund turned to meet her husband's eyes. He was watching her, waiting. He must have seen something in her face because he began to speak without her having to ask. His voice was soft and saturated with bitterness.

'I got a call last night asking me if I could confirm or deny that Markovic Constructions were involved in building a brothel. Of course, I denied it. Names and dates were put to me, but I still denied it. I had no idea . . .' He rubbed his hand over his jaw. 'I rang a few people and found, to my amazement, that we had built the brothel and now owned a share in it. It was all quite legal.'

'And you didn't know?'

'No!' He glared at her, then swallowed his anger. 'No, I didn't. It was all done without my knowledge. I would never have allowed such an undertaking.'

'Have you visited this place, Mark?'

He stared at her as if he were astounded. 'I've just told you, I didn't even know about it!'

'You said you'd sue. How can you if it's the truth?'

'I'll tell my own story, through my solicitors. And if any of the media have overstepped the mark in their enthusiasm for a good story, I'll sue them.'

'Will that settle it? End it?'

Mark laughed angrily. 'End it? I doubt it. I'm considering whether I should resign from the company board, dissociate myself. That might help. The Melbourne house is lit up with flash-bulbs. I can't go there. I can't go into the office. I'm not allowed near any government officials—they're afraid sympathy from them will be seen as sympathy for my supposed sleazy dealings. So I've come here, to Colonsay. No-one will find me here, not for a while anyway. Not until I've sorted out a strategy to beat them. I still have a few weeks until the by-election.'

'You intend to fight this, then?'

'Of course I do. What choice do I have?'

The fire was growing hotter. Rosamund moved away, brushing herself down while she thought. She had every reason to distrust Mark, and yet his words rang true. 'All right,' she agreed. 'You can stay for a time. Although it's not what you think, Mark. Colonsay isn't a happy old family mansion.

There are things . . . Ah, well.' She shrugged as his expression altered to blank disbelief. 'You'll see for yourself. I'll go and make up a room for you. Did you bring any luggage?'

'An overnight bag. I didn't have time for any more, and I didn't want anyone to guess I was leaving.'

'Kerry will be in with some sandwiches.'

'Thank you.'

She looked down at him. The firelight shone in his grey eyes, accentuating the sleepless shadows. 'Mark, you said to me once that a brothel was a good investment. Do you remember that?'

He blinked and shook his head. 'It probably is. That doesn't mean I'd want to be involved in one.'

'That's the truth?'

'For God's sake, yes!'

She turned away.

'Rosie?'

Rosamund paused at the door, not looking back, waiting.

'Rosie, I'm sorry.'

Sorry for what? For landing on her like an exorcist on the run, with the dark powers of the media about to descend on him? Or sorry for being such a bastard? She didn't ask, she didn't want to know, just closed the door quietly and firmly behind her.

****

Colonsay was a house shut off by bereavement, a grey house. The weak winter sun gleamed coldly on window panes and stone. Alice made her way down the long driveway, the cold, still air causing her toes and fingers to ache despite thick boots and gloves. She felt a hundred years older than when she had left. An old woman, grown shrivelled and withered inside, her dreams long dead. The only dreams she had these days were about revenge.

Cosmo had returned, as Meggy had said he would. Alice's father had seen him yesterday, out riding. So this morning Alice had set off to do what she had to.

'Mr Cunningham has guests.' Mrs Gibbons eyed Alice with barely concealed dislike, the mild affection she had once bestowed upon her gone.

'I need to speak to Mr Cunningham,' Alice insisted. 'It's important. I'll wait.'

'Oh, will you, miss!' the cook mocked. 'Well, if you want to wait you can be of use while you do it. Here, cut these up.'

Alice didn't argue. She removed her coat and gloves and sat down at the kitchen table with the peeling knife. Meggy was busy scrubbing a pot in the scullery and didn't come in to greet Alice. In silence, they all worked. As if nothing had changed.

****

'Why is he here?'

Gary sounded angry, and something more—he sounded worried.

Rosamund tightened her grip on the receiver.

The hallway was so thickly shadowed, the ceiling light barely made an impression. Outside, heavy rain was broken by growls of thunder and brilliant streaks of lightning. It was like warfare, the old-fashioned kind, with cannons and muskets.

'Haven't you seen the newspapers?' she asked.

There was a pause. 'No. I've been down to the boat, to make sure everything is secure.'

'Well, read them, Gary, and then you'll know why he's here and why I can't tell him to get out.'

'It's not a personal thing, then?'

'No. It's not a personal thing.'

She heard him sigh, followed by the crackling of static on the line. She remembered the warnings about speaking on the phone during a thunderstorm, but she didn't want to hang up yet.

'Rosamund?'

'What?'

'Be careful. And Rosamund?'

'Yes?'

'I love you.'

She opened her mouth to tell him she loved him, too, and then couldn't say it. She didn't know whether she did, and she didn't want to lie just to make Gary feel better. She probably would have, once, but she was trying to put that woman behind her.

'Goodbye, Gary,' she said instead, softly, and replaced the receiver.

If Kerry was fazed about having Mark stay, she didn't show it. In fact, she appeared to revel in it. 'Tomorrow night we'll eat in the dining room,' she announced with a smile. The prospect of a proper, formal Colonsay dinner appeared to excite her even more.

'Kerry . . . Mark mightn't want it too formal. He

mightn't even want to sit with us at all.'

Kerry brushed that aside. 'It will do Mr Markovic good to forget his troubles for a while. I'll hunt out the silver candle sticks and the good crockery. There's little enough of it left, but what there is is very good indeed.'

'I didn't know.' A gleam shone in Rosamund's eye. 'How good?'

'Too good to sell to a secondhand dealer,' Kerry replied sharply. 'And if you're going to open Colonsay as a guesthouse, you'll need to keep a few of the plates.'

'You really think I should do it, don't you? Throw Colonsay open to the paying public?'

'I believe your choices are limited. Of course, now that Mr Markovic is here—'

Rosamund interrupted her before she could finish. 'Where is Mark at the moment?'

'In the library. He has his mobile phone in there and he's been making calls all afternoon.'

'Damage control.'

'I've taken him in lunch and an afternoon snack. Perhaps you could take him another cup of coffee?'

'Perhaps I could,' Rosamund said.

As she made the coffee she did a mental stocktake of herself. Surprisingly, everything seemed to be in order. In fact, she felt remarkably well. Before, Rosamund had always felt as if she were balancing on a slippery slope—her feet had never been able to find purchase. Now she was climbing, and with each step it got easier.

She wondered at herself. Her estranged husband's career was about to be blown to pieces by a nasty scandal and he had come to hide out in her haunted house; and Rosamund had lately discovered her famed great-grandparents were part of a hushed up murder-suicide.

Was her inner strength a recent thing, born of the adversity she had faced since she came to Colonsay? Or had it always been there, hiding beneath the unhappiness and insecurities, just waiting for an opportunity to be set free?

The library felt warm and cosy. Mark was by the window, silhouetted against the grey light, mobile phone pressed to his ear. The room was almost dark, apart from the window and the glow of the fire. With the neglect so pleasantly camouflaged, Rosamund might almost have believed Colonsay had never changed.

Mark glanced around at her, but she couldn't read his expression with only his dark shape against the light outside. The rain was still pelting down, turning the ground into one huge muddy puddle. Frederick and his crew wouldn't have been able to start work today even if they'd wanted to.

Mark spoke again into the phone, his voice husky from overuse. Rosamund moved towards the door.

'Wait!'

He meant her, but she pretended he didn't and kept walking. Outside in the hall, she drew a deep breath of relief. Mark's presence was affecting her more than she wanted, more than she wanted him to see. Perhaps she should have told him to go, instead of taking pity on him. She had no business with compassion after what he'd put her through.

A clatter and a snatch of song from the kitchen brought Rosamund back to earth. She glanced towards the other end of the hall, the silent end. And it was silent, she could feel it, despite the rain and the continuing storm. She couldn't go near that room today. The library, too, was off limits, but for a more flesh-and-blood reason.

Slowly, Rosamund mounted the stairs and turned into the west wing. It was dry enough, the tarpaulins appeared to be keeping out the worst of the weather, but Frederick would have to do something soon. They could not go on like this forever. Rosamund continued walking through the rooms, feeling the past thick about her, like smoke from a badly lit fire. Her house, her people, her past.

Her grandmother had slept in this room. Ada, the baby of the family. And Bertie must have had his room nearby. She had seen his stone in the family plot. He had died as a boy, before his parents, when a train struck him on his way back to school in Melbourne. An unfortunate accident. Ada had rarely spoken of him, and Rosamund had often wondered whether the deaths of Cosmo and Ambrosine had over-shadowed all else to such an extent that Bertie had been forgotten. Ada had called him weak, and dismissed him. No-one could ever have called Ada 'weak'.

Suddenly she was aware of the faint scent of honeysuckle twining about her.

Rosamund stopped abruptly, all thoughts of her own past forgotten. She looked about anxiously, trying to pierce the shadows. A cold breeze came from somewhere and with a shiver Rosamund folded her arms tightly across her chest. Now the honeysuckle was stronger, closer.

'What do you want?' she asked, her voice strained. 'I know you're there, Alice. What do you want?'

Abruptly, the sweet smell intensified. It filled Rosamund's head. Claustrophobia gripped her and with it came emotions as strong as ocean waves. Hatred and sorrow, longing and despair. Savage, shattering emotions. They rolled over Rosamund, drowning her. Gasping, she tried to keep afloat.

'Alice,' she managed, but her voice was only a whispery shell. 'Help me to understand.'

The sensation of being suffocated began to diminish, drawing away with the receding thunderstorm. Rosamund blinked, and with a shudder opened her eyes. The tarpaulins over the windows rustled and fluttered. She felt drained, as if someone had pulled out her emotional plug and all her energy had escaped. Swaying on her feet, Rosamund turned towards the door, only to stop with a shocked cry.

'Mark!'

He was leaning in the doorway watching her, his face a combination of light and shadow. Rosamund swallowed and pushed her hair back with a shaking hand. She wondered how long he had been there.

'What were you doing?' he asked quietly, as if he didn't really care. But she wasn't deceived.

'Nothing, just looking around. Excuse me, I have some things to do.'

He didn't answer, or move, just kept watching her. Rosamund walked towards him, acutely self-conscious. He was blocking the doorway, and to leave she'd have to brush by him. The thought frightened her. Why was she suddenly so afraid of Mark?

Just as she reached him, he stood aside. She slipped past, out into the corridor. Relief washed over her.

'Rosie.'

He had deliberately waited until she thought she had escaped. When she didn't stop, he reached out and caught her arm.

'Rosie, I want you to tell me the truth.'

'The truth?' she managed. Her head was aching in an odd, echoing way. 'What are you talking about?'

He shook her slightly and she pulled her arm away, facing him across the narrow space. Behind her, she was uncomfortably aware, were the steep stairs into the attic.

'What is this Gary Munro to you?'

Anger came to her rescue. It took all else in its wake and she let it. 'What the hell business is it of yours?'

'You're my wife.'

'A fact you were prepared to forget. You're going to divorce me, aren't you? Only you haven't had the guts to come and tell me yourself, you'd rather send Peel-Johnson.'

'Rosie . . .' He looked away. 'When you're in the position I'm in, it's like a maze. You lose sight of your start and you can't find your finish. You just wander through it, and every day you have a new direction to choose. You just hope it's the right one.'

'And I was the wrong direction, is that what you're telling me?'

'Sometimes you think you're doing the best thing, they tell you you're doing the best thing, and even though deep in your heart there's a voice telling you what a prize bastard you are, you don't listen to it. You listen to them.'

He was watching her, waiting. All at once Rosamund understood. 'Very nice,' she whispered. She squeezed her fists tight at her sides. 'So now you've

'One of Mr Marling's buttons, sir.'

He looked at her as if she had gone mad. Alice sighed. He had no suspicions then. He did not understand, not yet. She would have to explain things more particularly.

She made her voice calm, although her blood was pounding. 'I found it in Mrs Cunningham's bedroom sir. Under the day-bed. I found it there, sir, after Mr Marling had been visiting at Colonsay.'

His attention was caught now. His frown darkened, blue eyes turned to slate, like the bay before a storm. 'I see,' he said, and now she could see that he did. He turned away and stared into the fire. Alice held her breath, waiting, but he didn't move again.

What had she expected? At the very least, a violent explosion of anger and pain. She had even hoped he might rush up the stairs to confront his wife and damn her adulterous behaviour in thunderous tones. But he did none of those things, just stood silent and still. Perhaps, decided Alice, his pain was too great to be acted upon yet.

'Thank you, Alice,' he said at last. It was a dismissal. With a sense of anticlimax, Alice left the room.

CHAPTER 19

It was early afternoon before Rosamund was able to set out to see Mrs Gibbons and her daughter Rae. She hadn't slept well during the night, awoken by sounds real and imaginary, and thoughts of Mark and Gary and the past. Consequently she had slept in.

The weather had improved slightly. At least it wasn't raining. The car stuttered a few times up the driveway—she hadn't driven since she arrived at Colonsay—but soon warmed up. Rosamund kept her eyes on the graveyard as she passed, but didn't see any old men in red coats. Today, all was peaceful.

Rosamund turned on to the Geelong road for the short time it took her to reach her destination. There was no sign of the swamp which had been drained in the 1960s to make way for the new housing development. Small brick houses clustered together, street after street. The builder hadn't had much imagination, or perhaps in those days it wasn't considered necessary to inject a bit of creativity into a housing estate.

The Gibbons's house was in the second street. Rosamund parked outside and, as she climbed from the car, she saw the net curtain twitch. Her shoes tapped on the concrete path to the front door, and when she pressed the bell she was greeted by a rendition of 'Greensleeves'.

'Mrs Markovic.' Rae, looking younger and less certain than she had the day she spoke with Rosamund at Colonsay. Her arm was tied in a sling about her neck, her fingers protruding awkwardly from a thick plaster cast.

'Rae, how are you?'

Rae relaxed a little and wriggled her fingers. 'Better than I was. Frederick wants me back at work next week. Just light stuff.'

'At Colonsay?'

Rae looked uneasy. 'I don't know, maybe.'

'Is that Mrs Markovic?' came a voice from inside the house. Rae glanced over her shoulder and shouted back.

'Yes, Mum.'

'Well, let her in, then.'

Rae grinned. 'Sorry. Come in. My mum's through here.'

The house was small and cluttered after Colonsay, but at least, thought Rosamund, the roof didn't leak and it was warm. And there were no ghosts. Mrs Gibbons, her dark hair greying and her eyes bright, looked up from her place on a couch by the electric heater. Her smile was warm and friendly.

'Mrs Markovic, I'm Sue Gibbons.'

'Rosamund, please. How do you do?' She stood and allowed Sue Gibbons to observe her.

'Mum!' said Rae, and pulled forward a comfortable-looking chair. 'Sit here, Mrs Markovic. Mum has a few things to show you.'

The 'few things' were spread across the couch and onto the floor. Rosamund didn't know whether to be pleased or daunted by the prospect confronting her.

'Mrs Scott—Kerry—said you were interested in the Colonsay servants but didn't want to go into the Historical Society,' Sue said briskly. 'I can understand that. Nosy lot of busybodies. Well, I've chased up some things for you, Rosamund.'

'So I see. I'm very grateful for this, Sue.'

'Don't mention it. Are you going to live at Colonsay with your husband? It would be lovely to have a family there again. Though, of course . . .'

She trailed off, looking embarrassed, and Rosamund realised that she would have seen the newspapers. She probably thought that was the real reason Rosamund didn't want to show her face at the Historical Society.

'My husband hasn't done anything wrong, Sue.'

'Of course he hasn't, of course,' she said quickly, but exchanged a glance with her daughter that said they believed otherwise. 'Now, here are the household accounts books that Kerry was talking about. You see, they date from 1880.'

The books were rather like ledgers and had a strong musty smell about them. Rosamund had grown almost inured to old smells since returning to Colonsay. The pages were ruled, with entries for payment and name and type of work done. Several books concerned Cosmo and Ambrosine's time at Colonsay, one was filled out by a man who signed himself A. Kirkwood, and the rest were in Ada's handwriting. Ada had begun her entries after her marriage, in 1917, and continued them almost until the date of her death. The spartan nature of the ledger was enlivened by her comments on the character of those she employed. Most were unflattering. 'More hair than sense', she had written over one name, and Rosamund couldn't help wondering what the 'busybodies' at the Historical Society had made of such things, particularly since there were still descendants living in the area.

'I'm interested in who was employed at Colonsay just before Ambrosine and Cosmo died,' Rosamund said.

'Here's the book for 1900–1901.' Sue handed her a mould-spotted ledger.

Rosamund opened it at the wages page for May 1901 and ran her finger carefully down the list. There was the cook, Mrs Gibbons, at the head of the list. Then followed a bewildering number of names, including a governess, a nurse, a groom, stable-boy, gardeners, kitchen maid and housemaid. The housemaid was Alice Parkin, and Alice Parkin was twelve years old.

'Oh God,' Rosamund whispered, peering intently at the page. Alice Parkin, the brown girl, the Alice in Marling's portrait. A twelve-year-old housemaid at Colonsay.

'Are you all right, Mrs Markovic?' Rae was watching her curiously.

'Yes,' Rosamund pulled herself together. 'It's just so . . . so moving, seeing the names.' She didn't care if Rae thought her a sentimental fool. Better that than the truth.

Returning to the book, Rosamund saw that Alice's employment at Colonsay had not been for a lengthy period. She had begun in late 1900 and finished in 1901. Hardly long enough, surely, to have developed an urge to haunt the house after she had gone. And where had she gone? Unfortunately, there were no clues to the name or whereabouts of her next employer.

Rosamund was still staring at the entry for Alice

when she noticed another familiar name. Meggy, the kitchen maid. Meggy McLauchlan, fourteen years old. And there, a little way beneath her, Jonah McLauchlan, groom, twenty-eight years. Meggy and Jonah were brother and sister.

'Do you know of a place called Tinyutin?' she heard herself asking aloud.

Sue looked thoughtful. 'No, I don't think so.'

'It's on the Murray River. At least, it was there in the 1920s.'

'Rae, get the atlas.'

Rae obliged, pulling a solid-looking atlas from book shelves near the television. While Rae searched the index, Sue handed Rosamund more documents. There was a long, admiring entry in a book on Port Phillip pioneers, and a copy of the land grant to the Cunningham family on the Bellarine Peninsula, and a later grant in southern New South Wales. Here was an obituary notice for Cosmo's death, and a photograph of the State funeral procession, with a black border. The Historical Society had done him proud.

'Here it is.' Rae shuffled over, holding the book open with one arm. 'There, just north of the Murray. In New South Wales.'

A tiny dot. Tinyutin. 'I believe the McLauchlans moved there after Cosmo died,' Rosamund said. 'Meggy and her brother. Do you know anything of them?'

Sue Gibbons shook her head. 'No. The name Meggy McLauchlan doesn't ring any bells with me.'

'Wait on, didn't Cosmo have land up that way?'

They pulled out the land grant again and tried to match it to the atlas, without much success.

'The McLauchlans could have been brought to

Colonsay from Cosmo's property on the Murray,' Sue said thoughtfully. 'It used to happen.'

Rosamund picked up a small booklet on the Old Soldiers' Home, and the sight of the old men, some in scarlet greatcoats, gave her another nasty shiver—the faithful layer of flowers on Ambrosine's grave had looked very like this. Inevitably, there were photographs of Cosmo and Ambrosine at various official functions, and one of Cosmo shaking hands with the local mayor. He was a handsome man, an impressive-looking man. Rosamund couldn't help a sense of disbelief that he had been the perpetrator of such a brutal deed.

'Can I take this with me, just for a day or so?' Rosamund asked, holding up the household accounts book for 1900–1901.

Sue, after a few moments of doubt, agreed. 'Before you go,' she added, 'I'll show you my husband's family tree.'

She unrolled a formidable scroll of paper and held it out. It was very detailed.

'Look,' said Rae, 'this is me, and this is Dad, and here's his father, and there's the one you're interested in. The cook.'

Rosamund leaned closer. The cook, Dorothy Sewell, had married Arthur Gibbons and then been widowed when she was forty. There were three children from the marriage. She had been remarried in Melbourne at the age of fifty-five to a Mr Harry Simmons. His occupation was given as showman.

Rosamund looked up in surprise. 'But wasn't Harry Simmons the man they found in the swamp?'

Sue and Rae exchanged a glance. 'No, not that I ever heard,' Sue answered. 'Where did you get that?'

'Kerry. She said my grandmother was certain the body in the swamp belonged to a Harry Simmons, who had been a showman. He lived there when she was a young girl and she remembered him. She, my grandmother, was in touch with the authorities and they thought it was Harry Simmons, too.'

'Well, it couldn't have been him, could it?' Rae laughed. 'Remember, Mum, how Gran used to say that her mother and old Harry were such a funny pair? Running off together at their age. Eloping to Melbourne. It was a family scandal, after the cook had been so respectable all those years.'

'I remember, Rae,' Sue said. 'I'm just surprised you do.'

'I prefer the juicy bits.'

Sue Gibbons searched in a folder at her side and pulled out a yellowing newspaper cutting. 'Here, this might interest you.'

Rosamund took it with a brief glance. It was about the body in the swamp but she wasn't about to be sidetracked from her own objective. 'So, Harry Simmons married the cook and went to Melbourne?'

'That's right.'

'What about the other servants? Did you ever hear what happened to them? Alice Parkin, for instance?'

A frown flitted across Sue's face. 'Alice Parkin? There were Parkins around here, but they're all gone now.'

'Perhaps, if you've time, you could look into it. I'd be interested to know if Alice was a local, and where she went to. I'm interested in all the servants who were there at the time of Cosmo's death.'

changed your mind, is that it? Suddenly you realise you can't live without me?'

He shrugged. 'It's the truth.'

'No, it's not. The truth is that you realise how bad it would look if your wife asked for a divorce just as your shady business dealings are uncovered. Just at the moment you need her standing smiling by your side. Predictable, Mark.'

She marched into the east wing and slammed her bedroom door behind her. The air in here was cold but she barely noticed. She was hot with her own righteous anger.

****

'Alice?'

Cosmo looked older, thinner. Alice felt an immediate pang of sympathy for him. He had lost his son. He had lost Bertie. How doubly bitter must that knowledge be when he had never accepted Bertie for what he was. Alice was certain that, if only Cosmo had understood, he would have appreciated his son so much more.

Ambrosine could have helped in that, but she had cared more for herself than for her husband or her son.

Alice took a breath. 'Sir, I have something to tell you.'

Her seriousness captured his attention. He nodded at her to continue.

Alice stretched out her hand and opened her fingers. Cosmo frowned at the ivory button.

'What is it?'

Sue Gibbons looked puzzled but nodded her head. 'If you like.'

Rosamund sensed that she needed a stronger motive. 'I'm ... I'm thinking of writing a book about it.'

It was obviously the right thing to say. Sue's eyes lit up.

'That would be great!' Rae cried. 'Wouldn't it, Mum? A book about Ambrosine and Cosmo.'

'A novel, do you mean?' Sue asked.

'No, oh no, I want it to be a factual account. Which is why I need to know all I can about the servants.'

An hour later, after tea and biscuits, she drove away, the household accounts book on the seat beside her and her ears ringing with good wishes and offers of help. She should have felt guilty about the lie, but somewhere between telling it and leaving she had begun to believe that she really would write a book. Not just about Ambrosine and Cosmo, but about Alice, too, and what had happened since she came home to Colonsay.

Mark *would* be pleased.

Rosamund dressed for dinner. Her only concession to Kerry's hard work was her hair style. She had swept her dark hair up on top of her head, an attempt to copy Ambrosine in the portrait. The end result was, if not precisely the same, at least a decent attempt. The mirror showed her a woman whose eyes were filled with secrets.

A loud knock on the front door broke her reverie. She went to the window. Gary's car was parked at the front, half obscured by the pile of wood and other refuse still awaiting collection.

Gary! What on earth was he doing here? The thought of Mark and Gary, together, made her feel queasy. Quickly, slipping on her shoes, Rosamund hurried to her own door.

Downstairs, Kerry stood with Gary in the entrance hall. They both looked up as Rosamund descended the stairs. 'Gary's just come from the hospital,' Kerry said, her voice full of relief. 'The poor man who fell off the scaffolding is going to make a full recovery. Isn't that wonderful, Rosamund?'

Rosamund nodded, still looking at Gary. 'Yes, it is,' she answered quietly. Then, 'You could have rung instead.'

'I was heading home, and Colonsay is only a slight diversion, so I thought I might as well drop in on the way. All right?'

So he wasn't as ignorant of the consequences of his visit as Rosamund had feared. She had placed her hand on his arm, as if to steer him towards the front door, when Mark came out of the library. Rosamund dropped her hand and Mark paused, perhaps sensing the sudden tension, before striding forward with his politician's smile.

'Gary. Have you come to join us? I believe Kerry has prepared a dinner fit for at least two kings.'

Rosamund said, with desperate cheerfulness, 'Gary's just given us some good news about the workman who was injured. He's going to be fine.'

'That is good,' Mark replied, still smiling.

'But he can't stay, can you Gary?'

'Oh but surely, now you're here . . .' Mark raised an eyebrow in inquiry.

Kerry cleared her throat nervously and avoided Rosamund's eyes. 'There's plenty to go round, Gary.'

Gary also avoided Rosamund's gaze. 'Thank you, I will stay. If you don't mind—'

'Not at all,' Mark cut in. He turned to Rosamund. 'We don't mind, do we, Rosamund?'

It was then that she knew for certain, with a sinking sensation, that Mark was well aware of what he was doing.

'You three go in. I'll fetch the soup.' Kerry escaped into the kitchen.

Rosamund moved to follow her, but Mark caught her arm in a deceptively casual grip and led her into the dining room. 'You look beautiful with your hair like that, Rosamund.' His voice was warm and possessive, a masterpiece of acting skill. He pulled out a chair in the middle of the table, and Rosamund sat down. Mark took his place at the head.

'Stunning,' Gary added, and took the chair at the other end.

Kerry brought in the tureen and proceeded to ladle out the soup. The smell was rich and inviting. 'A fine, thin chicken soup,' she said. 'I found some recipes in an old cooking book. A dinner menu for fifteen guests! I've had to reduce it slightly.' She sounded disappointed.

Kerry had lit candles, their wax ghostly in the gleaming candle sticks. Rosamund tried not to calculate how much each one would sell for. The flames dipped and wavered as if stirred by a breeze. There was hardly a room in Colonsay without a draught.

Mark complimented Kerry extravagantly on the soup, making her blush. Even now, Rosamund thought in disbelief, he can't stop. Gary watched the scene without speaking, his healthy good looks somehow out of place in this formal atmosphere.

As he bent his head to taste the soup, he caught Rosamund's worried gaze and winked.

'Was your boat safe from the storm?' she asked.

'Yes. The mooring's sheltered from south-westerlies.'

An awkward silence fell. Kerry was looking into her soup and Mark was watching the candles.

'Is it true what they're saying in the newspapers?' Gary asked coolly.

Mark set his spoon down. 'Some of it. Enough of it. Why, do you want to interview me and get the "real story"? I imagine you could ask a six-figure sum for something like that. The money would keep you until you finished your book.'

Gary's mouth twisted. 'No, I don't want the true story, or any story. I'm only interested because it affects Rosamund. Legally, you're still her husband.'

Rosamund stiffened. The tension in the air which until now had been simmering invisibly below the surface was suddenly palpable. 'Gary,' she said warningly.

The two men ignored her. 'Legally?' Mark repeated, and the amusement in his voice couldn't quite disguise the dislike. 'I am her husband, yes. Legally and in all other ways.'

'I don't think so. You've lost the right to claim that.'

'Gary! If I have to, I can fight my own battles. But right now is not the time.'

The stiffness went out of him, his smile said sorry, and other things. Despite herself, Rosamund flushed and looked down at her soup. Mark's silence was more dangerous than anything he could have said. Why didn't Gary take him seriously?

They finished the soup. Kerry cleared the plates and brought in the second course. It was salmon, set in little moulds and arranged with slivers of vegetables and sprinkled with shallots.

Rosamund poured herself some more wine.

'What is the publication date for your book?' Mark asked silkily, sipping from his own glass. 'Do you have one?'

'It's open at the moment.' Gary took a mouthful of salmon. He hadn't touched his wine.

'I have friends in publishing. Which publishing house are you contracted to?'

Gary mentioned a name, but Rosamund could see he was unwilling.

'I see.' Mark smiled over his glass. 'I don't think you've been entirely honest with my wife, have you, Gary?'

Gary's eyes narrowed. There was a stillness about him that Rosamund hadn't seen before.

'I don't suppose you have a monopoly on dishonesty, Mr Markovic.'

Mark laughed, dismissing the jibe. 'After I heard your name, I asked a few questions, Gary.' He turned to Rosamund. 'It seems that his book is a thinly disguised exposé of me and you, Rosamund. The hopeful Premier and his wife. His neurotic wife, I believe was the word used.'

'Gary?' Rosamund turned to face him. 'Are you writing a book like that?'

He sighed. His eyes were apologetic and she felt a rush of betrayal. 'They wanted me to. I'm not saying I didn't think about it. I was in the right place and I had the journalistic qualifications.'

'A book about Mark and me?' she repeated. Her throat was aching. 'Is that what this is all about? Research?'

He reached out and caught her hand, hard, so that she couldn't pull away. 'No, it isn't. From the moment I met you, I knew I couldn't do it. I wouldn't do it. Rosamund, *think*, please. He's trying to damn me in your eyes. Don't let him. You know I wouldn't hurt you, you *know* it.'

Rosamund blinked, tears shining in her eyes. He was willing her to believe him, to understand, his own eyes full of love. She relaxed a little. 'Why didn't you tell me?' she asked in a hurt voice.

'I would have, if I'd been going ahead with it,' he said. 'But I rang my publisher to say I'm not. The deal is off. I'll return their cheque when Enderby lends me the money.'

Mark shook his head. 'You believe him? He's having you on, Rose. He's a journalist! He probably knew about the story on me—they're all in each other's pockets.'

'I knew something was going on,' Gary said, and carefully put down his fork. 'I didn't know exactly what.'

'You could have warned Rosamund.'

'Why?' Gary looked directly at him. 'It had nothing to do with her.'

'What, the papers are full of lies about us and it has nothing to do with her?' Mark's face was livid now, his anger had broken free at last.

'Mark—' Rosamund began.

'The lies were about you, not her. If they were lies. I grant you, some of the more sensational press have gone over the top, but I've read a number of reports by reputable journos and they're well put together, well researched and fair.'

'Is it fair to ruin a man's reputation, his life?' Mark shouted.

Gary didn't flinch. 'I believe so. When that man is hiding something the public should know. More than fair, when you consider what the reports left out.'

Mark had been breathing hard but now he seemed to stop altogether. 'What did you say?' he whispered.

'You heard what I said. You know what I mean. Do you want me to say it here, in front of Rosamund?' Gary's eyes were glittering.

Rosamund banged her spoon against her plate. 'Stop it! Both of you, stop it! We're here to eat a meal, not to tear each other apart. Mark, shut up. And you too, Gary.'

The two men turned away from each other. Gary glanced at Rosamund with a sheepish look. 'Sorry,' he said. 'Sorry, Kerry. The food's delicious. Any more of it?'

Mark took longer to calm down. He was pale in the candlelight and his hands kept moving, rearranging the cutlery, his cuffs, the napkin. 'Yes, Kerry,' he added his apology, 'I'm sorry. Please continue with the meal.'

Slightly mollified, Kerry left to bring in the next course of perfectly cooked roast lamb.

Such a grand effort, thought Rosamund, should have been accompanied by witty conversation and lots of laughter. The sort of gathering Cosmo would have shone at, and Mark, too, in other circumstances. But the words that had been spoken sat heavy on the four of them, and Rosamund found more solace in the wine than in the food. She drank steadily, in a way she had not done for some time.

'Zephyr rang this morning.' Gary sipped his own wine, watching Rosamund over the rim of his glass. 'She's been having dreams, very vivid dreams.'

'Has she?' Rosamund heard the reluctance in her voice. She didn't particularly want to think of Alice tonight.

'She wants to try again.'

'Oh?'

'Tomorrow.'

Mark would be here, but it couldn't be helped. He would just have to go to his room and stay there, like a naughty child. The thought made Rosamund smile.

'Tomorrow will be fine.'

'Try what again?' Mark was looking at Kerry.

She dabbed at her mouth with her napkin. 'Oh, well, Gary has a friend who talks with . . .' She dabbed again. 'Really, Mr Markovic, it's nothing to do with me.'

Mark's eyebrows rose.

'She's a psychic,' Gary said flatly. 'She communicates with the dead. Perhaps she could resurrect your political career, Mr Markovic?'

Rosamund bit her lip.

Mark gave her a sharp look. 'Is that nonsense still going on?' Then, at Gary, and angry once more, 'Are you encouraging her in this?'

Rosamund sat up straighter. 'I don't need Gary to tell me what to do. Can't you understand, Mark? I am my own person and I do what I want to. I don't need your permission any more.'

Gary gave a shout of laughter and clapped his hands. 'I think I hear the sound of a worm turning!' he cried.

Kerry shifted uncomfortably. 'There's dessert, if anyone's interested.'

Mark cleared his throat, turning on the charm

again. 'Thank you, Kerry, that sounds marvellous.'

Gary gave a snort of disgust. 'You're unbelievable. I'll give the pudding a miss, if you don't mind, Kerry. I think I'll go to the library and wait for coffee.'

When he had gone, Kerry and Mark exchanged a look. Rosamund, angry with both men, said nothing. Each mouthful of crème caramel felt as if it would choke her, but she swallowed it down. When they were finally done, Kerry went to make coffee and left them alone.

'Your paparazzi friend seems a little stressed,' Mark said, folding his napkin.

'Please, can you let it rest, Mark? I'm tired of your childish games.'

'I didn't start it.'

Rosamund stood up, pushing back her chair clumsily. She was more than a little drunk. 'Are you feeling threatened, Mark, is that it?'

'No. Should I be?'

'What did Gary mean when he said the newspapers had left something out?'

Mark's eyes stayed on hers but she sensed a shift in him. 'Ask him, I don't know what he's talking about. Another thing you might like to know about Gary Munro, Rosie. He spent some time in a psychiatric hospital.'

'You really are a bastard, aren't you?' Rosamund walked towards the door, trying to keep her legs steady. The room was tilting but she managed not to slide off the floor.

'I love you, Rosie. I want you back.'

'Grow up, Mark.'

She reached for the doorknob, only to encounter Mark's fingers. They closed on hers, hot and tight.

'Rosie,' he whispered. 'Please. I'm sorry. I've been a fool.'

She didn't want him to kiss her but his mouth covered hers. Instead of an expression of love it felt greedy, suffocating. Rosamund put her hands up to his shoulders to push him away. 'Let me go!' she demanded and, dizzy with wine and emotion, her hair falling down, she escaped out into the hall. But Mark was close behind her.

The library was very warm and instantly Rosamund longed for cool air. Ignoring Mark she sank into one of the leather chairs and leaned her head back, eyes closed, wondering if she were going to be sick. You've done it again, she told herself. Rosamund Cunningham, drunken fool. Don't you ever learn?

'It's all about winning with you, Mark, isn't it?'

He didn't answer. Rosamund turned her head and saw that he was tapping out a number on his mobile phone. Where was Gary? Had he gone to help Kerry with the coffee? Rosamund moved restlessly and her eye caught something shining near the fireplace. She frowned, trying to make it out. Gleaming silver, it hung in space against the wallpaper. What was it? Had Kerry hung some sort of ornament there and not told her? Some sort of blade—

'Coffee,' Kerry announced loudly as she entered the room.

Rosamund blinked and the shining thing was gone.

'Here,' Gary came over and put his hand around hers and lifted a coffee cup to her lips. 'Drink.'

She sipped and coughed. The coffee was so strong it almost made her hair stand on end. 'Gary,' she wailed.

'Drink,' he said again grimly. 'I asked Kerry to make it like this for a reason.'

She drank.

Near the window, Mark was speaking on his phone, shoulders hunched over, voice muffled. Kerry took a cup of coffee and set it on the table beside him. She stayed to draw the curtains.

'Sober up, Rose,' Gary breathed in her ear.

'I will . . . I am.'

'You're not. Drink up.'

She drank more of the strong coffee and felt slightly more alert. 'What are you afraid of?' she managed, pushing Gary's hand away. 'That I won't be able to fight him off?'

'Well, will you?'

Rosamund let her eyes slip away from his. She sat up straighter and tucked her hair behind her ears. 'I'm all right,' she said quietly. 'Or I will be, soon. Don't worry about me, Gary, I can handle myself. I know Mark. He won't do anything.'

Gary sat back on his heels. 'I don't think you do know him,' he said softly.

'I'll be all right. How are *you* feeling?'

He smiled. 'Surprisingly okay. The spirits must be taking a holiday.'

'Either that or they're happy with our progress.' She told him about the visit to the Gibbons and what she had discovered. 'I have the book upstairs.'

'I'd like to take a look but it probably wouldn't be a good idea, would it?'

Rosamund touched his lips with her fingertip. 'Maybe not just now.'

Kerry cleared her throat. 'More coffee anyone?'

Mark finished his call and turned to face them. Suddenly he was all business. 'I'll leave you now.

I have some more calls to make. Thank you for the meal, Kerry, it was magnificent.'

Kerry looked flattered. 'Do you need anything, Mr Markovic?'

'No, I'm fine. Oh,' he paused at the door, 'who owns the dog? I saw it in the garden this morning. Little dog, long hair, and a ribbon—' He frowned, looking at their faces. 'What have I said?'

Rosamund shook her head. 'Nothing. We've been trying to catch it. It must be lost.'

Mark nodded, though he still looked suspicious. 'Good night then.' He bent and kissed Rosamund's cheek in passing, as if everything were perfectly normal between them. Amazement at his arrogance stopped her from responding.

Kerry went out to pack the dishwasher, refusing all offers of assistance. Gary leaned back in his chair and looked at Rosamund.

'What was that about?'

'Mark just doing what he does best, being Mark.'

'He seems to think you'll come when he whistles.'

Rosamund shifted restlessly.

'You had me worried tonight, Rosie. Do you always drink that much?'

'I'm sorry.'

He studied her face thoughtfully. 'Is it really over between you two? Because there's something you should know, Rose. He's a creep.'

'Gary, whatever you might think about Mark, I know he wouldn't hurt me.'

'Maybe Ambrosine thought Cosmo wouldn't hurt her, either.'

Rosamund flinched. 'Touché. But Gary, it was so different then. A woman in Ambrosine's position couldn't leave her husband without a shocking scandal, and when that husband was a man as powerful as Cosmo, perhaps it was just easier to be unhappy.'

Gary ran his hands through his hair. 'I don't know, Rose.' He sounded defeated. Leaning forward, he took up Marling's book and flicked through it. Suddenly he gave a gasp.

'Gary, what is it?'

He looked up, his face blank. 'This is the man I saw that day, in here, sitting right where you're sitting. The grey man, the ghost. It was Henry Marling.'

Rosamund leaned forward to see the page. Henry Marling's handsome face gazed back at her, a twinkle in his eye. 'He was a close friend of Cosmo's, we know that. He would have stayed at Colonsay many times.'

'Rose,' Gary closed the book with a snap. She could see he had made up his mind about something. 'Marling was painting Ambrosine's portrait. He was here at Colonsay. He was handsome and intelligent. What does that say to you?'

Rosamund looked startled. 'He was Ambrosine's lover!'

Gary nodded. 'Cosmo found out. Perhaps she told him she was leaving him and he lost it.'

'Do you really think that's what happened?' Rosamund had slumped, and sadness filled her, the aftermath of too much to drink.

'Perhaps I should write a book about that,' he said wryly.

Rosamund sat up straight again. 'Then it will have to be a collaboration. I've already told Sue Gibbons *I'm* writing a book about Cosmo and Ambrosine!'

Gary gave a chuckle. 'You're on.' He sobered.

'Rosie, look, I'm sorry I didn't tell you about the other thing. I'm sorry you found out through Mark. I wanted to tell you, but it felt like a betrayal that I'd even contemplated it, even for a second. And besides, I'd already decided to turn them down.'

'Gary, if I'd still been the sulky girl you remembered from the past, would you have gone on with it?'

He shook his head. 'No. I try not to be too judgmental these days. I'm not perfect myself.'

'I wouldn't say that.'

His smile was warm, stroking her.

'You'd better go to bed. Zephyr's coming tomorrow, remember?'

'Oh God, I forgot.'

Reluctantly, Rosamund followed him to the front door.

'I wish you didn't have to go,' she whispered.

He put his arms around her and kissed her slowly. 'I'll see you in the morning.'

He had turned towards the car when she said. 'Gary, I do trust you.' He didn't know it, but it was something she had never said to Mark.

'Thank you.'

She watched him drive away. The air was cold but invigorating, more sobering than any coffee.

****

'I want to go home,' Meggy hiccupped. She looked up at Alice through tangled hair and red-rimmed eyes. 'I want to go home, and Jonah says he won't leave. There's bad things stirring, Alice. I feel them. I want to go home.'

Wisely, Alice held her tongue, but Meggy's next words caused her heart to jump.

'Jonah says the master knows something, and madam's in trouble and he can't go. He says what sort of servant would he be if he went now?'

Alice saw the flicker in Meggy's eyes and knew there was something else, something she wasn't telling. Perhaps Jonah saw profit for himself in the rift between Cosmo and Ambrosine, and that's why he insisted on staying.

'What do you think the master knows about madam?' Alice asked softly.

Meggy shook her head, lank strands of hair falling over her brow so that her eyes were veiled.

Alice swallowed her impatience and put an arm about Meggy's shoulders. She thought, It's begun, Bertie. Cosmo will punish Ambrosine and that will be our revenge. She deserves to be punished. Someone should pay for what happened to you.

'I want to go home,' Meggy was whispering. 'I want to see the evening shadows stretching out over the plains. Giants walking, that's what Jonah always calls them.'

Her words caused a ripple of recognition deep in Alice's memory. Who else had said that? But the answer did not seem important enough to persist with, and Alice let it slip.

CHAPTER 20

'Mrs Markovic?' Frederick Swann sounded crisp and businesslike over the phone. 'I think we'll be ready to start work again tomorrow. How do you feel about that?'

'I feel wonderful, Fred!' She did in fact feel remarkably wonderful, with little trace of a hangover after last night's efforts.

'Good. How are, eh, things?'

'Things are wonderful, too. Colonsay appears to be a normal house again.'

He was obviously relieved to hear it. 'The power of prayer is not to be belittled,' he told her. 'You might remember that in the future, Mrs Markovic.'

'I will, Fred, I will.'

After she had hung up, Rosamund looked uneasily down the hall towards Ambrosine's sitting room. The door was closed and all was quiet. Had whatever was in there gone? Somehow she didn't think so, and she had no intention of testing it now.

Zephyr would be here soon.

Mark was in the library again, talking on the phone, calling in favours, trying to salvage something out of the mess. Rosamund stuck her head in the door and caught his eye. 'Can I speak to you?'

He nodded and wrapped up the call, watching her as he spoke. 'All right, then, fine, yes, okay, that'll be fine, I'll talk to you then.' Mark tossed the mobile onto the table. 'What did you want to say?'

'We'll be using this room. You may want to go elsewhere before Zephyr comes.'

'And this ghostbuster is a friend of the paparazzi? Do God and journalism go together? I would have thought they were mutually exclusive.'

'Can't you just let it drop, Mark?'

'No, I can't.'

Out in the hall the phone rang again. They heard Kerry answer it.

'Will you let me have Colonsay without a fight, Mark? I'll fight you for it if I have to, but it would be so much better if you'd just accept that it's mine. You can't be another Cosmo. Cosmo Cunningham is dead. Let Colonsay go.'

He shook his head. 'I need Colonsay, it's part of the package. I want you to be here with me, Rose. I thought we'd agreed to forget the past.'

'We've agreed to nothing!'

'Rose, you love me. I look after you. You'll fall to pieces without me.'

Rosamund shook her head. 'No, Mark. I'll fall to pieces *with* you.'

Mark stared at her, unconvinced. 'You'll change your mind.'

'Mark,' she breathed, 'do you really think people will forget what you've done?'

'I have friends. They won't desert me.'

She folded her arms as if to protect herself. 'Surely there comes a point when even friends can no longer help?'

He shrugged irritably. 'I'm not finished, Rose.

I'll fight this. Markovic Constructions has done nothing illegal. It was business, that's all. There'll be a lot of sympathy out there for me.'

Kerry knocked on the door and opened it. 'Sorry to disturb you. Rosamund, Enderby Munro was just on the phone. He wants to see you as soon as possible.'

She tucked her hair back and sighed. 'All right. Tell him this time tomorrow, okay?'

Kerry closed the door. Mark had already picked up the mobile and was busy punching out another number.

****

Alice had come to visit Meggy. She had walked from the town in the cool sunshine, a brisk breeze stinging her eyes and bringing colour to her pale cheeks. Her mother had been glad to get her out of the house and her father had taken the horse to Geelong on business.

Colonsay stood solid against a pale blue sky, the bare honeysuckle clinging to the wooden verandah posts and stone walls. Thorny roses dotted the front garden. Their foliage had all dropped, apart from a single red rose, like blood against the grey. Stone crunched under Alice's boots and she wondered if her planted seed had yet borne fruit.

It was the only thing she had thought of since her interview with Cosmo. Revenge and Bertie. Her whole life had become centred on that and nothing else. It was as if a fire burned within her, consuming every other feeling and emotion. A bright core within the darkness.

'What do you want?'

The voice was a stranger's. Alice glanced up sharply. He was near the fountain, a man in a shiny black coat. He looked Alice up and down.

It was not usual at Colonsay to have strangers ordering visitors about. Alice drew herself up. 'Who are you?'

The man frowned down at her. His hair was thin on top but, as if to make up for that, grew in thick, dark borders in front of his large ears. 'They're not receiving visitors t'day,' he said in a voice meant to intimidate. 'Come back t'morrow.'

Alice hesitated, but the stranger set his boots slightly apart, his thickset body blocking her way. She sensed he'd not cavil at putting his hands on her.

'Tomorrow then,' she told him. He grunted as she turned away.

Again the stones crunched under her feet as Alice retraced her steps. She felt his eyes on her back, and walked idly to the end of the driveway before she turned off into the paddock. She kicked the ground, pretending to dawdle, until she reached a stand of big pine trees.

Then Alice began to run.

There was something happening. Something strange going on. Bad things, Meggy had said. Alice sensed a silence at Colonsay that had nothing to do with restfulness.

****

Gary and Zephyr were waiting in the kitchen. Gary gave Rosamund a smile. 'How are you?' he asked.

'Better than I expected.'

Zephyr, dressed in a combination of mauve and lemon, gave her usual serene greeting. 'I've been dreaming,' she explained. 'Sometimes that can happen after I've been in contact with a spirit.'

'You mean, dreaming about Alice?'

Zephyr fixed Rosamund with a look. 'You know her name. That's good. Rosamund, this poor soul is greatly in need of help. She can't leave Colonsay. There is no peace for her. Past events have trapped her here. We must help to free her.'

'Just Alice?' Rosamund asked, remembering the man who called for Rosie and the visions she had of Ambrosine.

'There may be others but I think Alice is at the centre of it. She's stirring things up. If Alice can find peace, then they may well be at peace, too.'

When they entered the library to begin the session, Mark was still there. He glanced up at Zephyr and smiled his most charming smile.

'Sorry, I'll get out of your way.'

'Mr Markovic,' and she held out her hand. He took it briskly enough but Rosamund sensed his unwillingness.

'Mark,' Zephyr tipped her head to the side, 'I am getting a sensation of water. Cold water, deep water. Is there some problem in your life to do with water?'

Mark went pale.

Zephyr closed her eyes. 'Oh dear,' she murmured mildly, 'have you had an accident in water?'

'No,' Mark bit out, 'I haven't.'

'I must warn you. There is danger for you. A choice. I see water, deep water. Does this help you?'

He dropped her hand. 'No, it bloody doesn't.' Rudely, he pushed past her to the doorway, where Rosamund was standing. 'You told her, you bitch,' he hissed in her ear as he walked out.

There was an uncomfortable silence.

Zephyr was looking after him. 'Have I said the wrong thing?'

'It's all right.' Rosamund put aside her own anger to reassure her. 'Mark prefers to keep his weaknesses to himself.'

Gary arranged the chairs in a semicircle, as last time, and drew the drapes. Zephyr settled herself by the lamp and closed her eyes. She began her relaxed breathing. The trance seemed to happen more quickly this time, as if Alice were standing by her chair, waiting.

'Help me.'

'Alice? Is it Alice Parkin?' Gary spoke quietly.

'Yes. Alice.'

'Tell us what you want us to do, Alice. We want to help you. Tell us what you need from us, Alice.'

Silence. Zephyr's breathing grew ragged.

'Forgive . . . Alice.'

'What happened to you, Alice? Why can't you leave Colonsay? Tell us, so that we can help you.' Gary leaned forward, intent.

Zephyr sighed deeply and opened her eyes. They were different, brighter and younger. Slowly they passed over Kerry and Gary, and found Rosamund.

'Ambrosine,' she said, her voice coming from deep within. Rosamund swallowed. She was trembling.

'This is Rosamund,' Gary was saying. 'Not

Ambrosine. Alice, what happened to you? Tell us so that we can help you. Did you die here, at Colonsay? Is your body here?'

'I was flying . . . a storm petrel.'

'Flying?'

'There was no pain. I was flying.'

'Do you mean when you died?'

'Yes. I wanted to find Bertie but he wasn't there.'

'Do you mean Bertie Cunningham, Alice?'

'Yes. He was my friend.'

Silence.

'Alice, was there something weighing heavily on your conscience when you died?'

'Yes.' A gasp.

'Let us help you, Alice. Tell us.'

Alice's voice spoke again but the word was too low to catch. Zephyr's eyes fluttered and closed. She sighed deeply.

Gary moved to touch her arm and then glanced back to the others. 'She's coming out of the trance.'

'We were right,' Rosamund said quietly. 'Alice can't leave until we free her. If only we knew how!'

'It will come.' Zephyr said, her voice weary. She opened her eyes and now they were her own dark ones, with grey shadows beneath them. 'Poor soul, may she find peace.'

Kerry nodded. 'Amen.'

Rosamund was far away in her own thoughts. She was trying to imagine the Alice she had seen and Bertie Cunningham, as friends. And it was not difficult after all. Weak Bertie, like Rosamund, would always have been drawn to a stronger personality.

As Zephyr was leaving, she took Rosamund's hand. 'Your husband has a decision to make. Remember, it's his decision, not yours. We must all take responsibility for our own lives, Rosamund.'

****

It was easy enough to get to the kitchen door. No-one was guarding that and it opened to her cautious touch. The heat from the stove pressed against her, momentarily taking her breath. Mrs Gibbons looked up from the folds of her apron, her face blotched and soaked, her eyes like small red beads.

'Alice!'

Meggy stumbled towards her, flinging her arms about her. She was trembling, teeth chattering. Alice steadied herself.

'What are you doing here, girl?' the cook asked in a grating whisper. She glanced back over her shoulder as if afraid someone might be standing there. 'No-one's to be allowed in or out. Apart from the doctor.'

'Is there sickness in the house?' At school they had spoken about plagues and things. Could Colonsay be afflicted with something so dreadful?

Meggy groaned and lifted a ravaged face from Alice's shoulder. 'Dead,' she gasped. 'Alice, she's dead!'

Mrs Gibbons caught Meggy's arms and pulled her away roughly, pushing her down onto the stool by the hearth. Her fat fingers seemed unnecessarily cruel, her small eyes swollen with weeping. Alice knew that something bad had happened.

'The master,' the cook swallowed. 'The master.' But she didn't seem able to go on, and collapsed heavily into a chair.

'Madam's dead,' Meggy whispered, her voice muffled, bowed head in her hands. 'Killed.'

Alice could find nothing to say. Her mind, like a school slate, had been wiped clean. 'But . . . how?' she managed at last.

Mrs Gibbons's lips began to tremble violently, tears rolling over her wobbling cheeks. 'That sword up on the wall in the library. The one the old soldiers gave him. He cut her down with that.'

'Chopped her up like his bloody onions!' Meggy breathed.

Alice didn't speak. The enormity of what she had just heard filled her every pore. Madam was dead. Cosmo had killed her. He had killed her because of Mr Marling. He had killed her because of what Alice had told him. Alice's seed had grown far larger than she had ever imagined. Madam was dead. No more darkened rooms and headaches and hiding in her bedroom instead of bringing her son home from a school he hated. No more fine clothes and shoes, dressing up her beauty for Mr Marling while Bertie suffered. No more Ambrosine.

I'm glad.

The words slipped slyly into her brain. Bertie had died, and surely it was only just that Ambrosine suffer a similar fate? *I'm glad.* But still, the horror of it couldn't be so easily dismissed. And there was Cosmo—what would happen to him? The last thought stirred in Alice a need to know and she found her voice again. 'You must tell me what happened.'

The cook wiped her face with her apron. 'She . . . madam was having tea in her sitting room, with him, the master. They started shouting—'

'He were yelling,' Meggy said, lifting her head. She looked old. 'Yelling like a wild man.'

'Then he came bursting out of there and went into the library. When he come out of the library again he had the sword. Miss Ada, she were on the stairs, screaming, but he didn't notice. Or he didn't care.' She stopped, her breath catching.

Meggy took up the story again her voice barely louder than the ticking of the kitchen clock.

'He went back to her and locked the door. She was begging him, Alice. I heard her begging for her life. Her dog was barking, but then it stopped all of a sudden. Just . . . stopped. And she screamed and screamed and . . .'

The horror in her eyes was like a dark rushing wave, and Alice turned away before it swamped her, too. 'Where is he now?' she asked the cook.

'He got a horse, took off like a madman. Mr Kirkwood's sent out after him.'

Voices could be heard in the hall. Mrs Gibbons rose unsteadily, hands resting on the chair back, supporting herself. Meggy's head twisted sharply. The door opened and Alice saw that it was the doctor, and beside him a stranger. Not the servant who had been at the front of the house, but, by the cut of his clothes, a gentleman. He was white-faced but determined on some course of action, a resolve Alice recognised well.

'Mrs Gibbons,' he said quietly, addressing the cook. 'The doctor will see Mrs Cunningham now. We'll carry her up to her room. Will you begin heating water?'

There was an uncomfortable silence. Meggy put

her face in her hands again. Mrs Gibbons nodded at last, her fingers opening and closing on the back of the chair, opening and closing. Mr Kirkwood's eyes moved over Meggy's bowed head and rested on Alice. He frowned, white marks appearing either side of his mouth.

'Who are you?'

Neither Mrs Gibbons nor Meggy was presently capable of subterfuge, so Alice answered for herself. 'I'm Alice Parkin, sir. I'm the housemaid here. I've been away, but I was due to start work again today.'

Her crisp, clear voice seemed to impress Mr Kirkwood. He relaxed slightly, a spark of interest lightening the burden in his eyes. Turning to the doctor, he asked, 'Is this true?'

The doctor looked miserable, barely listening. A man forced into a position he did not relish. 'This is Alice Parkin,' he muttered, 'and she is a servant at Colonsay.'

Kirkwood glanced at her again, then nodded. 'No-one's to leave,' he said, and it was an order. The door closed.

The cook sank down again in her chair. 'But he loved her,' she wailed. 'I don't understand. He loved her!'

Meggy began to cry noisily.

Alice said nothing. Of them all, she alone understood why Cosmo had murdered his wife. She alone understood, and condoned it. But it was a knowledge she would never share with anybody else. Alice was good at keeping secrets.

****

Outside, the late afternoon sun was shining, as if making up for the rain. Gary had long ago taken Zephyr home, and although he had promised to return he had not done so. Mark was upstairs somewhere and Kerry was baking, judging by the mouth-watering smells coming from the kitchen.

Rosamund hesitated in the hall, nervously smoothing her hands on her jeans. Slowly, cautiously, she approached Ambrosine's sitting room. This was where it happened, where Ambrosine had died, brutally, at Cosmo's hand. Somehow, Alice had been mixed up in their tragedy and now, for whatever reason, she could find no peace.

Rosamund grasped the doorknob and pushed. The bottom of the door jammed, and she pressed against it, forcing it open. As usual, the air smelt stale and dank, and the light was poor. Rosamund stepped over the threshold and peered into the shadows.

The room had not always been like this. Once, it must have been as beautiful as Ambrosine herself. Had she entertained Henry Marling here, when Cosmo was away? They must have been a striking couple. Had Alice known about their affair? Rosamund could imagine her, an intelligent and curious girl, bored with her work, seeking entertainment. Twelve was a difficult age, and Alice Parkin must have been more difficult than most—

'Rosamund?'

Kerry touched her shoulder, an unspoken apology for making her jump.

'Should you be here?' she asked, eyes skittering nervously away from the shadowy room.

'This is where it happened, Kerry. I know it.'

She stepped outside and pulled the door to. 'Did Ada speak much to you about her mother? The few times she mentioned her to me, it was to tell me how happy she was. It was always Cosmo who held centre stage.'

Kerry followed her back down the hall. 'Not much, no. I got the impression she was not a strong woman, physically or in her personality.'

'I suppose Cosmo was pretty overbearing.'

'Wait a minute, I do believe Mrs Ada mentioned her mother was not from a wealthy background, not like Cosmo. It was a love match, according to your grandmother. I suppose such a thing was considered a little shocking in those days and in those social circles. Ambrosine's father had fallen on hard times—he was a farmer, or that sort of thing. I know her brother was in the Boer War and was killed not long after Ambrosine died. Mrs Ada always said she might have had a different upbringing if he had lived. Not that the Kirkwoods, the family who cared for her until she met your grandfather, weren't very kind.'

They had reached the kitchen and Rosamund began to make coffee. 'Poor Ada. How could any child cope with all that and grow up to be normal?'

'Mrs Ada was perfectly normal,' Kerry said stiffly. 'Do you know,' she went on more thoughtfully, 'I believe Ambrosine came from the country north of the Murray River. Yes, I'm sure that was it. I can remember Mrs Ada telling me that her mother was never very fond of the sea, and that was why.'

'Tinyutin?' Rosamund asked.

'I beg your pardon?'

'It's the name of a little town up that way. Cosmo had land there, too. They must have been neighbours, or near enough. That was probably how they met. The rich and handsome Cosmo, riding by, notices the beautiful but poor farmer's daughter. Deal done. Poor Ambrosine, I wonder if she had much of a say in it?'

'She was probably very grateful.'

'You're probably right.'

'Well, that's all I can remember. I'm sorry I haven't been more help.'

Rosamund smiled broadly. 'You know, Kerry, you amaze me.'

Kerry coloured.

In the hall the phone rang.

'If that's the press,' Rosamund called after Kerry as she hurried to answer it, 'tell them I'm not home.'

****

The doctor had gone. It was Kirkwood who had taken over the household, and Colonsay ran to his bidding. Alice was not even sure who or what he was, other than a parliamentary friend of Cosmo's, but he appeared to have a great deal of authority. He gathered together the Colonsay staff in the drawing room, and they stood in a huddle like victims in a war, waiting to hear what he would say. Perhaps, like powerless people everywhere, they were hoping he would make everything better again.

Alice shuffled, waiting, ignoring Meggy's murmured, 'Where's Jonah? Is Jonah here?'

'This is a terrible day.' Mr Kirkwood's voice

was low with grief. He lifted his head and allowed himself to take in their white, drawn faces. 'A terrible day. Mrs Cunningham is dead and Mr Cunningham . . . well, we think now that he has taken his own life. He was seen going out in his boat and he hasn't returned.'

A moment while this was digested. Alice moved uneasily. Cosmo dead? She hadn't meant for that to happen. That hadn't been in her plan. She shivered and felt a stir in the people about her, as though they were experiencing the same emotions.

'Mrs Cunningham has been murdered by her husband, cut to pieces with a sword, and now, through remorse or guilt or fear, or all three, her husband has killed himself.' Mr Kirkwood repeated the last five words, allowing each one equal weight. Mrs Gibbons whimpered and covered her shaking mouth with her plump hand. Others began to cry.

'The truth can be very cruel sometimes,' he went on when they were ready to listen again. 'Sometimes it can be kinder to tell lies. Just for a moment I want you to imagine this. What if Mrs Cunningham wasn't murdered by her husband? What if she was ill with, say, influenza and died suddenly. She had a weak heart. It gave out under the stress of her illness. And what if her husband, overcome with his shock and grief, went out in his boat, out into the bay, and let himself drown. What if it happened like that?'

He was a clever man, thought Alice. She could see the lightening of the faces about her, the sudden interest. Even Mrs Gibbons's lips had stopped trembling.

'If it had happened like that, then the Cunningham name would be unsullied. Mr Cunningham would retain his rightful place in the history of this country, his key importance in the writing of our new Constitution and the equally important part he has played in the new Federal Parliament. He will be a hero, the more so because of the tragic circumstances of his death.'

'That's true,' someone whispered.

Mr Kirkwood smiled briefly in their direction. 'And Mrs Cunningham. What if it happened as I say? Dying so suddenly, still beautiful, still loved by you all, by the whole nation. She could rest peacefully, don't you think? Or would you prefer people to remember her as a bloody thing upon the floor, cut about so savagely she is hardly human at all?'

'No!' Mrs Gibbons's wail struck at their hearts.

'And what of yourselves? Will you, as the servants of the Cunningham family, be viewed with sympathy and compassion, or with ghoulish fascination? Will you find it an easy thing to gain new employment when the truth is known about your last employers and their ghastly deaths? Naturally such a thing has not occurred to any of you yet, but it must be thought of.'

Yes, Alice agreed, after the shock had worn off these people would begin to think of themselves, of their own futures. What had happened here at Colonsay would do them no good in terms of new employment. Mr Kirkwood was very clever to remind them of it.

'Newspapers can be very cruel,' he went on softly. 'People can be very cruel. The truth is not always in everybody's interest.'

'People will see the truth though, won't they?' someone asked.

Mr Kirkwood hesitated. 'If it is thought that

Mrs Cunningham died of influenza, the doctor will place Colonsay in quarantine. No-one will be allowed in or out. No-one will see. We can keep the truth to ourselves. I can do that for you, for us all. I can make sure that the Cunningham name remains as bright as the star it should be, and that Colonsay becomes a house of remembrance rather than a place for ghouls and seekers after scandal. But you will have to obey me, and you will have to make promises you must keep for the rest of your lives.' He looked long into the faces about him. No-one dissented.

'So,' he went on, and allowed himself a sigh of relief. 'Your loyalty will not go unrewarded. In return for your promises, you will be given the opportunity to go to new jobs in new towns. And you will each receive a sum of money.'

It was irresistible. Alice could see he had won them over, each and every one of them. She sensed the same willingness in herself, despite what she knew and felt about Ambrosine. She would do it, but it would be for Cosmo. Surely it was only right and just that such a great man be remembered as such, and not be vilified as a wife-murderer because Ambrosine had been unfaithful?

'Who will give me their hand on this matter?' Mr Kirkwood stepped forward and they swamped him with their hands and their promises.

****

Kerry's face was carefully blank. 'It's Gary Munro and he wants to speak to you.'

Rosamund took her coffee with her. 'Gary?'

'Rose.' There was a note in his voice that had her antennae quivering.

'Where are you? I thought you were coming back after you dropped Zephyr off?'

'I got a call from one of my contacts in Melbourne.'

'You mean, about the file on Cosmo?'

'Yes.' He hesitated. 'Not much good, I'm sorry. I found mention of a man named Kirkwood. Ada lived with him and his family after her parents died. He was *in loco parentis*. Had control over Colonsay and Ada's money. Seems to have done very well out of it. Ada never asked to have Kirkwood's dealings looked into, but I have a feeling she should have.'

'You mean he stole from her?' Rosamund gasped.

'May well have helped himself, but it was never proved.'

'Gary, that's horrible! But why didn't she prosecute him?'

'Kirkwood was an important backroom man in the Federal Government. He probably knew about Cosmo. Ada wouldn't have wanted that to come out, Rose.'

'No wonder she never trusted anyone.'

'Maybe. This is all supposition.' He took a quick breath. 'Where's Mark?'

'Around somewhere. Why?' And when he hesitated, 'Gary, there's something else, isn't there? Tell me what it is.'

After a moment he said, 'Rose, your husband's about to be investigated by the State Police. It's supposed to be a secret but the media already know. They're baying for his blood. Nothing they like better than to bring down a hero. Tell him to get out now.'

Rosamund put down her coffee mug, spilling it, burning her fingers. 'I don't understand. Mark said he knew nothing about the brothel. And anyway, they're not illegal in Victoria.'

'Rose,' he murmured, 'poor Rose. Hell is about to break loose around you, and it'll be worse than anything Alice could dream up. Come and stay with me. Will you?'

She felt as if she were losing her sanity. 'Gary, will you tell me what's happening!'

He gave in. 'Mark's been lying to you. Not only did he know about the brothel, he used it to his own advantage. He's been entertaining there, giving some of his politician friends, and others, carte blanche. No wonder they're a hundred percent behind him—they wouldn't dare be otherwise. But there's more.' He paused. 'Allegations have been made about underaged girls. That's what the police are interested in.'

Rosamund felt cold. She was pressing the phone so hard to her ear it hurt.

'I'm sorry, Rose, I'm sorry. He's corrupt, and he's about to be disembowelled by the police and the media and all the people he's let down. I'll come and get you.'

She hardly heard him. 'But he can't have known, Gary. Mark wouldn't . . . he'd never—'

'It's true, Rose.' He said it sharply, in one swift stroke severing any false hopes she might have had. 'Believe me, it's true. You said you trusted me last night, then trust me now.'

She felt her fingers unclench and the receiver fall, knocking the coffee mug onto the phone book and herself.

'Rose? Rose?'

She could hear Gary's voice, tinny and far away. Fumbling, she got the receiver back to her ear. She had to hold it with two hands. 'I'm sorry, Gary. I can't talk now. Later . . . later . . .'

She hung up.

Above her, on the stairs, one of the treads creaked. Rosamund jerked her head up. Mark was looking down at her, and she knew from his face he had overheard her conversation. There was no point in pretending, even had she been capable of it.

****

Mrs Gibbons poured more of her tonic into her teacup and drank it down quickly, eager for its blurring effect. She had told Mr Kirkwood that she would wash madam and lay out her body, ready for the coffin.

'No-one else'll touch her,' she'd added, between belligerence and tears. 'It'll be done with love, sir.'

He'd agreed, comforting, offering any help he could give. The others were set various tasks. Someone had to make their way into the town to give out the news, and to inform the families of the servants that they would not be able to return home. Colonsay was a house under quarantine.

Ambrosine's little dog Cleo had been bundled up in a sheet and lay in the yard, awaiting burial. In the sitting room, only the blood remained. And there was so much of it. The button-back couch where Ambrosine had sat and read her brother's letter was only fit for burning, as were the rugs on the floor.

'We'll need plenty of washing water,' Mr Kirkwood informed Meggy and Alice. Meggy promptly leaned her head in her arms and wept. Alice sighed, and gave Mr Kirkwood a direct look.

'I'll see to the water, sir.'

He nodded, and she could see he was impressed by her clear head. 'My man, Gray, will help you in any way he can.'

Alice had already encountered Gray, with his shiny black coat. She wondered if he had told Mr Kirkwood about their meeting in the garden, and then knew he had not. It would reflect badly upon Gray.

'Thank you, sir.'

'Good girl, Alice. You'll be rewarded for this, you know. I'll see to it personally.'

The thought of the reward kept her at her task. And when the smell and sight of the blood became almost too much to bear, Alice reminded herself that soon she would be in Melbourne, and she need never return to Colonsay ever again. It helped.

'Jesus,' Gray whispered, when they first walked into the sitting room. He went a sickly colour, like potatoes gone mouldy. 'Looks like someone's slaughtered a bloody pig,' he muttered, eyes following the splatters of blood on the floor and walls, the great arc of it speckling the ceiling.

'Get the scrubbing brush,' Alice told him grimly. 'And take down the drapes. They're not fit for anything now.'

Gray glanced at her sideways, but he did as she told him. As time passed and they worked together, silently and grimly, she sensed a change in his feelings towards her. Where before there had been a kind of contemptuousness for a lowly servant girl, the superiority of a man over a woman, there was now confusion and fear. Afterwards, during the days when Colonsay remained in quarantine, he kept away from her.

Alice didn't care. Mr Kirkwood had offered her a position in his own home, and she had accepted it. Gray could like it or lump it, as far as she was concerned. She would miss Meggy, perhaps, but no-one else. And even Meggy had changed from the amusing girl she had been, mainly because of Jonah.

He had been missing since the day it happened. At first Meggy had said nothing, but then concern and a growing fear for his safety had sent her at last in to see Mr Kirkwood. They had searched and asked questions, careful not to stir any undue interest, but nothing was found and no-one had seen him.

'He's run off,' Alice said. 'He probably heard all the commotion and took fright. Not that I blame him, Meggy. He'll have gone home.'

Meggy tried to believe it, but Alice could see in her heart she didn't. No-one was very interested. Everyone was in mourning for Cosmo and Ambrosine, and there wasn't anything left over for such as Jonah. Meggy's small grief was soon swallowed up in the larger one.

CHAPTER 21

Mark closed the library door.

Rosamund could hardly bring herself to turn and look at him. Her chest was hurting and a sickness was churning in her stomach. Although she herself had done nothing wrong, she felt guilty.

She spun around. 'Oh God, Mark, why? Why? Didn't you realise you'd get found out? Did you believe no-one would care?'

He had been leaning against the door but now he stepped away from it. 'I don't know what you're talking about.'

'You did, didn't you? Mark Markovic, another name for God Almighty!'

He stood in front of her. For the first time she saw the rage blazing out of his eyes.

'You don't know what you're talking about!'

Rosamund held her ground, although he frightened her as he had never frightened her before. Maybe because she had never seen him clearly before.

'I think you really did believe you'd get away with it,' she said, amazement struggling with pain in her voice. 'That you could do anything.' Tears flooded her eyes. 'Don't you see that what you've done is wrong? Or does the end justify whatever means are necessary?'

'I'm telling you I'm innocent, you stupid bitch.'

Rosamund wiped her eyes and took a shaky breath. 'Gary says there'll be a police inquiry. He told me to warn you. Get away while you can, Mark.'

'And his advice is, of course, disinterested.' Mark was cold and in control. 'Well, maybe it is time to go, but you're coming with me, Rose.'

She pulled back but it was too late. He caught her arm, drawing her in tightly against him. 'I said you're coming with me. Everything was all right until you left. Everything was going so well. You'll stand by me, Rose, just like a proper wife, whether you want to or not.'

Stand by him? Did he really mean that? Couldn't he see past his own single-minded ambition to the truth? 'Mark,' she managed. 'I won't come with you. It's over. Finished. Do you hear me, Mark, it's finished!'

'Shut up,' he said, his voice hard as stone. 'We're walking out to the car now. No hysterics, no bloody stupid nonsense. I love you, Rose, and you're coming with me.'

She laughed, but he pressed his hand over her mouth, cutting the sound off. They were out in the hall, Rosamund could hear Kerry in the kitchen. Mark squeezed her viciously, his arm about her waist.

'No tearful goodbyes,' he mocked.

The BMW was outside, its previously gleaming exterior splattered with dried raindrops and fallen leaves. The pile of old timber and other rubbish lay between the car and Colonsay. Rosamund stumbled around it but Mark held her up. His face was white and strange, as if the soul of the man she had known had slipped out and something else had taken its place. He had to remove his hand from her mouth so that he could dig the keys out of his pocket.

'Mark! Gary says they know. You can't run away. It won't matter whether I'm there or not. You—'

'*Gary says*,' he caught her pleading tone perfectly. 'This is all his fault. And yours. Rose Cunningham, spoilt little girl, worthless woman. A wife should stand by her husband. A wife should be grateful. I gave you *everything*, but you never thought I was good enough. Not for a Cunningham.'

Rosamund turned her head to stare at him. 'That's not true!'

'Isn't it?' He unlocked the car doors with a press of a button, pushed her hard against the vehicle while he opened the passenger side door. Then he tightened his grip on her arm and climbed into the car, shuffling across to the driver's seat and dragging her in after him.

'Mark,' she tried again. 'Please. I'll come with you. I will. But not like this. Let's pack first. I need a change of clothes. At least let me get a toothbrush! This is crazy.'

He glared at her. 'Close the door.'

She met his eyes. He was rigid with the effort it was taking him to remain calm. She sensed the violence lurking under the surface. It had always been there, and once upon a time it had even attracted her. No longer. Now she had had a taste of what life could be like without Mark, and it had been as sweet as summer berries. She was not about to give it up.

She tried a new tack. 'Mark,' she said dully, in her old, beaten voice. 'I'll come with you. I know I'm nothing without you.'

It was what he expected. She felt his relief, although she had bowed her head and couldn't see his face. 'I'm glad you're seeing sense, Rose.'

'I . . . I can't manage on my own.'

'No, you can't.' He said it gently, as an adult to a small child. This was the way he liked her, Rosamund knew. Helpless and acquiescent.

'You'll take care of me, won't you, Mark?'

He gave a bark of laughter. 'I always have. Shut the door and we'll get going. You'll see, Rose, everything will be all right. I'll make it all right.'

Even in her role of the beaten wife, Rosamund was amazed at his self-deluded arrogance. Couldn't he see that nothing was all right, that it could never be all right ever again?

She sighed, 'Yes, Mark,' and felt him relax. She leaned towards the open passenger side door and, as he moved to insert the key in the ignition, Rosamund lunged. His hand struck out—she heard her blouse tear—and then she was on the muddy ground. And up, running.

'Bitch!' he screamed out furiously. 'You bitch, I'll kill you!'

The pile of broken timber was in front of her and she veered away, expecting Mark to jump out and follow her. Until she heard the car start up. Rosamund dared a glance over her shoulder.

Mark accelerated with a roar of the powerful engine. Mud sprayed up in a great arc behind him. The car was coming after her.

Her throat felt raw. The cold air was hurting her chest and she coughed and sobbed. With a wordless sound of anger she threw herself to one side as the car closed on her. She rolled over and over in the wet dirt, skinning her hip and knee, jarring her unfit body.

Several metres on, Mark had brought the car to a screeching stop. As Rosamund tried to sit up, she saw it begin to reverse, cold air pouring like smoke from the exhaust. The carbon monoxide stung her nostrils.

And then, before her terrified gaze, something began to take shape. A wavering, incandescent form; a column of light rising up between Rosamund and the car.

The car, which had been accelerating, slowed, then stopped. Rosamund saw Mark's face, a white, horrified blur. For an endless moment everything was still, and then he put his foot down, and the car flew forwards, up the driveway, away from Colonsay. Away from Rosamund.

The light hovered just above the ground. It was like a kaleidoscope, moving, swirling. And yet . . . there was a face in it. Rosamund felt what little strength she had left drain from her. A narrow white face and brilliant, intelligent eyes. The girl's hair and skirt were blown by a breeze that didn't exist in Rosamund's world. There was not a sound.

'Thank you, Alice.' Rosamund finally found her voice but her words were a croak. 'You saved my life. Thank you with all my heart.'

The ghost shimmered a moment more and then began to fade. Rosamund always swore she heard it say goodbye.

Ambrosine had been buried simply, at Colonsay. There would be a state funeral for Cosmo. His body had never been found, but the inquiry had made a finding of death by his own hand.

Alice's final duty as a servant of Colonsay had been to attend Ambrosine's funeral. She had trailed behind the glass-sided carriage, its froth of white roses filling the interior and covering the coffin, bowing her head and pretending to a grief she could not feel. Instead she thought of Bertie, grieved for Bertie.

Oh well, it was all part of the promise she had made to Mr Kirkwood.

At the burial Alice stood with her parents. They were well back, outside the picket fence which marked the Cunningham family plot. Nearby, Petersham stood in his cleaned and brushed red coat, tears running freely down his red-veined cheeks.

By now Alice was so used to shutting off her emotions, she felt little. Neither did she believe this was strange or unnatural. Rather, the opposite. Although sometimes, at night, she'd wake to the smell of blood, as if it had caught deep in her throat, and then she would cough and cough to try and dislodge it. Other than that, she was her usual self.

Mr Kirkwood had told them all that Miss Ada had gone to stay with his wife in Melbourne, and Colonsay would be closed up. A caretaker couple from Geelong would be living there. For the time being. In the longer term, as the house was Ada's, it would be up to her what to do with it. Mr Kirkwood added that the arrangements for them all had been made.

Meggy was going home. She had rallied slightly,

but sorrow still pulled at her mouth and shadowed her eyes. Mrs Gibbons wept into her broth, and seemed to have aged a decade. Everyone avoided the sitting room, as though the sight and smell of blood would always be there, in their minds, although Alice was rather proud of her cleaning.

The morning the servants left and the house was closed, Alice walked home past the Cunningham burial ground, past Ambrosine's new grave. Petersham was laying roses, his back stooped and shaking with his grief. Alice looked the other way.

****

'It was as if he had to blame me, because if he hadn't, he'd have to blame himself. And Mark Markovic was never wrong.' Rosamund shrugged. 'I'm not making sense, am I?'

'You're making a lot of sense.' Gary was sitting opposite her at the kitchen table, two mugs of steaming tea between them.

'Do you think he'll come back?'

'I doubt it.'

'I don't think I could look at him again, Gary.' She bit her lip, forcing the trembling to stop.

'You should get a restraining order. You'd have no trouble, after what's happened.'

Rosamund put her hands around the tea mug and felt the heat, welcoming the pain. To feel physical pain, you had to be alive, and she had very nearly been dead. 'Alice saved me, you know,' she murmured with wonder. 'She did. And now she's gone, isn't she?'

Kerry nodded from the stove. She lifted her head, like a dog sniffing the air. 'The house definitely feels different. Whatever was here is gone.'

'Alice is at peace,' Gary said quietly. 'I feel it, too. Colonsay is at peace, Rose.'

Rosamund's eyes blurred with tears. 'It was all so awful, Gary. I still can't believe Mark could do such a thing. Whatever we might have gone through, and however bad things had become, I thought I knew him.'

'There's always a part of ourselves we hold back.'

'Is there, Gary?' She wiped her eyes again. She had been crying for hours. 'Have you got some dark secret, too?'

He pulled a face. 'You've seen me at my worst, Rose, and I think I've seen you at yours. It's all up from here.'

Despite herself, Rosamund laughed.

'Rosamund.' Kerry's voice was soft, a warning. She was standing in the open doorway into the garden. A pale trickle of sunlight ventured inside, and with it, one paw at a time, a small, unkempt dog with a dirty blue ribbon tied to the top of its head.

Rosamund caught her breath.

The little dog paused, looking about with big brown eyes, and then took a couple more steps into the kitchen. The dirty, matted tail wagged hopefully, the ears lifted.

'Here, dog,' Rosamund whispered, and slowly held out her hand.

The dog stepped backwards and then forwards, dancing on the spot, uncertain. Loneliness and desperation fought with distrust.

'Come on, boy . . . girl? Come on, pup.'

Kerry was quietly closing the door behind it, blocking off its escape.

The black button nose stretched out and the terrier drew close. Rosamund let it investigate her trembling fingers. Suddenly a rough pink tongue gave them a tentative lick, and then another. Rosamund's wan face lit up with a joyful smile.

'You're real,' she gasped. 'You're real, after all!'

The following day was cool but fine. Gary drove Rosamund to see Enderby, leaving Kerry at Colonsay. She had been busy brushing the knots out of the newly washed dog. They still hadn't decided on a name for it.

Kerry had rung the police, but no-one had reported a missing dog. The local radio station and the pet shelter had also proved fruitless. So, for now at least, the dog belonged to Colonsay. Another stray, Rosamund thought, looking for refuge.

Gary and Rosamund had opened up Ambrosine's sitting room, and Gary had clambered across the various boxes and furnishings and discovered the hole in the floor which the dog had been using as an entry point. It had made a comfortable nest for itself in a pile of old blankets. As for how it had entered the remainder of the house when the sitting room door was closed, Gary believed that was quite simple. The outside doors were often open during the day, especially when Fred and his crew were working. Once inside, there were plenty of places to hide in a house as large as Colonsay.

'So much for ghostly hounds!' Kerry scoffed, apparently forgetting everything else that had happened.

Enderby Munro was where he had been before, sitting by the window. This time the sun was shining through, making patterns on the floor and highlighting his craggy face. He gave his big smile as soon as he saw Gary and Rosamund.

'You came!'

'Of course we came.' Rosamund bent and kissed him, and watched with surprise as two patches of hectic colour stained Enderby's cheeks. 'You said it was important. What is it?'

'Just some unfinished business I have with you, Rosie.' He eyed her closely. 'You're looking a bit peaky. How are things at Colonsay?'

Gary stepped in. 'Everything is just fine.'

'You'll be staying on then?' Enderby wasn't about to give up his secret easily.

'Yes. I'm going to make Colonsay my home.'

Enderby screwed up his eyes in another smile. 'That's what I wanted to hear! Now, I want to give you my scrapbooks. No thanks needed. They're about your family, and when I'm gone Gary will probably burn them.'

Rosamund glanced at Gary. 'That's . . . Thank you, Enderby, I'll treasure them.'

Enderby nodded as if he had expected nothing less. 'There's another thing, too. A document I . . . found, when I worked for the government. You might be interested in it, Rose.'

'A document?'

Enderby was searching in the side of his chair, scratching about with arthritic fingers. 'Where is it? If that nurse has taken it, I'll—ah, here it is!'

He produced a long brown envelope and waved it in front of their faces. 'This is it, Rosie. You take it and read it when you feel like it. No hurry.' He thought that was funny, and laughed loudly.

'No hurry,' Gary muttered as they drove away. 'Why didn't he tell us that before?'

'And spoil the fun?' Rosamund protested. 'Will I open it?'

'Sure. Maybe it's a treasure map.'

'If only!' Rosamund ripped up the flap and spread the single sheet on her lap. 'It's a list of the Colonsay servants,' she said after a moment. 'Alice Parkin is here, Mrs Gibbons, the cook, Meggy McLauchlan . . . Jonah isn't. It looks as if they all received a sum of money. It's signed by A. Kirkwood.'

'Pay-off,' Gary said. 'They kept quiet and Kirkwood kept them happy.'

'The date is August 1901.'

'Another piece of the puzzle.'

'I don't need proof, Gary. I already know what happened.' She reached over to touch his face. 'At least one good thing has come out of all this.'

'Only one?' he said, but he was smiling back. 'Do you want to go to lunch somewhere, just me and you?'

'I'd love to, but I'd better get back. Fred Swann said he had a few things to discuss with me. I promised I wouldn't be long.'

Frederick Swann had arrived early that morning, and Colonsay again resounded to the sounds of full-blown restoration.

'How will you pay?' Gary asked.

Rosamund closed her eyes and rested her head against the seat. 'I don't know. I imagine there will have to be some sort of settlement, when I divorce Mark, but with everything else that's going on, who knows when I'll see it? Perhaps I can borrow against it?'

'Use the Cunningham name,' Gary said. 'It still

counts for something, around here anyway.'

But she didn't want to face her problems just yet. She was still bruised and aching from her encounter with Mark, inside as well as out. She wondered what he had made of Alice, and where he was now. The story had yet to break, but Gary had said it was only a matter of days. A storm was gathering about Mark, and it looked to be a bad one.

'Prepare yourself, Rose,' Gary had told her earlier, 'because you'll have to take some of the flack.'

Once, that would have terrified Rosamund, but now she sensed that, although it wouldn't be easy, she could face it and find a way through it. Just as she had done with Colonsay.

'Rose?'

She opened her eyes and saw that they were almost home. The turn-off to the Colonsay driveway opened up before them, to the left was Cosmo's column. I was lucky, she told herself for the twentieth time. Ambrosine wasn't.

Gary was glancing in the rear-vision mirror. Rosamund turned and looked back through the rear window. A police car was following them. As Gary drew up in front of Colonsay, Rose opened her door and stepped out to face the police. The air was very cold, and somehow she knew that what they had come to tell her was not good news.

He was young, the same constable who had come to the house that first time to investigate the noises in the attic. It seemed ironic that he should be here now. 'Mrs Markovic? I'm afraid I have some bad news. Your husband's clothing has been found on the beach. His car was in the car park. We've assumed he went swimming some time yesterday. We're assuming he's drowned.'

CHAPTER 22

Alice Parkin clicked her tongue and looked down at the catch in her stocking, a little tear just above her ankle. She had wanted to look her best. Not, she supposed, that the young man waiting for her would see a hole in her stocking. Things had not progressed that far, not yet. But she was fond of him, and he of her, and she had hopes.

The ten years in Melbourne had gone quickly. She had moved from her position with Mr Kirkwood soon after arriving—Gray had made things awkward, and Ada's angry misery had made Alice uncomfortable. Now she worked as a chambermaid in a big hotel in Flinders Street. The job suited her, and she had a room to herself in a respectable boarding-house nearby.

Alice was happy and, she told herself, had forgotten all about Cosmo and Ambrosine and Colonsay. Sometimes she even forgot about Bertie. She liked to think, when she did remember, that she had in some way helped to see justice done. Righted a wrong.

She was late.

Smoothing her narrow grey skirt, Alice turned to walk down the hill, where there was a stop for the horsedrawn tram. She had hardly gone five steps when a passing face struck her as familiar.

Slowly, she turned, holding her hat with one hand and her purse with the other. A handsome, well-dressed man was about to enter the tobacconist's. Alice realised, with a dizzy lurch, that it was Mr Marling. She must have spoken his name, for he turned, then drew closer.

He looked older, though still prosperous. She had, of course, read about him in the newspaper. He had had an exhibition recently. She hadn't gone, although she had wondered whether the sketch he had once done of her had been part of it.

'Alice Parkin,' she told him now when she accepted he couldn't place her.

His hand closed on her shoulder and she realised with surprise that he wasn't nearly as tall as she had remembered. His eyes, too, were different, faded, as was his hair. Only his *joie de vivre* had not diminished.

'Alice Parkin? Alice Parkin!' The memory made him smile. 'I think of Colonsay. I remember those wonderful days.'

'Do you, sir?' She considered, with a rush of dark emotion, whether he really thought of them as wonderful. It had been Mr Marling's fault, almost as much as Ambrosine's, that she had died. How could he not know it, somewhere deep in his heart? How could he not realise the damage he and Ambrosine's affair had done?

'Cosmo was a man of his class and education, I suppose,' he went on, and she could tell by his expression he was far away. He seemed to be speaking to himself, rather than her. 'A bigot and a bully, although it's unfashionable to say so now. He's God's golden boy, isn't he? I am awaiting the day when they throw a public holiday and declare it Cosmo Day.'

Alice felt shocked and repulsed by his words. He didn't seem to notice.

'Ambrosine was different. So gentle and sweet, and so trapped. Sold off to Cosmo like a sheep or a bushel of wheat, the object of a deal done between Cosmo and her father. Cosmo saw her and wanted her, and the father wanted his debts paid off. What did it matter what Ambrosine felt or thought? We should protect the weak, shouldn't we, Alice?'

She didn't know what to say. She didn't want to think about Ambrosine and the sitting room. She didn't want to think about the blood.

'I saw Ada Cunningham not long ago. She reminds me of Cosmo. It was the boy I used to feel sorry for. He took after his mother, poor little devil. The image of her, if you looked into his eyes. That same trapped, gentle soul. She tried to protect him, but she was having enough difficulty protecting herself. I did have hopes, though, that she would leave Cosmo one day. She never spoke of it, Alice, but I knew she was desperately unhappy. Did you never notice that? Desperately unhappy.' He shook his head. 'Well . . . they're dead now.'

Alice swallowed. Something was thudding in her head, hammering to get out. No, she thought. No, no, *no*! How dare Mr Marling? What did he know or understand? He pretended to care, but at the time he had only cared about holding that weak and selfish woman in his arms. Distracting her from her son, breaking her husband's heart.

'You loved her!' she burst out furiously, and then could not retract the words.

Mr Marling took a step back. There were more lines on his face than she remembered. He seemed puzzled by her manner. 'I suppose I did,' he replied at last. 'She was a beautiful woman. But I was never her lover, Alice.' He laughed deprecatingly, and there was a gentle note of regret in his voice that spoke of opportunities lost. 'I would never have been able to paint Ambrosine, if I had been her lover.'

But the button! a voice within Alice cried. *What about the button?* And, then, as if she had known it all along, she saw what must have happened. The stitching on Mr Marling's blue waistcoat had broken and the button had fallen off. The dog Cleo had found it and carried it into Ambrosine's bedroom. Mr Marling had never been in there.

Automatically, Alice returned his good wishes and goodbyes. From the end of the road, the horsedrawn tram was approaching. She no longer thought of the young man she had planned to meet, or the hole in her stocking. People passing by turned to look at her strangely, but she did not notice that either. She was remembering, words and scenes flashing through her mind like trains, roaring and shuddering. Steam, hot and acrid, was in her eyes and throat.

The world was tilting, turning upside down. Inside out. Alice began to walk blindly across the road. She didn't hear Mr Marling's voice call a warning. A wagon rattled towards her but her eyes were fixed on the sky. She didn't even feel it strike her.

It was nearly two months since the police had come about Mark. They hadn't found him, and Rosamund didn't expect they would. The police still assumed that he had gone swimming, got into difficulty and drowned, although there were others who suspected darker intentions, people who didn't doubt the brothel business would have destroyed his political ambitions. Rosamund of course knew that Mark would never have gone swimming. She knew he had gone into the bay with the intention of killing himself. Just like Cosmo.

She tried to imagine the cold salt water and Mark's deep fear of it. His acceptance, finally, that his dream was over. Perhaps there had even been a moment of peace for him, before the end. Rosamund hoped so. She had loved him once.

Frederick Swann had continued to work on Colonsay, and Rosamund was making some progress in the garden. The little dog often accompanied her—Kerry had named it Tangles for want of something better. Rosamund had found real solace in digging in the soil and planting new life. There would be no pool, after all.

Mark had left everything to an organisation for under-privileged children. Rosamund had received a bequest, probably just enough to pay for the renovations. Graham Peel-Johnson, acting on instructions, had changed Mark's will shortly before he died. Rosamund, at first stunned, now found it amusing. To continue to survive, Colonsay would have to become a guesthouse after all. She was sure that Alice, if not Cosmo and Ambrosine, would have seen the funny side of it.

The press had besieged her for a couple of weeks, and some of the stories on Mark had been brutal. Rosamund had begun to believe that Ada was right to have fought to keep her privacy. But now the story had cooled. Something else had come along; in the media, there was always something else.

One of the stranger things to come out of it had been the re-release of 'Grey Skies', Rosamund's old hit. Last time she looked it was number two on the Top Forty.

Sue Gibbons had rung, asking if Rosamund could return the household accounts book she had borrowed—there had been some questions asked at the monthly Historical Society meeting. 'Are you still planning to write that book?' Sue asked.

Rosamund had to think a moment to remember which book she meant. 'I . . . I'm not sure. Maybe. I might have lost my taste for exposing skeletons to the light of day.'

'I checked through the other household accounts books, the earlier ones,' Sue Gibbons went on. 'There was a reference in one of them to Meggy McLauchlan coming from a property called The Meadows, near Tinyutin. It belonged to Mr McKay, who I believe was Ambrosine's father.'

'So, Meggy was Ambrosine's servant, not Cosmo's. I wonder why we always assumed everything was Cosmo's?'

Sue didn't know the answer. She rang off, with a reminder about the return of the book.

Rosamund retrieved it from Ada's box of personal papers. While she was at it, she flipped through the contents—the letters and red appointment book—retracing familiar ground. She had never finished reading the bills and when she opened an envelope from a local grocer she realised a foreign letter had been hastily bundled inside. The writing was familiar.

Meggy McLauchlan's. The second time her name had come up today.

Rosamund sat down on one of the cracked leather chairs and opened the crumpled paper. The letter was grubby and appeared to have been refolded hastily rather than folded along its original creases. Rosamund carefully smoothed it out.

Tinyutin, 17th June 1920
Dear Miss Ada,

You write you'd rather not hear from me again. I suppose you don't want to remember the past, or is it just some bits you don't like? I know all those bits. Jonah told me. He said you saw him and your mother together in the stables that day, when the horse nearly trampled you. He said your mother was sick with worry you'd tell your father, and tried to make you believe it were a secret.

Is that why it happened? Did you tell him? I always knew he had a temper, and he treated your mother like one of his horses, didn't he? She was his. He'd probably have killed her for loving any other man, but how much worse to have her loving a black man. 'Cause she did love him, Miss Ada. She'd loved him all her life, since the days at Tinyutin. They'd met when they were young, when Jonah worked for her father. They'd grown up together. When she married your father it broke their hearts. Then Jonah began working on Cosmo's place, and Cosmo came to visit, liked his way with horses and brought him back to Colonsay, and so they met again. And they still loved each other just as much, more. I wished it weren't so. I tried to make

Jonah see the danger. I begged him to leave, but he wouldn't leave her, you see. He'd never leave her.

Do you know where he is, Miss Ada? I think you do. You know everything. I wish you'd tell me, so I can bury him proper. He wanted to lie at Tinyutin, on the plains. He always said the shadows were like giants walking across the land.

Meggy

Filled with sadness, Rosamund set aside Meggy's letter.

The answer had been here all along, the reason why Cosmo had killed his wife. It had had nothing to do with Mr Marling. Ambrosine hadn't been having an affair, she'd been in love. She and Jonah had been childhood sweethearts, separated by a parent's cruelty and the attitudes of the times. Ambrosine, the daughter of a property owner, no matter how poor, could never have married a groom like Jonah, especially not a black groom. It would have been unthinkable. So she had married Cosmo.

And then, through a twist of fate, or maybe Jonah's manipulation, Jonah had gone to work on Cosmo's property north of the Murray, and Cosmo had decided to bring him south. To Colonsay. To Ambrosine. And it had started up all over again.

Rosamund imagined Ambrosine sneaking out of the house at night to meet her lover. Had she waited to pull on her robe and slippers, or had she been too impatient, running through the wet grass with bare feet, her long silk nightdress clinging damply at the hem . . .?

Rosamund felt tears burning her eyes and blinked them back. It was over, they were dead. And, she truly hoped, at peace. With a sigh, she glanced back through Meggy's words. A strange idea began to take shape in her mind.

An hour later, Gary came and found her. He bent and kissed her, his face and hands splattered with paint from his work in the west wing bedrooms. He saw the dreamy look in her eyes. 'What is it?'

Rosamund handed him Meggy's letter and waited while he read it, watching the changes of expression on his face. When he had finished he looked at her with a soft exhalation of breath.

'It was all Ada, then? She told Cosmo, and Cosmo lost it. No wonder she couldn't leave Colonsay,' he added. 'She was bound to the place as much by her guilt as her love.'

'Yes, you're probably right. It seems wrong to blame her, though, doesn't it? She was a child, a little girl. She was probably frightened and confused. How could she be expected to stay quiet about something like that? Ambrosine should have left Colonsay while she had the chance. If she had gone with Jonah, none of it would have happened.'

'A big ask for those days, Rosie. Imagine the scandal.'

'I know. I don't think she had it in her. If she had, she'd have run off years before, when her father first arranged her marriage to Cosmo. She had her chance then, and she let it slip away.'

'We don't all have your strength of mind.'

Rosamund pulled a face, then sobered. 'There was something else that struck me as interesting when I was reading Meggy's letter. What about

Jonah? Meggy seems to think Ada knew where he was buried—he must have been dead, then. And do you remember that list your grandfather gave us with the names of the servants on it? Jonah wasn't on that. So, between the time of Ambrosine's death and August 1901, Jonah was dead too.'

Gary went to sit down, then remembered his paint-stained clothes and changed his mind. 'You'd think if he'd died a conventional death his sister would have known about it.'

'Yes, you would.' Rosamund gave him a look.

'You know where he is, don't you?'

'I think so.' She reached down into the box and brought out a yellowed newspaper cutting. 'Do you remember that household accounts book I borrowed off Sue Gibbons? I was searching it out today and I remembered a cutting in it that I'd never read. It's a story on the body they found in the swamp when they were draining it in the '60s. See, here.' She pointed out the relevant line.

'"The only item of clothing still identifiable on the body was a pair of brown riding boots",' Gary read aloud, and looked up inquiringly.

Rosamund reached into the box again and handed over a crumpled receipt with faded ink.

'"One pair of brown hand-sewn men's riding boots, ten guineas. Ambrosine Cunningham."' Gary raised his eyebrows. 'Do you mean it was Cosmo's body? I thought he drowned?'

'No, Cosmo did drown. It was Jonah. Of course, it was Jonah. Ambrosine bought him the boots for Christmas, riding boots because he was a groom and no-one would notice boots, whereas anything else might have been remarked upon.'

Gary did sit down then, ignoring Rosamund's pained expression. 'I wonder what happened.'

'Perhaps Cosmo met up with him as he was leaving the house after he'd killed Ambrosine. Or perhaps he met him beforehand and went on to murder Ambrosine. I've always thought Ambrosine's murder was a spur-of-the moment thing, but maybe it was premeditated. Jonah and then Ambrosine.'

'You can't prove it's Jonah.'

'I can't prove it, Gary, but I know. I wonder where he is now? I'll have to find out. He should be buried at Tinyutin, with Meggy.'

'Why not put him in with Cosmo and Ambrosine?'

Rosamund kicked him and he protested. He knelt by her chair and wrapped his arms around her, and they mock-struggled. After a moment, Rosamund rested her head against his, her fingers tangling in his springy hair.

'Gary, Ada must have known where Jonah was. Not when Meggy wrote to her, in 1920, but later, when they were draining the swamp. Kerry says she was always on the phone to the council, and that she had some tale that the body was that of Harry Simmons, who wasn't dead at all. She was trying to throw them off the trail. The receipt, too. Why else would she have kept that receipt and no other? She knew, and kept that secret, just as she kept the others.'

'There was one secret she didn't keep though, wasn't there?'

Rosamund sighed. 'Poor Ada. She suffered for her sins. First Kirkwood stealing from her, then her husband dying and the years alone here at Colonsay. Maybe that's why she doesn't haunt, because she paid for her mistakes while she was alive?'

Gary kissed her lips softly. 'Can you live here at Colonsay with all these memories, Rosamund? Will you be happy here?'

She smiled. 'Yes, I think so. I *am* happy. As long as you'll live here with me?'

'I thought you'd never ask.'

EPILOGUE

It was dusk. The child ran along the narrow twisting path between the tall spires of late-autumn hollyhocks and sprawling daisies. Moths flitted in the fading light, and her long fair hair was a pale blur around her pale face. Behind her, drifting out through the open kitchen door, she could hear her mother's voice, and Kerry's answering, and the clatter of a meal being prepared.

There were guests at Colonsay tonight and she was to keep out of their way.

The path widened and opened into an alcove with a seat set in front of a huge mound of philadelphus. In spring this was a mass of sweet white flowers, but now the rough green leaves were colouring and beginning to fall. The child picked her way around it, seeking the deeper shadows where sometimes a stray cat prowled. Occasionally she had given it such a fright it had run all the way to the fence.

Carefully, she climbed over a thick old branch—she didn't want to catch her new overalls. A curtain of leaves shielded her secret place and she pushed it aside eagerly. And stopped.

There were a man and a lady standing there. They must have heard her arrival and been as surprised as she was. But they weren't cross. They couldn't be, because they were smiling. She wondered if they were guests, even though they were dressed so oddly.

The lady wore a long skirt, like the ladies in the photos her mother had. She was very pretty, even in the half-dark the child could tell that. The man had a scarf tied around his throat, and a coat, and checked sort of trousers. They both looked very odd, but very happy.

'Ada!'

Her father was calling her, his voice loud in the stillness. She turned instinctively towards the sound. When she looked back, the man and the lady were gone.

It startled her, but only for a moment. Once she'd found an old button, and fallen asleep with it clasped in her hand, but it had gone again in the morning. And once in the night, as she lay in her bed, an old lady with a cane had come and peered curiously into her face. She had pointed to herself and then Ada, and seemed to be trying to say something, but Ada didn't know what. Things like that happened at Colonsay. She'd learned not to be afraid. Her father told her the past could not hurt her.

'Ada!'

'Here, Daddy!'

Ada turned and ran back the way she had come.

AUTHOR'S NOTE

Those who know the Bellarine Peninsula will recognise Drysdale in the town near Colonsay. Changes to it and the surrounding area have been made for the sake of the story. I also apologise to the members of the local historical society, who are very hard-working and definitely not 'nosy busybodies'.

The Dark Dream
Lilly Sommers

From the bestselling author of *The Glass House* and *The Bond* comes a gripping story of passion and survival.

Who is Ella Seaton? Waking face-down in the mud by Seaton's lagoon, her head throbbing from an ugly wound, a young woman struggles to come to terms with an unfamiliar world. Who is she? Why can't she remember? Was she on her way to the goldfields at Bendigo? Or escaping from them?

All she has are snatches of a dark dream, a dream which holds memories she is too terrified to face.

Adam, a handsome young goldfields merchant, befriends her on the road, but Adam is a man with secrets of his own.

As she travels from the danger and excitement of the goldfields to polite Sydney society, Ella begins to unravel the threads of her past to confront the startling truth. A truth that will change her life forever.

When Shadows Fall
Lilly Sommers

The floor groaned as my uninvited guest stepped inside. With him came a gust of cold air and the smell of the river. I saw a shadow pass my doorway. A big, black mass that had no shape, no definition. Yet I sensed his glance towards me . . . Then his footsteps carried him on, moving towards the back of the cottage, into silence.

Kate O'Hara rents an old stone cottage on the banks of a Tasmanian river to try to get some peace after the death of her husband, and to plan her future.

But there are mysterious footsteps in the night. The soft plash of oars on the river. An old picture of a boatman hanging on the cottage wall. And a rent in the fabric of time itself . . .